right the first time

SHAFER U
BOOK 1

KRISTEN VAIL

Developmental editing by Eleanor Boyall

Line editing by Nancy Smay

Proofreading by Sarah at Reed Editorial Services

Cover design by Books and Moods

lenni

I SHOULD HAVE WORN an underwire bra.

I glance at my watch—eleven minutes until class starts—and pick up the pace, cursing my earlier decision to wear the cute little bralette with the spaghetti straps and exactly zero support.

"None of your usual granny bras," my best friend Jade had warned, insisting that if I wanted more than innocent flirting from Shafer University's star quarterback, I'd better get used to bras made from lace, string, and little else. Jade doesn't approve of my crush, but she's so desperate for me to like a boy—any boy—that she's set aside her own feelings about him to stoke mine. Now I sort of wish she hadn't. I like my granny bras with their wide, padded straps and fifteen hooks. Who cares that they're hideous? The only living thing that sees me shirtless is the withering philodendron on my nightstand. I press my notebook to my chest and cross my arms to minimize the bounce. Reeve Dalton had just better be worth it.

I've powered through a few rounds of flirting with Reeve in our Applied Statistics class with no idea where it might go. I'm not even clear why it began. I'd like to think the fact he started chatting me up the first time I wore a tight shirt to class is a mere coincidence, but so far, the evidence isn't there.

A small part of me suspects he's been using his charm and killer smile for nefarious purposes, and any day now he'll lean over, letting his masculine scent overwhelm me, his lips brush my ear, and smoothly inquire as to whether he can cheat off me during our upcoming exam. It wouldn't be the first time I've gotten that question from a guy way out of my league. But so far, Reeve's shown no hint of an ulterior motive. And with Jade's encouragement, I've decided I'm not leaving class today without an invite to one of the football team's legendary postgame parties. Not because I like those parties; on the contrary, I'm uncomfortably aware how much I stick out in places crowded by beautiful, cool people. But an invite would mean something is actually happening between me and Reeve. And am I ready for something to happen? I don't know yet. But I'm ready to step out of my all-work-no-play world and find out.

I'm damp with sweat by the time I reach the mathematics building, the late-summer heat combining with my jacked-up nerves to make me feel like the least sexy version of myself. I try not to imagine the frizz situation surely unfolding on top of my head. I almost trip on the stairs leading into the building. Wedge sandals to walk around campus all day? What was I—er, Jade—thinking? I haven't worn a heel since the Freshman Formal, and now I remember why. Not only can I barely walk without my ankles threatening to snap, but even an extra two inches makes me conspicuously tall. I hate being conspicuous.

I fan myself with my notebook to dry the sweat at my temples. Walking inside offers no relief, only the smell of decades-old wood paneling baking in the Midwestern heat. As one of the oldest on Shafer University's century-old campus, the mathematics building lacks air-conditioning and is basically a giant oven for the first month of school.

When I open the door to the sweeping lecture hall, there's Reeve strutting his way across the room. And there's that familiar little spark of excitement in my chest. I head for my usual seat, wishing I had the courage and social skills to walk up to him and insert myself into the conversation he just struck up with a group of people a few feet away. One of them mentions the football party on Saturday and my gut churns. Does Reeve hand out party invites like candy, or am I going to have to invite myself to this thing? Jade keeps reminding me girls don't need invitations to parties, but it's not about getting in. It's about getting invited by Reeve.

From the corner of my eye, I see him glance my way, and suddenly nerves wash away my excitement completely. But I tell myself this feeling is good. For once, my nervousness isn't about my grades or what my editor will think of my latest article or what my mom's voice will sound like the next time she answers her phone. This is the opposite of all of that. I'm letting loose for once.

I pretend not to notice Reeve and his friend approaching, but of course I do; everyone does. I wipe my suddenly sweaty palms against my jeans, trying to be subtle. I can't do this. Maybe today I'll just settle for flirting. There's plenty of time to get an invite from him.

"Hey, Red," Reeve says as he takes the seat next to mine, leaning over me so I can practically feel his deep voice. He must have all of this practiced to perfection, the nickname and the sexy voice, and the whole thing, but I don't care. I'm eating it up. Who even am I?

"Hi." I try to keep my smile coy and cute, but I'm overeager, so I probably look like the Cheshire cat.

Two seats down, Reeve's friend Cameron gives me a cursory

glance before turning his attention elsewhere. Reeve and Cam are a study in beautiful contrasts. Aside from their chiseled good looks and superior football skills, I can't imagine what the two have in common. Reeve is impossible not to notice with his loud laugh and self-assured smile and that gorgeous blond hair that's styled differently every week. Cocky as he is, he's not above chatting up anyone who's willing to listen. And who on campus isn't? Meanwhile, I barely know the sound of dark-haired Cam's voice. He's definitely got that silent, holier-than-thou air about him. Even his gaze is selective and intentional, like he refuses to waste time looking at anything that doesn't interest him. He doesn't grab your attention like Reeve does. Somehow, though, he's harder to look away from.

Unfortunately, he's also an asshole.

"You coming to the game this weekend?" Reeve asks.

I hesitate. Would a yes score me an invite to hang out afterward? The game's hours away, a fact I only know from listening to the sports writers' chatter in the school newsroom. Do girls actually drive for hours just to watch these guys? My apartment's five minutes from our home stadium, and I've still never seen a game. "I don't think so," I say sweetly. "Schoolwork and all that." Am I smiling too much? My teeth feel dry.

"Bet I'll catch you at the next one," Reeve says confidently. "Nice top, by the way." Briefly, his gaze drops to my chest, taking in the lace bra and the deep scoop of my tank top before returning to my face.

"Thanks." My delight is totally out of proportion with the meager compliment, but a crush is a hell of a drug—one I haven't dared let myself taste in so long. *Perfectly reasonable after what happened,* I can hear my old therapist reassuring me. Maybe, but I'm tired of being perfectly reasonable. I don't know why Reeve has suddenly decided to pay attention to me, unless he got bored of flirting with all the beautiful, stylish girls who usually swarm him, and he figured, why not try the opposite? But his lapse in judgment is the most exciting thing to happen to me since my grandparents gifted me a vintage typewriter last year.

And they call these the best years of my life.

"So, Red," Reeve says, "party at the football house this Saturday. You should come by, bring some of your girls."

And just like that, he drops it in my lap. I didn't even have to work for it. I feel an unexpected wave of disappointment—I was supposed to earn that invitation. This was going to be a test of how much I actually want Reeve, and he just pulled the rug out from under me. But the feeling is fleeting. I'm off the hook.

I smile belatedly, finding my voice. "Post-game celebration, I take it?"

"You know it. Win or lose, we're partying." He holds my eye. "You should wear your signature color."

I think it's only an innocent reference to our school mascot, the Red Phantom, but my body responds to it like a compliment, radiating with pleasure.

When Professor Richards walks in the door and students settle into their seats, I let out a deep breath and face the front of the room. I got what I wanted, even if it's far less satisfying than expected. Now I can stop pretending I know what I'm doing and focus on something I'm good at.

When class ends, Reeve nods to me. "See you Saturday."

That's when I spot the T-shirt at the bottom of my bag and remember my little brother. My stomach drops. Am I really going to embarrass myself in front of Reeve and his friend just to make my brother smile? I yank the shirt out. Yes, I am.

"Hey, Reeve?" I say as he's turning away. "I know this is weird, but would you mind, um, signing an autograph?" I feel my cheeks redden as I hold up the shirt.

Reeve looks pleased and throws a quick look at Cam that's surely full of meaning, but even if I could decipher it, I wouldn't want to. Cam, meanwhile, just blinks at me. Much like he did freshman year—the first and last time we spoke—when his dickhead football friends spilled booze all over me. I look away and fumble in my bag for the marker I brought.

Reeve spreads the T-shirt across the desk, smoothing it expertly. "Where do you want my name? Across the chest?" He winks.

"Sure, that's great," I say eagerly. Then I catch his meaning. "Oh, no, actually this is for my little brother so . . . yeah, it's not like that." My cheeks are pure fire. This is even more humiliating than expected.

Reeve shrugs like he's not sure he believes me, but he proceeds with a careful and elaborate signature across the dead center of the shirt. Then he hands the marker to his friend. "Cam?"

Cam looks at me for a brief second and then nods. "Yeah, sure." He produces a small autograph on the shirt sleeve and hands back the marker.

I grin in spite of my embarrassment. Signatures from two of Shafer football's very best? Gus is never going to take this shirt off. "Thanks, guys. You just made my brother's year."

"Anytime," Reeve says and the two of them walk out.

I drag my eyes away from their imposing figures and gather up my things. I have one more man to talk to before I leave class.

Darren Pierce sits at the end of the third row typing on his laptop, his tight curls a little frizzier than usual, his light beard neatly trimmed as always.

As sports editor for the school newspaper, Darren is kind of my new boss. Temporarily, anyway. He glances up as I walk toward him and does an unmistakable double take through his tortoiseshell glasses. I flush, wishing the walk to the third row wasn't so long, and tug the neckline of my top to hide the lacy edges of my bra. Damn Jade for making me think I could pull off this look. Who cares if Reeve likes it? I need Darren to take me seriously.

"How's it going, Lenni?" he says when I reach him. "You're all dressed up again. You know, if you're angling to start a weekly fashion column, I'm not the one you need to impress."

"Ha. Definitely not," I say, pretending to find him funny. But jeez, how much of a slob do I usually come off as? I'm not wearing an evening gown and stilettos here, it's fitted jeans and a tank top. "No, I just wanted to run a few questions by you for this volleyball article. I'm not sure I'm on the right track."

I sit down and show him what I've written, feeling like a freshman reporter all over again. Sports really aren't my thing —I usually write for the Arts and Lifestyle section—but when one of our sports reporters went on abrupt hiatus from school last week, I faked a little enthusiasm and volunteered to cover whatever the other sports writers couldn't get to. If I don't make editor by next year, I can say goodbye to any chance of admission to a great grad program . . . and any chance of saving my family from imploding.

After Darren suggests a few edits for my article, I thank him and stand up. Over by the door, Reeve has stopped to talk to two pretty girls that I'm sure have never snapped an ankle walking in heels. Cam stands silently at his side. The foursome blocks most of the exit, but of course no one complains about having to squeeze past. I'm hoping they leave before I do.

"One more thing, Lenni, while I have you here," Darren says, standing up. He lowers his voice. "It's not looking like Bella is coming back this semester," he says gravely.

"Really? Is she all right?" I'm dying to know why the bright and hardworking Bella is suddenly MIA, but the editors aren't talking and the rumors of her having a secret drug problem are just that: rumors.

"I think she'll be okay after some time at home. But how would you feel about helping fill in the blanks a while longer? Now, don't freak out," he adds quickly, "we're already working on bringing in a new reporter—"

"Definitely!" Sure, this next month threatens to drown me in schoolwork and my part-time job at the fine arts library, but I don't say no to anything for the paper. The more I stand out as a student journalist, the sooner I can support my family.

I glance again at Reeve's group just beyond Darren's shoulder. At that instant, Cam's head turns from his friends, and his eyes shift directly to me. I want to look away because I don't know what to make of his stare—no one ever stares at me like this—but I'm trapped in his gaze.

"You can think about it," Darren assures me. "This is a busy time of year."

I force myself to look at him, but I'm not seeing him at all. "No need," I say quickly. "I'm all in."

Darren expresses some sort of gratitude that I barely hear while I flick my gaze back to Cam. The vivid amber of his eyes blazes bright even from across the room, and the dark arches of his eyebrows betray a focus that makes me uncomfortably aware of myself. My heart, perfectly at ease an instant ago, is hammering in my throat. And then it's over. The boys disappear through the doorway while I sit staring at the spot Cam just occupied and recovering from the intensity of his eyes.

And suddenly, I'm not thinking about Reeve at all.

cameron

"DID you see what Lenni was wearing?" Reeve smirks as we walk out into the hallway.

"Hard not to," I say. Lenni in a tight top might be the reason I fail Applied Statistics this semester. Now that she's suddenly started wearing clothes that aren't two sizes too big, it's impossible to ignore the fact that her body is nothing but soft curves as far as the eye can see. I pull out my phone for distraction because I know what Reeve's going to say next and I'm not in the mood.

"You know why? 'Cause I told her I liked her in that tight top. She's under my thumb."

I don't want to admit he's right.

"All of a sudden she's proud of her tits and we're all richer for it," he continues. "Call me an asshole, but I do have a knack for making girls feel good about their bodies."

"You're skilled at spreading joy to a certain subset of the female population, I'll give you that. Too bad you usually follow it up by making them cry."

Reeve laughs. "Don't be jealous. Now that Kira's finally set you free, time for you to break some hearts of your own. Let's see what kind of friends Lenni brings on Saturday night. I bet she rolls with a few hot little bookworms."

"Suddenly you're into chicks who can read? Let's pray your evolution from complete Neanderthal doesn't affect your throwing arm."

"Evolution? Don't get crazy. I'm just trying to spice things up for all of us. You can thank me when some nerd chick is in your bed wearing glasses and nothing else."

But not only am I not interested in Lenore's—er, Lenni's friends, I'm hoping she doesn't even show up Saturday night. This thing with her and Reeve is still new and already I can't stand the awkwardness of being in the same room as them. See, what Reeve doesn't know is that she and I have a history. And I'm starting to think Lenni doesn't even know it herself.

"Man, I'm starving," Reeve says as we cut across campus. "You coming to lunch?"

"Not today. I need to hit this study session before my exam tomorrow."

Reeve barks out a laugh. "Study session? What happened, grades are slipping down to a solid A-minus?"

I tell him, kind of sheepishly, that the girl who usually leads the student study sessions is out with mono and our professor asked me to lead today's group. Even though Reeve and I have known each other since seventh grade, I feel weird sometimes talking to him about grades. He's smart as hell, but learning disabilities—most of which were diagnosed late—have always made school challenging for him. He plays it cool, but I know our academic differences get to him.

But today, he nods approvingly. "That's cool, Cam. It's about time your teachers recognized your grades aren't dumb luck."

"Thanks. Hey, Lorenzo needs to know if you want in on the poker game Thursday. I'll spot you." Lorenzo, our middle linebacker and my freshman roommate, hosts a poker night that's almost always more fun than hitting the bars.

"No can do. Big Dina's in town Thursday, remember?"

"Oh, right. That's good, man. Bet she's pumped to see you on the field."

Reeve nods and rubs the back of his neck. "Yeah. . . we'll see."

Reeve's mom, Dina, hasn't always been around, and secretly I wonder if he's better off because of it. I hate seeing the nervous quiet that comes over my normally brash friend when one of her rare visits is on the horizon.

"Is that your whole night?" I ask.

"Probably. I figured I'd take her for dinner in town."

"Yeah, that reminds me." I take my wallet from my pocket and pull out a silver gift card. "Here." I hand it to him.

Reeve looks at the card, then at me. "What's this?"

"Can you read?"

Reeve checks the card again and his eyebrows jump. "Bistro Violette. Hold up, what? You're giving this to me?"

"It's not really for you, it's for Dina. I'll let you take her, though."

Reeve smiles. "Come on, man. Seriously? This is the nicest restaurant between here and Chicago. And wasn't this a gift from Kira's family?"

"What am I going to do, walk in there with my dick in my hand and ask for a table for two? I don't need it."

"There's not one chick in this town who wouldn't give her left tit for dinner with you at Violette." He holds the gift card out to me.

"Take it. Tell Dina I owe her one."

"At least come with us."

I shake my head. "That's all you."

Reeve taps the card against his open palm and looks at me like he's trying to figure out what to say. Finally, he smiles. "Yeah, all right. Thanks, Cam." He gives my chest a smack with the back of his palm. "Think I need a suit for this place? Can I borrow one off you?"

"Yeah, like you could ever fill out the shoulders." I squeeze his shoulder, then push him away. "Nah, shirt and tie are all you need."

"Good. I'd probably bust right through the crotch of your little suit pants anyway."

I laugh. "Keep the dream alive, man."

THE STUDY SESSION GOES FINE, if not a little awkwardly. I could practically smell the skepticism coming off the other students when they realized I was leading for the day, but I get a kick out of proving to people that I'm not some dumb jock. Those students just better ace the exam.

I'm leaving the library after the session when I spot Lenni lingering between the stacks, searching for a book. She's thinking; I can tell because the tip of her tongue is touching her top lip, a move I always catch her making when she's concentrating in class. She's out of sight within seconds, but I know what'll happen next. I'll be thinking about her for the next three hours until practice starts, and then my mind clears of everything but football.

I don't know why this keeps happening. In the last two years, I've caught sight of her barely a handful of times on campus, but ever since this weird flirtation between her and Reeve started, I swear she's everywhere. And she's definitely not the girl I remember.

· · ·

Shafer freshman orientation took place during the hottest, muggiest three days of the entire summer. Even though my mom's house is only twenty minutes from campus, all incoming freshmen had to stay in a dorm, and on our last night, I'd skipped out when the dudes I was rooming with went trolling for girls. I was still holding on to my high school girlfriend—a relationship doomed to end undramatically three weeks later—which made for a good excuse to wander campus and be alone.

I'd stumbled across a sunken garden in the middle of campus, a small rectangle of grass enclosed by shrubs, gnarled trees, and spiky ornamental grasses. A low stone wall doubling as a bench ran along all four sides of the space, and lights hidden among the plants cast exaggerated shadows. I sat down at the far end of the garden, where an old, eroded fountain bubbled away. No one was around. Immediately, I breathed easier.

I was thinking about the school year ahead and that, come August, this spot might be the only place on campus I could be alone when, suddenly, I wasn't alone anymore.

A girl wandered down the steps, her eyes on the ground like she hadn't even realized what she'd just walked into. The first thing I noticed was that she was wearing men's basketball shorts and a baggy T-shirt. The second thing I noticed was the way the garden lighting shone on her wet, tear-stained face.

Instinctively, I stood up like I was being summoned. She saw me and stopped short, her expression caught halfway between crying and surprise. "Oh." She looked around. "Are you . . . ?"

"No," I said, not even knowing what she was asking. I sat and motioned to the empty space between us to let her know she was free to be. "Go ahead." Just as naturally as if this raggedy garden was marked on the campus map as the Place to Feel Your Feelings. She nodded and found a seat in the corner farthest from me, then pulled her legs up onto the bench and retreated into herself.

I was glad she wanted to be left alone and that I didn't have the uncomfortable job of trying to soothe her. Growing up with the mother I did, I'm used to women's tears, but a stranger is a different business. But after a few minutes and a few soft sobs out of her, I felt like a complete dick.

"Do you need help?" I asked. "I can call someone for you."

She shook her head quickly. "I'm okay. Just . . . there's nowhere to be alone on this campus, is there?" She sniffed.

"I was wondering the same thing."

We returned to silence. Reeve texted to ask where I was, but I didn't answer and instead turned my phone to silent. I knew I should leave soon—I felt for the sad chick, but she'd killed the mood. Then I heard a snuffling sound; she was chuckling.

"I just realized what you meant when you said you were wondering the same thing. You found the one place at Shafer you could be alone, and I walked in and ruined it. Sorry about that."

"No, I just meant I get it—wanting to be alone."

She looked at me like she was hoping I'd keep talking.

"So no," I said, suddenly self-conscious that I'd outed myself as someone who needed alone time. It didn't fit with the unfazed image we freshmen all seemed required to project. "I don't mind you being here."

It got quiet, but the mood had changed. Instead of two strangers silently trying to ignore each other, we were two strangers together in silence. At least that's how I felt. And the way her body relaxed, and her tears dried up, I think she felt it too.

"If I tell you why I'm here, will you tell me why you are?" she said after a while.

I looked over to find her directing a small smile at the fountain in front of her. I wasn't sure what to say and while I hesitated, she slung her gaze my way. "Sorry. I thought at first that was too weird of a question to ask a stranger, but then . . . " She trailed off.

"No, your first instinct was right, definitely too weird. Luckily, I'm kind of a weird guy."

She chuckled, looking embarrassed. Her grin transformed her face, wide and bright and showing off perfect white teeth. It was the first authentic laugh I'd earned in a while. Girls are always suspiciously quick to laugh at what I say.

"Why am I here?" I said thoughtfully. My brain readied a generic excuse sure to get her off my back, but I stopped. I didn't want her off my back. "I guess I needed a break from the freshman orientation scene."

"What scene is that?" Her tone told me she already knew.

"The one where everyone pretends they're chill as fuck about leaving home forever."

"When we're really scared shitless, you mean?"

"Right. Everyone acts like an unfriendly asshole to prove how not scared shitless they are."

She nodded.

"I guess I do it too," I admitted. "But at least I do the normal thing and show up here to have a proper cry all alone."

She laughed. "Oh, so you came here to cry too? Why didn't you say so?"

"Seemed indecent, stealing your thunder."

"I'm done if you'd like to have your turn."

"Nah. I think I'm better now." At this, her expression seemed to glow.

Loud voices erupted from somewhere near the dorm, a few

guys shouting and a girl laughing. Coming closer. She looked at me, putting her finger to her mouth; *be quiet.* I slid over a few inches, so my back was against a bushy shrub. The plants made a thin wall, but someone walking by would only have to peer between a couple ornamental trees to see beyond them. We looked at each other as we listened to the group approaching. The moment built. Humor danced in her eyes, like she was about to laugh, which made me want to laugh. It was silly; we had nothing to hide. By the time the voices were right behind me, my heart beat hard in my chest. Maybe we had nothing to hide, but if someone walked in, it wouldn't be just us anymore, and in the moment, that felt like the worst thing that could happen.

When the group passed and their voices finally faded into the distance, we both let out the laugh we'd been holding in.

"Close one," I said, and she nodded enthusiastically.

And that was the way it went; skipping the small talk and going straight for the things we were too embarrassed to tell our own friends. But mostly laughing about them. She told me about growing up with a single mom and the much-younger brother who was clearly the bright spot in her life, and the fiction she wrote in her spare time. Later, when she hesitantly asked me if I'd really come here to have a cry, her gullibility made me realize instantly, I had a little crush on her.

It didn't hurt that she had the most perfect lips I've ever seen. But it went beyond that. She was easy to be around in a way I wasn't used to. It wasn't just that she was undemanding. I knew plenty of girls who acted happy to go along with whatever I wanted to do, laughed at whatever jokes were told. What drew me in was how certain I felt that she wasn't trying to make me believe she was anyone except who she was. She wasn't any particular type of girl, and she didn't need me to be any particular type of guy. She didn't ask if I played sports or if I planned to join a frat or what my major would be. I was glad not to share.

It was an instant friendship, deep in the way only temporary friendships can be. We didn't even exchange names until the night was almost over. She'd introduced herself as Lenore.

When we said goodbye a few hours later, I watched her walk out of the garden, wishing there was more to it than that. I wanted more of her. The air felt thick with humidity and my own guilt as I headed back to the dorm. Even though I hadn't flirted with her, I felt something I'd never felt for my girlfriend, for any girl. I just didn't know what it was. It took me months to figure it out, months of hanging out with self-important athletes and the preening girls who wanted to claim us. Lenore didn't want anything from me except conversation.

She didn't treat me like anyone in particular—not an athlete to be fawned over or a dumb jock to roll her eyes at. I didn't have to be Cam Forrester, devoted son and winning receiver and future pro athlete. I didn't feel the urge to mention my GPA to prove that it was more than my skill at catching a football that landed me admission at Shafer. With Lenore, I could just be.

I knew what I saw in her. A girl who knew who she was, even if she didn't always like it. Someone willing to show me who she was, even if it embarrassed her. That wasn't something you did in my circle. But it was all a one-off.

I didn't see her again until months later at some house party where I got way too drunk. I was there with some guys from the team, and under the dim glow of a flickering porch light, one of them gestured too wildly with his plastic cup and sent a wave of neon-red jungle juice straight into the chest of a girl walking by. It took me a minute to realize the girl was

Lenore, and in my slow drunken state, another minute to react. The guys I was with weren't too slow, though. They laughed or smirked, some of them having the decency to try to hide their smiles behind their cups, but all of them responding like dicks. I remember fumbling uselessly, trying to think of something to say as I yanked a damp beach towel off the deck railing and handed it to her. I couldn't believe it was her. But she barely looked at me as she took it.

"Hey," I'd said, thinking she'd recognize me instantly. "We were—"

"Chill, Prince Charming," one of my teammates said loudly, clapping me on the back. "She looks better now anyway."

Lenore had looked hotly at him, then gave me a quick glare as she turned away. And that was that. I remember staring at her back as she hurried off, my brain yelling at my mouth to say *something*, even just her name, but nothing came out.

After that, ignoring each other became the norm. I never saw her at another party, never had a class with her, just spotted her once in a while crossing the quad or starting up the stairs as I came down. She didn't acknowledge me, and I pretended not to care. But her indifference stung. Apparently our night in the garden hadn't meant as much to her as it had to me. That or maybe she didn't even recognize me as the guy she met at orientation. I *had* cut my hair the first week of practice after Coach told me I looked like I should've been shoving flowers down the barrel of an M14 rifle.

Whatever her reason, it doesn't matter now. The other week, she showed up to our Applied Statistics class wearing this tight red top which was impossible not to notice because a) she's stacked, and b) I've never seen her in anything that didn't look like it was borrowed from a boyfriend. That top was like catnip for Reeve, and when he told her how good she looked, she lit up like a Christmas tree. And ever since, I've been watching him play his game and her fall for it like a lost puppy, and wondering what the hell happened to her.

Now I know she doesn't hate me for being an athlete; I'm just waiting for the moment she offers to do Reeve's homework for him and enters into full jersey-chaser mode. So the question nags harder at me: Why is she pretending not to know me?

cameron

I HATE this part of the day. Class is over, practice starts in thirty minutes and my brain kicks on the anxiety.

It wasn't always like this. Sure, practice has always been brutal. The wind sprints, the Oklahoma drills, the occasional vomiting when mid-eighties temps and Coach's sadistic streak combine into stomach-churning misery. But I never used to care. This year, apprehension hits me in the gut as soon as my last class ends and my mind shifts into athlete mode.

The locker room is quiet today, reminding me I'm not the only one who feels the change. Reeve nods when I come in but he's getting dressed silently, for once not in the mood to broadcast who he slept with this week. Lorenzo doesn't look up from tying his shoes as I walk by. Even Cash, known as much for his enthusiasm as his solid running back skills, skips his trademark "Chin up, motherfucker" and chatters mindlessly about baseball stats while he changes a few lockers down.

It all comes down to two little words: the draft. Our entire football careers, it was the distant dream, the prize you focused on in those shitty moments when you wondered why you ever picked up a football in the first place. The future you swore was yours when you were riding high. But here we are. Junior year. We're closing in on our last chance to prove who we are on the field. Everything we've worked for is right there on the horizon, just out of sight. Or else it's not there at all and never will be.

Something in these last few weeks has turned the pressure that I always accepted as an athlete into a suffocating weight I can't get out from under. It's not the first time I've had mixed feelings about football. Senior year of high school I was burnt out and one bad game away from quitting the team entirely, and it wasn't my love of the sport that stopped me, it was Reeve. *Not an option*, was all he said, but the subtext was clear: not senior year, not when you have colleges after you, and not when football is the entire foundation of your friendship with a guy who's more like a brother.

This is different, though; it's not burnout. This is love and hate, fear and need, a constant push and pull. I feel like I can barely breathe during those hours before a game, walking into the locker room, pulling on my gear. Then I step out onto the turf and play begins and my head clears, and I remember: Oh, right, I fucking love football.

It's ones against ones and we're running our newest plays. First play, I beat my man to the outside. Reeve hits me in stride going down the sideline, and nobody can catch me. On the next play, I pick on the safety. We run play action and I go to the post and tear right by everybody. Two for two. We line up again. This time, it's a bootleg to the opposite side and I run all the way across the middle. Reeve finds me. I put a move on the first guy and split the other two defenders, and I score again.

Our offensive coordinator nods his approval. "Play like that on Saturdays, Forrester, and you might be on your way to breaking the record for touchdown catches in a season."

I acknowledge his compliment, trying not to make too much of it, but I already hear the words echoing in my head, where they'll stay all week, reminding me my big plans might not be all that far out of reach.

We're walking off the field when an ugly voice pipes up behind me. "Break the record for touchdown catches, huh, Forrester?" I turn to see the smug face of Mason Connery, a little shit of a backup receiver. "You got a long way to go before you beat my brother's record."

Mason's older brother was a phenomenal wide receiver who graduated from Shafer last year and was snatched up in the first round of the draft. He was basically my idol freshman year. Too bad his younger brother inherited half his height, a fourth of his talent, and not a drop of his charm.

I give Mason a tolerant smile. "Spend a little more time on the game and a little less up your brother's ass and maybe you'll see some playing time this year."

"Oh, yeah?" His voice is bitter; he's getting ready to turn up the charm now. Mason never fails to make up for his small stature and shitty personality by being a complete asshole. "Maybe if you racked up a few more yards, that hot-ass girlfriend of yours would still be sucking your dick. Oh, sorry, *ex*-girlfriend."

My shoulders tighten, but I force the tension back down. Mason's not the first guy on the team to have something to say about my recent breakup with one of the most beautiful girls on campus.

"Bet she's getting hungry," he says a little quieter. "Maybe I'll give her my number."

Up ahead, Reeve and Cash are heading for the locker room.

"Good luck," I tell Mason as I walk away. "She's got a height requirement and you're about a foot short."

"Connery being mouthy again?" Reeve asks, eyeballing Mason over my shoulder when I catch up to him.

I nod. "Napoleon complex in full effect today."

"Want me to smash him into a locker?" Cash asks.

"You do you. Nobody would miss him."

Sometimes I feel bad for Mason. He walked onto this team thinking he was a big shot just because his brother was a stud. Even guys who gave him the benefit of the doubt early on are starting to turn on him. It's painful to watch sometimes. But then he starts in on my ex sucking his dick, and suddenly it feels good to know that if there are two things that unite our team, it's winning games and hating Mason.

I'M SHOWERED and half dressed, standing in front of my locker when my phone rings on the bench behind me. Busybody that he is, Reeve grabs it before I can see who's calling.

"Hey, Minnie," he answers, turning casually back to his locker with the phone pressed to his ear like my mom was calling just to talk to him. Which she probably was. Reeve lived with my family on and off through high school, so my mom is like his second mother. She's definitely seen more of him than his real mom. It's only as I'm walking out of the locker room and heading home that the two of them manage to wrap up the gabfest and Reeve hands me my phone.

"Hi, doll," comes Mom's melodic, southern accent.

"Hey, Ma. How's it going?"

"Just fine, just fine. How was practice?"

"Good. Hey, before I forget, did you get the patio thing resolved with the contractor?"

"Oh, he's taking his sweet time, but he'll get to it."

"When, in January when the ground's frozen? Just send me

the dude's number already, please? I'm sick of him jerking you around."

"You threatening the man won't see my patio finished any faster."

"Yeah, I know, you catch more flies and all that. I'm not going to threaten him, I just want to remind him you have a grown son who's not half as sweet and charming as his mother when she's being taken advantage of."

"Honey, dealing with a lazybones contractor is a piece of cake compared to what I've pulled myself through."

"I know, Mom." She's walked through hell these last few years, and she's managed to do it without her beauty-queen smile ever faltering, but if you know her well enough, you know that what my father did has changed her irreversibly. Maybe I can't fix that, but I can get her patio finished sooner.

"I have other news for you," she says brightly.

"Just promise you'll send me the guy's number if he doesn't show up by the end of the week, okay?"

"Sure. Can we carry on now? I wanted to tell you I'm thinking of bringing a few friends to the game this weekend."

I hesitate. I know where this conversation is headed. "I didn't realize you were coming. It's an away game."

"I'm aware."

"That's a three-hour drive."

"We'd make a weekend of it. I've been talking you up to my girlfriends, and they'd love to catch a game."

"Fine by me, but if you're looking for a guaranteed win, this one isn't it."

Heavy silence. "Oh?"

"They're ranked number three, Ma."

"I know what they're ranked."

"So it'll be a tough game; their receiver is probably best in the nation."

"I see." I can hear the wheels turning in her head. A game where her son doesn't dominate every second he's on the field? And with friends there to witness? Bad news. "I wonder if perhaps this isn't the right weekend for a game."

"Your call, Mom," I tell her. "I'm almost home so I'm gonna go. Just let me know about tickets."

"Sure thing, I'll think about it. Love you, doll."

She doesn't need to think about it; she's not bringing anyone to a game where I don't shine bright enough to justify her constant bragging. I couldn't care less if my mom's friends see me up against a better athlete. What I can't do is let my mom down, not after everything she's put into my football career and not after the shit she's been through. My mom deserves to see a dream come true.

It's just too bad her only dream is me signing a pro football contract. Because the closer I get to the end of my college ball career, the more I worry it might all end right there.

lenni

"OKAY, HOW ABOUT THIS ONE?" I hold up a fire-engine red minidress to my body.

Jade looks up from the rack of jeans she's combing through and groans. "Oh my god, *Red*. Get over it!"

We laugh, attracting the attention of the salesgirl tagging secondhand T-shirts a few feet away. Her eyes linger on Jade, whose hair color du jour is baby blue. "Is that a no?" I ask.

Jade takes the dress from my hands and places it back on the rack. "Unless Reeve is taking you to a rave for your first date, that's a hard pass."

"Please. I don't think Reeve does dates."

"True. And if he did, it would be something totally unoriginal like dinner and a movie. I mean, calling you Red? Seriously? So lame."

We both know she's right, just like we both know I secretly swoon over said lame nickname. Therefore, I choose to say nothing.

Jade eyes me. "Okay, what exactly are we doing here? You want something short, tight, or otherwise sexy, my closet's the place to go."

We're in my favorite consignment store—my favorite because it's basically the only place I can afford to shop and because the owner always gives me a heads-up when a cool band tee comes in. And I'm not exactly sure what I'm doing here except trying to find the perfect clothes to transform me into whoever it is I seem to be turning into.

"I wish," I tell Jade. "You know my ass wouldn't fit into anything you own."

"Reminds me, I need to try your lower body routine." Jade runs a hand absently over her butt. "But for real, what are we doing here?"

"Finding an outfit for the football party."

"If Reeve was worth a damn, he'd like your boyish style."

"I thought you were excited to help me shop outside the men's section."

"I am! I fully support your newfound body confidence and your style and all of it. I especially support you finally having a crush, I'm just wondering why it has to be him." Who knows the exact moment Jade decided she hates Reeve Dalton, but if she ever changes her mind, hell will freeze over. Jade's decisiveness is almost as admirable as it is frightening.

"It doesn't have to be him," I tell her. "It just is. He's the one that stoked the feeling. That's all."

I poke through the clothing rack again, starting to hate what this crush is becoming. It began as just a feeling: The feeling of being invisible all my life and then, without warning, finding the attention of the most wanted guy on campus concentrated entirely on me. Who wouldn't crave more?

"You know what I think?" Jade's green eyes flare. "I think you just like the attention."

I sort faster through the hangers.

"You do!" Jade declares. "I can't believe it, but you do! Two-plus years of living together and I'm finally rubbing off on you."

I bite back a smile. I've never liked attention, especially from guys, which worked out beautifully because I rarely got any. And it's only now that I'm basking in the glow of Reeve Dalton's gaze that I have to acknowledge how crappy it is that I used to feel superior to girls who got off on male attention. "Maybe I do," I admit. "In small doses and from certain people."

"And Reeve is certain people because he said you look good in red?" She curls her lip like she finds this repulsive.

"He said he'd never seen me in that color before and I should wear it more often." I've already told her this story, but stuff like this never happens to me, so she's going to hear it again. "Which means he's been watching me long enough to notice what I wear."

"Because he sees all women as prey. A hunter can describe a deer's coat color in fine detail, I'm sure."

"He was nice to me before the red top."

"When?"

"First day of class. I was late, almost every spot was filled, and he took his backpack off the seat next to him so I could sit down."

"Whoa, basic human decency? You're right, that is impressive for a dog."

I sigh. Trying to change Jade's mind is a waste of time. Besides, she's probably right. Reeve might have manners, but he wouldn't have looked at me twice if not for the fact that one morning, liking what my weightlifting routine had done to my body, I took a risk and wore the only tight shirt I own to class.

"You are so far above that fool it's not even funny," Jade can't help but add.

"I never said I was planning on doing anything with him. I'm only talking about how he makes me feel."

"Which is what?"

"Like I'm one of *those* girls: fun, easygoing, knows how to have a good time."

"I don't think you want Reeve to consider you a girl who knows how to have a good time." She gives me a meaningful look.

"Why? You're usually a cheerleader for casual hookups."

"Because you don't do casual sex. You don't do casual anything."

"That's the problem. Flirting with this guy for a few minutes before class is the most exciting thing I've done as a college junior. Maybe I need more casual sex. Or casual something in my life."

A slow, conspiratorial smile spreads over her face. "I remember you. You're that girl who used her bra to sling water balloons at unsuspecting guys from the top floor of our dorm the first week of college."

I smile at the memory of spending the first month of freshman year carefree and optimistic. I chalk it up to being drunk on freedom and false hope for turning my life around in every conceivable way. You meet one amazing person when you arrive at college and it's easy to start thinking like that. But I shake it off. "That's not me anymore."

"Oh, come on. You can plan your future and worry about your family and still blow off steam once in a while. All I'm saying is ease into it. I mean, when's the last time you even kissed someone? Freshman year?"

"No way! It was this year."

"When?" Jade narrows her feline eyes like she's zeroing in on prey. Why did I even open my mouth?

"January." I turn away and feign interest in a table full of costume jewelry.

Jade follows me. "January first, you mean?"

"I guess."

"January first at 12:01 a.m.?" She laughs. "At the New Year's party where everyone had to kiss whoever was standing closest to them at midnight? Lenni! I bet you didn't even use tongue!"

"A kiss is a kiss."

She shakes her head. "Not with Reeve Dalton. I guarantee a kiss leads to getting naked with him. What if he asks you to spend the night on Saturday?"

I don't tell her about the text Reeve sent me earlier, the one suggesting I stay over Saturday night after the party and promising he'll make me a mind-blowing plate of French toast the next morning. Before I share that with Jade, I need to figure out why, after the initial thrill of reading those words, I've felt nothing but anxiety ever since.

"I might not even go to the party." I sigh. "Look, I'm just enjoying this crush for what it is. I haven't let myself have fun with a guy like this . . . ever."

Her eyes soften. "Who could blame you? You've been through a lot."

I look away and nod. I trust Jade more than anyone in the world, but I hate talking about my past. "I need to force myself to move on."

"Force yourself? I don't think so." Jade reaches out to squeeze my hand. "But I get what you're saying. You should have your fun and not have to worry about defining it . . . yet."

"I sense a 'but' coming on."

"But Reeve Dalton isn't relationship material. Just FYI."

"Please. A relationship is the last thing I want, especially not with some athlete."

"All right, I'll lay off you. But I reserve the right to gag every time I hear him call you Red." Jade's phone chirps. "Oh, god," she says as she reads the text. "Sam has lost his damn mind."

"What?"

"You know how he keeps track of everything? Apparently today is the anniversary of our first date." She holds up her phone to show the picture her boyfriend sent, which features the two of them leaning in close. She rolls her eyes, but she's smiling.

"Aww. I remember that night." Jade had been unenthusiastic and on the verge of canceling, having only said yes to a date because she was in a dry spell. But by the time she came home that night, she was practically in love. "So what did he get you this time? A hot-pink Maserati?" Sam is a masterful and generous gift giver.

"He says he's treating me and a friend—obviously you—to a spa day on Saturday. Ooh, he must have a Design, Build, Fly meeting. Those always go for hours."

"That's really sweet."

"He's so cheesy," Jade says, her voice brimming with affection. Sam is cheesy sometimes, but he's also the perfect boyfriend. Our friends love to give Jade and Sam crap for having such a picture-perfect romance, but I think they're the sweetest. Who doesn't dream of having the kind of love you never need to question? "So what should I book? Massages and manis?"

I shake my head. "I'm covering the volleyball game on Saturday."

"Girl, aren't you tired of saying yes to every damn thing your editors ask you to do?"

"The fact that they're asking me to do more is a good sign. Did I tell you Darren liked my volleyball article?"

"Of course he did. You're such a good writer even I enjoyed reading it. I'm telling you, if those fools don't make you an editor by spring, I'm burning down the newsroom."

"Thanks, that'll definitely help me achieve my goals!"

"Yeah, yeah. Achieve this, Darren." Jade throws up her

middle finger. "Anyway, I'll tell Sam we'll do the salon thing Sunday instead."

"No, don't change it for me. Take Madison, she could use the pampering." Our friend, Madison, is fresh off a devastating breakup. "Besides, I'd just end up picking off the nail polish an hour later."

Jade makes a sad face. "I'll miss you."

"Tell you what, let's get breakfast Saturday morning and you can help me agonize some more over what to wear to the party." I quickly add, "If I go."

"Deal. But you know it's not your outfit you need to figure out."

I know, I know.

A guy like Reeve has plenty to offer a girl that doesn't include a relationship. I'm just not sure that girl is me.

lenni

I'M on my way to class and I'm nervous as hell.

It's not the sweet butterflies-in-the-stomach nervous either, it's the Reeve-Dalton-is-too-much-for-me-to-handle nervous. Last night when I should have been working on edits I got swept up in a text exchange with him that left me wondering if I'm in over my head. I know getting asked for nudes is just another Wednesday for some girls, but not for me. And when I coyly said no, he rolled with it and said he prefers the real thing anyway. Like us getting naked together is inevitable. I keep telling myself to just see where this flirtation might go because maybe the star quarterback is exactly the kind of guy to teach me how to loosen up and leave the past behind. Dive into the deep end. Go big or go home.

But the closer I get to the possibility of actually being alone with him, the more my nervousness feels like fear. What if Reeve isn't the guy you experiment on when you're just learning how to have a crush again? There's no way I could live up to his expectations, sexually and otherwise. And I know better than to trust him.

When I get to class, Reeve's not there, but his friend is. As I take my usual seat, Cam looks over at me and flashes a brief, liquid smile that jolts me back to the look he gave me the other day. Suddenly he deigns to acknowledge me? Must be Reeve's doing. I stumble through a greeting and quickly turn away to pull out my laptop. No wonder he smiles so rarely, that thing is like a loaded weapon.

When I glance over again a minute later, he's reading a book I recognize from my other class.

"Are you in Writing for the Digital Age?" I ask.

"Uh-huh." He doesn't take his eyes off the page.

"I've never seen you there." It's not that I'm calling him a liar. But that class is well-known as one of the toughest upper-level electives, so yeah . . . maybe I am.

"I'm in the Thursday section."

I wait a beat before answering, trying to make my voice neutral. "That's the honors section."

He looks over at me. "I know." The little smile he gives before turning back to his book is triumphant and oh, so arrogant, but can I blame him? I had him pegged as a meathead.

I shrug like I'm not overly impressed by this revelation, then, when it's safe, sneak a sidelong glance at him as he reads. Jet-black lashes line his eyes, the kind any girl would kill for. In profile, his lips curve into a subtle pout, pillowy and tantalizing, like surely he has to be an amazing kisser because how could those lips not feel as perfect as they look? The back of my neck prickles, and I'm suddenly acutely aware of every inch of space that separates his body from mine. Without Reeve there to suck up all the oxygen, I realize Cam might be the most gorgeous man I've ever laid eyes on.

And ice freaking cold, I remind myself.

I force myself to look away, but his image still lingers. How are these guys even more attractive in person than on those cheesy football posters plastered all over the student union? Not that I have a problem with the posters; the guys look ripped to hell, biceps bulging as they run down the field in those shiny, tight football pants. Something about that silhouette really does it for me. Skintight pants, thick shoulder pads, and those big, strong hands football players always have? Uh-huh. I wouldn't complain if Darren asked me to give women's volleyball a rest and cover a football game or two. I'd fail spectacularly, sure, but I wouldn't complain.

Up front, Professor Richards clears his throat and shuffles a few papers, and I'm brought back to earth. It's ten o'clock on the dot.

I look over at Cam. "Think I should take notes for Reeve until he gets here?"

If I thought his earlier smile was a sign of something warming between us, I stand corrected by the chilly look he gives me. "Reeve's not coming," he tells me, his voice laced with annoyance. "And no."

Jeez. Cameron Forrester may be hot, but he also doesn't let anyone forget what an elitist asshole he is.

As Professor Richards greets the class, a little wave of relief washes through me knowing I won't have to face Reeve and my indecision today. I push aside my lingering thoughts about him and concentrate on the sound of Richards's voice.

Only once during class do I get sidetracked, and that's when I notice Cam looking at me. Not my boobs, which account for half of what scant attention I get. And not my class notes, which account for the other half. He's looking at me.

If I was as experienced as Jade in being stared at, I'd know what to make of the look on Cam's face. It's not the stunned-by-your-beauty expression I undoubtedly wore when I was sneaking looks at him earlier, but it makes my cheeks burn hot all the same. Cam, though, is cool as ever, totally unfazed at being caught staring. I snap my gaze back to the front of the room and vow not to let my eyes stray again.

A normal person would give a casual goodbye, but when class ends, I'm still flustered by Cam's hot-and-cold demeanor, so I quickly pack up and leave. I'm just outside the door when I hear him call my name. Not Lenni but Lenore. No one here calls me that.

I turn around, a deer in headlights watching him approach. His expression isn't friendly, so I let my eyes drop to his body, taking in his impressive height and the sharp cut of muscles under his clothes. But just as he comes out into the hallway, someone says his name.

She's blond, whip thin, and I have never, and I mean never, seen her smile. I don't remember her name, but I know she's Cam's girlfriend.

He says something to her and looks back at me, taking another step in my direction. But she reaches for him, and I watch his resolve disappear. He gives me a final look and I can't help it; I roll my eyes. The image of the two of them together in all their genetic-lottery glory is just so. . . I don't know. . . vomit-inducing. Something about it snaps me right out of my fawning over him and back to what I already know: He's just another dickhead football player at Shafer—all style, no substance and zero regard for any of us little people.

I walk out of the building, but I still see Cam and his girl-friend in my head. Their combined beauty is infuriating. I've heard her mother was a famous Russian model in the '90s and her father is some European bajillionaire, but you don't need to know any vof that to guess that she—and therefore Cam and anyone else she associates with—is of the highest echelon of the social order. Her hair, her clothes, her rail-thin body just scream European wealth. I don't know why she's at Shafer

University, unless it's to bag a rich American athlete like Cam and merge dynasties.

And that's fine; to each her own. But I fail to see any love between her and Cam. Theirs is probably a bond built on him buying her diamond-encrusted vials of cocaine and her reciting his football stats while giving him blow jobs that leave not the slightest smear of her perfect nude lipstick.

It takes the entire walk to my next class spent analyzing Cam and his girlfriend—neither of whom I've ever had a full conversation with—before I remember it's Reeve I'm supposed to be obsessing over.

cameron

I WATCH LENORE—LENNI, that is—roll her eyes at me and walk off. And I'm officially baffled. She hates me.

Without Reeve around, I thought if I could get her to look at me for more than a couple seconds, I'd be able to read her. Maybe she did forget me. Yeah, I'd committed the steely blue-gray of her eyes to memory, but my face might've passed right through her, instantly forgotten after that summer night. But when she looked at me today, that wasn't indifference in her gaze.

Now Kira's cost me my chance to ask Lenni why she acts like the night we met never happened. "What is it?" I ask, trying to contain my irritation.

Kira glances at a departing Lenni. "Can we talk?" The question is only a formality because everything she asks for, I give her, and just because we're not together anymore doesn't mean that's changed. She closes her long fingers around my arm, and we start down the hallway.

"So what's up?" I ask.

"First of all, Cameron, how are you?"

My jaw tenses. "Come on, Kir, don't stand on ceremony. What do you want to talk about?"

She drops the painted-on pleasant expression. "Fine. I wanted to tell you I'm dating someone."

I wait for a stab of jealousy, but nothing comes. "Ok. Thanks for letting me know." I try to sound serious so she doesn't realize I don't care who she's started fucking.

"Alex Novik," she offers, not that I asked. She's watching me so I nod because there's nothing to say. This is the least surprising news she could have given me. Alex Novik is one of the dudes in her tightly controlled circle of rich European kids and the heir to some fortune. Like all of them. I look up ahead for any sign of Lenni, but she's long gone.

"Are you all right with that?" Kira asks insistently, and I realize she wants some kind of reaction from me.

"If you're happy with him, then yeah, of course I am."

I can tell by her silence she's unsatisfied with my answer. Kira was never very emotional and what she felt she always said bluntly, so I'm not sure what she expects from me now. But I can guess what she's thinking: Did we ever love each other?

After she broke up with me, I spent about a day on the same question. When you love someone, a breakup is supposed to hurt. Right? And when the person you love starts dating someone new, you're supposed to be jealous. And we both know I'm not.

Outside the building, I pull her off to the side. "Thanks for telling me, but you don't need to worry. I'm glad you're living your life. As long as he's good to you—"

"He is," she interrupts, lifting her chin.

"Good, Kir. You deserve someone who knows how to make you happy." I lean in to kiss her on the cheek. Her scent is familiar, but it stirs nothing inside me. "So I'll see you around." Total lie. Beyond attending classes, Kir and her friends have zero involvement in campus life.

I walk to my next class, remembering the relief I'd felt when Kira first told me we were done. Not because I was unhappy, but with the relationship over, I could put a check mark on it. I excelled at being the boyfriend she wanted: calling her every morning, listening to her complain about her parents, buying her pricey gifts—Kira's love language. She'd had her list of boyfriend requirements and I'd checked the boxes, but there was nothing more I could be for her. She tried on "girlfriend of an American football player" for a while and it didn't quite fit. Novik, on the other hand, is definitely the type who can help her reach her goal of being a wealthy, pampered wife who'd be flawlessly beautiful if not for the way her terminal discontent shows on her face.

Okay, so I've thought about this a lot. I guess it's easier to analyze Kira than it is to contemplate why I'm fine being in a relationship that doesn't make either of us happy.

So now I'm free and the girl I can't stop thinking about is Lenni.

I found out she writes for the school paper, and I've been reading her articles every time a new issue comes out. She's a talented writer and smart as hell. If she hadn't already proven that the first time we talked, she makes it clear every time she raises her hand in class. Her surprise when she realized I'm in the honors section of Writing for the Digital Age was almost as satisfying as if she'd been impressed.

Of course, it's not her brains I can't stop staring at. The first night we met I thought she was so refreshingly pretty with her loose hair and no makeup. But whatever you call this new style of hers, it brings her sexiness into sharp focus, and I can't look away. I hate being the stereotypical dude who starts drooling the second some nerdy girl slaps on eyeliner and a miniskirt (looking at you, Reeve), but damn.

The sight of her tits in a tight shirt makes me want to dive in headfirst. Her whole body sets me off. The way she walks into a room just . . . gets me. She moves like she's on a mission, all long legs and broad shoulders that make it impossible not to stare. The idea of her using that strong, muscled body, naked and on top of me has kept me awake every night this week. But so has the cold truth that if she's going to wind up in any bed in my house, it'll be Reeve's. And that has me even more heated than any fantasy I have about her. I can't understand why Lenni does the ditzy jersey-chaser schtick when she's around him. And whatever she's playing at, I'm not letting her get away with it any longer.

THAT NIGHT I stop home after practice to change into jeans. Four of us share the house, but tonight the only light comes from Reeve's bedroom. I knock on his door.

"Come in," Reeve calls over the music coming from inside. He's lying on the bed, tossing a neon-yellow foam football up against the ceiling and catching it again.

"Hey. Thought you'd be at dinner with Dina."

"Didn't happen."

There's a little clench in my stomach. I put my hands in my pockets and lean against the doorframe. "Bummer." I don't need to ask what went wrong.

"She said next month, maybe." Reeve keeps tossing the ball. "Heard you and Kira were chatting it up on campus today."

I shake my head. "Seriously? Someone actually told you that?"

"Slow news day. So does she want you back?"

"She just wanted to tell me she's fucking someone else."

He snorts. "Shocker."

"Like I care. You know Kira; stone-faced to the end, but she loves a reaction."

"Good for you not getting pulled back into the bullshit. You need a clear head this season."

"Come play poker with us. We could use another man," I say, even though I know what his answer will be.

"I'm good here." He stares at the ball in his hands. "Maybe don't mention anything about my mom to everyone."

"Wasn't going to." I turn to leave. "Meet up if you change your mind."

"Hold on." Reeve drops the ball and reaches for a pair of jeans on the floor next to the bed. He pulls something out of the back pocket—the gift card—and slings it across the room to me.

I catch the card but hold it out toward him. "Keep it for next month."

Reeve gives a subtle shake of his head as his eyes light on me. Then he picks up the football and his gaze goes to the ceiling again.

"Okay, I get it. You want to be wined and dined," I say, pocketing the gift card. "You and me. Bistro Violette. Next weekend. Let's give this town the football bromance they're craving."

A small smile cracks his facade as he throws the ball into the air once again.

lenni

I'M in the middle of drafting an article about the food truck scene around Shafer, and I've hit a wall. After telling my Arts and Lifestyle editor I don't get enough juicy stories, she'd assigned me this one with a cheesy grin and a promise that Cal's Burger Truck had the juiciest burgers in town. Oof. The story isn't without its perks—free food—but now that the eating is done and the writing has begun, I'm utterly uninspired.

My phone rings and I just about snap my neck looking for it. There are only three people who call instead of texting. I jump up and snatch my phone off the bed to see who it is. Mom. My stomach drops.

"Hey, Mom," I answer, sending up a quick plea that she's sober.

"Hi, love." My mom's clear, bright voice floods me with relief.

"Nice to hear from you. How are things at home?"

"Oh, good enough. Gus is driving me nuts bouncing off the friggin' walls," she says with a chuckle. "He's got a big Boy Scouts campout Grandpa's taking him to."

"I know, he texted me from Nana's phone the other day. Good for him. And how's work?" I try to keep my voice light, but my unnatural singsong tone betrays me.

Two years ago, Mom fell back into some heavy drinking habits after getting sober when I was in middle school. She lost her job, and she and my little brother Gus had to move in with my grandparents, who don't have much money. When Mom's working steadily, she earns just enough to keep them afloat, but she needs her sobriety to keep her job, and she needs her job to maintain her sobriety. Things could fall apart at any minute.

"I'm hanging in," Mom tells me. "My boss has finally come around to letting me adjust my work schedule on Thursdays so I can get to my meetings. I haven't missed one in seven weeks now," she says proudly.

"Mom, that's great! Look at you!" I smile. It's a small victory, but for our family, it's huge. "You should celebrate."

"Russ says when I make ten weeks in a row, he's gonna take me out dancing."

I whoop and my mom laughs. Russ is Mom's first boyfriend since she got sober this time around. I don't trust any man for shit with my mother, but so far, he seems to be a positive force in her life. Even Grandpa likes him enough that he hasn't mentioned the fact that Mom shouldn't be dating this early in her recovery.

"Listen, love," Mom says, "I wanted to tell you I ran into Pete Clemmons yesterday and we got to talking."

"Who?"

"Peter Clemmons? You know, he runs the town paper. You graduated with his son, can't remember his name but that cute kid who drove the souped-up blue pickup."

Ugh. AJ Clemmons. Another guy from high school I'd like to forget, along with my entire graduating class. Oh, what the hell, make it the whole town.

"Ok." I clear my throat. "And?"

"When I told him you were a journalism student writing for Shafer, he said he's starting some kind of digital media company. You know I don't understand that crap, but you would. He wants to talk to you about a summer position. He promised it would pay better than any college job."

This is what I hate about our family. It always comes down to money. Not because we're greedy and not because we value it above all else. Just because we've never had any, and barely scraping by is the closest we've ever come to financial success.

"Mom, I appreciate you putting in a good word, but I've almost got my summer lined up, remember? The internship?"

"Obviously I remember." I can tell by her voice I've touched a nerve. "But this is better. It pays real good and best of all, it means having you here. You know how much we all want you back home again."

My insides churn with guilt. I adore my family, but I'm never going back to my hometown. Not to the people who knew me and not to the humiliating memories. And no one, not even Jade, knows I ended up at Shafer not because of its renowned journalism program but because it was the best school I could get into that no one else from my high school was attending. My hometown is in my past forever. I just haven't managed to find the nerve to share that information with my mom.

"I'll give it some thought," I say tonelessly. Mom doesn't get that what happened to me isn't in the past. She knows the facts of what went down—the whole town does, for fuck's sake. But she doesn't understand the dark, unrelenting feelings that came with it and never left.

"Yeah, please do," Mom says. I hate the chill that's settled between us.

"I was thinking Gus could come up for the weekend next month," I tell her, hoping to bring us back around to the high note we started on. "I could take him to a football game, have him spend the night, and then drive him home Sunday."

"Oh, he'd love that! I gotta work weekends from now until Christmas, so I can't bring him, but Grandpa'd be happy to do it."

"Definitely. I'll check the calendar and give you a few options."

"Sounds great. I better get going to pick up Gus, but we'll talk soon."

I say goodbye and let the guilt sink deep.

I'm a crappy person for leaving home and never visiting, especially a crappy sister; my poor little brother has already been through so much in his nine years. But that guilt is my fuel to keep working hard. If I can keep it up, it'll be worth the sacrifices we've all made.

I've made vague mentions of my plans to my mom before, but they always sound childish and fantastical spoken out loud. Still, I know they're possible. I'm not abandoning my family. I just need more time. A summer internship, keeping my grades up and securing an editor position at the school paper will land me a spot in a good grad school, and then it's only a matter of finding a decent job in a city with a moderate cost of living. Then I'll move my family to me. Between Mom's salary, mine, and my savings, which I've been squirreling away since the summer after high school graduation, we can support all five of us; god knows we're experts at living on a shoestring budget. I don't need to make a million dollars. I only need to bust my ass hard enough to succeed, and I'm already doing a pretty decent job of that.

Now if I could just figure out how to craft a riveting article about campus food trucks.

cameron

MUSIC THROBS through every room of the house. It's Saturday night and everyone is high off our win this afternoon, which has turned this into the biggest party we've had since the start of the semester.

Reeve keeps calling it my re-release party, but it's the same tired shit: being congratulated on the game by guys too drunk to realize they said the same thing forty-five minutes ago, girls pressing their tits up against me, vying for bragging rights of being the first to sleep with me since my breakup. Still, it feels good to be free—Kira knew how to show up to these parties looking like arm candy, but she never knew how to enjoy them. Plus Lorenzo, who hardly parties anymore, let us convince him to get drunk in the name of his half birthday tomorrow and he's fervently working on some kind of dance routine that tells me he's seen too many '90s boy band videos.

And then Lenni walks in and the night takes a turn. I didn't expect her to show, mainly because I couldn't picture her in this scene. And she does look out of place. Despite her tight jeans and tank top, she looks almost matronly compared to most of the chicks walking around in miniskirts and tops that I'm pretty sure are just bras with some extra lace glued on. But she looks sexy. Her body is un-fucking-deniable.

She smiles at someone, that wide smile that's been etched in my mind since the night we met; that and every other detail about her. She was heavier then, with shorter hair that had this little halo of frizz that was extra noticeable with the garden lighting behind her. She was so pretty. Not the kind of pretty that stops you dead, but the kind that grows the longer you look at her, until finally you realize you've been staring for the entire conversation and you're wondering how you didn't notice at first glance that she could be the most beautiful girl you've ever met.

Reeve spots her and crosses the room to retrieve her, that "fresh meat" look flickering bright in his eyes. He's as bored with this scene as I am, and when Reeve is bored, he always manages to liven things up at someone else's expense. He won't mean to, but he's going to break Lenni's heart.

"Cam." A female voice purrs in my ear and a hand closes firmly around my arm.

I turn to see Alexis Truman smiling up at me. I knew she'd hunt me down eventually; I was just hoping I'd be drunk by then. "Hey." I angle my body away. I've been trying to slide out of this girl's grasp since we met last fall.

"*Such* a great win today," she says, leaning closer. "I, like, can't get over how good you are. Are you sore?"

"Sore?" I don't even want to know where this pickup line is headed. "Not yet."

Alexis should be attractive: tight body, nice curves, cute face. But somehow, she just . . . isn't. I have no problem with jersey chasers; they might be shameless, but they're honest about what they want. But Alexis has all the worst traits of a jersey chaser with none of the redeeming ones. She's clingy, gossipy, conniving. And more than once, I've seen her try to wheedle a relationship out of a guy when he's made it clear he's not interested in more than one night together. I'm just her newest victim.

Alexis starts talking about a massage class she took freshman year, but my attention is on Lenni, on her hip, to be exact, because that's where Reeve has his hand, his thumb making little circles on her hip bone. I have to work to unclench my jaw.

I know I have zero claim to this girl. Whatever I thought I knew about her from the night we met, I was wrong. That girl wanted to be protected, and she wanted something that Reeve won't give her. Does she remember that? I've been thinking for days about calling her out, but something settles inside me. I have to ignore her. She can be whoever she wants to be. It's not my job to save her from getting hurt.

I watch Lenni excuse herself from Reeve, a little smile on her face. Not the follow-me-to-the-bathroom-and-fuck-me kind of smile but the sincere, uncalculating smile I remember from the garden. Reeve stiffens, his hand lingering on her until she walks out of reach. I'm halfway across the room before I realize I just walked away from Alexis midsentence. Whatever. I was wrong. I can't ignore Lenni.

I follow her to the kitchen. She's standing against the wall, tucked up against our beer fridge like it's her companion, though she's empty-handed. I take a beer out. "Hey," I say.

She looks at me for a second too long, but I can't tell what she's thinking. "Hey."

I rip the cap off the bottle. What do I even say to her? And why am I nervous? "Having fun?" I'm such a bore.

She shrugs. "I guess so."

I don't believe her. It makes me wonder how she usually spends her weekends, but that would be a weird question to ask. This is nothing like the first time we talked. It was so easy then.

"I don't usually catch you around our parties," I say, which is about the lamest observation I could make, but I want her attention. Her gaze is trained on Reeve in the center of the room. Sasha James—perky blond jersey chaser extraordinaire—has just sunk her claws into him.

"Not my usual scene, that's true." She crosses her arms, hugging her elbows.

Her usual scene must be more interesting than this. I wonder about the guys she dates. I've never noticed her with anyone around campus, but that means nothing. Her boyfriends are probably at least intelligent enough to sustain stimulating conversation, which is more than I can offer her at the moment, but does she remember the hours-long conversation we once had?

Lenni is watching Sasha and Reeve's blatant flirtation, and it's getting uncomfortable. Reeve is like this; whether you're a guy or girl, he makes you the center of his world when he's talking to you, but as soon as his attention shifts, you're left cold.

But when Lenni turns to me, she doesn't look cold. "Is it always like this?" she asks.

"Like what?"

She gestures to Sasha and Reeve. "Girls literally hanging on you all night?"

My first instinct is to say no, to try to make her feel better, but I don't think that's what she's looking for. "Pretty standard."

I expect her to get upset or roll her eyes, but she only studies me for a few long seconds and then swings her gaze back to Reeve.

I'd like nothing more than to completely sink this budding

romance between her and my best friend, but my loyalty to Reeve demands that I at least try to salvage things. "It doesn't mean anything, though," I tell her. "Reeve's not a total dog."

She gives me a sidelong glance, a glint of humor in her eyes. "But is he somewhat of a dog?"

I open my mouth to tell her that's not what I meant, but I catch myself; that's exactly what I meant. "He's a good guy." Which sounds like a total deflection. "I mean, he doesn't pretend to be something he's not, right? Just look at him." She does, and while she looks at him, I look at her. I don't have a clue what she's thinking. "He's not for everyone." So much for being Reeve's wingman.

"Meaning?"

I probably seem like a shit friend trying to scare her off him, but this thing between them is so stupid. Who does she think she is, playing these bullshit games? Reeve is exactly who he presents himself as. Lenni is the one pretending to be someone she's not, and I just haven't figured out which version of her is real and which is posing. "Meaning, if you think he could end up hurting you, you're probably right."

And with that, I have her full attention. She turns her gaze on me, the spark in her steely blue eyes sending up a flaming red flag. I recognize that look—it might be the one thing she and Kira have in common. "What are you saying? That I should stay away from him?"

If I've learned anything from that look, it's don't fucking tell a woman what to do, but something makes me want to get myself in deeper with her. "I'm only suggesting you think hard about what you want from him."

"Think hard?" Her eyebrows shoot up. "You've got some balls saying that when you don't know the first thing about me."

"I know what you've told me."

"Which amounts to what?" She stands up straight. "Two sentences?"

I let out a short laugh. I've fucking had it with her. "All right, enough. I'm calling this bullshit already." I turn so my body is square with hers. "Are you seriously telling me you don't remember me?"

She gives me a look like I'm pathetic, which is fair given I'm not even trying to stop myself from acting like a child. "How could I forget? I never did get the stains out of that shirt."

I stare at her. "And?"

She pauses. "And what?" Her expression morphs from confused to irritated. "What happened, we sat next to each other freshman year and you can't believe I haven't been pining for you ever since?"

"No. We sat around a garden for four hours and talked about our lives."

Lenni freezes, blinks slowly, and stares at me, her eyes wide. "Oh my god, Cam. That was . . . you?"

She didn't know. It lands like a gut punch. "Yes, Lenore," I say quietly.

Her jaw opens like she's about to say something and then closes again, her eyes still locked on mine. I can practically see her brain realigning itself as her memories shift, every word and look we've shared no longer some forgettable exchange with Reeve's friend but instead a return to a night and a guy that came and went years ago. It did mean something to her. Now I'm sure.

"Wait." She squeezes her eyes shut and shakes her head quickly. "That guy—I mean you . . . you told me your name was Forrest."

My cheeks go hot. "I, uh, had grand plans to reinvent myself in college; totally douchey. That lasted until about hour two of football training camp."

"Oh." She looks out onto the party. "Well, I'd love to mock you mercilessly for that, but I guess I have my own name change to keep me humble."

"So you never recognized me?"

"You looked familiar, but I figured that was because you're on those stupid football posters all over campus. And it was dark that night. And you had all that hair falling in your face." She smiles briefly, though not at me.

"And you hardly ever bother to make eye contact with me," I can't help saying.

"It's not easy making eye contact with someone who walks around with his nose as high in the air as you do."

Damn, she didn't even hesitate with that one.

"Besides," she adds before I can say anything, "that guy—Forrest—doesn't seem like you." She says it with such disdain that I think I'm insulted.

"Like you know me?"

"I know enough. All you guys walk around campus like you own the place."

"All what guys? Football players?"

She shrugs primly. I don't understand the hostility coming from her, but it's getting my skin hot. Problem is, I can't tell if it's the bad hot or the good.

"Yeah, we're all the same. Except for Reeve, right?" The words are out before I can stop them.

The look she gives me could cut glass. "What's that supposed to mean?"

I want to tell her how blind she's being, how it's almost funny how completely twisted she has things. But why do I care? I've been watching delusional chicks make the same mistakes for years. No reason to let it bother me now. Except it does.

I turn to her and lean in close. Her scent hits me like a wall, sweet and spicy and dark. I'd forgotten I knew this smell. "Stick around and you'll find out."

Her eyes bore into me. I recognize their color but not the angry way they flicker at me. I pull myself away and walk off, leaving her alone.

lenni

IT'S HIM. Forrest. How did I not realize it before? One look into those amber eyes and there was no doubt. It's him.

Forrest—er, Cam—was the most beautiful guy I'd ever seen in the flesh and, sweet Jesus, he'd only gotten better. Sure, he was handsome when he was Cam Forrester, elitist athlete and best friend of Reeve, but something happened when he revealed himself. I'd stopped to see him. He was no longer some cold statue of male perfection. He was that charming boy that, for a few hours, I thought I knew.

I slip out the door of the football house and send a quick text to Jade, who was supposed to meet me after her date with Sam. I tell her the party was boring and I don't feel great, so I'll see her at home. But she'll have a hundred questions about Reeve that I can't handle until morning, so I plan to be in bed when she gets in.

I can't believe this. I can't wrap my head around Cam and Forrest being the same guy. How did our magical connection in the garden that night turn to disdain without my even knowing it?

The night we met I was lost. Not literally—the dorm I was

staying in for orientation was barely a hundred yards from the garden. But inside, I was completely disoriented. I'd been waiting years, maybe even since birth, to leave the town I grew up in, desperate to be somewhere nobody knew me. And then I got it: A campus of twenty thousand students and not a single one knew my name. It was a dream come true, and one that left me almost instantly disillusioned.

I'd thought the power of anonymity would reveal me as relaxed and sociable, perhaps even witty. I'd never been witty, not even before the high school incident, but I'd hoped to find it hiding somewhere within me. For the first time, I would use my real name—Lenore—and perhaps find myself as mature and sophisticated as the name suggested. But as I moved from orientation check-in to the welcome meeting to the dorm tour, I felt completely unchanged. I didn't want to converse with strangers and when I did, I was awkward and uncertain. My smiles were painfully forced. I couldn't stand the quick, assessing glances I received, girls appraising whether I was competition, a potential friend, or better off ignored. Boys simply assessing whether I was fuckable. I was locked up as tight as ever. The only thing that had changed were the faces around me.

Until that night, wandering campus, when I discovered what was different: here I could cry.

Back home, I excelled at holding it together for Mom and Gus. Of the three of us, my tears were the least justified, and with the shitty apartments we lived in, the walls were always too thin for my crying to remain private. But at Shafer, once the day's events were over and night fell, I had total freedom to walk the campus and seek an uninhabited corner.

I was crying quietly when I found the garden and the beautiful man inside it. I still remember the way he stood when he saw me, like some biologically driven act of chivalry.

He didn't know what to do with me, but everything he did was right. I'd walked into the garden lonely and overwhelmed, the weird crying girl who didn't want to be here and didn't want to go home. By the time I left, the loneliness had lifted. The garden was the first place at Shafer I felt okay.

His name was Forrest. I'd never considered what my dream man would be like until I met him and realized, he was it. With him, I didn't have to pretend I wasn't graceless and scared. The way he spoke to me without any hint that he'd expect something at the end of the night in exchange for treating me like an actual human was revelatory. Talking to him was safe. And the things he told me about his family and his unease about where life was heading made me think he didn't share these things with just anyone. Of course I'd thought he was gorgeous with his long hair falling over his eyes and half his face in shadow all night, but it was bigger than attraction. Looking at him, I felt hope unfurl inside me.

Forrest revived the dream that Shafer would be the start of something new and wonderful, that if I looked for good people, I'd find them. That there would be a thousand more nights like this.

As I pass the alley behind my building, two guys from the apartment below mine are throwing empty beer bottles up against the brick wall and cackling drunkenly at the spray of glass raining down. There haven't been a thousand more nights like that. There hasn't even been one.

But I'd carried that hope through the rest of the summer, imagining our next meeting, and into the new school year. I fed on the feeling for months, and for a short time, college was fun. I made a few friends, went to a few parties like normal girls do, always expecting this would be the night I'd run into Forrest again, always regretting I hadn't gotten his number. But I didn't see him or any other guys like him. And the more I looked, the more I hated what I saw.

All around me, my new friends were crying over boys who never called after a hookup, who slept with their sorority sisters, who ignored them after a night together. I wasn't missing out on anything. I gave up on Forrest. Maybe he'd decided not to attend Shafer after all, or maybe he'd lied and he was never a student here, just some local kid wandering campus. I stopped hoping for love, and I stopped caring; it was an easy transition back to a role I knew. And I gave up on all the Forrests I'd believed were just around the corner. My family was suddenly in crisis back home; that was the love I needed to focus on.

And now here he is, and he's not Forrest at all. Okay, maybe I can blame some of his cold behavior on the fact he thought I was blowing him off, but that doesn't change what he is. Cam is a conceited, swaggering athlete. A rich boy who dates rail-thin blondes he probably handpicks from some European modeling agency portfolio. Just another jock with a pack mentality. And most offensive of all, he's arrogant enough to think he can tell me what's best for me. Like he thinks he knows me. Does it matter that the girl he met that night would never have even a spark of interest in a guy like Reeve? Why should it? That girl isn't me anymore.

Back home, my apartment is mercifully empty. I change into comfy pajamas and move halfheartedly through my bedtime routine.

No, Cam is the one I need to stay away from. It doesn't matter how he made me feel years ago or that just thinking about his perfect face makes my insides tighten up with longing. Reeve is the safe choice here; I know what I'm getting with him. Fun and nothing more. Except as I lie in bed, all that fluttery excitement that Reeve inspired has gone cold.

When I hear Jade come in and open my bedroom door, I pretend to be asleep. If I tell her what happened, she'll have some sort of indignant, emotional reaction, and I don't need that clouding my thoughts yet. I need to process this my way. Rationally.

I lie awake for hours, replaying every memory I have of Forrest and Cam, his face and his voice. I keep getting tripped up on his smile. The image of it pulses in my brain, a painful, throbbing reminder of everything that's changed. I thought I'd stopped wishing for Forrest to walk back into my life years ago, but now I know that's not true. I was always hoping for him. But finding Cam feels like losing Forrest all over again.

lenni

THE NEXT MORNING, I'm woken up by the weight of Jade on the bed.

"Lenni," she trills. "Wake up, lover girl."

I groan and force open my eyes. Jade is looking bright as sunshine, and I can already see the questions tumbling from her head. Meanwhile, I just want to go back to sleep. Sleeping in is one of my few vices, and after a fitful night thinking about Forrest—okay, I have to stop calling him that—I need it more than ever.

"So," Jade says. "Obviously your night wasn't filled with quarterback-induced orgasms. What happened?"

I throw my arm over my eyes to shield them from the sun. "I told you. The party got boring, so I chose sleep."

"Clearly something happened for you to up and leave ol' Dreamboat behind."

"I think the crush is fading."

"There's something you're not telling me." She pulls my arm down and I squint up at her. Jade is like a bloodhound for secrets.

"Everything was fine. All I can say is I saw him talking to

another girl—you know exactly the type—and they just looked right together. I realized we would look all wrong."

"Right, because he's a caveman and you're a total goddess who shouldn't have contact with a guy like that outside of a well-paid tutoring session."

I snort out a laugh. "What do you have against him, anyway? Did you witness him killing a puppy or something?"

She rolls her eyes. "Whatever. I'm not advocating for you two as a couple, but who cares what you look like together? If other people don't like it, that's their issue."

I sigh and close my eyes again. "I don't have the energy to care right now. I just want sleep."

"Too bad, we're having brunch with Madison, remember? Better get up. She's expecting a graphic recap of your night with Reeve."

Forty-five minutes later, Jade, Madison, and I sit outside at our go-to brunch spot, a cheap little café that serves microwaved croissants and calls itself French. I quickly scan the other tables to check for Cam, not because I've ever seen him here but because I'm now terrified of him popping up before I can figure out how to handle him. Ever since we walked out the door this morning, I've been operating with an uncomfortable sense of self-consciousness, like I've been exposed.

Jade was kind enough to fill Madison in on my wholly anti-climactic evening with Reeve as we walked over, and Madison still looks disappointed.

"Are you done with him?" Madison asks.

"I don't know yet." I haven't thought about him since I left last night. There's no room in my head for anyone but Cam right now.

"You know I'm a big believer in intuition," Jade says as our waiter slides a plate of eggs in front of her. "So if something is steering you away from Reeve, follow it."

"You're only saying that because you hate him," I point out.

"I just think your affections should be given to a more worthy man."

"Hmm." Do I tell her she's wasting her breath? I chew on a piece of bacon and prepare to sound as casual as possible before my next question. "What do you guys know about Cameron Forrester?" I look first at Madison and then, with trepidation, at Jade. She's looking at me like a dog with its ears perked up.

"What's there to say?" Jade asks. "Football god, gorgeous, exclusively dates girls who could pass for supermodels."

"Don't forget rich kid," I say, both satisfied and disappointed that her assessment lines up perfectly with mine.

"Sounds like you know all there is to know."

I dip a piece of bacon in maple syrup. "I was just wondering if either of you have ever talked to him."

"He's in one of my classes," Madison offers.

I stop eating. Madison's schedule is studded with honors courses. "Which one?"

"Freedom of Expression and Communication Ethics."

Jade cocks her head. "Interesting. I've heard smart jocks exist, I've just never seen one in the wild."

"He's definitely smart," Madison says. "He has some thoughtful things to say in class. Doesn't talk much, though."

"You have any sense of what he's like?" I dare to ask.

Jade points her fork at me. "Wait, why are we even talking about him?"

I ignore her and wait for Madison's answer.

"Not really, just a quiet guy. Oh, but you know what? I've seen him at Cooper's Park playing with a little kid. Tossing around a football and that kind of thing." Cooper's Park is a sprawling park near campus where a lot of students head to run or play basketball or sit in the sun.

"Like a group volunteer thing with other football players?" I wonder.

"Who knows?"

Huh. Cameron Forrester a do-gooder? I'm not sure I buy it. Forrest though? That, I could believe.

Jade seizes on my silence to once again demand answers. "I want to know why you're asking about him all of a sudden. Are you into him, Lenni?"

"No," I say quickly. "He and Reeve are BFFs, I think. And at the party last night, he warned me off Reeve. I can't figure out why he'd do that."

This of course isn't the main reason I want dirt on Cam, but it's a question that needs answering. It was easy to shrug off his words last night when he was a stranger to me. But I have to remind myself that I know this guy, or at least I once did.

"Weird," Madison says. "That's not in the wingman hand-book, is it?"

"Maybe Reeve's crawling with STIs and Cam's just trying to slow the spread. He's probably hoping for a job in public health." Jade takes a delicate bite of toast.

I roll my eyes. Anyway, it wasn't my health Cam seemed concerned with, it was my heart. I just wish I knew if he was speaking out of genuine concern or simple bitterness that I'd forgotten who he was. He expects me to trust his advice simply because we were friends for a few hours? Well, joke's on him; I don't trust any man. Save for my grandfather, every guy I've ever known has disappointed me. Why add another one to the list?

***

"I think I should sleep with Reeve," I announce to Jade that night as we sit on the couch eating fried rice and Thai curry out of take-out boxes.

She swallows a mouthful of food and looks at me, eyebrows raised. "Whoa."

"Look what he texted me this morning." I pull up my messages and hand over my phone.

Jade looks warily at the screen, like she's afraid of what she's about to see. "Spent the entire night picturing you naked on top of me," she reads. "You know how to leave a brother wanting more." She rolls her eyes. "Wow, he must have worked hard on that one. What a douche."

"Okay, it's not great, but he clearly wants to sleep together. This isn't a fun little challenge anymore for me to see if I could actually get him interested."

"It was never a challenge, hon. Guys like that will sleep with anyone as long as there are no strings attached. Anyway, you told me this morning the crush had faded."

"But that might be an advantage. I can go into this with clear goals and not get bogged down by petty emotions."

She tries unsuccessfully to stifle a smile. "Those goals being getting laid and . . . getting laid? This is a hookup, not a prospective career path."

"What I mean is the fewer feelings involved, the less likely I am to wind up wanting more than he's willing to give."

"Pro tip from someone who's had a lot more casual sex than you: if getting emotionally entangled with a man is going to be problematic, that's not the guy you sleep with. Really, Lenni, there are so many sweet guys out there who would love to let you experiment on them. Sam has some super cute nerd friends."

"I don't want them." I dig around my food but don't take a bite. "I want Reeve."

Jade's smile fades. "You're serious about this."

"I think so." What I'm actually serious about is ignoring Cam's advice.

"If you don't like casual sex and you don't like him, why would you want this?" Jade asks.

"Because I'm tired of my past having a hold on me like this. Maybe I would like casual sex if I tried it."

"Okay, I respect where you're coming from, but . . . Reeve? You're trying to move on from shitty guys with him?"

"Is there any actual rationale behind your hatred of him?" I ask. "Seriously. What did he do?"

"He didn't do anything. I just know what type of guy he is, and he's the last man I'd pick for you at this moment in your life." Her eyes are round and sincere. "I don't want you getting hurt."

I look at my food. "Why would I? It's just sex. I'm not gunning for a marriage proposal."

"I know that. But I don't want you to . . . you know."

"No, I don't."

"To try to make up for what happened in high school."

"I'm not," I snap, more forcefully than I mean to. I soften my voice. "I'm not, Jade. I'm in control of this."

Despite the years that have passed, talking about the high school incident never fails to bring on a fresh, hot wave of shame. When I was sixteen, one of the popular football players from my math class invited me over for a study date, and even though I was a chubby nerd and he'd never spoken to me before, it didn't occur to me to be suspicious of his invitation. But instead of studying, he wanted to drink, and I went along with it. I drank too much, couldn't find the words to tell him no and ended up giving him a blow job. Days later, I found out he'd secretly filmed the whole thing—and that the teammate who'd dared him to do it in the first place was busy sending the video out to anyone who wanted it. That was the part that sank me deep into depression. Because that teammate had been my friend since I was ten years old.

Ben Brashman lived two doors down and was the closest male friend I'd ever had. Our families got together for barbecues every summer, and Ben and I bonded over our shared interests in comics and the fact that we were both the children of single moms who worked long hours. In high school, we drifted our separate ways, him toward popularity and me toward invisibility, but we still chatted in shared classes, still gravitated toward each other at those backyard barbecues full of boring adults. We weren't best friends, but I was certain he had my back. I trusted him.

Later, when the boys were kicked off the team and one of them lost his college football scholarship, I felt nothing. After that, I stayed far away from guys. I'm not a virgin, but by the time freshman year was over and the only thing I could remember about my hookups was being drunk and being afraid, I decided I was done.

Jade's watching me. "You know the last thing I ever want to do is sound like someone's mother, but have you ever considered alternate methods for tackling your emotional baggage?"

"Such as?"

"Therapy?"

I shake my head. "Can't afford it."

"They have free counseling at the Student Health Center."

"Gee, months of counseling at Student Health or sex with a beautiful man? I wonder." Actually, both give me anxiety in equal turns.

Jade shrugs. "Honestly, it's what I would choose too. But let me say this and then I'll never say it again. If you're going to put yourself out there with a guy, he should be worthy of your trust."

I work at spearing a chunk of chicken with my fork. "It's not about trust, it's about sex." Trust is far too complicated an issue to weave into a short-term project like Reeve.

"You're a big girl." She sighs and puts her food on the coffee table. "If this is what you decide to do, I'll try to keep my mouth shut."

"Thank you." I have no intention of putting my heart on the line for Reeve Dalton, and if he's using me? Good. I'm using him too. I want to be like my friends; I want to have crushes and kiss boys and not feel this fear anymore. What better way to get there than with someone who probably knows how a woman's body works better than I do? Besides, Cam needs to learn he's not qualified to tell me how to live.

"Just know that if he breaks your heart, I'm never going to say I told you so," Jade says. "You can cry on my shoulder while I plot out his castration and subsequent murder."

I smile at her. "Promise?"

"Promise. You know how sharp I keep the kitchen knives."

lenni

"I FUCKING HATE THIS PLAN," Jade says petulantly as she watches me lay a lacy bra and thong out on my bed. Red, of course.

I try to picture myself two hours from now, sitting in Reeve's bed waiting for him when he walks in from Friday night team dinner, and a rush of nerves hits me. Quite a different setting from the newsroom where I typically spend Friday evenings.

"I think it's sexy," I say, though sexy is far from what I feel.

"Walk me through it again," she orders, and I know she's looking for more flaws so she can talk me out of it.

"It's not the Normandy invasion, Jade. I get naked in his bedroom, he walks in and—surprise!—we fuck." Of course, sometimes it's the simplest of plans that can make us so nervous we want to puke. "What, you think he might turn me down?"

"Of course not." Jade flops onto the bed while I shrug off my robe and put on the lingerie. She reminds me of my mother before my first and only prom, wringing her hands over every possible tragedy that might befall me. "I just have a bad feeling."

"Well, I need to get out of my own way and Reeve's going to help me do it." I give her a sharp look. "You said you'd support me."

"I support your decision to sleep with him, I just don't see why you have to go about it this way."

"Because I'm in control. I'm deciding where and when, and he can either acquiesce or not, but I'm calling the shots. That's just how it's going to be. End of story."

Jade looks impressed.

I take a deep breath as I hazard a glance at myself in the full-length mirror on the door, trying to will myself to feel as confident as I sound.

I'm not so worried about what'll go wrong tonight as tomorrow morning. I worry that nothing has changed and that a night with Reeve will end in the same disappointment as with every other guy, but I'm ready to stop wondering. I don't care if Reeve is an asshole. I'm tired of giving men power just because they're popular or athletic or they've slept with the entire female student population. I can make that power work for me, not against me.

I adjust my boobs inside the barely-there bra and pointedly ignore the dimpled skin on the backs of my thighs. "Well?" I turn toward Jade for my final assessment.

She whistles and looks me up and down. "Your only potential problem is him busting a nut in his pants before he can get his hands on you."

I laugh and let myself believe her.

I'M IN.

It's scary how easy it is to waltz into the football house and up to Reeve's room without any explanation, but being a girl has its advantages.

Once inside his bedroom, I strip down to my underwear, feeling like the world's biggest fraud. I mean, who does this? Women in movies with perfect bodies, sure, but what about real girls? I can't believe I'm here. I don't have the seduction skills or the body confidence for this shit.

But then I think of Cam and my resolve strengthens. I think about getting dressed and slinking home defeated, and I know I can't give my fear that much power. I want this.

I get comfortable on Reeve's bed and put on a sexy playlist Jade helped me put together. I try to adopt a casually seductive position, then realize it's impossible, at least for my body. A few minutes pass while I scroll my phone. Thirty minutes, forty-five. My nerves have just about worn a hole through my stomach, so I text him.

> Lenni: Hey. What are you up to? Plans tonight?

He responds within a minute.

> Reeve: Heading home now. Game tomorrow morning so I probably won't see you tonight.

I wiggle my fingers, trying to come up with the perfect response. Do I tell him I'm here? It'll kill the surprise, but suddenly I'm imagining everything that could go wrong. There are too many people around. What if someone else walks in? Or he comes in with five friends in tow?

> Lenni: You will if you come up to your room now.

His response is immediate.

Reeve: What do you mean?

Reeve: ??

It won't be long now.

I'm RIGHT. Within a few minutes, voices drift up from the front porch. I spring out of bed and look out the window. Reeve's taking the steps two at a time, with Cameron behind him—damn, he looks good—and a redheaded woman teetering in black stiletto boots.

Butterflies swarming my stomach, I dash back to the bed, fluff my hair and wait. Someone pounds quickly up the steps. God, let it be him. Footsteps come down the hall, the door opens and there's Reeve.

His jaw drops when he sees me on the bed.

I smile.

He looks fucking horrified.

Instantly, I know I made a colossal mistake.

"Lenni. Jesus Christ, what are you doing here?" His eyes are wild as he glances over his shoulder into the hallway.

"I wanted to surprise you," I say.

"No." He shakes his head furiously. "No, no, no. You can't do this. You can't be here."

I'm frozen on the bed. "What do you mean?" My voice quavers. "What's wrong?"

"You gotta go. I mean it," he insists, waving his hand rapidly toward the door. "I'm sorry, but I've got a situation and you've gotta get the fuck out of here. Now."

I hesitate for a second, paralyzed by confusion and humiliation. Reeve comes toward me and takes my arm. "Please, Lenni. Now!"

I'm shaking as I stand up, but I still have the strength left to yank my arm from his grip. Reeve is muttering panicked curse words and apologies, but I barely hear any of it. Then someone else is in the doorway. Cameron.

He looks at Reeve, then at me and his face registers shock. "Oh, shit," he says, taking in my near nakedness.

My humiliation is complete.

"Can you fucking believe this?" Reeve spits the words at Cam. "Is she still downstairs? You gotta keep her downstairs, man. I gotta deal with this."

Even through my shame, I manage to glare at him because I know I'm the *this* he's talking about, and fuck him.

"You shouldn't have done this," Reeve says, answering my glare. "You're putting me in a real bad spot."

The tears of humiliation threatening to fall boil into tears of anger, but before I can say anything back, Cam takes control. "Lay off her," he orders Reeve. Then, looking at me, "It's not her fault."

"Reeve?" comes a female voice from downstairs.

Panic lights up Reeve's eyes again. Who is this woman he's so desperate to hide me from? "I'm coming down," he calls back, looking at Cam with a pleading expression.

"Go," Cam tells him. "I'll take care of her."

Reeve obeys, hustling out of the room without sparing a glance at me.

Cam and I are alone. We stare at each other for a few awful seconds as the abject mortification of the situation bears down on us.

"It's okay, Lenni," he says gently. "It's okay."

The kindness in his voice is too much. Without warning, my waiting tears rush forward. I feel excruciatingly vulnerable, and I flash back to a day in fourth grade when I threw up in front of the class and my sweet, well-meaning teacher tried so hard to reassure me while making sure she didn't come anywhere near me.

My tears have an energizing effect on him. He scrambles to pick up my clothes from the floor and he's somehow produced a towel that he throws over my shoulders, all while assuring me that it's okay, not to worry, and skillfully averting his eyes from my body.

"Come on," he says once I'm covered. "You can change in my bathroom." He must see the fear on my face because before I can protest, he glances out into the hallway. "Don't worry, no one's out here. No one will see. Come on."

I follow him, still crying but not fully believing what's happening to me. He leads me into his bedroom, shuts the door, and steers me toward the bathroom. There's a door at the other end, presumably leading to Reeve's room, and Cam is quick to flip the lock on it. "Go ahead and change," he says, backing out into his room. "I'll, um, wait out here."

Speech is impossible, so I just shut the door. Alone in the bathroom, I sink to the floor, ball the towel up around my face and let out the only remaining tears I'll allow myself. God, I hope he can't hear me.

Then I dry the tears and jam myself into my clothes, wishing I could take off the lingerie and throw it away and never think of it again. It's trash. It's not me and it never was, and I should have known that the second I looked at it. I *did*. But I ignored what I knew. I splash cold water on my face, which only makes my mascara run darker under my eyes. Then I stare in the mirror and try to figure out how the fuck I'm going to walk out of this bathroom and face Cam. I can't do it. I actually can't.

My gaze stops on a small, frosted window above the toilet. An escape route? But no, that's ridiculous; my ass would never fit. I close my eyes and force myself to breathe slowly and deeply. I have to go out there and deal with this.

When I open the door, Cam stands up from his seat on the bed and looks at me, his face a mixture of concern and uncertainty. It's kind of cute. "You all right?"

I nod.

He's trying hard not to look at my body, and my cheeks burn to realize it's because he knows exactly what I look like under my clothes, right down to the size of my areolas. My shame must be palpable because he clears his throat and says, louder than necessary, "I can take you home."

An odd little part of me resists, wishing I could stay locked in this room forever, but I don't blame him for wanting to get rid of me as soon as fucking possible. "I'm only a couple blocks away, don't worry about it."

He shakes his head. "It's dark. And I think it's about to rain." He doesn't wait for a response, and I don't argue; tonight his presumptuousness is a comfort, not an annoyance. He opens his closet and pulls out a rain jacket, which he hands to me.

I put it on. I think I thank him, but I'm not sure. I'm operating like a robot, still not certain what's happened and more than anything, just grateful someone else is in control.

We move into the hall, but when I hear voices coming from downstairs, I freeze. No way I can face Reeve and the woman he rebuffed me for.

Cam's warm eyes settle on mine. "Only one way out of this house."

"Is he going to freak out if I walk downstairs?"

"Just pretend you're with me and no one will ask questions."

I follow him down the stairs, hoping against hope that Reeve won't be anywhere between the steps and the front door but, of course, my luck is shit. He's standing with his body in a protective stance near the redheaded woman, and even though I avoid his eye, a fresh surge of shame hits as I feel him watching me. I want to disappear. The door seems miles away. Then I feel Cam's hand close around mine.

"We're out," he says to Reeve and the woman with a nod. "See you guys later."

Reeve's gaze rakes over me, but I won't look at him. And even though I know Cam taking my hand is just an act, the feel of his strong fingers around mine makes Reeve briefly cease to matter.

Once outside, I breathe a little easier. Rain is just starting to fall, leaving polka dots on the sidewalk, and Cam walks close to me, though his body is rigid. Free of the house, I finally have the wherewithal to start putting the pieces together.

"What was that?" I ask without looking at Cam.

He hesitates. "That was Reeve's mom."

"That's his mother?" I let this sink in. The woman was older, but she didn't look like someone's mom, not with her stylish clothing and stiletto boots and long, vibrant hair. Not with her bloodshot eyes and the smears of mascara on her cheeks. "Okay, so my timing was off," I say bitterly. "Why was he such an asshole about it?"

Cam doesn't answer at first. "Look, don't repeat this, okay?"

I nod. Like I want anyone hearing a word of what just happened?

"She needed a place to crash for the night. And Reeve works hard to keep his family life separate from his life here. I guess he didn't want you to see the messiness that is Dina Dalton." He pauses. "And also, Reeve can just be an asshole sometimes."

Yes. And didn't I know that already? Wasn't I told? Cam warned me this could happen and now it has. I want to hate him for it. I cross my arms tight over my chest, so they don't brush his. But I steal a glance at him, and in the shadowy glow of the streetlights, he looks exactly like the guy I remember meeting in the garden. There's no way to hate that person. Nor can I find any excuse to hate the person that just rescued me from complete humiliation.

The rain begins to fall harder. I stick my hands in the pockets of Cam's jacket and my fingers close around something cold and hard. I pull it out; it's a little toy sports car painted glossy royal blue.

I hold up the car. "Still playing with toys at your age?" I ask, trying for a joke even though I don't feel lighthearted in the slightest.

Cam smiles. "So that's where that went. My little brother's been wondering about that thing for a month."

"I didn't know you had a little brother."

"Yeah, Liam."

I try to picture Cam lying belly down across from his brother, driving toy cars across the carpet. "I have a little brother too. He's nine."

"I remember. Is that him?" He nods at my phone, which I've just taken out of my pocket. Gus grins at me from my lock screen.

"That's him."

"Cute kid. He's got your dark curls. My brother's a towhead."

"Sounds adorable."

"You see your brother much? I know your family lives a few hours away."

I forgot how much I told him about myself. "Not as much as I should. But he comes up for weekend visits sometimes. He loves coming to football games."

Cam gives a little smile at that. Then we lapse into silence.

As we round the corner, my building comes into view, and I stop. "You can leave me here."

"I'll walk you to your door," he says brusquely. Then, a little gentler, "Please."

We keep going.

"Do you live with anyone?" he asks.

"Yeah, with a friend."

"Will she be home?"

"I think so." It's early enough that Jade will still be getting ready to go out, thank god. As much as I don't want to recount this little horror story, I don't want to be alone tonight.

"Good," he says.

We're silent as he follows me inside my building and up the stairs to the second floor. But as I start down the hallway, he reaches out to stop me. His fingers are featherlight around my wrist, but their effect is like a thousand elephants. I can't feel anything but his hand.

"Listen, Lenni." He turns so we're face-to-face, his body blocking my path. He looks into my eyes, and as hard as it is to meet his gaze, it's even harder to look away. No one should be so gorgeous.

"I know how you must feel," he begins.

"No, you don't," I hear myself blurt.

He blinks, struggling for words, and I feel a small sense of triumph to see that the great unshakable Cameron Forrester is, well, shaken. "You're right." His voice is deep, like he just woke up from sleep, and in the silence of the hallway, I feel the raw sound of it in my veins. "But I know it must be bad. And I just want to tell you not to sit with that too long. You didn't do anything wrong." Here it is again, that singular, intense gaze that reaches straight down into me. "I mean, any guy would give a couple years of his life to have you offer yourself up like that. Believe me."

Now I have to look away because the question that immediately pops into my head is, *Would you?* He's waiting for a response, but all I can do is nod. He steps back and we walk on.

I unlock the door and there's Jade, standing in our tiny kitchen, pouring herself a drink. She looks up at me and I watch her expression transform from surprise to alarm as she takes in my blotchy, mascara-stained face, and then Cam just behind me.

"Oh my god." She rushes to me, knocking a capped bottle of vodka over on the counter. "What happened?"

Suddenly, I'm on the verge of tears all over again. "I'll tell you later," I manage to say shakily.

Jade slings a protective arm around me and hits Cam with a look of both interest and accusation. Jade's looks alone can feel like an inquisition, and I see Cam ready himself to defend against her silent barrage.

"I was just bringing her home," he tells Jade, then looks at me. "She's okay," he says in that same gentle tone he used in Reeve's bedroom.

His words stir something inside me, and tears spill down my cheeks.

"Thanks," Jade says coolly. She puts her hand on the door, ready to close it on him. "I've got her now."

"Bye, Lenni." He gives me a final look before the door shuts in his face.

lenni

TUESDAY. My first class with Reeve since the incident-that-shall-not-be-named, and I'm praying he won't try to talk to me.

He sent me an apology text on Saturday that was brief and may or may not have been sincere. I didn't bother answering. Not because I hate him but because I don't care anymore. I acted like a complete idiot, and I paid the price. I pretended to be someone I'm not, pretended that trust meant nothing to me when really, it means everything. All I'm taking away is gratitude that I figured it out before I developed any real feelings for him.

My comfort today is my clothes. With dread sitting heavy in the pit of my stomach this morning, pulling on my old baggy jeans and the XL T-shirt worn thin by hundreds of washings felt like crawling into bed at the end of a long day. Maybe I did look good in those tight tops and maybe I was even a decent enough flirt to get invited to parties by Shafer's star quarterback, but I was painfully uncomfortable. It wasn't me. I led myself so far from who I want to be.

When I open the door to the lecture hall, Cam is in his usual seat without Reeve by his side. I quickly avert my eyes. I can feel him watching me as I climb the steps toward the back, where I've decided I'll sit for the rest of the semester. The weight of his gaze stirs up a hundred tiny sparks of emotion, but I push them away. Jade and I already talked about this: don't chastise yourself, don't play the what-if game, and don't analyze his actions. And while Jade was talking about Reeve, I was talking about Cam.

Despite my promise not to chastise myself, I spent the weekend awash in humiliation and regret, and it had little to do with Reeve. What I kept replaying was Cam's face when he walked in and saw me. What must he think of me? Desperate. Easy. Predictable.

For two years, he remembered me as someone who could hold a conversation, who he could open up to and share secrets with. Now I've obliterated that. Now I'm the girl who gets naked and offers herself to guys who don't want her.

I indulge these thoughts until Professor Richards starts the lecture, and then I try to forget the last four days. I take good notes. I share what I wrote with the girl two seats away who missed one of Richards's wordy explanations. But I keep looking down at where I used to sit. Reeve hasn't shown up. And Cam looks good enough to eat.

His dark-brown hair is just long enough to hint at the waves I remember from the night we met. I thought he had the best hair, all thick and wavy and hanging over his eyes. His face is perfect in profile: straight nose, curving lips, razor-sharp jawline. My stomach does a little flip. Some people are born with it all.

My eyes trace the line of his long, tanned arm stretched out on the armrest. I stare at his hand and his strong fingers. That's the hand that held mine, the hand that made me feel, if only for a few seconds, that I was safe and I was strong. With every second that passes, a hollow, yearning feeling unfurls inside me until my whole body strains with the strength of it. I watch as his fingers curl slowly into a fist and then out again, a move I swear he designed just to torture me. Desire hits me like a stab. I picture his fingers curled around my waist, then my thigh. I can't believe how much I want him.

Finally, I turn my eyes to the front of the classroom and shake off the confusion of lust and fondness I suddenly feel toward Cam. Just because he had the decency to take pity on a crying, pathetic girl doesn't make him a hero. He's a cocky, spoiled athlete like all of them, and if I need proof, it's that he calls Reeve Dalton his best friend.

When class ends, I take my time packing up. I don't want to risk running into Cam as we walk out. But as the seats around me clear, I look up and he's coming up the steps toward me. A sick feeling takes root in the pit of my stomach.

"Hey," he says when he reaches my row. "Nosebleed seats, huh?"

I shrug, useless for speech of any kind.

"So I don't get a hello or anything?"

"Um, hello?"

"I just thought after what happened . . . you know?" His mouth lifts into a hint of a smile.

I swallow hard. "You think I should be thanking you, right?" Suddenly I'm angry. The truth is, I probably should be thanking him, but my humiliation is so overwhelming, I don't even want to look at him. I want him to leave me alone. "Look, Cam, just because—"

"No," he cuts in. "I don't mean you owe me anything. I just thought we're . . . friends."

I stare at him, caught in the earnest expression in his eyes. *Friends.* My anger melts away.

"Anyway, I wanted to tell you Reeve dropped the class. He's

missed too many." He shifts his backpack on his wide shoulders. "So if you want your old seat back, you're in the clear."

He gives me a final nod and turns to go. I watch him until he disappears through the door, his words echoing in my head in time with my shallow breaths.

It's a stretch to call it a kindness; he was really just stating facts, wasn't he? But my heart doesn't take it that way. Just at the moment I needed Cam to be the biggest asshole possible so I could once and for all turn my back on male arrogance and never look back, he had to go and invite me to sit next to him. And my fragile heart fucking eats it right up.

I WALK into the newsroom on Wednesday and breathe in the mingled scents of new electronics and old wood. I thrive on the hurried atmosphere that's baked into the walls of this place, especially when my mind is spinning.

Darren is on me as soon as he spots me. "Pretty nice write-up on the volleyball game this weekend," he says, settling on the edge of the desk next to mine. "I want to go over a few things before the next one, but you're getting the hang of it. Next question, how much do you know about football?"

"Can I dodge that question if I remind you I'm a quick learner?"

"That's why I had you in mind. You know the game against Reynolds coming up?"

I nod. Everyone knows. Reynolds University is Shafer's biggest rival, making the annual matchup the most hyped game of the regular season. But covering a football game for the paper is miles out of my wheelhouse.

Darren smiles at what I imagine is a look of sheer trepidation on my face. "Slow your roll, I'm not asking you to cover the game. What I want is more along the lines of a profile; a short one. A little fluffy, but fun, something that even students who aren't big football fans will read."

Sounds like a lot of pressure for a fluff piece. "A profile of who?"

"To be determined—Coach Haskins will pick someone—but I want a player who's a local boy to reflect on what it's like to grow up watching this big rivalry and now find himself playing in the game. Definitely an upperclassman, maybe even a captain if Coach is in a good mood."

Great. Just great. I can think of two upperclassmen who happen to be locals, and they've both seen me naked in the last week. My fingers tap dance against my thigh. I have a "no saying no" personal policy in the newsroom. I love taking the assignments that no one else wants, being the person who always says yes. But this? Nay. Nope. No fucking way. "I wouldn't even know what questions to ask," I tell Darren.

He shakes his finger like he's scolding me. "You figure out what questions to ask; that's what journalists do."

"It's just a little out of my comfort zone."

"Good! You're bored with volleyball, and it shows in your writing."

I tuck my hair behind my ear and force myself to keep eye contact with Darren. "Sorry. I knew my article could have been punchier, I got a little—"

"It was fine, but I know you have bigger aspirations around this newsroom. I want to see you write something that sizzles."

"You just called this interview a fluff piece."

"Then make it more than fluff," he dares me.

All the uncertainty brewing inside me hardens into resolve, and I remember why Darren was my favorite person on staff long before he became my editor. I can do this profile, and I can make it a hell of a lot more solid than a fluff piece.

Darren nods like he's reading my mind. "I want to see you start pitching ideas. I know you think you don't have the sports experience to come up with stories like you do for Arts and Lifestyle, but do it anyway." Someone catches his eye across the room, and he stands up. "You've got a lot of competition for an editor position."

"I think the writers would riot if I became sports editor."

"It's not about that. What you do in our little section of the paper reverberates all over the room." He walks away but glances over his shoulder. "You know that by now."

I spend two hours making edits and chatting with the other writers in a successful effort to forget the profile, but on the walk home, I finally confront it. I have to do it and I have to do it well, no matter who's on the other end of the interview. Anyway, it might not be Reeve or Cam that Coach Haskins picks. Surely they're not the only locals on the team.

But I happen to know Reeve ends up in a lot of football interviews. He's the captain, he's the star quarterback, and that charming, loudmouth personality of his makes for some great quotes. Cam? Seems to me, Cam speaks mostly with a closed mouth and gorgeous eyes, which doesn't exactly translate well in print.

Instinctively, my cheeks flush with heat, a confusion of embarrassment, regret, and, well, let me just face it, my overwhelming attraction to him.

I'm stuck on what he did for me. He helped me when he didn't have to, and instead of doing the normal thing and ignoring me in class so we could both pretend the awful incident never happened, he had to go and treat me like a human being. Everything I've learned about him in the last few days is tempting me to believe maybe he's not just a stereotype.

But then . . . he is. He's a rich, popular athlete with an exclusive taste for girls so pretty they make you want to smash your mirrors. Those are facts. And if I was writing a story on Cameron Forrester, that's what I'd have to go on, not the hot, fluttery feeling I get when I think about him. I can't let myself forget that.

"You're looking grim," Jade says when I walk into the apartment. She's sitting on the counter, spooning ramen noodles into her mouth, her feet crossed in their white combat boots.

I sling my backpack on a kitchen chair and flop down. "I found out I have to interview a football player and he has to be a local guy. Darren's hoping for a captain." I give her a look.

"Shit. Talk about bad timing." She shoots a healthy squeeze of sriracha into her noodles. "I don't suppose you get to choose who to interview?"

"Apparently it's up to the coach." I stare down at my hands and pick at the last bit of blue nail polish on my thumb.

"Reeve always gets those interviews," she says gloomily.

"Of course."

She puts down her bowl and looks thoughtful. "Don't forget, you're the one in charge of the interview." She smiles. "We could come up with questions that put him on the spot. Like, let's see . . . 'Where do you see yourself in five years when you've been outed as an overhyped creep and no one wants you on their team?'"

"Jade," I begin.

"The point is, you're controlling the interview; you've got the power."

"I don't want the power. I just want to avoid him."

"You know, Cam's a captain too." She raises an eyebrow.

I look at her. "He is? You sure?"

"How many games have I endured with Sam? I'm sure. They have three captains." She watches me and when I don't answer, a flicker ignites in her eyes. "Your silence is screaming at me. You like Cam, don't you?"

"No."

"You know he and the Russian broke up, right?"

This shouldn't make me happy, but it does. And Jade can read me like a book, which is why she must have chosen this moment to drop that bit of gossip. Time for a diversion. "There's something I haven't told you about him," I say.

She leans closer, almost drooling.

"Remember I told you about that guy I met at orientation? Forrest?"

"Uh, yeah, you didn't stop talking about him the entire first semester of freshman year."

"I just found out that was Cam."

She pulls back, looking a little confused and a lot disappointed; this isn't the secret sex-filled romp she was hoping to hear about. I make my explanation brief: the long hair, the different name, our heated exchange at the football house.

"So that's why you were asking about him at brunch," she concludes. "You're into him."

"No!" I say quickly. Met with her smile, I add, "If I am, it's probably just because I associate him with that summer."

"If? Give it up, girl, you'd bang him right here if he knocked on the door."

I cross my arms. "I'm still trying to figure out whether he's even worth liking. Or whatever—banging."

She picks up her bowl and starts eating again, then looks up to find me watching her. "Wait, you actually want my opinion?"

"No, but we both know it's coming, so just get it over with."

She smiles down into her ramen. "You want my opinion."

I grunt.

"Is he worth liking?" Her eyes flare dramatically at the word *liking*. "I guess that depends how you want to judge him, based on how he treats you or on the company he keeps."

"You're saying he's Reeve's best friend, and that about sums it up?" I don't expect the jag of disappointment that hits me.

She frowns. "I don't know what I'm saying."

Jade has an opinion about everyone and everything, and she doesn't need more than ten seconds of reflection to form said opinion. But even she doesn't know where to land on Cam.

"What?" she demands when she catches me smiling.

"You think he might be a good guy, and it's killing you."

"You wish. When has a guy like that ever turned out not to be an asshole?"

I can't deny she's got a point.

"Rule of thumb: if a guy can be an asshole and still manage to get laid, he'll be an asshole."

"You really hold the male species in high regard, don't you?" I tease.

Jade grins. "Fuck 'em all."

THAT EVENING, I hit the university gym for a slow, heavy strength-training session. It's where I do my best thinking. I try to calculate the odds that Coach Haskins chooses Cam for the interview, knowing the whole time it'll be Reeve because my life is just like that.

The gym is dead and given the space and time to linger at the squat rack without having to accommodate impatient gym bros, I set a personal record for back squats. Nine months ago, I couldn't have done one proper bodyweight squat. It feels incredible, and as I slide the heavy weight plates off the barbell, I have to hold back a smile, so I won't look like a lunatic.

When I leave the gym, my mind is set. I'm doing the interview, no matter who's on the other end of it. I can handle Reeve and whatever he thinks about me. I don't even like the guy; I don't think I ever did.

cameron

"SO BRING YOUR GODDAMN A GAMES." Coach Haskins looks at us in turn from under his gray eyebrows. It's our weekly captains' meeting and we're just about to wrap up, which is good because I'm starving. "All right, last thing real quick here. Dalton and Forrester, which one of you wants to answer a few questions for the Daily Phantom about the game against Reynolds? They want a hometown boy."

"I'll do it," Reeve says to the surprise of no one.

"Good. The girl will contact you about it."

Reeve hesitates. "The girl?" I know what he's thinking. There's only a small handful of writers who usually interview the team, and they're all dudes.

Coach is scribbling something on his clipboard and doesn't look up. "Yeah. Lainey or something."

Suddenly I'm not hungry anymore. Reeve and I look at each other. I don't know what my face says but his clearly reads, *Oh, shit*. As it should.

Coach looks up from his paper. "Problem, Dalton?" Before Reeve can answer, he adds, "Don't go bringing personal shit into this, remember?"

Reeve clears his throat like he's about to make a speech, and his brow furrows in concentration. He's digging deep for some elaborate excuse. Reeve is the king of bullshitting.

"I'll take this one," I say.

Reeve's eyes cut to me. Coach glances between the two of us. Even Tim, our other captain, is staring. I don't volunteer for interviews, ever. I ignore the looks and nod at Coach.

"Fine," he says, eyeing me a second too long. "I'll give her your info."

Reeve squeezes my shoulder as we walk out. "Thanks for saving my ass. You're the hero we all need right now."

I nod instead of saying that I didn't do it for him. I don't have a clue how it works at the paper, but I'm wondering if Lenni was given this assignment or if she actually asked for it. And if she asked, why would she want to be anywhere near a football player after what happened?

Later, Reeve and I grab dinner at a pizza spot off campus. He makes a point of saying how overrated he thinks Reynolds University's top-ranked wide receiver is. He must be sensing my nerves about our upcoming matchup. What he's careful not to mention again is Lenni.

He hasn't said a word about what went down in his bedroom that night, which means he feels guilty—Reeve rarely has a problem laughing about other people's embarrassment—but apparently not guilty enough to apologize to her. I'm tempted to tell him how shook she was after he left that night, but she wouldn't want that. What happened when it was just me and her feels private.

Memories of that night linger in my head, and not just because of how hard it was to see her cry.

I've gone to sleep every night thinking about her curves barely contained by that lacy red getup she wore. I knew she was stacked, but damn, her body is fucking solid. Big, juicy ass, thick thighs, and soft, pillowy tits. Jesus. I should feel guilty thinking about her this way when it was probably one of the worst moments of her life, but a man can only do so much once an image like that is burned into his brain. At least I haven't let myself jerk off to her. Yet.

Dammit, it's enough to make me wish she was a jersey chaser who wants nothing more than a long night with me and some bragging rights to follow. But I don't think that's Lenni. I just don't know what is; that's why I need to forget her.

I don't date girls who aren't perfectly explicit about what they expect. As far back as I remember, that's the only way I know how to relate to women. If a woman doesn't tell me exactly what she wants from me, I can only disappoint her.

Besides, I need to keep my head in the game. Lenni is a distraction I can't afford, not if I want to get drafted. And I do; at least I think I do. Most days.

As we're leaving the pizza spot, my mom calls; it's like she knows I'm doubting the path she's set me on since birth.

"Hey, Ma," I answer, waving to Reeve as he heads off to the library and I turn toward home.

"Hi, doll. How was practice? You're taking care of yourself?"

"I always do." I nod as I pass a guy from my ethics class.

"Good. The last thing you want right now is an injury." If Mom could cover me in bubble wrap all through college, she would; anything to get me to the pros intact.

"I know. What's new with you?"

"Well, you know how eager I've been to show you off this season. I was thinking I'd come the week after the Reynolds game and bring the whole crew. Rick and Gloria and their kids, and the Wiltons along with their daughter," she says, naming two of the families Mom is tight with. Then her voice turns girlish. "And I'd like to bring Harris too. He's just dying to meet you."

I roll my eyes. Harris is my mom's shiny new boyfriend, and I couldn't give a shit about meeting him. Why put both of us through the farce where I pretend he could be a good father figure and he pretends to be one? Meanwhile, we both know what landed him here: Minnie Forrester is pretty, rich, and insatiably hungry for attention.

I'm about to tell her fine when I remember who else I invited to that game. My stomach knots up. "You're already coming to the Reynolds game, right? Can't this crew come with you then? It'll be a better matchup than the next game anyway."

"Harris might have a hunting trip that weekend. Is there a problem with me attending both?"

"Sort of. I already have guests coming to that game."

Mom chuckles, but I can tell she's confused. "Surely there's enough room in the stadium for another few."

"And I'll be busy after the game too."

"With who?" Mom's honeyed voice has lost its honey.

Guilt grinds at me. "Serena and Liam."

In the dead silence that follows, a car horn blares from somewhere across campus and someone shouts angrily in response. I clear my throat unnecessarily. Then, finally, Mom says, "Cameron." And for the moment, that says it all.

All my life, my mom called me "Cammy" and I hated it; it's a name fit for a toddler in pigtails. My dad was Cameron, or occasionally Cam when Mom had downed enough wine. Then Dad was gone and the whole messy life he'd kept hidden from us spilled out, and suddenly I was Cameron. You'd think she'd never want to utter the name again after what he did to her, but instead she reclaimed it—for me. Cue my short-lived reinvention of myself as Forrest . . . Forrest Forrester. Yeah, didn't think that one through very well, did I?

"Why would you do that, Cameron?" Mom wants to know. "Why would you invite her?"

"Liam's been asking to see me play."

"I had no idea you had that kind of relationship with the woman." It's not a statement but an accusation.

"You know I talk to her."

"Yes, well, I didn't know that amounted to a relationship of this sort. You're treating her like family, Cameron!"

"Liam is my family, and the kid needs all he can get."

"Oh, hell's bells, with the amount of money that woman has gotten out of us, she could buy the child a new father. And what are people going to say when they find out your so-called brother has a mother not a decade older than you?"

"No one here cares about our family drama."

Mom sighs slowly, gathering herself. "Honey, I know you want to do right by the boy, but you are not responsible for your father's sins." Because that's all Serena and Liam will ever be to my mom: sins.

"I gotta go, Ma. I'm sorry. Pick any other Saturday and I'm all yours."

"I'm your mother, Cameron, and I should be able to attend any Saturday I want. It's not as though I'm there every weekend."

I sigh. "So you're asking me to uninvite Serena?"

"I suppose I'm only asking you to decide what's more important."

Not what, *who*. That's what she means. So I'm trapped. "Fine. I'll talk to her."

After we exchange a quick goodbye, I sit down on the brick stoop in front of my house. The street is quiet, and as usual, no one's bothered to turn on the porch light. I feel like a shit son. Mom's pissed, which is one thing, but she's hurt too. All because I went off script.

In the beginning, when we found out that Dad not only had a mistress but had fathered her son, I hated Serena almost as much as Mom did. I even hated Liam. He was just some dumb little kid whose father never wanted him. Until I realized that's what he was: a clueless kid whose father had barely been in his life and never would be again. I couldn't hate him for that.

Mom thought I'd take her side no matter what because for so long, I did. It was just me and her, hurting together, trying to pick up the pieces Dad left when he blew up our family. And now that I'm trying to be a brother to Liam, she's hurt even more. Story of my life. Either meet expectations or live with the guilt of letting down the people you love.

I pull out my phone to check the time, suddenly wanting to hear my little brother's voice. He's not much for phone conversations, but he has a birthday coming up, and I bet I could get a nice monologue out of him if I asked what was on his wish list. But it's past his bedtime, so I settle for searching the internet for a replacement for the blue toy car Lenni took home with her in my rain jacket. I know she'd give it back, but I like knowing it's with her.

Turns out they don't sell the exact car anymore, but I find a new-in-box version on a resale site for ten times the original price, which still only amounts to about twenty-five bucks. I order it, feeling a small sense of victory. So maybe there's more to life than living up to expectations.

lenni

IT'S a tale as old as time. I've gotten what I wanted, and now I don't want it anymore. No, scratch that, I still want it. I'm just terrified of it.

I'm interviewing Cam today.

At first, it seemed like an unbelievable stroke of luck that I could not only avoid the painful awkwardness of interviewing Reeve but actually have an excuse to talk to Cam. But I realized a Reeve interview would have been easy. I know him, I know how I feel about him, and I know I could have been aloof, straightforward, and professional. But Cam—who he is and my feelings for him—is a mystery I don't know how to approach.

I'm a wild mix of butterflies and dread as I take one last look through my interview questions. They're solid, and if I stick to them, I'll get through it. Problem is, there's so much more I want to ask him off the record.

We agreed to meet in one of the small courtyards behind the main library that are always empty. I arrive early and set out my notebook and laptop, then double check that my phone is recording without issues. I resist the urge to check my reflection in my phone camera; this is an interview, not a date. Besides, no amount of primping could make me look like the sort of girl Cameron Forrester dates. Just to drive home the point, I even opted not to wear makeup.

It's a choice I regret the instant he steps out into the court-yard. He looks so damn good, the incredible color of his eyes intensified by the sunlight. He doesn't even have the advantage of makeup and hairstyling, so how does he look even better than usual?

I swallow hard and stand on shaky legs. I take in his tall form, the wide, strong shoulders in his white T-shirt, the damp hair. He's fresh off football practice and a shower. Yum.

"Lenni." His deep voice stirs up those butterflies again.

"Hi, Cam. Thanks for meeting me." Out of habit, I extend my hand to him.

He looks at it and hesitates, but then shakes it. "Nice to meet you too," he teases.

Is he flirting or making fun of me? Trying to act professional is somehow making this even worse. "This is an interview, remember? I'm a journalist." I don't feel like a journalist, though; I feel like a little girl playing pretend. I take a steadying breath and direct him to the table. He sits opposite me, lacing his fingers together in front of him. His hands are huge, strong. I tear my eyes away.

I go through my usual spiel, explaining how everything will be recorded and the overall gist of the interview. He nods. He's done this before. I warm up with a little small talk: football practice, school. I've got my work cut out for me because Cam is well-known as a man of few words, and so far, he's living up to his reputation. His answers are polite but brief.

We roll quickly through my first few questions, establishing the basics. He was born and raised here in Shafer, on the north —in other words, wealthy—end of town, started playing football in sixth grade, and like all good boys in town, has been a Shafer fan since birth.

Then onto the questions I hope might yield a few stellar quotes for the article.

"Did you ever dream of playing for Shafer when you were a kid?" I ask.

Cam hesitates. "Actually, no. Back then I was convinced I'd end up at Oxford. For lit, not football."

"Quite a pivot to a football scholarship at Shafer. What happened?"

"What can I say? Life takes you where it wants you."

I pause to give him time to elaborate, but he doesn't. "Can you say more about that?"

"About how I haven't always dreamed of attending Shafer? Better not. The written word is forever, isn't it?" He winks, triggering a visceral sense of longing somewhere inside me. I forgot he could be playful like this.

"Nothing's written until I write it," I remind him.

He nods. "Then let's back up. Life takes you where it wants you." Then, in a voice brimming with fake enthusiasm, "And for me, it chose the greatest university in the world." He places his hand on top of my phone to cover the microphone and leans in close. "Your editor will eat that up."

Surprised, I let out a laugh. "No touching." I slide his hand off my phone, committing to memory that image of my fingers on top of his. When we touch, the heat of his skin moves right through me.

I try to push down my flustered feelings. I knew this interview would challenge me, but I thought it would be the awkwardness of the Reeve incident. Instead, it's the undeniable electricity that sparks in me every time I look at Cam.

"Okay, so from Oxford dreams to football star . . . when did you start to believe you might be the guy on the field that everyone is cheering for?"

"Sixth grade." His smile is so damn cocky. He's quiet, yes, but modest? Not so much.

"Sixth grade. I take it you were a confident kid."

"I think it was more my mom that had me believing I'd end up here. As soon as she saw I had a talent for football, she was painting fantasies of me being a star athlete lighting up the TV screen every week."

"I bet there's a few thousand parents out there who'd like to know your mom's secrets."

"If I gave away my mom's secrets, I'd never hear the end of it. But she's a big believer in putting on a happy face. You know, make the whole world believe you've got it all and eventually, you will."

Something in his dubious expression tells me he's throwing a bit of shade at his mom, so I move on to the next question. "Would you say that you owe your athletic success in part to growing up in a town like Shafer?"

"Definitely. For better or for worse, being raised in a college football town shapes your view of success. And that's the flip side. Football dreams don't seem so far out of reach, but sometimes they blind you to other ones."

"Other dreams? Which ones?"

"All of them. Anything else I excelled at or enjoyed. I never gave a second thought to any of it."

It's the most interesting thing he's said in this interview—and, of course, completely at odds with the tone of the piece I'm striving for. I hold back, hoping maybe he'll say more, but he just glances around. He doesn't want to go there.

"So as a hometown boy, you must have watched this rivalry play out from the stands a time or two. Did your parents bring you to games as a kid?"

"All the time. It was usually my mom that brought me throughout the season, but the Reynolds game was the one Saturday Dad would attend every year."

"Sounds like a great tradition. Your parents must be thrilled at the idea of watching their son out there for a third year in a row."

He nods. "Actually, my dad passed away a few years ago."

My heart drops like a stone. "God, I'm sorry. That must have been really painful."

"It hurt," he says, though his voice lacks any self-pity. "But everyone's got their tragedies."

I want to reach across the table and touch him to let him know he's not alone. Or maybe to remind myself that I'm not alone. "I'm sorry for saying sorry." He gives me a puzzled look. I sound like a fool. "I mean, people always say it, but it's hollow."

He holds my gaze, his eyes achingly kind. "People mean well. They just don't know what to say."

"Yeah, but I should know better. I grew up without a father."

"I know, you told me."

"I did?" I rarely tell people unless there's no way around it.

Cam nods. This is the part I normally want to fast-forward through: the look of pity, the awkwardness in the air. But there's none of that from him. Nothing has changed except me wondering what else I forgot I told him.

And this, of course, is why I might have told him anything. He makes it so easy. I've been trying to convince myself the night we met was an anomaly, some precise mixture of his beautiful face, the night air, and the fact we were strangers. An atmosphere we could never recreate. But now I think it was just Cam. Because I know who he is and we're in the ugly concrete courtyard of the library and not even my nipples are strangers to him, yet here's that feeling all over again.

"I wonder which one's worse," Cam says. "In the battle of the shitty dads," he adds when he sees my questioning look.

"Sorry, but I'm going to go ahead and declare mine the winner. It's not your dad's fault he died. Mine decided to peace out as soon as my mom had a pregnancy test in hand."

"Definitely a top contender for shitty dad," he concedes. "But mine pretended to be a good husband and father while making a huge mess behind our backs. By the time we found out, he was gone."

"Okay, that's really bad."

"Call it a draw?" Cam offers me a wry smile.

"Definitely. Better luck next time, Dad." It shouldn't be this amusing to talk about our crappy fathers, but somehow it is. I look into his eyes, feeling emboldened. "You know, I owe you an apology, Cam."

"For stealing my rain jacket?"

"Oh. Shoot. Sorry, I keep forgetting." I don't, actually. It's still hanging on the corner of my closet door and every time I think, *I need to return that*, I decide not to.

He smiles. "I'm kidding. Keep it."

I think I'm blushing. Damn it. "No, I wanted to apologize for being kind of bitchy to you. Especially that night you tried to warn me about Reeve."

"That was nothing. You didn't know me."

"I'm sorry for that too."

He waves me off. "It's not your fault I'm utterly forgettable."

I laugh. "Stop, you're totally memorable. And don't take my word for it, just listen to every girl on campus who's ever glimpsed your football poster in the student union and then made it her mission to memorize your height, weight, birthday, favorite foods, childhood nickname, and touchdown stats."

"You know, I was wrong about you. You'd actually make a great jersey chaser."

"Yeah, you wish." I make the mistake of giving his hand a playful slap and electricity races through me. So maybe it's not always easy to be around him; not when we touch. When we touch, I can barely breathe. I pull my hand back, the playfulness between us gone.

"I want to apologize to you too." He rubs the back of his neck. "I was a dick about your thing with Reeve."

"Didn't stop me, unfortunately."

"I guess I was pissed off you didn't acknowledge me." He looks off to the side. "And maybe a little territorial."

Territorial? It's caveman bullshit for sure, but damn if it doesn't make me want him more. "The thing about Reeve, though—"

"Doesn't matter," he says. "You don't have to explain."

"So you get it?" Maybe then he can explain it to me.

"No, but you don't owe me an explanation. I wouldn't want to have to account for how I ended up in certain girls' beds."

I push down the jealousy that flares at his words. I need the reminder that even if he's more discreet than other football players, he's still probably bedded half the girls on campus. He's not for me, no matter how open he's been, no matter how strong of a connection I feel to him. No matter how much I want to run my fingers along the light stubble he's sporting on that laser-cut jawline and wrap my fingers around the back of his neck and press my mouth to his soft, full lips. Um, where were we?

I straighten up and see Cam looking at my phone with knitted brows.

"Are we still recording?" he asks.

"Oh my god." I forgot we were in the middle of an interview. "I'm sorry. I'll erase the personal stuff, obviously."

"No worries. Isn't forgetting you're being interviewed the mark of a great interviewer?"

"I'm not sure, but let's go with that."

He smiles. That smile gets me every time. Must concentrate. Must be professional. Must pretend it's never occurred to me to wonder what he looks like naked.

"So any other questions?" Cam asks.

I look at my list and groan.

"What?"

"I had a few other ones, but they're total fluff. I mean, really cheesy."

"Cool. I love cheese."

I sigh, feeling like a huge dork. "Okay. What'll be your celebration meal Saturday night after Shafer beats Reynolds to a pulp?"

"Cheese?"

I try not to laugh. "Don't be cute."

"Now how am I supposed to do that?" He gestures toward his face, and I let my eyes linger on his perfect features longer than I should. I hate that these little antics of his work so well on me. I thought I was better than this.

"All right, so cheese and what else?"

"I don't know." He eyes me, and I sense something coming. He's smiling, fully confident, totally feeling himself. I don't trust it. "What would you like to eat?"

"What?"

"If Shafer beats Reynolds and we celebrate together. What would you like to eat?"

"Why would we do that?" My heart thumps uncomfortably.

"Because we're friends."

Oh my god. What is he doing? I clear my throat. "We're still recording, remember? This is an interview."

"Oh, right, right, right." Is he mocking me? "In that case, I'll be at the student union sinking my teeth into a tray full of juicy

Red Phantom burgers." He leans back, satisfied. "There, another Easter egg for your editor."

I cross my arms. "You like to act all modest and quiet, but I think you actually love giving interviews, don't you?"

"Just trying to make your job easier." His eyes are steady on me. I don't think we've broken eye contact in minutes.

I lick my lips, my mouth suddenly dry. "Then stick to the script, Forrester."

I can't account for what's happening between us. We're playful, we're serious, we tease, we apologize. Whatever it is, it crackles. And I can't get enough of it.

Then something shifts. Cam looks past me, and his smile drops. He leans forward, getting ready to say something, when behind me, I hear hushed, girlish voices. Irritation flashes across Cam's face.

"Look who's here!"

"Cam, babe, hi!"

The girlish voices are no longer hushed. I don't need to turn around because immediately the girls are at his side. Alexis Truman, a jersey chaser so prolific that even I can name half her conquests, and her friend whose name I don't know. Both are blond, tanned, manicured, and have killer eyeliner game—seriously, I want to ask how they do it—but neither of them has bothered to glance at me, the sight of Cameron Forrester too enticing. And now Alexis has her long pink nails pressed into his shoulder.

I feel Cam watching me, and I deserve an acting award for how hard I'm trying to appear unfazed. But I really, really want this chick to get her hands off Cam and out of my interview.

"Hey, cutie," Alexis says, leaning over Cam.

"Hey," he says tightly.

"Are you . . . studying?" she asks after giving me a cursory glance. Because of course that's the only reason Cam would associate with someone like me.

"Lenni's interviewing me for the paper, so it's not a great time."

"Oh." Alexis gives me another look but won't be defeated. "Then can I wait for you? Brielle and I are on our way to grab a little bite. Join us?" She finishes it off with this perky little one-sided shrug that even I find sort of sexy. How does she do that?

But Cam barely glances at her. "You go ahead. Lenni and I might be a while." He fixes me with a look that I can't read, but I stare back because I'm powerless to do otherwise. That is, until Alexis lets her fingers graze his jawline and then it's all I can see. That and visions of them naked and sweaty together.

"Actually, we're all done here." I stop the recording and begin to gather up my stuff.

Cam sits up. "I thought you had more questions for me."

"No, we covered everything. You're free. Thanks for your time."

Alexis glows with delight.

Cam frowns, his face pinched in annoyance, but I don't care. It doesn't matter how good I feel when I'm around him, he's not for me. He's for Alexis Truman and Kira the Great and girls like that. It's not even about beauty. I just know he and I aren't a possibility, and the longer I'm near him, the harder it gets to remember that.

I stand and turn to go inside, but Cam is right behind me. Just as I reach the door, he puts his hand out and leans on it. I turn to him. He's close, very close. At my height, I'm not used to guys towering over me, but he's so close that I have to tilt my head to look at his face. "Yes?" I make the mistake of breathing, and the woodsy smell of his skin immediately weakens me.

"Why are you rushing off?" His muscled arm is so close it's

almost touching my hair. He's got me trapped, and I don't hate it.

"The interview's over. You can be with your friends now."

"You don't have any more questions for me." He's not asking, he's challenging.

A dozen questions flash in my mind, and none of them have anything to do with football. "Nope, I've got what I need."

He nods. "Good."

"Thanks again."

He watches me from eyes a thousand feet deep. Eyes I can't look away from. And just when I think, *I'm not going anywhere,* he steps back and I'm free to go. "Anytime."

I shake off the spell of his gaze and pull open the door, but then he says my name. I turn back to him.

"What if I want to call you? About the interview."

Alexis and her friend are watching us with curious stares. "Then call me," I say.

"I don't have your number."

"Yes, you do. Same one you used when we set up this meeting."

"That was email, remember? Let me get your number." Behind him, Alexis's expression has gone from curious to pissed.

I hesitate, but he pulls his phone out and waits expectantly. I give him the number.

"Thanks," he says, sliding his phone back into his pocket. "I'll call you."

"I'll just get in touch if I have questions about the interview."

He smiles like this is funny. "And if we beat Reynolds?"

"Excuse me?"

"What will you want to eat?"

What is he doing? I feel unbearably warm and I'm sure I'm

beet-red, pleasure and embarrassment converging to make me feel like I'm running a fever. "You haven't won yet."

All the way home, all the way through dinner, all the way through homework and studying, and getting ready for bed, I wonder if he's in bed with Alexis. This is easy. I wonder about him and Alexis to stop me from wondering about him and me. Our connection, our attraction, the fact that he actually suggested we celebrate together. Nope, can't go there.

Better to focus on the facts. Cameron Forrester has sex with Alexis Truman despite the obvious fact he can't stand her. That's who he is.

Cameron Forrester is not for me.

cameron

IT'S hotter than it should be for fall, and sweat spills down my forehead. Maybe it's the weather that has me off my game today, but nothing is going the way I want on the practice field.

Our offense is installing new plays this week and so far, I've messed up every one. First, I run the wrong route and cause an interception that has our offensive coordinator shaking his head. Then I'm wide open on a post route, and I drop the perfect pass from Reeve. I can just feel Mason smirking from the sidelines.

After, I take my time in the shower, hoping most of the guys will have cleared out of the locker room. I'm not in the mood to hear talk about the upcoming Reynolds game.

Unfortunately, Mason is one of the few left when I come out. He's staring at his shirtless self in the mirror, but his attention shifts to me, and I can tell he's weighing whether it's worth giving me more shit. Because he has more balls than brains, he speaks up.

"Lookin' a little creaky out there, huh, Forrester? Sad to think you peaked sophomore year."

Coming from almost anyone else on the team, it might have

meant something, but Mason is such a worthless little nothing I can't be bothered to get riled up. "Almost as sad as watching you try to flex in the mirror," I say, opening my locker.

He walks over as I start getting dressed. "I noticed your game is off ever since you got dumped by the hottest chick at Shafer. Was that your secret all along? No more superpowers without that sweet pussy?"

I slam my locker door harder than I mean to. My feelings for Kira are long gone, but I can't stand when girlfriends and exes get dragged into this bullshit. "You know what would be great? If you could put on a shirt and scuttle back to your own locker. Thanks."

Mason laughs. "Hit a nerve, huh?"

"Nah, Connery, I'm just a little sad for you, that's all."

"Sad?" He sneers.

"Hearing you try to talk about pussy reminds me you've never had a girl give you the time of day unless she was too drunk to speak." I take a step toward him. He doesn't flinch, but I catch the flash in his eyes.

"All right, all right, chill." He laughs, trying to play it off like he's not a punk who's worried I might beat his ass. "Think I haven't seen just as much pussy as you have? Let me prove it."

"Don't." I turn my back to him and rub a towel through my hair, but before I realize what he's doing, his phone screen is in my face and I'm looking at a picture of a naked girl on a bed. Not a professional photo or some Insta-model pic, but a regular girl, asleep or passed out. I knock his arm away, but it's too late; despite the fact the photo's dark and underexposed and I only look for a second, I think I know who the girl is. "Get that shit out of here," I snap.

Mason is grinning like the creep that he is. "Come on, don't be such a boy scout, dude."

I don't know what annoys me more, that he took the picture

or that he actually thought I'd be impressed. "Why would you show that to me?"

"Because you're a dude. At least I thought so."

I throw my towel down. "You're even stupider than you look, Connery."

"Why's that?"

"Because you just showed something illegal to your team captain. The team captain who can't stand you."

His smile wavers. "How is that illegal?"

"I'm guessing you don't have written consent from that girl to show her nudes in public, right? That makes it illegal, dumbass." Actually, I'm bluffing. I don't know a thing about the legality of it, but common sense tells me the law isn't cool with this kind of shit.

"Chill," Mason says, but his casual tone sounds forced. "It's an innocent picture. I'm not gonna go posting it or anything."

I honestly hate this kid. "Delete it," I order him.

"You don't know that I don't have her permission. Maybe she likes the whole team seeing her titties."

"I know the last thing that girl wants is any proof she slept with you. Delete it for your own sake, you stupid asshole."

"Fine."

I watch him delete it. "Now from your recently deleted folder."

He rolls his eyes. I feel like such a dad right now.

"Delete it," I say again, getting in his face a little.

"Delete what?" comes Reeve's voice behind me.

I look over my shoulder to find him watching us. Great. I thought he'd left. Now we have a bigger problem. I'm pretty sure the girl in the picture is Sasha James, one of the chicks Reeve occasionally hooks up with. And even though his hookups are strictly no strings attached, he wouldn't take kindly to finding out Mason Connery slept with Sasha too.

In the few seconds it takes for Reeve to reach us, Mason and I have a little stare down. He gives me a tiny nod.

"Nothing," I tell Reeve, who's looking at Mason like he knows something's up. "It's nothing."

Reeve looks between me and Mason. "Good. Then move, Connery. You're blocking my locker." He gives Mason a little shove.

Mason says nothing—a first—and moves back to his own locker. I watch him from the corner of my eye as he fiddles on his phone, then glances at me and mouths the word *done*.

I just shake my head.

"You want to get dinner, or are you hitting the books tonight?" Reeve asks, shutting his locker.

"I should study. My ethics class is kicking my ass," I say as we head out. "But if you're not going out tonight, let's catch the game at nine."

"Yeah, I'll be home. See you then."

I head toward the library, even though the last thing I want to do is study. A beer in front of a baseball game sounds like a much better way to end this day, preferably in a crowded bar where it's too loud to think. I need to stay focused on improving my game, not on Connery and his antics, and definitely not on Lenni, who refuses to get out of my mind.

Her flirtation with Reeve aside, the interview made one thing clear: she's exactly the girl I remember. Despite the entire interview being about football, it's obvious that if I'm going to impress her, it won't have anything to do with my on-field performance. I forgot how easy she was to talk to, and how that feeling of connecting with her, even over our dads, gets in deep and sits with me for a long time.

Too bad she has to look as good as she does, otherwise she could be a friend. But sitting across from her yesterday, watching her bite those heart-shaped lips every time I said something she didn't know what to make of, I couldn't stop thinking about what she tastes like or what it might be like to make her moan.

Of course, going after her would be complicated. Messy. The kind of risk I don't usually take with girls. I remind myself of that as I walk by the building that holds the newsroom. I glance at the time—almost seven thirty. I'm pretty sure she's still in there; she told me she stays until at least eight on Wednesdays.

I hesitate. The idea of seeing Lenni soothes that ball of frustration that's been sitting in my stomach since practice. Suddenly I'm craving her. I put my bag down on one of the little umbrella-covered tables across from the main doors to the building and sit down. To hell with complicated and messy. I want her.

cameron

I WAIT AN EMBARRASSINGLY LONG TIME. When Lenni finally walks out of the building, the first thing I notice is her T-shirt; baggy and ancient looking like everything she wears, but this one, with "The Gits" plastered across the front in bold block letters, catches my eye. It's the same one she wore the night we met.

Lenni looks startled to see me and then pleased. Then she looks like she's trying not to look pleased.

She puts her hand on her hip, smiling coyly. "Look, if you wanted the rain jacket that badly, you could have just called instead of stalking me."

"Ha! You wish. It's not the jacket I'm after, it's the blue car. Liam's been asking, and if I tell him I let some girl play with it, he'll be pissed." I stand up. "You might not know this, but you have cooties."

She laughs and I swear I feel it under my skin. She looks down at the ground before meeting my eye again. "I actually can't tell if you're joking about the jacket or not."

"I'm joking. You can keep the jacket; the car too."

"Well, thank Liam for me." She looks me over. "So if you didn't come for the jacket, what are you doing here?"

"Just needed a pick-me-up." I move closer to her, but not too close. "You walking home now?"

She nods. Her hands fiddle with her necklace, a teardrop-shaped slab of resin on a gold chain, and I wonder if I made a mistake by ambushing her like this. She definitely likes to be in control, like during the interview. But I like catching her off guard.

We fall into step together.

"So," she says, "bad day to be a football star?"

"See, that's the problem. I haven't exactly been playing like a star."

"That's not what I hear. You're one of Shafer's best." I wish it was a compliment, but clearly she's only repeating what she's heard.

"Do you know anything about football?"

"Sure. There are two teams, one ball, and a lot of injuries." She gives me a sidelong grin.

"I can't believe they haven't hired you for the play-by-play."

"So what's the problem?"

I wish we were talking about something else. "Guess I'm just not living up to expectations."

"Which ones?"

"Let's see . . . being the best receiver in the country, winning a national championship, getting drafted in the first round."

"Whose expectations are those? Yours?" She takes in my silence. "Can I say something that's going to sound harsh?"

"Careful, I'm more sensitive than I look."

She gives me a dubious look. "All right, here it is. Nobody cares about your football career."

I laugh. "Jeez. Wow. That's just . . . that's the meanest thing anyone's ever said to me."

"No, hear me out. You might have the entire college football fandom watching you and expecting an amazing professional career, and when it doesn't happen, they'll be disappointed. But a few months later, when there's a new crop of potential draft picks to obsess over, they'll forget you."

"Just when I thought you couldn't get any meaner," I joke. I guess there's some comfort to be found in the logic of her words; somewhere. Up ahead, a few food trucks sit parked in the lot next to a row of frat houses. The smell of grilled meat wafts through the air, and suddenly I'm starving.

"I'm sorry." She looks over at me. "That was supposed to be reassuring. Take the pressure off? I guess it didn't work."

"I forgive you. Just promise you won't start an advice column in the school paper." I nod toward the lot. "You a food truck kind of girl?"

"Always. I hear next month we're getting a curry truck started by some chef that won a cooking show."

"Curry from a van? Sounds like trouble."

"I'll give it a shot. I've kind of made it a personal mission to eat at TV-chef restaurants anywhere I get a chance."

"Let me know how the curry experiment goes. So you hungry?"

"I can always eat."

I feel disproportionately triumphant at getting a yes out of her. We divert toward the parking lot and survey the options. "Let's see. Burgers, ramen, barbecue, or burritos. I read Cal's Burgers is damn good; wonder where I read that." I head toward the burger truck.

Her head swivels toward me. "You read my article?"

"I always do. What do you think, single or double?"

We stand in front of the menu posted on the front of Cal's truck, but while I'm reading it, she seems to be reading me.

"You read all my articles." She sounds unconvinced. "So what do you think?"

Uh-oh. Is this a test? Her mouth is pleasantly relaxed, but her eyes definitely aren't, and her arms are crossed. Danger! Definitely a test. "I like the positive spin you put on everything. I'm saving that one about graduation anxiety for next year. I gotta say though, even you can't convince me the women's volleyball team has a chance at a winning season."

She makes a sound that's not quite a laugh. "Yeah, I had to dig deep for some optimism on that one." I think I've passed the test. She looks at the menu. "Definitely get a double," she tells me. "Because I'm having a double and cheese fries and possibly even a shake, and if you're a gentleman, you'll at least try to eat more than me."

"I'm a huge gentleman, just wait and see."

I skip the double and get a triple, one-up her cheese fries by picking the cheddar bacon ranch option, then order the largest milkshake they have and ask them to sprinkle bacon on top. Then I throw in a basket of onion rings. She holds back her laughter as I order, looking slightly embarrassed, then puts in her own. She lets me pay without making a thing of it.

When we sit down, Lenni pauses before turning to me. "I really am sorry for what I said about nobody caring whether you get drafted. I guess I thought it was this brilliant perspective." She twists her straw around in her shake. "It wasn't."

"I know what you were saying. It might've helped if it was the fans I was worried about."

"Then who is it?"

"My mom, I guess. She decided a long time ago who she needs me to be, and anything less would be a shocking disappointment." I'm tempted to tell her the other part of it; that some days I just want to prove to my father—wherever he ended up—how much he gave up when he decided one family wasn't enough for him.

"She needs you to be a first-round draft pick?"

"She needs me to be the best at what I do. I'm the winning athlete. Period."

"Well, not to sound trite, but don't you think your mom just wants you to be happy?"

I snort. "You don't know Minnie Forrester."

"I remember you telling me she was a beauty queen. And a southern belle. What else should I know about her?"

"Look, my mom's a good mother and a nice lady and all that, so don't get the wrong impression. But her greatest strength is projecting the image she wants people to see. And she wants everyone to think we're the perfect family, especially after my dad died and we realized our family was even more fucked up than previously known."

I'm waiting for her to ask what my dad did, but she doesn't. "So part of the perfect family image your mom wants is you being a professional athlete?"

"She's been telling her friends I was destined for the pros since I was in high school. Anything less would suggest that maybe Minnie Forrester doesn't have it all."

"That's a lot of pressure."

"It's not all her," I say as guilt creeps in. "I want to make it happen too. My mom completely devoted herself to my athletic career from day one. She saw a little flash of talent and she made sure I didn't waste it. She deserves the payoff." I shrug. Lenni is studying me with a look I can't read and that I'm really hoping isn't pity. "Okay, now tell me all the ways your family is screwed up."

"Got a week to spare?"

"For you? Sure."

She looks up at me, her cheeks flushing pink with a small, embarrassed smile. But the smile fades quickly.

"That bad, huh?"

She dips a fry in cheese sauce and keeps her eyes down. "My mom's an alcoholic," she says. "She's sober at the moment, but that could change at any second; literally. A few years ago, she and my little brother had to move in with my grandparents because she couldn't hold down a job. And my grandparents had no money to begin with."

I probably have guilt written all over my face. For all my family's issues, money was never one of them. Money might not save you from problems, but it can definitely soften the landing from the fallout.

"I really haven't been around for them, especially my brother. And I know my mom wants me to come home for summers and after graduation, but I won't go back to my hometown. I just haven't worked up the nerve to tell her that. So yeah . . . guilt city."

"Why won't you go back?"

I see the storm clouds in her eyes before she breaks my gaze. "I hate everyone there. I hated high school. I just had a . . . bad experience, I guess." She swallows hard.

My mind goes to that night in Reeve's bedroom. My chest hurts at the memory of her tear-stained face stricken by humiliation and confusion, and it hurts more to think maybe that wasn't the first time she felt that way. I want to punish whoever did that to her, including Reeve.

I put down my burger, suddenly not hungry. "Doesn't sound like a place worth going back to."

"Unfortunately, my mom doesn't get that."

"Does she know what you went through?"

"The whole town knows. But she seems to think it's all in the past, that I shouldn't still let it affect me." She shrugs. "But we're not one of those families that talks openly about feelings, you know? So I can't blame her for not getting it."

"Sounds like we have one more thing in common."

"What's that?"

"Problems without solutions."

"No, I have a solution." She sits up straighter. "Once I start working, I'm moving my family out of there too."

"A girl with a plan; I'm impressed. Told you, you're always on the lookout for the positive."

"Well, it won't all be sunshine and roses. I'll be eternally poor, but that runs in the family." She looks around at our table covered in wrappers and half eaten food. "Are you done? You never even touched the onion rings."

I slide them toward her. "Want one?"

"I'm stuffed."

I take a big bite of one, then shove the rest aside.

Lenni's watching me, looking amused. "I hope you don't plan on kissing anyone after that."

Instinctually, I look at her lips, then busy myself gathering up wrappers to throw away. I wonder if she can tell how much I want her.

On the walk to her place, she tells me about her classes and her grad school plans while I try to figure out where we stand. I know there's more than just friendship between us—I can feel it, hear it, almost taste it. It's right there. But one wrong move and I could kill it.

When we reach her building, she turns to me. "Thanks for dinner. I hope I was the pick-me-up you needed." She smiles like she doesn't totally believe my excuse for, well, stalking her.

"I can finally call it a good day."

I watch her take the steps up to the front door. Her jeans are too loose for me to make out much of her ass—the one part I didn't get an eyeful of in Reeve's room—but the bare skin on her lower back peeks out, and she's got those two little dimples there. Sexy.

Almost to the door, she turns slowly back to me. Her expression has turned mischievous, like she's about to tell a dirty joke, or maybe I'm just horny. "You never answered me. Are you going to be kissing anyone tonight?"

For a split second, my eager ass thinks she's asking me to kiss her, but no. She's up there and I'm down here and there are people around and I've seen the "kiss me" face on enough girls to know that's not it. But she wants to know if I'm hooking up with anyone, so she knows whether to be jealous. And she wants to know bad enough that she's asked twice.

I'm sure I'm grinning like a cocky bastard, but I don't care. This feels better than any touchdown catch. She wants me.

I take my time answering. It's almost a shame I can't tell her yes just to see what jealousy does to her, but I'm not going to lie to Lenni. "No. Are you?"

She laughs, surprised to find the question turned back on her. "Definitely not. But ask me again in five years, maybe I'll have a different answer."

"Nah, I'm not gonna make you wait five years for a kiss, baby," I tease her.

She shakes her head and blushes. "Good night, Cameron."

"Night, Lenni."

Just before she opens the door, she adds, "By the way, I don't believe you."

She's gone before I can ask which part she doesn't believe.

On the way home, I manage to keep my smile contained, but I can't help walking with my chest puffed out.

Reeve is in front of the TV when I get back. "Hey, I thought you were studying," he says.

"Not yet."

"Where were you?"

"Just walking Lenni home."

He lifts a can of beer to his lips, keeping his eyes on me, then swallows. "That's a little weird, don't you think?"

"Not really. Give me a beer."

He hands me a can. "You like her?"

I want to deny it, but he knew the answer before he asked. He's witnessed every crush I've had since middle school. "There's something about her."

"I'd say there's two. Two big, juicy things."

"Not that." I give the back of his head a shove and then find a seat on the couch. "I like being around her. She's different." *Blah.* I hate the clichés coming out of my mouth.

"Yeah, I guess. Different from Kira for damn sure. But maybe that's why you're after her; trying to wash away the old with something new."

"Quit talking like you're some wise fucking elder statesman."

He holds up his beer in cheers and takes a huge swig.

It hits me then I have no reason to keep pretending I have no history with Lenni. "Remember at orientation when I met that girl I told you about?"

"The night the rest of us got laid and you wanted to be left alone? Yeah." He keeps his eyes on the TV. "You said nothing happened with her."

"Nothing did happen. But that was Lenni."

His head swivels toward me. "Why didn't you say anything before, you weirdo?"

I shrug, wishing badly that I had. "You were into her, and she was into you."

"Eh, not really," he says, confirming what I already knew; Lenni was just a game. He looks thoughtful for a moment, then turns back to the TV. "Still, you and her?" He shakes his head and makes a disgusted face.

"You were just jerking her around. It shouldn't bother you I'm talking to her."

"Doesn't, I just think it's crazy. Any girl on campus would hop into your bed at the snap of your fingers, and you pick her?"

"Crazy because you think she belongs to you? She wasn't even a hookup."

"She would have been, except she fucked it up with her shitty timing."

"Yeah, okay. And you seemed real broken up about it too." I stare at the TV, trying not to think about what almost happened between them. I can't even entertain how different things would be if Dina hadn't been in the house that night.

"Look, I'm not into her. I was flirting with her to see where it would go; it didn't mean anything."

"Great."

I finish the rest of my beer and get up to grab a few more from the kitchen. Studying isn't happening tonight. Reeve doesn't like more than a few cans before he switches to bottles so I get two bottles for him. Back in the living room, I hand him the beers and he nods his thanks. We watch TV in silence for a few minutes and then he looks at me.

"She's not your type at all, Cam."

I consider this, calling up the familiar images of her body covered in nothing but a few inches of red lace, her hair in wild curls around her shoulders, the smile she gives when I've made her laugh.

"Actually," I tell Reeve, "I just figured out exactly what my type is. And you're wrong."

Cameron

SATURDAY. Game day.

Finally, something important enough to distract me from thinking about Lenni.

We've been texting almost every day, at first just her following up on the interview and making sure we were both clear on where the interview material ended and the personal stuff began. But now it's more than that; now every time my phone beeps, I get a little rush thinking it might be her.

It's pretty pathetic, really, the person I've turned into. I don't lose my cool over girls. I don't daydream about them when my head should be in the game. And I definitely don't go fumbling for my phone when one of them texts. Except maybe freshman year when Maya Lopez, two years older than me and a perfect ten, finally quit playing hard to get and let me know her bed was open to me.

But this is different. Maya Lopez was about winning, proving to myself and the guys in the locker room that yeah, I could have whoever I wanted, even the most unattainable. I checked that box. This thing with Lenni couldn't be more different because she's not an accomplishment I can achieve and move on from. She's a feeling I can't get enough of.

But today I need to keep my head. Reynolds is undefeated, Shafer hasn't beat them in four years and if we want a shot at the conference championship, this is a must-win. And when it's all over, whether we win or lose, I have to paint my face in a smile and meet up with Mom, her friends, and her new man.

Yep, armed with her insatiable need to boast and an extra dose of overconfidence in her son, Mom decided this was the game to bring her whole crew to so they could witness this future megastar single-handedly crushing the country's number-five ranked football team. But no pressure or anything!

I'm up before anyone else in the house and take a long, cool shower, part of my ritual before a high-stakes game. I drop my head under the spray so the water beats against the back of my neck, filling my head with white noise.

This game doesn't have to be hard if I don't make it hard. I can make my body do just about anything I ask of it. Physically, I'm all there; I'm the strongest I've ever been, and the fastest receiver Shafer has had in at least a decade. And even though I've had some drops, I've got the hands to make tough catches at crunch time. We can win this, and I can be the difference.

I just need to get out of my own head. Or rather, I need to kick everyone else out of it: Mason, Reeve, Mom, and her friends. Definitely Lenni. I've been wanting to ask if she's coming to the game, but actually, I don't want to know. It doesn't matter. I can only make this happen on my own.

When I get out of the shower, there's a text from her.

Lenni: Good luck today. You won't need it.

It's cute because she knows nothing about football or what I need. And now I'm smiling and wishing that I could impress her just by winning today. I put down my phone and start trying to forget about her.

WE FUCKING CRUSH.

Reynolds has a better record, a better ranking, and is superior on paper, but on the field, we make them look like frauds. Reeve made all the right throws, Cash was running angry, Lorenzo laid the wood, and any ball that Reeve put near me I hauled in. So maybe carrying a mountain of pressure on your shoulders is the secret to success.

The locker room is a total zoo after the game, everyone riding high. Somehow it all came together today, almost too perfectly for explanation, and I know that no matter how many wins we bag this season, we won't get another one like this. The feeling fucking rocks.

We linger in the locker room after showering, no one eager to head out for meals and parties and congratulations from friends and fans just yet. Not because we don't love the accolades—they embarrass me, but I don't hate them—but because right now it's just us, and in here we don't have to share the win with anybody.

While I throw on clothes, Cash leans against the locker next to mine in nothing but his underwear and starts dissecting the best plays of the game. He's talking more to himself than me, but I get it; reliving the highlights is half the fun. While Cash talks, I check my phone. There's a bunch of texts from friends and girls sending congratulations and asking where I'm partying tonight. Nothing from Lenni, though.

Reeve comes up behind Cash and squeezes his neck. "Cash, man, take a breath." He looks at me. "How are you not smiling right now? What, two touchdowns isn't good enough anymore?"

"Lay off," Cash says. "It's his first major win since the Russian kicked him to the curb. He's busy fantasizing about how many girls he's gonna fuck tonight to celebrate."

"Then he should be grinning from ear to ear," Reeve says.

"Keep out of my daydreams," I tell them. "No dudes allowed."

When Cash moves off to finally put some clothes on, Reeve takes his place. "You were a total stud today. Swear to god, you're going to have your own highlight reel on ESPN tonight."

Lorenzo, walking by, whips his towel against my ass. "Fuckin' right!"

I smile. "We pulled off a huge one."

"We still celebrating with Mama Forrester tonight?" Reeve asks.

"If you're sure you want to sit through dinner with a bunch of fifty-somethings. I don't really have a choice."

"Yeah, man, I want to see Minnie. Besides, I need to check out this new man of hers; hopefully this one's got a full set of balls."

"You know she doesn't like her men that way anymore. Anyway, come prepared to charm; she brought friends."

Reeve pretends to pop his imaginary collar. "Sweet. I never put an age cap on female admirers."

"Be ready by quarter to seven. Oh yeah, and I know this is a big ask, but try to look a little better than me." I give his unshaven cheek a couple sharp pats. "The more those ladies paw at you, the less heat on my ass."

Reeve rakes a rough hand through his hair and smiles. "Done."

. . .

By the time 6:45 rolls around, my mood has crashed and burned, and I'm dreading dinner. I don't mind seeing Mom sitting there glowing under her imaginary spotlight. I've lived that my whole life, and better her be the center of attention than me. But I don't know if I can take another three-hour meal of her spouting off inflated stats from my season and making promises about the championship game tickets she'll score her friends in two years.

And Lenni still hasn't texted me.

I'm starting to think I blew her interest in me way out of proportion. We've had a few decent conversations, and she thinks I look good. That's all. And if there was anything more, I probably killed it by getting all cocky with my joke about kissing her.

I take a quick glance in the mirror before I head to Reeve's room to round him up.

Maybe I'm coming on too strong with Lenni, walking her home after Reeve's little tantrum, waiting for her outside, buying her dinner. Maybe she knows I got dumped and she feels bad so she's putting on a smile while secretly hoping I drop dead.

Who am I kidding? I don't understand this girl at all.

Three hours later, Mom is drunk, Reeve has bailed, and I'm in hell.

Things got off to a rocky start when Reeve and I showed up to the restaurant to find Mom in the company of just one of her friends—Harris nowhere in sight.

"That's all over now!" she'd declared, but offered no further details, just introduced Reeve to Mrs. Wilton and then we made our way to our table like we were kicking off some majorly awkward cougar double date. Reeve wasn't bothered; my mom adores him, and the feeling is mutual, and while Mrs. Wilton is nipped and tucked a little too tight, she's not half bad, especially for a guy like Reeve who objectifies women indiscriminately, regardless of age.

It was okay for a while. Without an audience to impress and with Reeve to shoulder half the burden, Mom didn't take the bragging too far. She didn't bring up Serena or Liam or Dad.

"You look happy, honey," she'd told me when Reeve and Mrs. Wilton started bantering about classic cars. "I never told you this, but I didn't much care for Kira."

"You never had to tell me, Ma."

"You knew? How could you tell?"

I laughed. "Uh, body language, tone of voice, the way you referred to her as the Russian Robot."

Mom smoothed down her hair and smiled primly. "Did I?"

My phone, on the table next to me, lit up with another text. It was Tracy, a girl I'd made out with a few times last year before I met Kira, asking if I'd like to celebrate my win with her tonight, and followed by a winking face emoji. It wasn't the first winking face I'd gotten in the last four hours.

Mom sat back and swirled her wine. "You're popular this evening. Special girl asking for you?"

"Just some friends." The special girl definitely wasn't asking for me; she hadn't texted me in thirteen hours, not that I was counting.

"That's probably better. You have your whole life to fall in love, but your football career is made now or never."

It didn't matter that she was right. It took us back to a place I didn't want to go, and the tolerable part of the evening ended right there. Mom started going hard on the wine. The Harris saga finally unfolded—Mom insisted she broke up with him because he was a bad tipper and rarely looked waitstaff in the eye, but her version of events has never once featured her being dumped, stood up, rejected, or humiliated in any way, so the truth could be literally anything. Whatever happened with this guy, she's taking it pretty hard. It was . . . uncomfortable. I felt for my mom, but no guy wants to see his mother getting weepy, especially over some 60-year-old patent lawyer she's been sleeping with for a month at best.

When Reeve's phone started blowing up, Mom insisted he go have fun with his "lady friends" while wrapping her fingers tightly around my wrist, just in case I got any ideas.

So here I am in hell. And I need a savior.

lenni

"LENNI? LENNI! FUCKING EARTH TO LENNI!"

Jade leans across my field of vision, and I realize that while I've been reading and rereading the text message that just popped up on my phone, she's been repeating my name.

"Who is it?" she asks over the music pumping from the dust-coated speakers at The Phantom, our local dive bar.

"No one."

"It's him. I knew it. Look at your smile!"

I ignore her and reread Cam's message.

"I told you if you ignored him all day, he'd eventually come begging for your attention. You have to play games with guys like that."

"Don't listen to her," Sam tells me from the other side of our high-top table. "I hate games."

Jade kisses him on the cheek, leaving a faint neon-pink lip print. "You're not a guy like that, baby," she says gently.

"You just called me a loser, didn't you?" Sam laughs.

"You're not a loser," she says. "You're dating me."

"I wouldn't know how to play games if I wanted to," I tell them. I've been itching to text Cam ever since the football game ended, but I was afraid he'd be busy, I don't know, having a threesome with supermodels or whatever these guys do to celebrate a big win.

But no, it's almost 11 p.m. and he's at dinner with his mom and her friend. Could there be anything more endearing?

"So what did he say?" Sam asks. Sam is easily the sweetest guy in Jade's long dating history.

"He's wondering what I'm up to."

"At 11 p.m.? Booty call!" Jade drunkenly declares.

Sam shakes his head. "If that guy wants a booty call, he's not calling Lenni. No offense, Lenni."

"Well, answer him," Jade tells me. "I want to know what he wants."

"All right, shut up for a minute and I will."

Jade closes an invisible zipper over her lips and smiles at me. By now I've told her every thought and feeling I have about Cam, and while she pretends to hate him and everything he stands for, I think she's actually dying for something to happen between us. The idea of it—something actually happening between me and Cam—feels both imminent and impossible. I can no longer blame my feelings for him on the magic of the night we met or even the way he rescued me, not after the time we've spent together and the undeniable spark that tethers us anytime we're in the same room. But someone like Cam wanting someone like me doesn't happen outside of cheesy movies. And isn't he the one that used "friends" to describe us?

I start typing.

> Lenni: Good game today (or so I've been told by people who understand football). How's dinner?

Cam: Painful. Mom just got dumped by her latest dude and she's on her fifth glass of chardonnay. You do the math.

Lenni: Your poor mom! How about listening to her?

Cam: I have been . . . we sat down to eat at seven! At this point I've listened to her cry about the guy for longer than they actually knew each other.

Lenni: Lol

Cam: What are you doing?

Lenni: Out with Jade and her boyfriend at The Phantom.

Cam: No man on your arm?

My stomach tightens. I love and hate where this conversation is going.

Lenni: No.

Cam: How many dudes have hit on you tonight?

Lenni: Gosh, so hard to keep count. I think zero?

Lenni: So what are your plans tonight?

Cam: Getting out of here ASAP. Can I come meet you guys?

I don't know what to say. I only know two things: Cam is a bad idea. And I really, really want him.

"He wants to meet up," I tell Jade and Sam.

Jade gives Sam a triumphant look. "Of course he does."

"No, with all of us," I say.

"Oh. Well, I guess if he has the balls to come out . . ." She trails off in favor of downing what remains of her vodka and soda.

Sam and I exchange a look. Jade hasn't been this drunk in a while, and she's teetering on the edge of belligerence. "Are we staying much longer?" I ask.

"Yes," slurs Jade.

"No," says Sam.

I look down at my phone and read his text again. The question feels heavy, like a hundred questions all in one. Is that ridiculous? I'm probably being dramatic and self-important. Cam doesn't need me for company, he could have anyone. But then isn't that what makes the question so significant?

Lenni: We're not going to be here much longer. Jade's drunk and needs to get home.

Cam: Disappointing. I need an excuse to bail. So much boyfriend talk.

Lenni: Some son you are!

"You told him no, didn't you?" Jade is watching me through watery eyes. "That's good. That's the game."

Which tells me I've made a mistake. I don't like playing games. Jade might know what she's doing, but when it comes to men, Jade and I have nothing in common. Regret flares inside me. "Are we out of here?" I ask.

"No, just one more round! Please?" She turns to Sam with a pleading face. As though he's ever told her no.

"One more," he concedes. "Plus a glass of water for you before we walk out of this joint."

Cam's name flashes on my screen once more.

Cam: Okay, my mom just started a sentence
with "When we were physically intimate . . . "
Help!

I laugh, and Jade opens her mouth to no doubt offer more helpful tips, but Sam takes her hand. "Come on, babe. Let's get that last round and leave Lenni to figure it out herself."

With a few moments of solitude to work with, I scramble for some response that might get me what I want without getting me hurt. I wish I was brave enough to just come right out and ask what he wants. But I'm not, so I deflect instead.

Lenni: Why are you asking me? I bet there are a
few dozen lingerie-clad blondes who'd love to
be your excuse to leave.

Cam: I don't want them to be my excuse. I
want you.

I smile and let his words drip all over me. Cam could own the world if he told the right girl, *I want you.* Jade would tell me to wait, but too late, I'm already replying.

Lenni: If you don't mind putting up with my
obnoxiously drunk friend . . .

Cam: So should I meet you at The Phantom or
at your place?

Something is actually happening. No, it's already happened. He knew the minute he texted me that my saying yes was inevitable, and maybe I did too.

Lenni: The Phantom.

Cam: I'll be there.

My chest feels all fluttery, and I don't know if it's because I'm excited or because I just made a huge mistake. *Damn it*, I think when I see Jade and Sam heading back with drinks in hand; it's the latter. Because Jade is wasted. She's going to be obnoxious to Cam. She wants to hate him, and without enough fuel for the hatred, she'll go looking for it.

I force a quick, halfhearted cheers, hoping Sam will take Jade home before Cam even gets here. Half of Jade's drink sloshes over the rim when we clink glasses. Good, good; less alcohol for her to throw back.

"Cam's going to meet me here," I announce, trying to sound nonchalant. "Just to say hi."

Jade is surprisingly sedate at the news. "Nice. I'll get to meet him—again." She delivers the word "again" like she's stabbing someone.

"I guess if you're still here, sure." I give Sam a meaningful look, which he meets with a subtle nod.

"Here, babe," he says, sliding a glass of water toward Jade. "Get this down or you'll be hurting tomorrow morning."

Yes, good. I might actually have a chance of facing Cam without the burden of Jade's hostility to deal with. Then, over Sam's shoulder, I see him walk through the door.

If this were a movie, the music would stop, the crowds would part. There'd be a spotlight on him, maybe even a fog machine sending up curls of blue-tinged smoke that dance slowly around his stunning, chiseled features. In real life, of course, nothing visible changes. But inside me, everything shifts completely, because even though I've watched him walk through doorways before, he's never done it looking for me.

He scans the crowded bar, and I stand up on weak legs to go to him. He looks goddamn delicious.

He's wearing a crisp white collared shirt and a skinny black tie, but he's loosened the tie and shirt collar, and opened a few buttons so a tiny but dangerous triangle of chest shows. His sleeves are pushed up, revealing strong, tanned forearms that make me ache with each step I take toward him. I've never been so unprepared for anything in my life.

His face relaxes into a smile when he sees me. I try to smile back, but I'm not sure I pull it off. My heart is pounding and I'm sick with nerves. I don't want to feel this way about him; it's too powerful, too far beyond my control.

"Hey," he says.

Now I'm smiling for real. "You got here quickly."

"We were just up the street at Salvatore's."

"Ah, so that's why you look like you just stepped off the pages of GQ." Salvatore's is one of the most expensive restaurants in town, and even though it's only two blocks off campus, I've never been within shouting distance of the place.

Cam doesn't argue. "Thanks for meeting up."

"You might not be thanking me in a minute. Jade's drunk and she's got a bit of a prejudice against football players."

"Been there, done that."

"She's a really good person when she doesn't have a dozen drinks in her, I promise."

"Relax, Lenni. I get it, I have drunk friends too."

I take a deep breath and turn to lead him back to our high-top. I can feel his eyes on my body, and I find myself wishing I'd worn something my size instead of a baggy T-shirt. For once, I don't want to be invisible.

We're interrupted twice on the fifteen-second walk by people congratulating Cam on the game, and when we get back to the table, Jade is just coming out of the ladies' room. Despite her drunkenness, the double take she gives Cam is unmistakable. Ha! Even she can't believe how good he looks tonight.

"Jade," I say, "this is—"

"Oh, I know who you are," she tells Cam. We all wait for her to lay out for us her cutting assessment of him, but she leaves it at that.

"Right," Cam says. "Well, nice to officially meet you, Jade."

"Let's all have a drink," Jade suggests.

"We already had our last round," says Sam.

"Cameron hasn't," she counters.

All eyes go to Cam, who looks trapped. But he's been warned not to fuck with Jade, so he nods. "I'd do one drink."

"Fine, but make yours a water," I tell Jade.

We order one more round. Sam, angel that he is, carries most of the conversation. Jade, in a shocking turn, sips her water and sits in silent judgment, watching Cam the whole time. Meanwhile, I just want this weird little social circle to break up and call it a night.

I don't know how to be around Cam with my best friend and her boyfriend watching. I hardly know how to be around him when we're alone; having Sam and Jade there feels like standing with one foot on earth and the other on the moon.

Cam graciously tolerates the near-constant stream of students interrupting to high-five him or congratulate him on some play. I try not to notice how pretty the girls who approach him are, or how even the ones that aren't that pretty have an air of sex appeal I couldn't capture on my best day. But somehow, every time he flicks that sizzling gaze at me, it's as though I'm the only person in the room. How does he do that?

With everyone's glasses finally empty, we head outside. Jade and Sam give us a little space when I turn to Cam.

"Thanks for coming out." I lower my voice. "Sorry if it was weird."

"What, you mean the unblinking stare down Jade gave me for a solid twenty?" He waves it off. "I barely noticed."

I laugh. "Next time she'll be normal, I promise." I fiddle with my necklace, unsure what to say next, and Cam's gaze follows my hand, settling at the base of my throat. "So where are you headed? Big party plans?"

He watches me. "No plans." A faint smile plays at his lips.

Oh. Suddenly I can't meet his eyes. "Come on. You can't tell me the MVP of the game isn't wanted at every party on and off campus tonight."

"I don't know where he's wanted, but I'm not partying tonight."

I hazard a glance at him, knowing that what happens next is entirely up to me. I'm so tired of this feeling of knowing that what I want to do when I'm near him is the opposite of what I should do.

"Oh, for Christ's sake, at least let him walk home with us," Jade yells from behind me.

My cheeks go hot. I hate my best friend sometimes.

Cam's eyes dance. "I wouldn't mess with her if I were you."

The four of us set off toward the apartment. I glance over at Cam, taking in the slope of his thick shoulders tight against his shirt and the light stubble on his neck. What would it feel like to unbutton that shirt and run my fingers over those shoulders? To lie down naked and reach up to touch that smooth, muscled body? I feel like I'm melting.

Sam is talking his ear off, but Cam turns, catches me looking and winks, and it's basically the hottest thing I've ever experienced. Somebody help me.

"I didn't know you two had so much in common," Jade says to the guys, and I realize I haven't followed a single word of the conversation. Sex fantasies will do that to you.

"Yeah, I don't know all that much about cars, but my dad was a car guy," Cam says.

Cars? What? I try to picture Cam racing a muscle car down the street, but in the image he's shirtless because why not, and then the car fades away and my brain is off and running with the picture of a shirtless Cam. I suddenly understand what people mean when they say they need to get laid.

"Are you visiting the car show next month?" Sam asks.

Cam nods. "I'm taking my little brother."

"We should all go together," Jade suggests, and honestly, I'd take the combative, bitchy Jade over this one any day. First, she hates Cam, now she's setting up double dates for us, and it couldn't feel more awkward. "Oh my god." Jade makes a disgusted face. "Cam and Sam. Yuck."

Cam looks at Sam and shrugs. "Must be fate."

"Ugh, it's too cutesy," she says. "I hate it."

"We're not the couple here, babe, so no worries," Sam says.

"Excuse me, we're not the couple, either," I can't help pointing out.

Jade ignores me. "I was wrong; the four of us will never work out. Every time I heard Cam and Sam, I'd puke."

I link arms with Jade, trying to steer her away from the guys. "The four of us aren't a thing," I whisper through gritted teeth. "Stop already."

"Oh, whatever. You know you love him."

"Shhh!" I hiss. I glance over my shoulder at Cam, who is mercifully several feet behind us and locked in conversation with Sam. "Just shut up about him, please? Things were better when you thought he was an asshole."

"Who said he's not?"

"Then stop shipping us like we're Draco and Harry."

"No, you guys are cute. He's barely stopped looking at you all night, and those puppy-love eyes you shoot him are too adorable. I've never seen you like this." Even through her alcohol haze, she sees what's happening.

At our building, Jade and Sam climb the front steps together. She gives me a sly look over her shoulder. "Come on, guys."

Cam and I stand on the street, watching them disappear inside.

"Quite the Cupid, isn't she?" Cam says.

I smile. "Feel free to ignore her. If you want to go—"

"I don't."

He's probably done this a thousand times: used that voice, those eyes, that body to convince a girl she's beautiful and special so he can have what he wants. But that's exactly how I feel when he looks at me like that. "All right." It takes everything I have to look him in the eye. "Then let's go inside."

NINETEEN

I TELL myself it's just for a little while. We'll all hang out and soon Jade will pass out, and then Cam will leave, and I'll go to bed lonely and maybe a little horny. Just the way it should be, better lonely than heartbroken.

But when we walk into the apartment, the common areas are empty and Jade's bedroom door is closed. And I just know I won't see Jade and Sam until morning. Damn. I fell into the trap.

I look at Cam. Well, not a bad person to be trapped with. "You want a drink?"

"I'll take a beer. Maybe some cheese if you have it."

"Cheese?"

"You owe me a celebration meal, remember?"

I bite my lip, hoping to rein in my smile. "I'll search the fridge, but might have to rain check you on that one."

"Anytime, anywhere."

I grab two beers from our desolate fridge, vowing to just nurse mine, while Cam makes himself comfortable on the couch. Under his long limbs, the couch looks small and unimpressive. I'm longing to sit close to him, close enough to feel the heat of his body, but I opt for the chair across from him instead.

"Congrats on your win today." I hold out my beer and we clink bottles.

"Thanks. Did you watch?"

"Of course. You looked good."

"Just trying to keep up with you." He takes a drink and watches me over the rim of the beer, his eyes promising that something is about to happen.

I wish I could bottle this feeling and sell it for millions.

"Jade's a trip," he says after a minute.

"She doesn't know when to stop sometimes. I'm sorry about all that stuff she said."

"About us?"

I nod, looking at his strong fingers wrapped around the beer bottle as a flush creeps up the back of my neck. Cam's hands have been the subject of scrutiny and wonder by thousands of people; I know enough about receivers to know that. But I can only think about his hands doing one thing, and it isn't catching a football.

"I didn't have a problem with it." Cam leans forward. "You know I'm into you."

My eyes jump to his. I can't believe he went there already. "Cam, I . . . I mean, you said . . . " I take a breath and try again. "I thought we were just friends." I'm such a liar. Like hell we're just friends.

"We were."

Raw desperation blooms inside me. Do I even have the strength to pretend I don't love what he's telling me? "Okay, but putting all feelings aside . . . "

His lip curls into a lopsided smile. "Why would we do that?"

"Because that—feelings—that's not how I make decisions."

"That's how everyone makes decisions."

"No, I don't think so."

"Okay." He looks unconvinced. "Fine. Feelings aside . . . what?"

"I don't date athletes."

"Because of Reeve."

"This goes back long before Reeve."

He cocks his head, looking at me like he's waiting for the punch line. "So . . . you don't date athletes, but you'll sleep with them?"

My breath catches in my throat. Maybe it's not an entirely hurtful, inappropriate, and overly personal question, but that's damn well how it feels. "I—" Shame heats the back of my neck. "Maybe you should leave," I hear myself say, too surprised to challenge him. I'm disappointed more than offended. Because I think I just figured out Cam's one of those guys who's sweet as sugar until you reject him, and then suddenly you're a fat, ugly whore who he would never have fucked anyway.

"Hold on, Lenni, I'm sorry. I'm not trying to be a dick here."

"Too bad, that's exactly what you're being." I stand up and hold out a hand for his beer. "I'll throw that away for you." I'm too stung to look him in the eye. And too embarrassed because he's exactly right; I was willing to sleep with someone I didn't know or respect. I don't like that about myself.

Cam sets his beer on the side table out of my reach and instead takes the hand I'm holding out. "Give me a break here." His voice is low and silky. I should pull my hand away because the heat of his skin against mine is weakening my resolve already, but I don't. "I like you, and you just told me it's never going to happen because I play football. So forgive me for trying to understand why Reeve was fair game."

"I never liked Reeve!" I yank my hand free. "I just thought he might be able to help me get over some . . . hang-ups I had.

Instead, he reminded me why I stay far away from guys like you."

He studies me. "Someone hurt you."

"That's right," I say sharply.

Distress flashes in his eyes, but he swallows it down. I watch the smooth movement of his Adam's apple in his throat. "I'm sorry. I shouldn't have pushed." He looks up at me, trapping me in the swirl of gold and yellow and brown of his eyes. "Will you sit down?"

I hesitate, and he probably thinks I'm unsure, but it's really just that his face is so mesmerizing I can't stop staring.

"Fine. I'll leave. But let me say one thing first. Whatever that asshole did to you, he did it because he was an asshole, not because he was an athlete. And I'm going to prove to you we're not all dicks."

God, I want him to be right. "That was two things."

Cam opens his mouth to say something, but then we both hear it, a loud banging coming from Jade's room. Our eyes meet and I think we realize at the same instant it's the unmistakable sound of a headboard hitting a wall over and over and over.

We both laugh. My cheeks are on fire. Jade is killing me tonight with the number of times she's made things awkward.

"Damn," Cam says. "I would've thought she was down for the count."

"I've been her roommate for two years. Jade can always rally."

Right on cue, the moaning starts.

"Oh my god," I mutter, dropping my head into my hands.

Cam is relaxed on the couch, looking amused and totally unfazed. I guess living in a house full of football players means this is just the usual background noise. And sure, I've heard Jade's, um, sounds of pleasure many times—Sam's a man of many talents, as Jade says—but I've never had to listen while sitting across from the guy I wish *I* was banging.

"You need another beer?" I ask him, though I can see perfectly well that his beer is barely half gone. "Come on, let's get you one," I say before he can answer.

He follows me obediently into the kitchen, which is only a few extra feet from the bedrooms, but I'll take what I can get.

"So," I say, "how'd you leave things with your mom?"

He scrunches up his face. "You know, I'd really rather not talk about my mother given the current atmosphere in this apartment."

I laugh. "That's fair. Would you—"

That's when I'm interrupted by the dirty talk.

The headboard I can handle. Moaning? Fine, I'll live. But the words I hear coming from my best friend's bedroom right now shock me into silence. Cam and I stare at each other. I can't make out everything she's saying, but here and there certain words come through crystal fucking clear. I put my hand over my mouth as a grin spreads slowly across Cam's face.

"God damn," he says. "She watches porn, doesn't she?"

I just shake my head and try to escape into a fantasy wherein I seek revenge on Jade in the most embarrassing ways possible.

A look crosses Cam's face that I know is trouble. "Come on," he says, moving toward Jade's bedroom.

"What? What are you doing?"

"Shhh. Come on."

"Cam, no!" I reach for his arm to stop him, but he's stronger, and he slips out of my grip, instead closing his hand around my wrist and pulling me behind him.

Now I'm left to decide whether having his hand on my body is worth the trauma of hearing my best friend getting banged out by her boyfriend. Cam's fingers are firm around my wrist, and I'm close enough to smell him; woodsy and fresh with a dark, vaguely familiar note that makes me throb between my thighs. Yep, totally worth the trauma.

Cam stops outside Jade's bedroom door and puts his finger to his lips. I want to be as far away from that door as possible, but the roguish look on his face, that rough finger against his soft mouth . . . lord, it could not be any sexier. I don't move.

He puts his ear to the door. Jade is becoming more and more explicit. I alternate between trying not to hear her and trying not to laugh at Cam's facial expressions as he listens. Sometimes he nods in approval, other times his eyes go wide and he shoots me a scandalized look.

Then we hear Jade say the word "thickness." We look at each other. A laugh builds inside me. Then Cam mouths it slowly, *thickness*. And I'm dying.

I turn and flee, clapping my hand over my mouth to stifle the guffaw, which erupts instead as a snort. Behind me, I hear Cam chuckle. I shove my face into a pillow to muffle the laughter that I'm powerless to stop.

Suddenly, I realize Jade's bedroom is silent. Shit! I turn around and grab Cam's hand, trying to pull him away. Clearly, he doesn't care if he's caught with his ear to the door, but I do. *Come on!* I mouth furiously, giddy with laughter and nerves.

He takes his time but gives in to me. I drag him out the door and down the back steps where, outside, in the cool night air, I can finally breathe.

For a minute, we just stand there recovering under the floodlights that illuminate the back of the building. Then we look at each other and start laughing again.

"I think we need to walk that off," I say, starting down the path that weaves through the apartment complex. For such cheap housing, the grounds are surprisingly nice, with tall evergreens, picnic tables, and carpets of thick green grass.

Cam glances at me. "I'm sorry about the Reeve thing."

"No, don't be. I took your question the wrong way. I'm too sensitive sometimes."

"I don't think so," he says mildly.

I sigh, breathing out the stress of the last few hours. Sometimes, when I least expect it, I feel completely at ease with Cam. "I'm sorry this night has been so weird."

"I like weird."

"Yeah, you weren't exactly clutching your pearls over Jade's dirty mouth. Can I assume you've heard it all before?"

The corner of his mouth twists. "Lenni Crawford, are you fishing for details about my sex life?"

"No," I say quickly, although I'm actually dying to know what he's into. Probably some crazy, advanced stuff I've never even heard of. Once again, my mind conjures up a vivid image of him shirtless in bed, his skin damp with perspiration, his muscles straining with effort . . . I swallow and bite down on the inside of my lip. "But since you brought it up," I say, emboldened. I look over at him. It's much darker here, with only a bit of light from the post lights scattered intermittently among the grounds.

"What do you want to know?"

Everything. Anything. "Who's the last person you had sex with?" I blurt out.

"That'd be my ex."

"You haven't been with anyone since?"

"Are you calling me a loser?"

"No, I'm just surprised."

"By now you should know better than to be surprised when you're wrong about me."

"What about Alexis?" Hearing the question in the air has me suddenly nervous. It's not even Alexis, it's everything she represents.

"Truman?" he scoffs. "Fuck no. You crazy?"

"What? She's pretty. And she clearly wants you."

"Yeah, she's also annoying, rude, vain, and can't take a hint."

"Jeez, you don't need to be so uppity," I joke, totally relieved. "Such a high bar you have for a one-night stand."

"Yeah, yeah. You sure like talking about sex, don't you?" He slides his gaze sideways to meet mine.

I can barely look at him when he says sex. That word rolling off his perfect lips makes me ache from somewhere deep inside. I make a noncommittal noise, deeply regretting where I've steered this conversation.

"Let's turn it back on you."

"I don't have sex," I say quickly. I feel his eyes on me. "I'm not a virgin. I just don't, you know, hook up."

"Okay," he says. "What about love?"

I let out a short laugh. "You've managed to find a topic I know even less about than sex."

"Shame, I was hoping you might know more than me. What's this over here?" He steps off the path toward a small piece of land half hidden behind some evergreen trees.

"I think it used to be a garden."

"Should we check it out?"

I look dubiously at the walled-in mess of overgrown plants and what I think used to be a gravel path. "Sure." I'll follow him anywhere right now.

The garden is darker than the rest of the grounds, but a few crooked stake lights still illuminate what's left of the narrow path. Cam slides behind me as we step over rocks and weeds. When I move just so, I can feel the warmth of his hand hovering at my back, ready to catch me if I stumble. I pretend not to notice. I pretend it doesn't make me feel safe.

The path clears after a few yards, and Cam falls into step

next to me, but the tight tangle of plants on either side forces us close. Butterflies flutter in my chest.

"You know what this place reminds me of?" he asks.

"Totally." This is a far cry from the manicured sunken garden on campus where we first met, but something about the atmosphere feels just the same.

"Must be something about the light."

"And the company."

He looks at me and nods. "And the company."

He's right, it's the light. The color of his eyes and the way the light sharpens the lines and curves of his face are just as they were that night. I need to stop staring at him. "You know, it was never that I forgot you, I just didn't recognize you. Back then you didn't seem like a . . ."

"Asshole jock?" he offers.

"Something along those lines."

"I'll ignore you implying that now I *am* an asshole jock," he teases. "So what did I seem like?"

The perfect guy. But I can't tell him that. Then he places a hand gently in the curve of my waist and steers me around a patch of mud. I can. "The perfect guy."

He snorts. "I knew you were high that night."

"Come on, like you don't know every girl on campus takes one look at you and sees her dream man."

He ignores this and catches my wrist, stopping me. "So what changed? Now you won't even consider going out with me."

"Me, I guess."

"You don't seem different. This feels just like it did back then."

He's right. There's still an easiness between us, a feeling that finally, we can stop pretending and just be. But I am pretending. I'm pretending that the way he looks at me doesn't weaken my heartbeat. I'm pretending that everything inside me doesn't quicken and fire when he says my name. I want to be the girl he met years ago, the one that felt so certain her awful past had no bearing on her future. She wasn't afraid of what she felt for Cam. But I'm not that girl; I'm terrified.

"I don't chase my feelings anymore, I chase goals. I need to stay focused on my plans."

"I respect that. But you said you don't date athletes, not that you don't date. Can I ask why we're on your shit list?"

I hesitate, not wanting to insult him when he's been nothing but kind to me. "Okay. But don't go getting all offended."

He puts his hands up in surrender.

"Here's what I think. Athletes have their big dreams, and you can't see beyond them. Your team always comes first. And everything else—friends, relationships—is secondary." I'm not ready to tell him that this is a theory born of experience. After I was filmed by that football player, there was a code of silence among his team; not one of them was about to give the others up. "And I think that love should always come first."

I'm startled to find him laughing. "Funny, I'm listening for the irony in your voice, but I'm not hearing it."

"Irony?"

"You just finished telling me how you need to focus on your goals and nothing else. But you're shitting on athletes who do the same thing? Irony."

"It's not the same thing! I'm talking about guys who put the game above their girlfriends. I stay out of relationships so I don't have to put anyone second." But when I say the words out loud, I feel like I'm lying to him.

"Not all athletes are like that," he says. "Not even close."

"Have you ever put love ahead of the game?"

"No." His voice dips low. "I've never been in love." I stare at him, caught by surprise and the unguarded look in his eyes. "We have more in common than you thought."

I force myself to look away. This is getting dangerous. "I guess there's more we don't know about each other than we do."

"I know enough to want more."

"More of what?"

"The girl I met that night." Something flickers in his eyes. "The girl who wrote mystery stories."

I cringe. I can't believe I ever told him about the stupid fiction I used to write. But he smiles at my reaction. I wonder what it would be like to see myself the way he does. "Why her?"

He looks thoughtful. "She was genuine, that was the first thing. Sweet. Real. A girl who follows her heart wherever it leads."

I feel a brief tug of sadness. That's exactly who I wanted to be.

"You were comfortable with not fitting in, and that energy was just . . . I don't know, hard to not get sucked into. It made me want to see where your life would take you." Humor flashes in his eyes. "And that girl didn't seem interested in judging me without knowing me."

Abashed, I offer him an apologetic smile. "Yeah, she was really something."

"You know what else she was?"

I look at him.

"Beautiful."

I roll my eyes. "I was fat." Actually, I liked the way I looked. But I knew what guys said about me.

"Fat? Are you crazy?"

"I was."

"You were beautiful, Lenni."

Without my permission, my body reacts to the compliment,

nerves firing like they've just woken up from a long, icy winter. "I was chubby."

"And you were beautiful."

I want to believe him, dangerous as it is. "You don't have to say that."

"I'm not allowed to think you're beautiful?" He leans toward me.

"When you've only ever dated a steady stream of flawless girls?"

A flash of annoyance quirks his lips. "I dated those girls for a reason."

"Which you already told me wasn't love. So I assume it was attraction."

"I liked those girls because they were the answer every time someone looked at me and wondered, 'What kind of man is he?' That was all I wanted from a girlfriend."

"What does that mean?"

"I don't know. I was hiding behind something with them, being what I thought people expected me to be, I guess." He shrugs. "Doesn't matter now. Point is, you can't tell me who I'm allowed to be attracted to. I know what I see when I look at you."

I stare off to the side because I can't meet his eyes. "I can't see what you do."

He leans closer, infusing my senses with his scent. "I'm sorry if only size-zero blondes do it for you. I guess you don't see the way guys practically break their necks watching you walk by in class, even when you're wearing those big, frumpy outfits you like. I guess you don't see the way I can't stop myself from staring at you." His voice is deep and throaty, and I can feel it skittering across my skin. "Or that brown hair and your perfect goddamn lips blot out the whole rest of the world."

I want to run away from him, from the pull he has on me.

But I need to know if his words are the truth. I look at him and his finger comes carefully under my chin.

"I've never been more attracted to anyone in my life," he says quietly.

Our faces are inches apart. And either I believe him, or I just don't care because his proximity and that single finger on my face have my body so completely alive I can't think straight.

His eyes drop to my mouth. My breath goes out of me and I feel myself give in. I need him to kiss me.

His mouth meets mine, and the pleasure of it shocks me. His touch is soft but certain. He glides his tongue along my lips, and I inhale, letting him in. His hand curls around the back of my neck to pull me closer but he doesn't need to, I'm already sinking into him, the feel of his tongue like a magnet drawing me in.

My body is humming. No, burning. No, melting completely under his touch and the taste of him. His scent up close is spicier, disorienting in the very best way.

I don't remember moving, but somehow I find my back pressed against the rough stone wall. The kiss grows deeper. The rocks scraping my back should hurt, but I only feel where Cam touches me. He makes a sound against my mouth, some breathy mix of a sigh and "Lenni." My name on his lips makes me shudder.

My hands seek out the steadiness of his body, settling on his shoulders. I feel in his muscles and the sound of his breathing that he's holding back. Somewhere in that realization, doubt falls away and for this instant I believe everything he's told me.

His lips move to my jaw, my neck, setting off fires everywhere they touch. I breathe him in and drop my head back. And when my eyes finally open to the night sky, the whole world has changed.

lenni

I DON'T SEE him again until Tuesday in class, and when I do, I can't stop smiling. All I've thought since Saturday night is *that kiss*.

Everything feels different now. My rational side keeps telling me that a kiss, no matter how mind-altering and magical, and all the other flowery adjectives, shouldn't change what I know to be true: that guys like Cam aren't for girls like me. But I think my rational side is being a bitter bitch this morning because she's not the one who kissed Cameron Forrester.

All throughout the silence of our test on inferential statistics, it's all I can do to keep from reaching out and touching him. He finishes his test first, which annoys me and turns me on. He's waiting for me outside the building when I finish.

"New rule," he says, watching me walk down the steps. "You can't sit near me on test days."

"I don't need to cheat off you."

"I know. I can't keep my eyes on my test when you're right there for me to stare at." He leans closer but clasps his hands behind his back, like he knows how much I want him to touch me, and he wants to see me go crazy.

"You finished your test before anyone else."

"And it was probably half-blank."

"Yeah, right. I heard somewhere you were valedictorian of your high school class. Is that true?"

"Can't remember." He smiles that winning smile and I think I actually sigh. "Hey, you free tonight after practice?"

Tuesday evenings, Jade and I usually order pizza and watch old episodes of *Pretty Little Liars* until Sam gets off work and picks her up. Then I put on a ratty old T-shirt and watch more episodes and eat room-temp pizza until my stomach hurts, at which point I tell myself how great it is that I don't have a boyfriend because I can take my bloated tummy and tentlike pajamas to bed without fear of judgment rather than slipping into cute panties and snuggling up to some sexy, shirtless guy. Mmm yeah, pretty free tonight.

"I think so," I tell him.

"Good. I'll pick you up around six."

"For what?"

He arches one eyebrow. "Surprise."

"Well, what do I wear?"

"Anything. Nothing. I gotta hustle. See you tonight."

I'm grateful he's gone before I can ask him if this is a date. I don't want to be the girl that needs to slap a label on everything. I don't know what we are. What I know is the way he kissed me. What I know is how I feel, and for the moment, that's good enough. Maybe eighteen-year-old Lenni was onto something.

At 5:55 p.m., I emerge from my bedroom. Jade puts down her slice of pizza to applaud, then gets up to give me the once-over.

"You look adorable," she says. "I knew that top would do it for you."

She's been tight-lipped about Cam and me, and half the time she refers to him by his jersey number instead of his name. But I asked her to dress me for my might-be-a-date, and she came through.

"Cute and sweet never fails," she'd assured me as she pulled a flowy white blouse, tags still attached, from the back of my closet. Then it was light-wash jeans, sandals, a loose ponytail with a few tendrils pulled out and blush, not bronzer.

Jade looks at me closely. "First date jitters?"

"I don't think it's a date. And yes." It's the anticipation that's getting to me, wondering what he has in mind for us tonight and beyond. And I just can't shake this nagging fear that I've got Cam—and us—all wrong. "Any parting words of wisdom?" I ask, reaching for my purse.

"Yeah. Remind yourself that he's lucky as hell you've agreed to spend any time with him. And that if he's as smart as you claim, he probably knows it too."

What I wouldn't give for Jade's confidence.

"Easy for you to say." I don't usually play the comparison game. Being thick and muscular is in my DNA, a fact I was good with until I started thinking about the girls Cam dates and realized we look like different species. Now I can't help but envy Jade's willowy proportions just a little bit.

She tucks a tendril of hair behind my ear. "Anyone can be thin and wear tight clothes and dye their hair. Doesn't compare to being naturally beautiful."

"I know you are, but what am I?" I say in a weak attempt to lighten my mood.

"His dream girl." She urges me toward the door and smacks me on the ass. "Now go prove it."

. . .

Cam is just walking up the street when I step outside. For a minute, I just watch him. He's dressed simply but looks incredible in jeans and a slim-fitting gray henley with the top buttons open. I can't believe he's here for me.

He smiles, and it's all I need to shake free of nerves and worry. I go to him and he wraps me in a hug, encircling me in the freshly showered scent of his skin. My brain conjures an image of us in the same embrace but under more favorable circumstances; like unclothed and horizontal. I pull away quickly. I can't spend the entire evening thinking about undressing him.

His gaze sweeps my body and suddenly I feel as sexy as Jade swears I am. The way his eyes burn tells me he doesn't wish I looked like Kira or Alexis or anyone else.

"You look really pretty," he says.

Gah, why is he so adorable? "Thanks. So spill it already; where are we going?"

"You'll see." He leads me in the opposite direction of downtown Shafer. "I'm not sure my idea is as brilliant as it seemed when it came to me."

How cute. He doesn't realize I'd find sorting recyclables brilliant if I did it with him.

A few short blocks later, we're in a part of town I've hardly seen; the historical part, if the buildings are any indication.

"Here we are." Cam stops outside a Victorian house painted cornflower blue. A wooden sign posted outside in gold lettering reads *Sarah Elizabeth Rowe House & Museum*.

And I'm confused. I don't know who this Sarah lady is, but I'm guessing her museum house isn't going to be an ideal place to get Cam to kiss me again.

"Sarah Rowe," Cam prompts me, his eyes hopeful. "You

know who she is?"

I shake my head politely.

"Oh." He sounds disappointed. "She was the first female journalist for the Daily Phantom. Back in the twenties, I think, when Shafer started accepting women."

"Really? I've never heard the name."

Cam looks serious. "Yeah, she went on to become a foreign correspondent. In South America mostly. Or maybe it was Africa." He cocks his head. "Okay, I'd never heard of her, either. I was just trying to find something you might be interested in. I stopped in yesterday to make sure it wasn't a total shithole, and the lady at the front gave me a whole spiel. If you don't want to go in, I totally—"

With every word, warmth blossoms inside my chest. "Stop," I tell him before he can apologize for the most thoughtful thing a boy has ever done for me. I wrap my fingers around his arm. "Let's go inside."

THE SARAH ELIZABETH ROWE house is about as interesting as most museums, which is to say not very. But my body doesn't know that because Cam stays as close to me as my own shadow, so I'm wound up like I'm about to run a marathon. I try to show interest in the exhibits. But inside me rages a silent, fierce energy that's only enhanced by the fact that the setting demands quiet propriety. And the brief, smoldering looks Cam keeps giving me tells me he feels it too.

We move from one dark, creaky room to the next, absently skimming the small plaques offering facts about Sarah Rowe's life. Upstairs and alone in her bedroom, I watch him read a sign next to a portrait of the Rowe family, and the tiny, precise movements of his lips as he mouths the words to himself make me dizzy with lust. I blink and turn my attention to the wood-carved canopy bed in the center of the room, which looks about as comfortable as a piece of plywood. Cam walks up behind me. When he speaks, his voice is barely above a whisper.

"You thinking what I'm thinking?" His lips nearly graze my ear.

My whole body warms because yes, I'm thinking about the same three-letter-word I've been thinking about since he showed up. I nod.

"Think she did it right here?" I can hear his smile.

It's such a juvenile question, but of course I was wondering the same thing. "It says she had four children so yeah, at least four times."

He leans closer until his scent is all I can smell. "What makes you think she only did it in bed? This was the roaring twenties, babe."

I stare at the bed, but what I see is an image of us. Not in bed, but up against the wall. Breathing hard, blind to everything but each other. My insides tighten with need.

I turn my head a mere few inches, and his mouth is right there. All decency falls away from me. I've lost control. I will have sex with this man right now if he makes a single move toward me. His lips part slightly, and like that's my cue, I turn into him. The warmth of his body is all around me. My lips find his, but just as my eyes close, voices rise outside the doorway.

I pull away just as two older ladies in floral-printed skirts walk in. I give them a polite smile to try to offset the weirdness of what they may or may not have just witnessed, but they're too busy eyeballing Cam to notice me.

I pretend to read the placard by the bedside table, but Cam steps close, stirring up my poor, overworked senses again. "Huh," he says, surveying the bed. The bass notes of his lowered voice fire up the tiny nerve endings in my ear. "Really makes you wonder about thickness, doesn't it?" For half a second, I don't understand, and then it hits me. I slap my hand over my mouth, but not before a cackle of laughter erupts.

Surely I have the attention of the two ladies now, but I don't stop to check in my rush for the door. Out in the hallway and still laughing, I glance back at Cam. He's wearing a boyish grin that only makes me laugh harder. We're done with the Sarah Elizabeth Rowe museum.

Safely outside, I let out the laughter threatening to choke me while Cam looks on, enjoying himself.

"What?" he says, an innocent look on his face. "I was wondering how thick the mattress was. What was your dirty little mind thinking?"

"Uh-huh." I give him a playful push. The solid feel of his chest under my palms is sobering. Cam's eyes light on mine, stopping time for a fleeting second.

Then he puts his arm around my shoulder. "Come on, perv. Next stop."

We walk around until we find ourselves at an ice cream shop that Cam says his grandfather used to take him to when he was a little kid. The owner behind the counter greets him by name, though I don't know if it's because Cam's a lifelong customer or a local celebrity. I order a vanilla cone with rainbow sprinkles, which Cam makes fun of, saying that's what he ordered the first time he came here at age three. He orders a mint chocolate chip milkshake, which I try to find mockable but fail.

We sit side by side at a tiny table outside and take turns looking at each other while the other watches the cars and people passing by. I'm not hungry and I barely taste the ice cream but finish it anyway.

I'm floating on a feeling, and even though I know it's dangerous to name it, I can't help myself. Hope. The last time I felt this way, I was someone else, a college freshman living for each day as it came, finally free of the twin strangleholds of my past and my looming future. I didn't know I could feel this way again. I thought that girl was long gone.

When we're done, Cam leans across the table toward me, his muscled upper body dominating the entire surface. "A historical museum and a vanilla ice cream. Was that the most boring date you've ever been on?"

He called it a date. "Definitely. Also the best date I've ever been on."

"No fair, that's what I was about to say." He reaches out and carefully tucks some loose strands of hair behind my ear. My skin prickles where his fingers touch.

"So say it."

"Okay," he says softly.

He leans down and kisses me slowly. His fingertips graze the side of my face, and the gentle way he presses his lips to mine makes me feel like my mouth is the only place in the world he wants to be. I finally understand the meaning of the phrase "read my lips." His are swearing to me that yes, this is the best date he's ever had.

He pulls away slightly, a languid smile on his face.

"You taste like mint," I tell him.

"You taste amazing."

He returns his attention to my lips, but now I'm craving more than his unhurried kisses. I open my mouth to bring him deeper, and his response is immediate. His hand moves to the back of my head, tilting me back slightly but insistently, giving himself a single degree of advantage. Our tongues dance for a few seconds, and then he lets me go, looking half dazed and half pleased with himself. Cockiness is sexy as hell on his face.

I swallow hard, heat swirling inside me. Here's another reason football players are dangerous. They won't just break your heart, they'll get you arrested for public indecency when you try to fuck them in front of an ice cream shop.

I watch him gather up our trash, my eyes zeroing in on the tiny, irresistible movements of his body. The liquid shift of muscles in his back when he lifts his arms, the curve of his bicep when he runs his fingers through his wavy hair. The way his hands move is obscene. I want to know what his hands could do to me.

Could he possibly want me as badly as I want him? I've heard that a kiss doesn't lie, but I don't know if I can believe that. What his kiss tells me is too good to be true. But maybe it's also worth taking a chance on.

"Where next?" Cam extends his hand as I try to get off my stool without looking totally graceless.

I check my phone. "Home, I'm afraid." I say it without looking at him because one look at his face and my resolve will crumble.

"Already?"

"I have to finish an article."

"That's too bad."

Three simple words, but the way he says them fills my head with a swirl of sexy images of where this night could end if not for my stupid article. *Goals. Must. Remember. Goals.*

"But," I begin, and the way his eyes light up gives me the courage to keep going because I need another date with this man. "If I finish it tonight, that means tomorrow night is free."

"Are you telling me Sarah Elizabeth Rowe didn't kill my shot at scoring a second date?"

"I think she guaranteed you one." Boldly, I slip my hand through his arm. His bicep tightens under my fingers, and he closes the space between us so that with every step our sides brush against each other.

"Hey, I almost forgot," I say as we walk. "I dug up some of the old stories I wrote."

"Oh, yeah? Did you strike gold?"

"Hardly. They were pretty bad . . . but not as bad as I thought."

"Told you." He nudges me with his elbow. "Can I read them?"

"No," I say quickly, then reconsider. "Maybe."

We're a block from my apartment, and though we're not actually on campus, we might as well be. We pass students in groups of threes and fours, most of them heading into the dive bar on the corner.

"You know what I think?" he asks with a sly smile. "I think you're rushing home to your mystery stories so you can write in a handsome brunette hero with a knack for crushing it on the football field."

I laugh, but suddenly his smile disappears. I follow his gaze up the sidewalk. At the other end of the street, heading our way, is Reeve with three other guys. But instead of continuing toward them, Cam takes my wrist.

"Let's cross here." He pulls me toward the crosswalk.

"Cam, I'm fine," I tell him as we wait at the corner for the walk signal. "I can face Reeve."

"No, I know." But he's barely listening. He glances back toward Reeve and the group, then hustles us across the street as soon as the light turns.

Something's wrong.

On the other side of the street, Cam looks back at Reeve again, his lips tight. Why is he so intent on avoiding his best friend? If it's not for my sake, and clearly, it's not, then it's for his.

And just when I think I'm turning nothing into something, he keeps on walking straight, the route that'll take us around the back of my building instead of hanging a left, the route that would put us directly opposite Reeve and have me to my front door in half the time.

It hits me like a blow to the stomach: he's embarrassed to be seen with me.

Of course he took me to the one place in town that's guaranteed to be free of college kids, he doesn't want anyone to see us together. Of course he doesn't want anyone to see us together. His dating history is stacked with solid tens. And I don't even rate.

I want to feel outraged, but I can't manage to feel anything except small and stupid.

If I was Jade, I'd stare him down and demand to know why the hell he doesn't want his friends to know he's out with me tonight. But I'm not Jade. So I hold it inside and avoid his eyes and walk faster so I can end this night as soon as possible.

At my door, I mumble an awkward, hurried goodbye. I barely look at him as I say it, but I know he's confused.

I want to believe I have it wrong, but how do I justify that? Cam being embarrassed of me makes so much more sense than Cam falling for me.

Everything I was so certain of twenty minutes ago seems like a joke. I'm his secret. And the only thing that's surprising is that I ever managed to convince myself that what we had was real.

"HI, GIRLIES!" Madison says when Jade and I step inside her sunny three-story townhouse.

Madison's parents bought her this place as a freshman, somehow bypassing the school rules that all freshmen live on campus. While the rest of us were crammed like sardines in our twin XL beds in cement-block dorms, Madison was living her best life in an airy bedroom with a king-size bed, walk-in shower, and balcony. The girl's idea of money problems is not being able to fit the wad of cash the ATM just spit out into her sleek leather wallet —she does her Neiman Marcus shopping in cash, so her dad won't get on her case. But she's never shown an ounce of snobbery, is uncompromisingly generous, and her parties are always lit.

"Happy Friday," Madison says, bringing us two glasses of pink sparkling wine. Behind her, a chic white bar cart brims with expensive-looking bottles of booze, not that I'd know the difference, but everything Madison touches looks expensive.

"Girl, pink bubbly?" Jade raises an eyebrow. "Friday isn't that happy."

"It is today. Lincoln just invited me to party with him

tomorrow night." Lincoln is the football player that Madison has been chasing the last few weeks. "Lenni, you should ask Cam if he's coming."

"Ugh." I roll my eyes and down half the glass of wine.

Madison looks confused.

Jade is quick to explain. "They went out the other night and he practically shoved her down a dark alley when he saw his friends coming."

"Okay, he didn't exactly—"

"For all intents and purposes, he did!" Jade insists. "Dude even had me fooled into thinking he wasn't a dirtbag. See, that's why if you're going to date a jock, better make it a dumb one." She nods at Madison. "Lincoln's a good choice."

Madison looks at me, motherly concern on her face. "What the hell is his problem?"

"Either he's embarrassed to be seen with me or he's dating someone else."

Jade shakes her head. "No chance that boy is embarrassed to be seen with you. You're hot as hell. And now that you've stopped wearing clothing three sizes too big, everyone on campus knows it."

"Oh, okay, so you think he has a girlfriend? Great. I'm a side piece."

Jade laughs. "Honey, you can't be a side piece until you've started fucking him."

Madison nods gravely. "What was his explanation?"

"For what?" I ask.

"For getting all weird like that."

I twist the wine glass in my fingers. "I didn't ask."

"Lenni!" she admonishes.

"What's the difference? Whatever his reason, it can't be something I want to hear."

"He could have a hundred good reasons. You're not even giving him a chance."

I take a generous swallow of wine.

Madison gives me a sympathetic look. "You like the guy? Then you need to talk to him."

"No, she doesn't," Jade says. "If he wants her that much, he'll come to her."

Madison shakes her head, smiling. "Don't take advice from this crazy. She's such a game player."

"Apparently so is Cam. Or just a player," I say. "Can we talk about something else now?"

Jade shrugs. "I wouldn't put it past him to be juggling multiple girls. Just because he's intelligent and charming doesn't mean he can't be a scumbag. But a girlfriend? I'd have heard by now."

"Totally agree." Madison hastily refills our glasses as though if she gets enough alcohol in us, all will be well. "If he had a new girlfriend, she'd practically be a campus celebrity by now."

I choose to believe them only because the idea of him having a girlfriend hurts too much.

It's been three days since our ill-fated date, and I still haven't grown the balls to confront Cam. I know the mature thing is to speak up, but that's not how things worked in my house growing up. I'm more comfortable with the shut-your-mouth-and-endure model.

He's texted me a couple times, innocent references to vanilla ice cream and the fact I still owe him a celebration meal since Shafer beat Reynolds. I left him on read for half a day, then gave short responses, but his ego wasn't deterred. He asked to see me this weekend, and because I'm a coward I told him I don't have much time for casual dating at the moment.

I haven't heard from him since.

Now I'm caught in the confused, ugly headspace of trying to forget him while simultaneously wishing he'd find a way to win me back. I know Cam feels something for me and I know he's attracted to me, I can't deny that any longer. A few weeks ago, I'd have sworn he wouldn't be caught dead dating some dorky journalism student, but every time I talk to him, he breaks another stereotype. Madison's right; I didn't give him a chance to explain himself. But I don't want to face the task of hearing him out and, once again, having to decide whether to put my heart on the line.

"So, you and Lincoln . . . things are happening?" I ask Madison, mustering up some happiness for my friend. With the way things ended with her ex—the guy she thought she'd marry—it's been a long time since I've seen her eyes light up over a man.

Madison tosses her sheet of blond hair over her shoulder. "We hooked up the other night. It was pretty tame, but I'm going to invite him to spend the night tomorrow after the party. He is so sexy, don't you think?"

"I don't get you two." Jade shakes her head. "Suddenly losing your minds over a couple of meatheads. Remember how much fun we used to have with the guys from the engineering frat? When smart dudes let loose, they go all out."

"You would know. Sam should be in MENSA," I say.

Jade smiles, absorbing the compliment, and I feel a little stab of envy. It isn't about Sam's IQ or that he can let loose, it's that Sam is hers. No question.

"So I need you girls at the party tomorrow night," Madison says. "I'm meeting him there, and I can't walk in alone."

I shake my head. "I can't do a party at the football house. What about Keeley and Shea?" Keeley and Shea are Madison's roommates and classic party-loving sorority girls.

"Keeley went home for the weekend and Shea works late.

And the party's not at the football house, it's at that big yellow house on the corner across from the liquor store."

"The lacrosse guys," Jade offers. As dismissive as she is of athletes, she certainly knows where all of them sleep. "We'll definitely be there."

Madison looks at me. "You have to face Cam in class anyway. At least if he's at the party we'll see if he brought a girl with him."

That's news I'd much rather receive secondhand. But she's right, I have to face Cam soon.

"Yeah, and besides," Jade adds, "I can't wait to dress you in a low-cut top and watch that fuckhead weep."

THERE'S no good reason to think I'll see Cam tonight, but I've dressed for a run-in all the same. I'm rocking a smoky eye, the only makeup trick I've ever perfected, and Jade straightened my hair, then helped me pour myself into jeans, heels, and a silky black top with a plunging neckline.

"You're beautiful, baby, but you need to wear a thong," Jade says when she sees me.

"I think the jeans are too tight in the ass."

"Not possible." We both check out my butt in the mirror. "You've been hitting the squat rack hard, haven't you?"

Yeah, that and the Hostess cupcakes; that cream filling and the little white swirl of icing on top have seen me through some tough times over the years. "I should just change."

"Go. Thong. Do it."

I do as told, finding the one thong I own—a midnight-blue strip of lace Jade bought me as a gag gift last Christmas—having thrown the red thing I wore that cursed night at Reeve's in the trash as soon as it came off. When I check the mirror, I wonder if Jade insisted on a thong for the shot of confidence as much as for the visual effect because, yeah, I'm actually feeling myself in this thing. Amazing what obliterating panty lines can do for the self-esteem.

I'm a ball of nerves on the walk to the lacrosse house. I don't want to see Cam, yet something about this thong and the fact that for once in my life my whole look is on point makes me think I could handle him tonight. I could look him in the eye and demand an answer, and he might just give me the truth. But do I want to hear it?

The house is beyond packed when we walk in, but I spot only a few guys from the football team. Madison finds Lincoln, Lincoln finds us drinks, and Jade and I find the dance floor. I have one basic move, but tonight it's enough.

Some guy comes up behind me to dance, puts his mouth to my ear and shouts, louder than necessary, "Lenni! Remember me?"

It takes me a minute, but yes, I remember him. Connor. No, Kyle. Lacrosse team. He kissed me freshman year and told me I had nice lips.

He leads me away from Jade, who lays a watchful eye on him but keeps dancing. It's hard to hear what he's saying over the pounding music, but we manage a shallow round of "how have you been?" over the noise. He's cute, though not as cute as I remembered. I know who to blame for that. He flirts with me shamelessly, which satisfies me mainly because it means this uncomfortable outfit is working. But when he takes my hand to lead me outside where we can talk without shouting, his skin doesn't shoot off sparks.

All I can think is, *I wish Cam was here.*

Outside, I can finally hear Kyle, but that's where I stop listening. That's where I realize I'm wasting his time because even if he makes a decent competitor for Cam on paper—handsome, polite, intelligent—he's not Cam. He inspires none of the feelings inside me that Cam does. No one ever has. And I realize then that I gave up those feelings—light and hope and all the shiny things every girl wants—for no reason. Literally. I invented a story about why Cam acted strangely on the street. I took the barest of facts and filled in the rest with my imagination. That's not what a good journalist does. And maybe my assumption is true, but what if it's not? What if I shut him out of my life over something I imagined?

"I need to go check on my friends," I tell Kyle when there's a break in the one-sided conversation he's holding.

If Cam's here, I'm finding him.

TWENTY-TWO

Cameron

"QUIT STEALING MY RAZOR," I grumble when I walk into the bathroom to find Reeve shaving on his side of the double sink. "For the fiftieth time, there's an industrial-sized pack of disposables in the cabinet."

Reeve pauses and looks in the mirror at the silver-handled razor poised under his chin. Then he holds it out to me, shaving foam and stubble still on the blade.

I shake my head. "Fuck it."

"Still with the shitty mood, Cam? Come on, man, you didn't have a bad game today."

I take a clean razor from the cabinet. "I didn't have a good game either, did I? I can't fucking afford anything less." I slam the cabinet shut, sending something inside clattering against the door.

"Damn, son, you need to hit the joint a couple times before we head out?"

"No."

"All right, then find another way to relax your sphincter, dude. It's Saturday night."

We shave in silence, and it reminds me of high school. In

those days, Reeve lived at my house most of the year and always used my stuff, even though my mom made sure he had his own of everything. And when he'd go back home to stay with his mother for a while, it was always weird to find my razor and hair gel and cologne exactly where I'd left them instead of somewhere on Reeve's side of the bathroom.

Reeve keeps checking my reflection in the mirror, and each time he does, his smile widens a little. I ignore him.

"It's girl trouble, isn't it?" he finally asks.

"Girl trouble? You sound like my grandpa."

"Pops is the man." He turns toward me and leans casually on the counter like his face isn't half-covered in shaving foam. "So I saw you out with Lenni the other night."

This catches me off guard, but I try not to show it. "Yeah. And?"

"And you've been out with the girl one time and you're already miserable. Doesn't that tell you something?"

"Yeah, it tells me you don't know what you're talking about." I towel off my face.

"Come on, Cam, you've been one surly motherfucker the last few days. You weren't even like this when Kira dumped you."

"Let's drop it. I want to booze, and I want to get out of this house. You almost ready?"

"Five minutos, hombre."

I rinse my razor, feeling guilty. I have been a dick lately, and Reeve's gotten the brunt of it because he's the only one who won't hold it against me. "Hey, fresh haircut," I tell him as I walk by, raking a hand through the undercut faux-hawk he's got going on. "Better reap the benefits of that tonight before Coach tells you you look like a clown."

I don't know why, but girls go batshit when guys on the team switch up their hair, and no one's into funky hairstyles as much as Reeve. Coach Haskins, on the other hand, isn't shy about letting everyone know he finds Reeve's sense of style a disgrace.

In my bedroom, I pull on a clean shirt and try to forget the past few days. It's been a shit week between my mediocre showing on the field, my lingering guilt over uninviting Serena and Liam to the game and, of course, Lenni.

She's blowing me off, and I keep thinking I should have taken her out for a classy dinner instead of a musty museum and a two-dollar ice cream cone. I mean, what was I thinking? But I know what I was thinking: Lenni doesn't care about fancy restaurants or which credit card her date pulls out when the check arrives. Lame as my plans were, I don't think she hated them. And I know she didn't hate the kiss. I can still hear the soft little sigh she made when I kissed her and feel the way she just melted under my hands. My dick stirs in my jeans.

So I come back to the place I've been in too long. I don't get Lenni. And it sucks hard because it's the only problem I can't work with. It doesn't matter how hot our kisses are or that being around her brings an ease I've never felt before. She's not the girl for me if I don't know how to make her happy.

THE PARTY IS LIT by the time Reeve and I roll up with Lorenzo. People spill out the doors, and beer cans and red plastic cups line the porch railing. Normally I put a time limit on parties like this, but tonight the idea of disappearing into a houseful of people and loud music has its appeal.

We're five steps across the front porch when a trio of sorority chicks descends on us. There's squealing about Reeve's hair, and Lorenzo and I laugh watching him waver between being pleased at the attention and annoyed that all those girly fingers might be shifting some perfect strands out of place.

Then one of the girls wraps her hand around my arm and leans in close.

"Hey, Cam. Great game today. You played so awesome." So either she didn't watch, or she doesn't understand football.

"Thanks."

I can't remember her name, but she hangs out with Alexis a lot. I almost ask her if Alexis is here tonight because goddamn, if she is, I'm outta here. I try to never be a dick to girls, but Alexis gets on my last nerve on a good day. Tonight I might just go off on her.

The girl looks me up and down and smiles like she's inviting me to reciprocate the compliment. She's pretty, but I'm not feeling it.

"Maybe I'll see you in there," I say and gesture my friends inside before she can respond.

Inside, we grab drinks and Reeve drifts off to introduce everyone to his mohawk while Lorenzo and I find Cash and a couple other guys from the team. It's hard to talk over the pounding music, and after a while we move out back.

That's where I see her.

Lenni's angled slightly away from me, pressed up against the house, but even if she were facing this way, she probably wouldn't see me because the dude drooling all over her basically has her caged in. I've seen him before. He's a lacrosse guy, and I just figured out I hate him.

I stare at them longer than I want to, completely caught off guard by how much it stings seeing her with someone else. She's not at home slaving away over articles. She didn't blow me off because she doesn't have time, she blew me off because she'd rather be here with him.

Lenni looks incredible: skintight jeans, heels, a tank top that does a hell of a lot more than just hint at her amazing tits. She didn't dress like that for our night together. Did she dress that way for him?

He's looking down at her with that unmistakable look of a dude who thinks "I'm in." The bitter side of me wants to laugh and tell him, "Good luck, man." Lenni can pull the rug out without even trying. But I don't wish him luck. I watch her laugh at something he says, her hands tucked behind her back and her boobs on full display. I curl my hand into a fist and imagine how good it would feel to knock it right into his teeth.

"Good," someone says behind me. Reeve has materialized from nowhere. "It's better this way."

"What's better?"

He nods toward Lenni. "She's showing you who she is."

I shake my head, irritation and bitterness colliding inside me. "Who is she, Reeve?"

"Jersey chaser in training. Last month it was football players, October must be lax dudes."

I spin to face him. "Dude, shut the fuck up already." I keep my voice down but I'm right in his face, all the ferocity I feel watching Lax Dude touch Lenni flowing straight toward my best friend. "Don't talk about her. Ever."

For once, there's not a trace of humor on Reeve's face. Behind me, our friends have gone silent. I feel a tentative hand on my shoulder.

"Everything okay?" Cash asks carefully.

I shrug him off without taking my gaze off Reeve. By now the surprise in his eyes has been replaced with a flicker of anger. "All right, Cam. Just chill."

No apology of course, just like he never apologized to Lenni for treating her like shit. I turn away, sick of looking at him.

Our friends are watching me warily. They're all familiar with the dynamic between me and Reeve. As much brothers as best friends, we'd kill for each other, and sometimes we want to kill each other. But I guess they sense this is something different, and they're right. I'm about ready to lose it on Reeve, and over a girl neither of us has even slept with.

I push past them toward the house, sparing a glance at Lenni. She hasn't noticed me.

Inside, I get myself another beer but don't drink it. She said she doesn't hook up and she doesn't do relationships, so she and Lax Dude aren't a thing. Of course, she also told me she doesn't kiss, and that lasted three days. Is she going home with him tonight? Maybe I ripped the Band-Aid off when I kissed her, and now she's gonna fuck every guy who looks at her right.

I think about embarrassing myself—going up to her, pushing him out of the way, telling her I'm not leaving until she tells me where I went wrong. It's not my style at all. She doesn't belong to me. Maybe they're actually together. But fuck it, I don't care if they're engaged. I can't leave tonight without getting something from her. Anything.

Then there she is, shouldering her way through the crowd. The man of the hour is nowhere in sight. She moves slowly, her eyes darting from one person to the next. I watch her stop in front of Lincoln Braggs, our fullback, and say something into his ear. He nods and looks around. It doesn't take him long to find me and when he does, he points, and Lenni's gaze follows. Our eyes meet across the crowd, hers steely and fierce. I forgot how prickly she can be, and if I thought for a brief second she had reconciliation on her mind, I stand corrected.

She picks her way through the party toward me, decidedly less determined than she looked a minute ago. I fight with myself to stay neutral, not to be as angry with her as I am and not to want her as much as I do.

"Hey," she says tightly when we're finally face-to-face.

I nod.

She opens her mouth to say something else but stops and

looks around like she expects to see the whole room watching us. It's not. She turns to me again. "Can we talk somewhere?" She almost has to yell to be heard.

I nod for her to follow me and lead us outside to an empty corner of the front yard where we face off again.

"Look," she starts, her chin jutting out defiantly. "I don't know what happened the other night."

"You can't know any less than I do," I say before she can continue. "We had a great night together and then you blew me off. That's about all I know."

"You forgot the part in between where you dragged me across the street like a dog on a leash."

I pause. "What?"

She looks down at the ground, her face contorting briefly like she's in pain. I've been so angry at her, at how much power she has over me. I don't do relationships like that. But looking at her face now, the anger's gone. "Were you embarrassed to be out with me? Or for your friends to see us together?"

"Are you fucking nuts? Where do you get that from?"

"From the way you acted when you saw Reeve!"

"No, I . . ." Then everything clicks into place. Of course she's pissed at me; that's exactly what I did. "But Lenni, that wasn't —okay, yes, I hustled us across the road, but come on. You think I'm embarrassed to be seen with you? Really?"

"Why else would you practically break into a sprint when you see your friends coming?"

I can't stand the way she's looking at me; like I disgust her. "Because I just had the best date of my life, and I didn't want to run into Reeve. He's . . . he's weird about me being into you. And he doesn't know when to shut the fuck up."

She stares at me, her eyebrows drawn tightly together.

"I just didn't want him to say anything to you."

She takes this in. "That's it?"

"Have we not been all over campus together? I sit next to you in class and make googly eyes at you every week. We drank at Shafer's most popular dive right after a huge football win. The whole school knows I'm into you. And you're really going to stand there and tell me I'm an asshole who's embarrassed to be caught in your company?"

She looks down at the ground. "Sorry. I guess—I guess I overreacted. Maybe I wasn't thinking clearly." She looks back up at me. "But you should have told me about Reeve. I can handle him."

"Yeah, okay, I should have. And you should have told me this was the reason you've been ignoring me." Anger flares back up again. "You think I'm that kind of person?"

"I'm sorry." She reaches out to touch my arm. "Don't be insulted."

I turn and look out toward the street so she won't see just how insulted I am. "I've never given you any reason to think of me like that."

"I know. I have some stuff to work on."

We exchange an awkward look, something still looming heavy over us. "It's Reeve, right?" I ask.

Lenni only blinks.

I think about Reeve and the ugly way I went off on him, but I'm not sorry. "Okay, I should have said this a long time ago. Nothing about how Reeve treated you is excusable, and I don't want you thinking that me being close with him means I condone his shit."

"I know you're best friends," she says like this is a fact she's just barely tolerating. "I don't expect that to change."

"It's more than that. Reeve lived with me for the better part of high school; he had family troubles. I know how he seems, and I know how he really is."

Lenni looks unmoved.

"My point is he acted like a total dick, but if that's who he really was, he wouldn't be my friend. He's just really good at hiding his decent qualities."

She puts her hands up to stop me. "I don't care about Reeve or what happened with him. It wasn't about that."

Silence settles over us. What happened to everything being easy between me and her? "I don't know what to say, Lenni. You could at least let me screw up before you give up on me." I shove my hands in my pockets. "I don't think this can work otherwise." I glance toward the street, ready to walk away. I'm embarrassed that I read her so wrong.

"Don't go, Cam." The panic in her voice is, ironically, reassuring. She's not ready to let this go. I wait, but I don't say anything else. It's her turn to explain. "I really am sorry. I know how I come off, but the truth is . . ." She swallows and comes closer. "I like you. So much. And I want to be the girl that jumps in headfirst, I'm just not."

"I never asked you to jump in headfirst. I'd say we've been wading in inch by fucking inch, wouldn't you?"

"You and I are so different. We're not coming at this from the same place."

"And that was fine with me. I can move as slow as you need me to. But I'm not fine with you thinking I'm a piece of shit. I thought I made it pretty fucking clear how much I liked you."

"Do you still?"

"Honestly? Right now I wish I didn't." I blow out a breath. "But in case you couldn't tell by the fact that I'm still standing here, yeah. I do, Lenni."

"Enough to work with me?"

"Tell me what you're asking for and I'll tell you if I can do it."

She blinks like she's thinking this over. "You deserve more trust than I've given you, and I'm going to work on that. I guess

I just need you to know where I'm coming from. I've got this baggage and zero relationship experience and . . . it's not a sexy combination."

I don't know exactly where she's coming from except a place of hurt. But I guess that's not so hard to understand. "Don't worry, I see that. You've been pretty obvious about it," I say, trying to soften both of us with some humor.

She gives me a grateful smile. "Does that mean you forgive me for freaking out?"

"I forgive you."

She closes her fingers around both my wrists and leans in. Her hips are dangerously close to mine. "Can I ask for one more thing?"

"One more."

"Leave this shitty party with me?"

lenni

I SHOULD BE HAPPY; I had Cam all wrong. He's not an asshole. But I think maybe *I* am.

I always thought if I found a guy who worked for my trust, I'd trust him. Simple as that. And here he is, doing his part. Why can't I do mine? Why is the strongest part of me urging me to run away, ignore my feelings for him, never see him again?

"You know what I like about you?" I ask as we walk slowly up the street and the music from the party fades away. "That you say what's on your mind. I can ask you a question and I know I'll get a real answer."

"Would you be insulted if I suggested you try it sometime?" He gives me a little smile.

"I'm going to. I promise." I reach for his hand because I don't like the distance between us. "But I need to know what you want from me."

He looks over at me, surprised. "A chance to be with you. That's all. What do you want?"

"I want the same thing," I say, caught in his eyes. "I'm just trying to understand you and what you expect from this."

"I don't have any expectations. Except that you try to trust me. What do you need to know about me, Lenni?"

I don't know where to begin so I pick the thing that shouldn't be an issue but is. "You never told me what happened between you and Kira."

He huffs out a breath. "Relationship ran its course."

"What does that mean?"

"I don't know. Every relationship gets to that point where you've gotten everything out of it you're going to get. You know?"

"I've never had a relationship."

I feel his eyes on me, but I don't look. "I like being with girls who are clear about what they want from me, and that was Kir. But once that part is fulfilled, there's not much left."

"What did she want from you?"

"Kira likes status. And appearances."

"And what did you get out of it?"

"Someone to be with. She's low drama. She did her thing and let me do mine. And I guess she looked the part. Maybe winning her when she wouldn't even speak to other guys I knew was kind of an ego stroke."

I have nothing to say to this. I guess he's honest, at least.

"No, I'm not explaining this right." He scrubs a hand over his face and tries again. "I know how it sounds, but it was more than that. We had a good time together. It's not some great love story, but it was what we both wanted. No one was being used, at least not without their consent."

We stop at an intersection and wait for the light to change.

He turns to me. "But what I had with her has nothing to do with you and me. I couldn't handle anything too real back then. Now I want more than that."

My whole body tightens. He's inches away, and I'm afraid to breathe, afraid of where one false move might land me. "Why?"

His eyes roam my face. "Because I know this girl. And when I'm around her, I realize that all the bullshit I've heard my whole life about following your heart isn't bullshit after all."

My heart skips a beat. I search his eyes for some sign of doubt, but it's not there. It comes to me now, a brief flash of clarity, what the word "real" means when he looks at me. Alive. Free. Already stumbling down the path toward something I've tried so long to stop wanting. I try to smile but feel unexpectedly choked by emotion. I nod and reach for him, hoping my touch might say what my mouth can't seem to. Cam accepts my awkwardness and drapes an arm around me.

The light changes and he takes my hand as we cross. On the other side of the street, he looks over at me, a playful smile on his face. "By the way, a dog on a leash? What was that about?"

Ugh. I did say that, didn't I? "You know, 'cause you dragged me across the street? Like a dog being dragged into a kennel. Or the vet's office or whatever." I ignore his laugh. "It made sense in my head."

"Damn, I better alert the animal shelter to put you on the blacklist for adoptions."

"So where are you dragging me now?"

"I'm just walking. Where do you want to go?"

He looks at me, letting me take him in—the wide, almond-shaped eyes turned up at their corners, the sharp cut of his cheekbones and his jawline making his bone structure an honest-to-god work of art, those lips that, even when I was busy hating him, I vowed to kiss one more time before I died. Desire curls inside my stomach.

"Home."

At my front door, I fumble with my keys while he leans against the doorframe and watches me. His stance is powerful and sure and reminds me that while I'm tall, he's much taller. In my apartment, we linger just inside the door. Cam trains that potent gaze on me, and I know he wants to say something, but instead he kisses me. I breathe him in as his lips close on mine. He's slow and careful when he backs me up against the door, and I'm completely under his spell, moving only in response to him. I want to let go. I want to just be. But something inside me is locked up tight.

"I want you so much," Cam whispers. "I want us."

This soft, sweet confession reaches straight down into my heart, and I pull back, overcome.

"I'm sorry," he says. "That was too much."

I shake my head. "I want us too. I'm just . . . scared."

He studies me, a faint line creasing his forehead. "What happened to you, Lenni?" His voice is so gentle, there's no mistaking what he's asking. It wasn't the question I was expecting, and definitely not the one I want to answer. But I need him to know.

Gently, I push him away, trying to shake off the kiss and the heady effect of his words. He's silent as I walk into the kitchen to get us some water and then settle on the couch.

"Before I tell you," I say, "promise you won't start babying me."

"Babying you? I'm not going to change how I treat you. I just want to know where you're coming from."

I nod. I don't have much practice telling this story, but I've thought about it enough times to know exactly how to make it succinct and low drama. "I was chubby when you met me, but that was after losing twenty or thirty pounds. I was fat in high school and had zero experience with guys. People said shitty things sometimes, but it wasn't like I had this sad, miserable existence. I had friends, I had hobbies, I played soccer. Life was . . . fine, by high school standards, at least.

"But when I was sixteen, this really cute football player invited me to his house to study, and I didn't even question it.

Apparently, I was not just overconfident, I also never learned a thing from all those cheesy teen movies from the nineties."

I try for a smile, but Cam looks back at me with a grave expression.

"You know, where the cool guy asks out the loser girl and it turns out to be a cruel joke?"

"I know them," he says quietly.

Great, he's pitying me already. I take a deep, steadying breath. I thought I knew how to tell this story. "Anyway, instead of studying, we drank; too much. And when he wanted me to, um . . . go down on him, I didn't know how to say no. I'd never even kissed anyone before."

Cam exhales loudly, his nostrils flaring.

"I found out later his teammate—my neighbor, actually—had dared him. I was a joke, and the whole school knew." I leave out the cruel detail about the video because it's salt in the wound, and I don't think he can handle it anyway.

I don't recognize the look on his face. I can feel the fury coming off him, can see it locked up tight inside the tense muscles in his arms and his curled fists. It should annoy me; I hate the macho shit. But something inside me breaks because I don't think it's macho bullshit. I think he hurts for me.

Cam lays his head back and looks up at the ceiling. His eyes squeeze shut.

I lay a hand on his arm. "I'm okay now, Cam."

"No." He sits up and looks at me. "I'm sorry. You shouldn't have to sit there reassuring me. I'm sorry." He pulls in a deep breath and takes my hand in his, tracing my fingers with his other hand. "I don't know what to say that you don't already know. You didn't deserve that." He looks down at our hands. "No one does."

I nod and we're quiet for a moment.

"I admire you, Lenni," Cam finally says. "The way you take what life hands out and keep on living."

I shrug. "What other choice did I have?"

"Kill him."

I roll my eyes, but Cam's face is serious.

"Kill them both. Lie in bed every night thinking about how much you want to smash their fucking faces in."

"Okay, that's exactly what I don't need. That's why I don't need you to keep Reeve away from me. I've dealt with assholes, and I can handle them."

"I apologized for that, but I was just trying to protect you. You can't expect me not to protect you."

I pull my hands gently from his grasp. "Who told you I want to be protected?"

"You did."

I shake my head. "Um, no, I didn't."

"The night we met. You told me every story you wrote had a strong, protective dude in it because you didn't have that in real life. You said," he recites, looking up like he's replaying it in his head, "'I never had a father or an older brother to make me feel safe. I always wanted to know how it felt.' That's what you said."

I stare at him, heat crawling up my neck and onto my cheeks. I did say that. I haven't thought about it in so long. It feels like a childish wish, some remnant of my broken upbringing that I'd rather forget. But he remembered. Emotion swells inside my chest. He was a stranger to me when I told him that, but I trusted him. Now that I know him, can I trust him again? I feel it like a living being, this trust I want so badly to place in his hands, this thing that's been building between us that only grows stronger every time I try to reason it away. I lace my fingers through his, my heart beating wildly. I want to tell him how I feel, but I'm so bad at this. All I can manage to do is say his name and hope that he hears, *Thank you* and *I'm sorry* and everything else I don't know how to say.

He looks at our linked hands and then at me. "Let me be the one to protect you, Lenni. Give me a chance to be the man you deserve."

A sound like a cry escapes from my throat, but I'm not crying. I think instead I'm melting because this beautiful man is asking my permission to be everything I want him to be. Yup, definitely melting. "Okay," I say.

I lean in and kiss him, the certainty in my lips making up for every hesitation in my brain. His kiss is soft for only a second before it turns rough, before he stops holding back. His tongue parts my lips. I open for him, sinking into his touch.

Strong hands pull me into his lap. All gentleness has left him. He grips my ass, pressing me to the hard thickness of his cock. Even through the barrier of my jeans, my clit pulses in response. I brace my hands against his chest, dizzy at the feel of this man that I've fought so hard not to want.

I kiss him harder, barely registering the pain of his teeth against my lips. He lets out a low, throaty chuckle. He knows how badly I want him, and I don't care. It only turns me on more. I want to be naked, writhing against him, pinned under his weight, drowning in his scent.

His hands slide down to my waist and, for a second, he just holds them there, conforming them to my curves like he's trying to memorize my shape. Then his fingers are at the hem of my shirt. He eases it over my head in a single, practiced move. My chest heaves in anticipation. His fingers move deftly at my back to unhook my bra, but when he takes the straps down, he moves achingly slowly; his fingertips graze my shoulders, my arms, leaving sparks of heat that radiate up and down my body. My nipples stiffen, standing at attention. His eyes are hungry as he peels the silky fabric away from my breasts.

"Fuck," he says hoarsely, my bare breasts inches from his face. "You know how long I've waited for this?" The feral look in his eyes floods me with desire and a sense of power I've never felt before.

"How long?"

"Forever." A tiny smile quirks his lips before he closes his mouth around my nipple.

I let out a moan, my back arching. My hips move involuntarily, grinding against him, seeking more. The wet heat of his mouth makes my breasts ache. I thread my fingers through his hair and urge him closer. I watch his perfect lips taking in my nipple. He makes a sound somewhere between a groan and a sigh, the sound of him losing control.

He moves to my other breast, his hand taking the weight of the one he just left. He flicks his tongue against my nipple, sucks it into his mouth and lets it go, his teeth a faint but dizzying tease against my sensitive skin. My eyes flutter closed. I'm slowly losing my mind.

The fabric between us, once a delicious tease, now feels frustrating. I tug at his shirt, and he gives me what I want, pulling it over his head, then lays me down on the couch and slides off my jeans.

He looks me up and down, and a sudden shyness washes over me. I'm aware of the softness of my belly, of my muscular thighs. But Cam's eyes are hazy with desire, his lips parted like he's about to devour me. He meets my gaze and swallows hard. That's all it takes. For the first time in my life, I feel beautiful. Perfect. Enough.

I reach for him, unzipping his jeans and pushing them down. My stomach flips at the outline of his swollen cock straining against the thin cotton of his boxer briefs. God, I want him.

I ease his underwear down and take him in. His cock is—

what else?—perfect. I look up at him and close my fingers around his thick shaft.

His response is a slow, liquid smile. "Like it?"

I run my thumb over his velvety head. "Love it."

He bends over me, easing me back onto the couch. His fingers hook inside my panties and pull them down, then toss them over his shoulder. "You're so gorgeous, Lenni," he whispers as he slides a finger between my legs, testing my wetness. Desire pulses inside my body. I have to concentrate on breathing.

"Hold on," I say, mustering the last bit of good sense left in my brain and sitting up. Jade could walk in at any minute. "Let's go to my room." I get up and take his arm, pushing him toward my bedroom. "Be right there."

In Jade's room, I rifle through her bedside drawer until I find the condoms, then take a handful because I'm an optimist and hurry back to my bedroom. I freeze in the doorway when I see him.

Cam leans back against my headboard, his fist moving slowly up and down his cock. He looks at me through half-mast eyes, inviting me in, and my breath catches in my chest. It's the most erotic thing I've ever seen.

I toss a condom at him. He catches it with one hand just before it hits his face; always an athlete. Then he smiles that cocky smile that has never not worked on me. My pulse beats hot. I'm done with foreplay, done with the teasing. I need him inside me.

His eyes take in my body greedily as I move for the bed. He grabs my arms and lays me down, positioning my body under his. I watch as he kneels between my legs and rolls on the condom.

Without warning, my doubts roar to life again. Does this really mean anything to him? He's done it hundreds of times, but not me. And when I did, I had no expectations of what would happen when it was over. But with Cam, I couldn't bear it if we were one and done.

He must feel my hesitation. His thumb brushes tenderly over my lip. "You want to do this?" he asks softly.

"I do."

"But?"

I swallow. "But I don't want our first time to be our last."

"It won't be. I could spend a thousand nights with you, and it still wouldn't be enough." He lays a kiss on my lips, soft as a feather.

It's not just about sex, we both know that. But this particular moment, his words and the ragged whisper they came in and the tease of his warm mouth set off something chemical in me. And this promise, which wasn't a promise at all, is enough for me tonight. Turning back would be an act of self-inflicted torture.

I open my mouth, deepening the kiss. I nip at his lower lip and pull him down over me. He grunts. I spread my knees wider, and we break the kiss to watch as he teases the head of his cock against my clit. My body trembles, far beyond my control. My hips rise off the bed, searching for more pressure, more of his touch.

His muscles are tight as bows as he holds himself over me, his breaths deep and steadying. I can feel how hard he's working to hold back. He wants to torture me. He pushes slowly inside me, making my breath hitch, then slides back out. Then again. Just enough to teach me how empty my body feels without him.

"Please," I hear myself whimper.

He ignores my desperation, pumps inside me twice before easing back out. I don't know if I love it or hate it.

Finally, he lowers his head to my breast. His lips close

around my nipple at the same time he thrusts inside me, filling me completely and tearing a jagged cry from my lips.

I lock my legs around him, not letting him go. This time he doesn't fight me. His hips find a deep, steady rhythm. Meanwhile, his tongue works my nipple in a rhythm all its own, hard and fast. God, yes. Now this is athletic talent. My nails press into the back of his neck, fingers twisted in his hair. I close my eyes, overcome by the frenzied sensations that wind me tighter and tighter.

When at last Cam pulls away from my breasts and comes up for air, his fingers find my clit. My body clenches around his length when his thumb makes contact; stroking, finding the perfect pressure, making my knees shake.

Tension ratchets higher inside me. My insides throb, aching for release. Cam's breath comes faster. I can feel him beginning to come apart, and I'm right there with him. But neither one of us wants to let go.

His brow furrows. He thrusts deeply but there's a desperation in his rhythm.

"Are you close?" he asks breathlessly. "I want to watch you come." Every word sounds deliciously dirty.

"So close." I'm right there, teetering on the edge. I just need a little more of him: his taste, his scent, his beauty. All of him around me.

I run my hands up his chest. His skin feels feverish. Drops of sweat leave glistening tracks along his temples, shoulders, his taut stomach. I wrap my hand around his neck and pull him close. I kiss him. I can barely breathe, but I can't stop. The heat of his mouth moves down my throat and spreads through me like fire. Finally, I spill over the edge.

I see his face as I come, his endless amber eyes. Swells of hot pleasure tear through me. I think I say his name, but maybe it's only in my head; *Cameron*. I want to possess him forever.

His fingers curl into my skin, bruisingly hard. His hips buck wildly as he loses control, roaring his pleasure. The sound is irresistible. I ride the wave with him until, slowly, the world around us fills back in.

There's no sound except our mingled breaths and my own thundering heartbeat as his body stills around me. He exhales, breathing my name against my ear.

I wait for my old fears to spring up again as I come to my senses, but there's nothing, only an unfamiliar feeling of contentedness. I don't want anything more than this.

lenni

I'M ALMOST AWAKE, swimming through hazy images that might be memories, might be dreams. Cam's hard, sweat-slicked body moving above me, his tongue on my nipple, his breathless voice saying my name. Did that happen last night? Weeks ago? Or was it only a dream?

I open my eyes and there he is, asleep, his hand resting on my hip. I prop myself on one elbow to look at him, moving slowly so I don't wake him.

The sheet rests dangerously low across his hips. His naked body is absolute perfection. Swells of muscle dominate his upper body, the tanned skin a tantalizing contrast to the paler strip of skin below his waist. My pussy aches, remembering the feel of him inside me last night.

But it's when I look at his face that my heart catches. He's relaxed in sleep, all those lines of worry and anger and pleading from the night before erased. I look at his lips and remember his tender words, and I know for certain I'm not turning back.

My heart led me here, and maybe someday I'll look back on that as my ultimate mistake, but I'm here and I won't go back. It scares me to know how deep I'm in. But when I look at him, the fear seems small next to the hope that surges inside me.

I lie down with my back to him and pull his arm gently around me. Do I even have the right to touch him like this? To move him to my liking? I don't know, but it feels incredible. He shifts onto his side, giving in to me. I shudder as the sleepy warmth of his body seeps into mine.

His arm tightens around me, and he slides his hand up to cup my breast. His face is pressed against my back so when he groans, the vibration sends a shiver up my spine. My nipple stiffens against his palm.

"Shit, honey," he says against my skin. "Was that for real last night?"

"I'm trying to figure out the same thing."

"We're pretty incredible together." He pushes my hair aside and kisses the back of my neck.

It's true. I've never had great sex before, but Cam and me? I finally understand why people are obsessed with getting laid.

Cam presses his hips against my ass, and my body strains with longing at the feel of his hardness. "I can't get enough of you," he whispers, kissing my ear.

Desire roars inside me. I roll onto my back and let my thighs fall open as Cam's fingers find the wetness already pooled between them. "Try to anyway," I say and pull him down on top of me.

AFTERWARD, he dozes but I'm due for a shift at the library, so I get up to shower. I take my time because my body feels deliciously spent and languid, but also because my mind is swimming with questions.

I was scared to sleep with him, not because of the sex but because of this moment: the morning after.

Now what?

I can't bring myself to ask him to define us, not yet. But how do I get through the next few hours or days until I see him again without driving myself nuts wondering what he's doing, who he's with, whether he's thinking about me like I'm thinking about him?

Back in my room, Cam stands shirtless at the window, looking down at the blue toy car—his brother's—that's been living on my windowsill since the night I realized I had no intention of giving back the rain jacket.

"Craziest thing," Cam says, picking up the car between two fingers. "My little brother has one exactly like this." He gives me a sly look over his shoulder that makes me warm with embarrassment and pleasure.

"No kidding?" I stand behind him and press my body against his. His skin smells like my sheets. "I hope it's brought him as much luck as this one brought me."

He puts the car back and turns around so I'm in his arms. "Luck, huh? Would that be the good kind or the bad kind?"

"You tell me."

"The good." He kisses me, twisting his fingers through my wet hair. "The great. Maybe even the marvelous."

"You're such a wordsmith in the morning," I tease, wrapping his arms tighter around me. I close my eyes, soaking in the warmth of his body and the pure comfort of this moment.

"You want some breakfast after that exertion?" he asks. "I make a killer egg sandwich."

"I wish, but I need to get dressed. I work at ten."

"Boo. Can we hang later?"

This feeling is bliss. "This afternoon, sure. My shift isn't long."

"I want to take you somewhere. And don't worry, it's not a museum."

"Thank god," I joke.

"Actually, it's even more boring, so there."

I laugh and kiss his cheek. But when I turn away to get dressed, he holds on to me.

"Hey, Lenni? I need you to tell me when I screw up like I did the other night. I don't want to go through all that wondering of what I did wrong again."

I look into his eyes. "You didn't do anything wrong. That was my own craziness."

"Either way, just tell me, okay? I want to make you happy. It's important to me."

"Okay."

He nods and releases me, then settles on the bed. I find some clothes, moving casually as though his words haven't just rocked me to the core. He wants to make me happy. I've never felt luckier in my life.

A sense of wonder moves through me when I think about how close I came to missing out on this. All because I chose to believe the worst about him. Because I chose to believe the worst about myself. I can't make that kind of mistake again.

cameron

JUST LIKE THAT, she's mine.

I've had my share of women before, girls every guy I knew had a boner for, girls who played hard to get like their lives depended on it.

But nothing compares to Lenni.

When I pull up outside her building, she's waiting for me on the steps, her legs looking a million miles long in a little pink sundress. I've never seen her in pink before, or in a dress. I wonder if she bought it just for me.

"Nice truck," she says as she gets in.

"Am I seeing things or are you wearing a dress?" I ask, silently thanking god for unseasonably warm, sunny days. Her dress checks all the boxes: short, tight, and low-cut. And if I know anything about boobs, she's not wearing a bra. She looks amazing. I don't even mind the button-down shirt she's wearing unbuttoned over top that looks like it came from the men's department. It just reminds me how many inches of her skin no one gets to see but me.

"I do own such things, you know. I just never wanted to

wear one until today." She gives me a smile that's ripe with meaning.

We take the highway south of town. She shoots me an occasional curious look but doesn't ask any questions, and the quiet between us is easy. Finally, when the only thing on either side of the highway is trees, I exit and we drive through the center of a tiny town until I turn down a long, tree-lined driveway.

Lenni reads the old wooden sign posted in the grass. "An orchard?"

I nod and park in front of the dusty brick house at the end of the driveway.

"Cool. I don't know if I'm dressed for harvesting fruit, but I'll try."

She's so cute. "No harvesting today. Come on, let's go."

Outside the car, I take her hand and head down a dirt road that leads into the trees. Lenni looks around, her gaze darting back to me like she's waiting for the punch line. "No one's here. What is this place?"

"Willis Orchard. Goes back a few generations on my dad's side."

"This is your family's orchard? That's pretty cool. I never pictured you with a future in apples."

"It's not operational anymore, not since my grandparents died. We just have a couple groundskeepers so it doesn't grow wild, but I love it here. It's kind of been my escape since I was a little kid."

"I would have thought this was paradise when I was a kid," she says, peering between the rows of apple trees. "We never even had a yard. Indoor kid here."

"Is that why you started writing?"

"I think so. The only real time I spent outside was at my grandparents' house. My mom was a mess, so my grandparents did most of the parenting. They had a tiny house and a tiny yard with this little garden patch of vegetables, and I remember spending hours helping my Nana, picking and canning vegetables."

"Man, my grandparents would have loved you. My work ethic was never quite up to their standards."

She smiles like she's trying not to. "I like to work, I guess. This is actually the first year since I was fourteen that I haven't had a job; a real job, I mean. The library gig is work-study."

"I don't know how you'd have time with all the hours you spend at the paper." I steer us onto a narrow grassy path between two rows of trees.

"Yeah, making editor is do-or-die this year."

"And what if you don't make it?"

She gives me a sharp look. "That's not really an option."

"But—"

"I need to help my family out. And money's the only way I can do it, because there's no way I'm moving back home after graduation."

I think about the guys from her high school who hurt her, two nameless, faceless nobodies who have become my enemies overnight. Anger bubbles up inside me. "Because of those guys?" I strain to keep my voice even. I need to figure out how to channel this anger into something productive because it's not going away, and it's not helping anyone. But since she told me what happened, not an hour has passed where some fantasy hasn't played through my head of making those dudes pay for what they did.

"Yeah. And there's just nothing there for me."

"Any high school friends?"

She looks over at the trees so I can't see her eyes. "They mostly . . . faded away after what happened."

"Shit friends," I mutter.

Lenni is quiet for a minute. "Some were. Others I just let go of. I didn't want anyone around."

"You ever think about going back for a visit? Just to check it out? Might not have the same power over you anymore."

"No," she says too quickly. When I don't say anything, she adds, "Maybe."

I squeeze her hand, wishing I knew the right thing to say. But she squeezes back and I think this is one of the reasons I'm crazy for this girl: I'm enough for her, even when I can't make it all better.

"So this was your childhood?" Lenni looks around in wonder. "It must feel good to be so deeply rooted in one place."

"Eh." I shrug. "There's such a thing as being too rooted. I'd like to call another part of the world home for a while."

"Wanderlust? Why didn't you go away for college then? I'm sure you had your pick of schools."

I want to tell her it's complicated, but the truth is that one word sums it up: Minnie. "I guess I felt guilty leaving my mom when she was in such a bad place." I probably sound like a total mama's boy.

"That's sweet."

"Anyway, playing football at Shafer is a dream come true for any kid who grows up in this town."

"Is it for you?" She watches me carefully.

"Of course."

"Really? Because we journalists have a knack for knowing what people aren't saying when they talk." Her eyes dance, lively and knowing. "And you told me in our interview that football wasn't your only dream."

Damn her for being so easy to talk to. "Okay, it wasn't my only dream as a kid. I also wanted to start a luxury hotel chain on Mars. I chose the path of least resistance."

"I'm not talking about your dreams as a kid. What about now?"

I roll my neck, trying to ease out the tension. I hate talking about myself like this. "I've thought about a backup career, maybe as a PR agent for athletes or a sports organization. I don't know, it's something I'm interested in."

The sun is low in the sky, and shafts of warm light cut between the trees as we walk. "I'm sure you'd be successful. You'd be successful at the Mars thing too, honestly." Her smile brims with an admiration I don't deserve. "You're the man with the golden touch."

"My GPA this semester would disagree with you."

"You're in some crazy honors courses. Madison's brilliant, and even she's struggling with that ethics class you're in."

Just the mention of ethics class gives me anxiety. "That one's killer. I just found out this midterm essay we have in a few weeks is fifty percent of our grade. Cue me repeating Freedom of Expression and Communication Ethics in spring semester."

"One essay won't tank your PR career."

"The PR thing is just an idea, anyway. I might do an internship next summer to check it out firsthand." I say this as casually as possible. "Just trying to be realistic. I can't bet my life on pro football."

I wait for the questions. Why wouldn't you make the pros? What would it take to get there? But there are no questions. Instead, she threads her fingers through mine and looks around, and something deep inside me settles down.

A breeze rolls through the trees and Lenni takes a deep whiff of the air. "This place is amazing. You're a real romantic, aren't you?" She raises an eyebrow like she's just uncovered a secret about me.

"Hey, no need for name-calling. That's a label I won't stand for."

"You are, Cameron Forrester. You so are."

"Fooled you. I just hoped this place would be boring enough you'd ask to go home and get in bed with me."

She laughs. "Nice try. I can tell this is your happy place."

"It was," I concede. "Of course, everywhere was my happy place if my parents weren't around."

"They fought a lot?"

"Hell no. Sometimes I wished they did. No, our house was always too quiet. My dad worked and traveled a lot, and when he was home, he and Mom didn't have a whole lot to say to each other. And my mom isn't a yeller. She's got that passive-aggressive candy-coated way of getting her feelings across like southern ladies do so well."

"Your mom sounds like an interesting woman."

"She's a fighter, all right."

Lenni slows her pace. "What did he do to her?" she asks quietly. My mind flashes to a memory of my mom standing at the bottom of the staircase in her silk pajama set, her face stained with tears. "He cheated. A lot. I think she suspected it for a while, but she didn't know for sure until after he died."

"Ouch."

"It wasn't just random one-nighters, either. He had relationships with other women. Bought them expensive gifts, took them on vacations, told them he loved them. That's what tore her apart."

Lenni doesn't look at me with pity the way most people would right now. She just holds on to my hand and looks ahead. "Seeing your mother hurting is just . . . there are no words."

I nod. Bingo. "What gets me the most is that he loved her like crazy, and he still did that to her. I never understood why we weren't enough for him." I shake my head. "If you're that screwed up, you don't deserve love."

"People mess up. Sometimes people who have it all just want more."

She's careful not to look at me. That's when I realize she's not talking about my dad anymore. It kills me to think Lenni worries I'd do something like that to her, but how do I promise her anything when I don't know where we're headed? Does she want to be my girlfriend? Are we just for now, or does she want to make this go the distance as much as I do?

Fuck it. I don't need labels. I need her.

I stop and pull her close, but she's grown shy and barely looks me in the eye. "Lenni." I tilt her head up until she meets my eye. "I'm not a stereotype, and I'm not going to let myself become one. I won't hurt you."

Her gaze is unrelenting as my words settle over both of us. I hear them again in my head and a brief flare of doubt hits me: Can I be sure I'll never let her down?

Then I think of Lenni hurting the way my mom's been hurt, knowing Mom will never be the same, and the doubt disappears. I won't be that kind of man.

"Say it again," Lenni whispers.

"I won't hurt you."

She takes a deep, shuddering breath and I realize she's been needing to hear this. "I don't really know how to do this, Cameron."

"Do what?"

"Be with someone. Trust someone. All of it." She exhales. "But I have faith in you."

I try not to let her see it, but her words hit me. Hard. I can't screw this up.

She reaches for me and gives me a slow, experimental kiss. Whatever my lips tell her, she must like it because she kisses me with a sudden hunger. Her hand finds mine and she pulls me with her until she's backed up against the wide trunk of a tree.

"Mmm." I take in the sweet taste of her mouth. "I like when you get pushy."

"Oh?" She looks up at me from under her eyelashes. "What else do you like?" She slides off her button-down, slowly wiggling her shoulders to ease it off her body and drawing my eyes directly to her tits. My body ignites like a match.

"These," I say, running my thumb over her soft lips.

She tips her head back and kisses me. The taste of her ratchets every muscle inside me tighter. My hands move down her neck to cup her breasts.

"These," I say against her lips.

Her nipples stiffen under my thumbs, making my cock strain against my jeans. I groan and Lenni lets out a soft laugh. She hooks her fingers under the straps of her dress, and I swallow hard, my eyes trained on her body when she tugs them down to reveal her naked breasts.

"Fuck," I mutter.

Out here, totally exposed, her body is even sexier. Hunger gnaws at me as I take in the sight of her taut, pink nipples and the milky skin of her full breasts. I dip my head, ready to take her perfect tits in my mouth, when something occurs to me. I mumble a few cuss words. "I don't have a condom."

But she just shakes her head and slowly slides to her knees. "I had something else in mind."

This girl fucking rocks.

I watch her push down my jeans and boxers. When my cock springs free, she hums appreciatively and takes me in her hand. I take a deep, ragged breath at the sight of her fingers wrapped around my shaft.

She looks up at me. "No one's working here today, right?"

"Does it really matter?"

Doubt flashes in her eyes and is quickly replaced with a smile. "Not to me."

But when I shift my hips toward her, I see her hesitation. "No one's here, I promise."

"It's not that." She presses her lips together. "I'm just . . . I haven't done this in a long time."

I look at her in surprise. "Oh. Well, we don't have to do it here." It takes all the strength I have, but I ease away from her and reach for my jeans. "Or at all if you're not into it. It's okay."

She tugs on my jeans before I can pull them up. "No, I want to. I really want to. I'm just not all that skilled."

"Just don't draw blood and I swear you can't go wrong."

She laughs a little nervously, but she nods and her attention returns to my cock.

When she takes me in her mouth, her heat seeps into every muscle in my body. I groan and shift closer. She teases me at first, wetting my entire length with her tongue, stopping here and there to bathe my cock head with attention. I wonder dimly if I should stop her, make sure she really wants to do this.

But then she lets out this low, throaty hum that sets my nerves on fire and I think, stop her? Seriously? I'm powerless. My whole world consists of Lenni's mouth on my cock. I want it to go on forever.

She's tentative at first, alternating between sucking hard and shallow on my head and taking my length as far into her mouth as she can. No, it doesn't feel like she's done this a hundred times and yes, she's driving me a little crazy, bringing me to the brink and easing me back probably without meaning to, but I love it. I vow to be the last guy she ever makes this crazy. It's not the picture-perfect porn blow job and that makes it even better. Because she's not doing it for the bragging rights or because she owes me; she's doing it because she wants to.

I close my eyes and stroke a hand down her cheek, feeling her soft skin move around my cock. "You're so good, honey," I hear myself mutter. I reach for the tree to steady myself.

There's no sound except the rhythm of my shallow breathing and the luscious, wet sounds of her mouth. That and the occasional soft sigh she lets out that must be designed solely to make me lose my mind.

I look down to watch my cock disappear between her perfect lips. Her gaze flicks up to meet mine, deep and intense, and it's the most beautiful sight I've ever seen. My body strains. I'm overwhelmed with sudden need—words swim inside my head, all the things I feel for her that I haven't found the nerve to say. But my body's needs win out against my heart's. I swallow back the words and give myself over to pure sensation. Pure fucking amazing sensation.

I think I say her name a couple times, but it might be in my head. She wraps her hand around the base of my cock and takes me faster. Everything is tight and wet. Perfection. I can't stop myself from thrusting into her mouth, but she takes it like she wants more. And then I'm gone, a billion stars exploding behind my eyes as I release into her. She takes everything I have to give. And when the stars clear, all I see is Lenni.

I lean my head down and close my eyes. I'm sure it looks like I'm just recovering from the best head of my life—which I am—but it's more than that. It's the feelings rushing me.

I think I'm addicted to her. I know I'm in too deep. And I'm afraid because I just realized this is what it's like to need someone.

lenni

THE LAST FEW weeks have been a heady blur of Cam's lips, his scent, and the feel of his arms around me. We spend almost every night together, usually at my place but sometimes at his. The occasional uncomfortable interaction with Reeve comes with the territory; I can feel how much he doesn't want me around, but he keeps his mouth shut. Cam and I cook cheap meals in my apartment, sit together in class and hold hands around campus. If I wasn't me, I'd hate us.

Tuesday evenings are the only ones we always spend apart because it's pizza and *Pretty Little Liars* night for me and Jade. But with winter creeping closer and the sun setting early, Cam likes to walk me home on these nights, coming by the newsroom on his way back from practice. I pretend to find this annoying even though I secretly relish his little shows of chivalry.

Tonight he's still in his workout clothes when he shows up, his skin covered by a thin sheen of sweat that makes me swallow hard. I still can't quite believe that when he smiles that wide smile, he's smiling only at me. Will it ever feel real? I kind of hope not.

"Sorry," he says, wrapping me in a hug. "We ran late in the weight room, so I skipped the shower. Didn't want to make you wait."

"Don't apologize." I breathe him in, salt and muscle and hard work, and run my hands up the firm muscles of his back.

"Come on, Handsy, better get you home. Jade's gonna have my ass if there's not still steam coming off the pizza when you walk in."

Recently, Cam has been concerned with winning Jade's approval. Again, the chivalry aspect is cute, but I'm pretty sure his mission has less to do with me and more to do with the fact that he can't fathom a woman not falling head over heels in love with him. "By the way, has she started calling me by my name yet?"

"Sorry, Number Eleven, you're still a jersey number to Jade. But don't I say your name enough for both of us?" I gaze up at him to see if he catches my drift.

His smile is liquid. "Say my name? More like moan."

I can't argue.

When he kisses me outside my door, I let my lips stray to his jaw and neck, the salty taste of his sweat drawing me in.

"Girl, don't start something you can't finish."

"Sorry," I say, not sorry at all.

Cam takes my hand and lays it on his crotch. Crude move but he makes it so damn sexy. "You sure I can't come in? All I need is five minutes."

"If Jade sees you cross that threshold on pizza night, you can say goodbye to your dick."

He glances appreciatively at my tight sweater. "But look at you, baby. Even Jade couldn't blame me." He skims his hands over my waist, his eyes dark with desire. That look is the reason I've added fitted clothing back into my wardrobe rotation.

For the first time ever, I wish pizza night didn't exist. No one has ever wanted me like Cam does, or made me feel half as sexy. Maybe this is how sex addicts start out, on the receiving end of Cam Forrester's lips.

But Jade has never ditched me for a boy, and I won't do it to her. "Save it for later, Forrester. You can come over after Sam picks up Jade tonight." I unlock the apartment before I can change my mind and close the door on him, watching him watch me until the very last second.

Lord help me if he ever loses interest.

Inside, the lights are off, and there's no inviting smell of hot pizza. Jade's door is ajar, her room dark. I reach for my phone, expecting to find a text from her saying something came up, but I have no new messages.

I scan my memory—did she tell me she'd be late tonight? No, I'm sure she didn't. And there's no way she forgot; Tuesday nights are written in stone. Something is wrong.

I flick on the lights. Jade's purse and backpack are by the front door like always. My heart thumps as I approach her bedroom door. Now I wish I'd invited Cam inside.

"Jade?"

No answer.

I push her door open all the way. From the dim kitchen light, I can see her lying on her bed, her back to me.

"Jade?" I say again.

Moving with strange slowness, she rolls over and sits up, her face alarmingly puffy and wet with tears. "Lenni." Her voice is so anguished that I run to her side.

"What is it, sweetie? What happened?!"

Her face crumples as she starts to cry. *Oh, god, someone's dead.* Her mom? *My* mom? "Jade, tell me! What the hell happened?"

She takes a long, shuddering breath. "Sam broke up with me." Then she starts bawling.

This is more shocking than anything she could have told me —and a massive relief compared to what I was imagining. But I don't tell her that. I sit on the bed and pull her close to me and hold her until she's ready to speak.

"He told me he's tired of feeling like a second-class citizen when he's with me," Jade says when her sobs subside, her voice bitter and hoarse. "Like, what the fuck does that even mean?"

I shake my head.

"And of course you know Sam, he couldn't just tell me to fuck off like a normal guy. He has to be all high minded about it, saying we both deserve time to think about what we want out of a relationship." She sniffs. "I'd respect him more if he just told me he wants to fuck other girls and that he'll let me know if I ever drift back into his jerk-off fantasies."

"I doubt that's what it is," I say gently.

But she's not listening. "He grows a little facial hair, and suddenly all twelve girls in his engineering program are throwing themselves at him. I never thought he'd be the guy who follows his dick through life, but here we are. And you know what? He won't even talk to me. He asked for a fucking month without contact. And I still don't know what I did wrong."

Jade dissolves into tears again. I stroke her hair and think about what a shitty friend I am because instead of hating Sam, I just keep wondering, what *did* she do wrong?

Sam worshipped her. Healthy or not, it was the kind of one-in-a-million love I know I'll never have because, well, it's one in a million. Sam always used to say that love at first sight was the first and last New Agey bullshit he'd ever believe in because he fell in love with Jade the instant he saw her face.

Eventually we get off Jade's bed and I order pizza. Jade cries. We watch two episodes of *Pretty Little Liars*. Jade cries again. I put her to bed and get in beside her and rub her back until I think she's asleep. I send Cam a quick text to tell him not to come over.

I'm almost asleep when Jade speaks, her voice thick. "Do you know why he did it?"

I blink away sleep. "Sam? Why he ended it? No, of course not."

"Because if you do, you can tell me. If you know what I did wrong, you have to tell me."

"I don't know why, sweetie, but I know you didn't do anything wrong."

Jade makes a snuffling sound. "I can't do this for a month."

"Don't worry. We'll find out."

I DECIDE to ambush Sam at his most vulnerable: leaving his Thermodynamics class. I've heard him lament that it's the only class where he's not among the top three students, and now I'll use his weakness against him. As Jade's best friend, it's only natural.

I have forty-five minutes to kill after my own class ends so I do a mini lifting session at the gym, smiling to myself. It feels so good to have a plan. I'm banking on finding Sam a shell of a man, even more broken than poor Jade is.

But when he steps outside the engineering building, he's actually . . . glowing? Goddammit. And he has a cute girl smiling at his side. My stomach drops.

"Sam!" I call, moving quickly to meet him.

He winces visibly, recognizing my voice before he sees me. I can't help but smile. I adore Sam, but after the way he hurt Jade, his discomfort spells my joy.

"Hi, Lenni," he says tightly as I step onto the path in front of him.

"Can I talk to you?"

His shoulders slouch, like he'd actually convinced himself this moment wasn't coming all along. Foolish boy, thinking his follies might slip past without consequence. He turns to the girl next to him. "Catch up with you tomorrow?"

She nods and gives him a little smile. I feel her curious stare as she moves past me, but I pretend she doesn't exist. I take her place next to Sam and we walk.

"I know what you're going to say, Lenni," he starts.

"No, you don't."

"I broke up with her because she thinks she's too good for me."

I stare at him. "What? That's crazy. She loves you, Sam. You don't see that?"

"I know she loves me, but it's true," he says with a sad sense of certainty. "Since our first date, I knew what everyone saw when they looked at us. A nerdy guy with a hot-ass girl a thousand times out of his league. I just didn't realize Jade saw it too."

"So you broke up with her because she's better looking than you?" But I only say this to stall for time. I know exactly what he's saying, and I've got a bad feeling that I can't honestly tell him he's wrong. Jade's fiery self-assuredness is magnetic, but sometimes even she can't see past it.

"You saw it." Sam gives me an impatient look. "In the beginning, she went wild for the flowers and the gifts and carefully planned dates. By the end, I had to do those things just to gain her approval. It was the minimum payment to be able to call her my girlfriend."

"So she took you for granted. It happens in serious relationships," I say as though I have any idea what I'm talking about. "That doesn't mean she thinks she's too good for you."

"You're telling me she doesn't know she could have her pick of guys?"

"She picked you, Sam."

He scowls and buries his hands in his pockets.

"Some people would die for what you and Jade have. Real love doesn't just get handed out like candy to everybody." Finally, a subject I specialize in.

He stops and faces me. "Would you take that, Lenni? If you were in love with some guy and no matter how much you did for him, you went to sleep every night worrying you'd wake up and he'd tell you that you aren't enough anymore?"

Some guy? No, I wouldn't take it. For Cam? Maybe I would. "I've never been in love, so how would I know?" I keep walking.

"I hope you wouldn't."

I steer the conversation back where it belongs. "Okay, so Jade believes in herself. At times a little too much, maybe," I admit. "But I know she never meant to make you feel like you didn't deserve her."

"Maybe not, but that's why I asked for time away from her. I need to sort it out on my own."

"Did you even tell her what you're telling me? Because she seems completely lost."

"I tried to. Maybe I—" Sam shakes his head, frustrated. "Maybe in the heat of the moment, I wasn't clear enough."

"Well, she's crushed. At least talk to her so she understands. Please?"

He doesn't agree, but I know the grumpy look on his face well enough to know he'll do it. Sam is one of those guys you can just tell grew up in a house full of women who got their way. When he sees my smile, he says, "Don't even think of thanking me. Jade's going to throw a fit, and you're the one who has to live with her."

I don't thank him, but I do give him a hug. "Glad we can still conspire behind Jade's back like old times."

Sam gives me a look like he doesn't like the sound of this.

"Kidding, Sam. I mean I'm glad we can still talk, like friends." He gives me a sober nod and I turn to go.

"Hold on, Lenni." When I stop, he closes the space between us and swallows. "It's good to hear you say that."

"That we're still friends?"

He nods. "Because there's something that I've been wanting to tell you. I just didn't know—what with me and Jade—if it was appropriate."

I lean away from him slightly. "Well, if it includes graphic details about your nights as a newly single—"

"It's not like that." He doesn't even crack a smile.

"Okay." My mind spins with uncomfortable possibilities. "Spill."

He hesitates, looking out across campus and then back at me. "First of all, Jade has never told me any personal details of your past, Lenni." He fiddles with the watch on his wrist and his gaze seems to have shifted from my eyes to somewhere just beyond them. "Only that, well, you had an unfortunate experience in high school . . . and while I don't pretend to know how that must feel, I couldn't help but wonder—well, given your position on the student paper and your aspirations for making editor . . ."

I think I should feel embarrassed, but watching the tips of Sam's ears turn bright pink as he sinks in his own awkwardness, I only feel sorry for him. "Sam, you're fine," I interrupt. "Just get to the point."

"Right. Well, I've heard rumors about a nude photo of a female student circulating around campus and apparently it started with the football team. An unauthorized photo, taken without her consent."

Dark memories claw at me, but I force them down. This isn't about me. "Who'd you hear this from?"

"Just a kid from my study group. He knows a guy who knows a guy . . . that sort of thing. He says it's easy to trace back to the football team."

"Have you seen the photo?"

Sam blanches. "I didn't ask for it," he says carefully. "I deleted it from my phone as soon as I saw it."

"And you think—" I swallow hard. "You think Cam might be involved?"

"Cam?" He cocks his head. "No, that's not what I was implying. I thought as a journalist you might have a duty to take it to your editor and see if the story might have some teeth."

"Oh." Relief washes over me. "Yeah, okay. Maybe I'll look into it."

"It's probably nothing, but it's been bothering me. When I heard, I couldn't help but think of you."

Immediately, I think, *With pity?* But I let it go. "Thanks for talking." For Jade's sake, I wish I had it in me to be cold to Sam, but I just don't. It's then I realize that aside from my grandpa, he's been the only trustworthy man in my life this past year, or ever. That's right, my friend's ex-boyfriend is my only male role model born within the last sixty years. I knew my life was sad, but damn.

"I'm not going to be able to make it all better, you know," he warns.

"Just talk to her."

He nods and walks away while my brain starts working overtime. If he won't make it all better for Jade, then I guess it's my job.

cameron

I WAKE with a vague sense of dread in my stomach.

The room isn't light yet, and I fight the crushing urge to hit snooze on my alarm, instead silencing it and sitting up before I can sink back into oblivion. I need to get in an hour in the weight room before my eight a.m. class. I tug on the blinds behind the bed to let in the sunshine that's just barely illuminating the sky outside. Pale light spills onto my desk cluttered with books, papers, and electronics, and I remember what that sick sense of anxiety is all about: I don't have a solid grip on a single thing in my life.

I pull on shorts and a sweatshirt, trying to ignore the unfinished internship applications on my desk that had me up until three a.m. Then I move onto trying to ignore the fact that I finally submitted my midterm essay for my ethics class last night and it's making me want to shit a brick. I shouldn't think about that right now. I shouldn't think about how I have zero sense of where my life will be after college or in a year, or hell, even a couple months from now. I should silence the barrage of questions. Is football my future? Or will I end up a nobody? Just some guy who might as well be named "wasted opportunity" because that's what everyone sees when they look at me. And the biggest question of all: Will Lenni be at my side?

Lenni.

That's the one I can't stop thinking about, the one I don't ever want to stop thinking about. Just the sound of her name in my head makes everything feel okay. All the shit that's weighing me down feels small and surmountable when I think of her and the way she moves through life.

I brush my teeth and check Reeve's room, but his bed is empty. Either he spent the night with a girl or he's already in the weight room, probably both. Grateful for the solitude, I grab a frozen smoothie and decide on walking to campus instead of driving for the extra thinking time.

Ever since that day in the orchard when I confessed to thinking about a backup career, I've wanted to tell Lenni I'm not just thinking about it, I'm planning for it. She'd know what to say. But I don't want to drag that mess into the world Lenni and I have created. In there it's sex and the smell of her skin and the feeling of being the luckiest dude on the planet. It's the one place that feels insulated from worry. Maybe that's why I haven't told her the real story of Liam and Serena either. Why bring that ugliness into something so perfect?

Of course that's not the only reason I haven't told Lenni my doubts about my future; the future is the one topic we carefully avoid, and I'm starting to wonder if that's because she doesn't see one for us. That's the uncertainty that's really eating at me.

If I knew she felt what I do, everything else would fall into place. But things are still new between us. Am I risking scaring off a girl who doesn't even do relationships by asking her where we're headed? Definitely.

Too bad I can't keep it in much longer.

THE NEXT NIGHT, I'm in front of the bathroom mirror trying to make my hair less of a mess. I'm surprising Lenni with dinner at this chic Vietnamese restaurant that opened downtown last week by some chef who won a cooking show, because she once told me she loves celebrity-chef restaurants. And if it sounds like I have a plan, I don't. But she needs to know what I feel for her. And somewhere along the way, I'm going to find the words for it.

The door's closed, but Reeve barges in anyway. "Hey, beautiful. What the hell are you doing in here for the last twenty minutes?"

"Date night. Where's that pomade stuff you stole from me?"

"Oh, yeah? With who?" he asks, reaching under his sink. When he hands me the pomade, I shoot him a look. Reeve can be a real passive-aggressive tool sometimes. He shrugs. "Just checking. I keep expecting one of these days you'll come to your senses and figure it out."

"Figure out what?"

"That she's not the girl for you."

I turn around to face him. "All right, dude, this is so old. What's your problem with her?"

Reeve checks himself out in the mirror. "Told you before. Not your type."

"That's not all it is."

He wets his hand and smooths down one side of his hair, not looking at me.

"I like her. And she's not going anywhere."

"Cool. And?"

"And so you need to tell me what's really going on, asshole."

His gaze swings over to me. He looks like a sulky little kid.

"Come on. I've dated girls you didn't like before, but you managed to act halfway decent around them. Remember Bailey?" Bailey was my girlfriend for a few months in high school, and the girl was even more attention hungry than Reeve. He couldn't stand the competition.

"Yeah, she sucked, but at least she was nice to me."

I give a short laugh. "That's it? Lenni's not nice to you? God, you are a delicate little flower, aren't you? She doesn't even talk to you."

"Right, Cam," he snaps, turning to me. "She hates me!"

I stare at him. Where's this coming from? "Okay, she doesn't exactly hate you. I mean, you were a total dick to her, and I'm still waiting to hear you apologize, but that doesn't mean—"

"I'm going to apologize to her, Cam. Let me do it in my own time."

"I am. If you were doing it in my time, you'd have said sorry before she left your bedroom." I take a breath, trying to cool the heat rising in my head. I hate this subject. "Anyway, so what if she's not your number one fan? You two don't have to be buddies."

He looks away, scowling at the window instead.

I should let it go—he can act like a toddler if he wants to— but I can't. Reeve has had my back on everything, big or small, since our first season together as scrawny kids. He doesn't have to like Lenni, but he does have to accept her.

"I like her, Reeve. You know that. More than I've liked anyone in a long time."

His expression doesn't change. "Yeah." He's still giving the window the stink eye.

"So tell me why you refuse to be on my side for the first time in my life."

He finally looks at me. "I don't like her talking shit about me."

With that, it all clicks into place. "You think she's going to turn me against you? Seriously?" I throw a soft punch at his shoulder. "Like I don't already know what a massive asshole you are? We've lived together since eighth grade. Believe me, dude, I had it figured out by day two."

Reeve gives a halfhearted smile. "Yeah, okay."

I turn back to the mirror and unscrew the lid of the pomade, but Reeve's still wearing an expression that reminds me of Liam after Serena tells him no more cookies. "I'm not going anywhere," I say, keeping my eyes carefully off his face. I feel his gaze on me for a second, then he nods. "So quit being an asshole around my girl and help me with my hair. It looks like crap."

Reeve appears behind me in the mirror, his self-assured smile back in place. "Relax, man, you look slick. The only reason you're doubting yourself is you're standing next to me. Your outfit, on the other hand, is shit."

"What do you mean?"

"That tie? Christ, is that from our old school uniform? You look like you're getting ready to knock on doors and spread the gospel."

"I'm taking her to a nice dinner."

"Then dress like a man, not a third grader on Easter Sunday. Hold on." He heads for his room and comes back a minute later with a slim silver tie.

"Silver? God, you're tacky."

"Trust me."

He watches impatiently as I swap out my tie for his, then steps in to adjust my work. "There. Now you look slick."

We both step back to check the final product. I nod. He's right, I do look pretty damn good.

"Thank me later when you're enjoying a nice, sloppy blow job," he tells me.

"Shut the fuck up."

We both laugh.

lenni

I SHOULD BE AT HOME RIGHT NOW. Cam's taking me somewhere nice for dinner tonight, and a novice like myself needs time to figure out an outfit, hair, and makeup without looking like a child playing dress-up. But the story Sam told me is haunting me like a ghost—I can't stop thinking about her, this girl I don't even know—so instead I'm sitting in the newsroom waiting for Darren, who's knee-deep in conversation with one of the sportswriters.

I wonder if the girl in the photo even knows her picture was taken. Would she want her story to go public? I didn't. I wanted to die. Not that anyone wrote about it in the local paper, but in my desperate little town, gossip hits a lot harder than some article on page four of The Daily News.

I felt weak, though, not like one of those women who stands up and puts her face on a scandal, knowing her strength might spare other women from future trauma. Maybe this girl in the photo will do what I couldn't.

And isn't it my obligation to at least find out if there's any substance to this story? If nothing else, I have an obligation to expose whatever dickhead football player thought it was okay to humiliate a sleeping girl to boost his shaky grasp on his own masculinity. To expose him and every other guy who looked at that picture and thought nothing of it beyond the sick idea that it's his right as a man to treat her humiliation as his entertainment because women don't exist beyond three narrow categories: family, fuckable, and useless.

I unclench my jaw—I have to try twice before the pain eases—and glance up at Darren. He and the other writer are now rambling about some pro football trade and they still haven't acknowledged me. Bet if I'd worn a push-up bra and a tight top, I would've gotten greetings before the door closed behind me.

I stand up. "Darren?" It sounds more like a bark than a question. "Can we talk? At your desk?"

I see him exchange a look with the sportswriter, but he falls into step behind me as I head for his desk in the far corner of the room.

"Everything going okay?" he asks once we're out of earshot.

"I just wanted to mention a tip I heard."

He nods. "Shoot."

Suddenly, my confidence wanes. It's really just gossip and speculation I'm working with here. But Darren is looking at me expectantly, and I think he might just be impressed by my initiative. "Someone I know was sent a nude photo of a female student that was supposedly taken without her permission. This source says it's easily traced back to the football team."

Darren holds up a hand. "Heard that one before. Someone emailed us anonymously with the same tip."

I feel a sudden sense of loss. I've been scooped before I've written a single word? "So?" I demand. "Do you have a writer on it yet?"

"This is a tricky one. I don't know that we'll ever have a writer on it."

"Why not? This could be huge."

"Yeah, with huge legal ramifications, Lenni."

"You're not going to touch it because there might be some legal issues involved? That kind of fear is exactly why guys continue to get away with behavior like this while the victims just suffer in silence."

"All right, Lenni, okay, okay. I never said we're not touching it, but we're not diving in headfirst, either. I don't know about you, but bringing down Shafer's athletics department isn't on my list of editorial goals this year."

I take a breath and remind myself that if I ever hope to make editor, I better avoid insulting Darren's journalistic integrity. "No, I just think this isn't the sort of tip that can be ignored."

"Agreed."

"So put me on it."

"Sorry?"

"Put me on the story."

"There is no story. We don't have a single fact to go on yet."

"Right. Let me dig up a few facts and we can go from there."

Darren smirks. "Oh, no way."

"Why not?"

"First of all, you're not an investigative journalist."

"And second?"

"Ever heard of conflict of interest?"

"What's that have to do with me?" I ask, knowing exactly what it has to do with me.

"A story about the football team from the girlfriend of a captain? Not gonna fly."

His words hit me with a mix of thrill and uncertainty. The word "girlfriend" implies a sort of ownership that I'm not sure I'm entitled to, one that's been heavy on my mind lately.

Darren laughs and I realize I'm blushing. And smiling. "You thought I didn't know, eh? Football players at Shafer can't blow their noses without the whole school knowing about it. And," he adds, standing up straighter, "as sports editor, you better believe I hear everything that goes on in that world."

Then maybe he can tell me whether Cam and I have a real future together.

"Anyway," I say pointedly, "this isn't about Cameron or even the team. It's individual players' off-the-field behavior. Even if I don't write the story, at least let me help gather information."

"I'll say it again, it's not a story yet. If you have a reliable source, send them my way. But don't go digging around like you're some PI." He crosses his arms. "I mean it, if that photo exists, you don't want any connection to it."

"I get it."

I walk back to my desk as it dawns on me that the shortest path from me to the truth about this supposed photo isn't Sam, it's Cam.

Can I really ask him if he knows anything about the photo? More importantly, can I really expect the truth? It's a dangerous question to bring into our relationship when I hardly know where we stand.

Jade drops me at Cam's house just a few minutes late—with her help, I cut my prep time down to a respectable forty-five minutes—but Cam is already outside when we pull up, just grabbing a charger out of his car by the looks of it.

I thought I knew what handsome was until I see Cam Forrester in a shirt and tie. His hair falls in effortless waves and his crisp white shirt highlights his golden skin and the impressive build of his upper body. He could sell those slim-cut pants for a million dollars, they look that good on him. Even Jade's jaw falls open. "Damn!" She turns to me. "Get it, girl."

But when I get out of the car, it's Cam's turn to stare. My cheeks flush hot with pleasure and embarrassment. I'm not the girl who gets those kinds of looks, and I don't know if I love it or hate it.

"You look stunning," Cam says. "I mean . . . wow."

I blush harder. "Thanks." I reach up to kiss him because I'm much better with kisses than compliments.

"Come upstairs, I need to charge my phone for a few minutes before we go."

We pass Reeve on the stairs, who nods at me. "Hey," he says. I wait a beat but there's no nastiness to the greeting, no steely look to accompany it. It's the first time he's spoken to me like he doesn't hate the sight of me with his best friend.

I give him a nod in response.

"How's the Jadester?" Cam asks when we reach his bedroom.

"Hanging on by a thread. Sam finally called, but he refuses to meet up with her to talk things over."

"So he's even smarter than I thought."

"Why?"

He plugs his phone in and gives me an impish smile. "That's the danger zone. Meeting up to talk things over always leads to sex, and then she's emotional and things are even messier than they were before."

"Sounds like you speak from experience." I keep my tone light, but the idea of him having that experience with another girl makes me burn.

"Anyway, Jade will pull herself together," he says, not taking the bait. "Sounds like the relationship ran its course."

"That's exactly what you said about you and your ex."

"Because that's what happens. It's natural."

And this is the guy I chose for my first relationship? "Not always," I say, wishing I didn't sound as hopeful as I feel.

He looks up and his face softens. "No, not always." He walks over and lays a silky kiss on my lips. His fingers find the back of my neck and pull me closer, deepening the kiss. And as much as I want to fall under the intoxicating spell of his touch, I don't let myself. He feels my resistance and stops to look at me, his hand still warming my skin. "We're not Sam and Jade," he says softly.

The moment suddenly feels huge, precipitous. I need to know what he feels—not in kisses and touches, in words. Are we for real, something solid enough to grasp onto every time something threatens to break us apart? Or could this end even faster than it began?

My pulse pounds in my throat. "Then what are we?"

He looks down at me and bites his lip. Is he nervous? "You're my girl, Lenni. My only girl. And you—" But he breaks away, his face contorting in frustration. "Okay, the reason I planned this night was to have this exact conversation. I just hoped I might have a drink or two in me so I could come off a little smoother."

I hold on to him until he meets my eyes again. "You don't have to be smooth."

He nods and tries again. "I don't know what to call what we have—what we've had since the first time I looked at you—because I've never felt anything like it before. But I know I don't want it to end." He exhales. "You and me, and that's it. That's all I want. I just hope you want it too."

Everything inside me slackens, relief weakening me. "I do, Cameron. It's all I want." I bury my face in his shoulder and try to breathe like a normal person instead of someone who just got the best news of her life. "Just you." Being alive has never felt this good.

"I guess I ruined the surprise, didn't I?"

I laugh shakily but hold tighter to him, soaking him in. "Sorry. I'm getting makeup on your white shirt".

He kisses me. "Screw the shirt." His hands slide down my body, waking up a million nerve endings that haven't felt his touch in too long. His cock presses hard against my lower belly.

He skims his hands back up my body, tracing my curves. His eyes follow his fingers with a hazy look of lust. Just like that, I'm buzzing with need.

"What about dinner?" I whisper, though I'm already loosening his tie. I unbutton his shirt slowly, top to bottom, fighting the urge to rip it straight off.

"Screw dinner," he growls.

The sight of his half-naked torso makes my breath come faster. I have to work to stop my fingers from shaking as I undo his buttons. Finally done, I run my palms up his smooth skin, watching his chest rise and fall.

"Are you sure? You might never get a table again if you're a no-show."

His answer is a searing kiss that blots out the rest of the world. Strong arms wrap around my waist and my thighs as he lifts me. He sucks my bottom lip into his mouth, nipping at me with his teeth. I hear myself moan.

I'm lowered onto the edge of the bed. Cam stands over me, steps out of his pants and boxers and shrugs the shirt off his shoulders. He leans over me and goose bumps race across my skin as the heat of his body spreads through mine. He kisses the sensitive skin on my throat.

"I don't want to be anywhere but here," he whispers. "With you."

His teeth close around my earlobe, sending parallel streaks of electricity shooting through me. My fingers curl into the skin of his back. His hands aren't gentle when they yank my dress up to my waist or pull my panties down to my knees. The roughness of his touch makes me desperate with desire.

"How do you want it?" he asks, his voice muffled against my skin.

"Any way you want." I don't care how I get it as long as I get it.

"No." He leans back to look at me, but his fingers slide between my legs and move slowly in and out of me, a soft, stroking tease. "Tell me how you want me to fuck you. Tell me exactly what you want."

I've never told a man what I wanted. Maybe I've never even known myself, but his words are electric. My imagination ignites. I know what I want. I want to spread my legs for him. I want him to take me fast and hard. And I want to watch it happen. I glance down at the mirror that hangs on the wall opposite the foot of his bed. "I want you to fuck me from behind."

I don't know who this girl is, the one who demands sex without a hint of self-consciousness, but apparently Cam likes her. He blinks, his eyelids suddenly heavy, and he reaches down to deliver a single stroke to his rigid cock, like he just can't resist.

I move and he follows like my shadow. I crawl to the end of the bed and position myself on all fours in front of the mirror. Cam is behind me on his knees. I spread my legs an inch wider for him and I watch his face transform in the mirror as he stares down at my body, his mouth falling half-open. The thrill of power rips through me. I can't believe I can do that to him.

"Lenni," he says gruffly, his gaze still heavy on my body.

I give my hips a little wiggle. "Come on," I tell him in the mirror. "Let's go."

He swallows and drags his eyes away to swipe a condom from his bedside table. His gaze meets mine in the reflection as he tears open the package with his teeth. My thighs tremble. He rolls the condom onto his waiting cock and centers himself between my legs.

His eyes blaze as they take in the most intimate parts of my body. With one hand steadied on my lower back, he guides himself to my entrance. His cock parts me and my hips jerk in response, then he withdraws. He licks his lips. The sight makes me ache to touch him, but I wait for him. He shifts his hips so I can just feel the heat of him against my damp skin. Then his strong hands close around my waist and he pushes himself roughly inside me.

The sharp pleasure of it makes me gasp. My head falls back as he pumps inside me, deep, steady thrusts that feel just barely within his control. No one's playing now. He brushes my hair aside and I arch my back to lift my ass higher for him. Hunger flares in his eyes. "Fuck, baby," he says breathlessly. "You are so sexy."

His hands circle over the rounds of my ass, then squeeze my flesh until I'm sure he'll leave bruises.

"Harder, Cameron," I command.

His gaze lifts to meet mine in the mirror. It takes all my strength not to squeeze my eyes shut and just let the pleasure take over, but I can't look away from him. I watch the tremble in his chin as he fucks me and the flex of his strained muscles. My breasts move in time with his thrusts. I reach down to cup one and Cam makes a strangled noise in his throat. He's mine.

I give myself over to the fury of desire, watching him through half-lidded eyes. In a faraway time, a long-ago Lenni, I'd be embarrassed at the way I'm spread out before him and all the flaws he could find on me. But I can't be. Under that lustful, animal stare on his face, I can't feel anything but how much I want this.

I shift back so he'll take me deeper. His thrusts grow frenzied. His hand slips between my thighs and finds my clit, stroking with unapologetic, single-minded purpose. My muscles are turning to liquid, barely able to support me.

"Cameron," I hear myself say, begging him for I don't know what. To make it stop? To make it last forever?

His face crumples, his expression needy. "I'm never going to forget the way you look right now." His voice is dark and jagged. It cuts all the way to my core.

I close my eyes and let myself fall. I'm on fire from the inside out, completely engulfed, blind with pleasure. I'm vaguely aware of the harsh sounds he makes and the weight of his body on mine as he comes. The steamy image of him behind me, all the power in his body concentrated on me, burns into my brain layer by layer. Nothing will ever top this feeling.

AFTER, I lay there in his bed, blissed out beyond any normal measure of contentedness. I feel like I'm high. His body, his touch, the fact that he belongs to me and no one else; it doesn't seem real. Surely a girl has to reach godlike status before she deserves something like this. I must have been sainted in a former life.

Coming back to life beside me, Cam turns and plants a kiss on my shoulder. "You make a really good boss."

I smile instead of being embarrassed. I do make a good boss.

"You want to do something tomorrow after practice? I should be done a little earlier."

"I forgot to tell you, my editor put me on a last-minute assignment so I have to go watch a dance show on campus tomorrow evening. Sorry. I invited Jade because I assumed you'd hate it."

"Thank Jade for taking that bullet for me."

Thinking about the paper gives me a bad feeling in the pit of my stomach, and it takes me a few seconds to remember why.

"What's wrong?" Cam asks, reading the worry on my face.

"Just thinking about something I heard." I didn't plan on bringing this up tonight, but after what we've said, it feels safe. Or at least safer than it did hours ago. "About athletes passing around naked pictures of girls. Have you heard about that?"

"Hate to tell you this, but guys get nudes from girls all the time. It's not just athletes."

"I understand nudes, but what about if the girl didn't send it out?"

"What, hacking into girls' phones for their pictures? No way. Not on my team." He turns to me. "Who told you about it?"

I try to look innocent. "No one. I just heard it mentioned in the newsroom."

"Ugh," he grumbles. "Don't encourage that crap, Lenni. Those kinds of stories do more harm than good. Someone hears a fake rumor about one guy and suddenly the whole football team is a bunch of sexual predators."

"That's not what this is."

"I only mean the full story is always more complicated." He shakes his head. "Anyway, I guess I won't see you until Saturday after the game. You coming?"

"What kind of girl misses a football game when her boyfriend is the sexiest man ever to take the field?" *Boyfriend.* I love saying this word.

"I don't know, ask the girlfriend of the sexiest man ever to take the field. I'm wondering about you."

"You know I'm not buying the modesty crap from you." I turn on my side and slide my hands up his chest. "If I looked like you, I'd never stop looking in the mirror."

"Why do you think I only date chicks with super shiny hair?"

I groan. "Your jokes could use some work, cutie, but I guess nobody's perfect."

Cam looks appreciatively at my breasts. "You sure about that?"

I lay back and sigh happily as he dips his head and runs the tip of his tongue around my nipple. "I'm sure. But you do make a girl want to get a little closer."

"Don't," he says. "You're already there."

Just then, my stomach growls with hunger, making Cam chuckle. "Oops. Are we too late for that dinner reservation?"

"Only an hour or two." He sits up. "I'll find us something down the street. You just lie in bed and stay naked."

I prop myself up on a few pillows, watching him get dressed. "Did I tell you my little brother's coming to the game?"

"That's this weekend? I forgot. Crazy 'cause Liam's coming on Saturday too."

"How sweet. You didn't tell me that."

"I wasn't sure it was going to happen until today."

An idea forms in my head. "Do we dare get these boys together? I mean it might be total chaos if your brother's anything like mine, but how cute would they be together?"

"Oh." His brow creases. "That'd be fun, but I think Liam's only in for the game and then he heads home. Early bedtime and all that." He watches me like he's waiting to see if I'll accept this.

"That makes sense," I say because it does. But something nags at me. "Maybe next time."

"Definitely. Liam would love you. So does your brother like football? Maybe we can meet up on Sunday and throw the ball around."

"You would do that?"

"Why not? It's no big deal."

But for a kid who's had the life Gus has had, not to mention the lack of male role models, it is a big deal, a huge one. "He'd love that, Cam. Thank you."

"Happy to do it. Especially if it makes you smile like that."

He leans down to kiss me, and the heady effect of his lips is immediate; my mind is cloudy with lust. But in the back of my brain, the ugly matter of the photo still lingers.

cameron

FRIDAY EVENING, after the team meeting, the guys are buzzing about the fact that we'll have not one but three pro scouts in attendance for tomorrow's game. Me? I feel like puking.

A year ago I would have been so jacked up I wouldn't be able to see straight. Tonight, I don't know what I feel. Maybe I wish it weren't happening at all.

I've played with a scout in the stands before, but this feels bigger, like an opportunity I might not get again if I'm not perfect out there. I know how good I am on the field. I also know it might not be good enough and that senior year might be my last as a football player.

And I could probably handle that. Mom might need to check into a mental clinic for a couple weeks and then rearrange all the family photos and mementos in the house to disguise the fact she ever had big dreams for me, but she'd live.

The person I can't disappoint is Lenni.

I thought telling her how I felt would help put all those doubts to rest, but it's only ratcheted up my anxiety. It doesn't make sense—I know that. She's my rock. She's the one who makes the rest of the world disappear with just a kiss. She's the only person in my life who honestly doesn't give a damn about football. But she's so sure that I'm capable of doing it all, of being the perfect student and the best athlete. Of making life happen exactly the way I want.

I just want to be the man she thinks I am.

On the way out of the building, I listen to Cash and Reeve trade theories on who's going to get what kind of attention from the scouts. We're just passing by the trainer's room when Mason appears with one of his minions, some backup punter who sports an obnoxious soul patch.

"Big day tomorrow," Mason says in our direction. "For some of us, anyway."

The three of us ignore him.

"Hey, Forrester," he calls after me. "Let me save you the pain. You're not making the cut."

I can tell Cash just wants to walk on, but I don't. And Reeve is always game for anything. I stop. "Funny, I hear a little boy talking, but no one's here." I feign confusion and glance around. Then I bring myself up to my full height and look down at Mason. "Oh, shit, there you are, little man."

Mason sneers. "Yeah, if height mattered, you'd be king. Too bad your talent doesn't measure up."

"Hey, you know what's gonna be hilarious?" Reeve says, not acknowledging Mason. "When the scouts get confused and start thinking some dumbass parents let their fifth grader loose on the field in a sea of men."

We keep walking. Mason mutters ineffectively behind us, but I don't get any satisfaction from his embarrassment. I should have ignored him. Acknowledging his bullshit means he's getting in my head.

Reeve and I wait in the hall while Cash grabs something from the locker room. My phone rings and I silence it—Mom again. Some girls chat at the far end of the hall by the exit doors, and Reeve checks them out.

"There's Sasha," he says. "Be right back."

As soon as he says her name, it hits me: the picture Mason showed me of Sasha James passed out in bed. I haven't thought about it in weeks. But is that what Lenni was talking about the other night?

Shit.

I replay our conversation in my head. She never said anything about the football team being implicated. And the sad fact is, there are probably girls all over campus who've had their naked pics passed around without permission.

But still . . . I didn't do anything about what I saw. I don't even know what I'm supposed to do. Tell Coach? The athletic director? Then it becomes a team issue when it's really about one stupid-ass worm of a kid whose name happens to be listed on our roster. I glance over at Sasha, feeling like a complete jerk. Does she know? Do I tell her Mason's been showing her picture around?

The only thing I'm sure of right now is I'm going to kill Mason Connery before this season is over.

As Reeve's walking back toward me, his phone rings, echoing loudly.

"Hey, Minnie," he answers cheerfully.

God damn it. Now I'm trapped. If only I didn't spend every waking minute with this neanderthal.

They banter for a minute, and even though I can only hear Reeve's side of the conversation, I know what it amounts to. She muses about all the hearts he's breaking and wonders whether he's getting enough to eat, he reassures her his heart belongs to her and nothing compares to her home cooking. She'll call him "Sunshine" at least once and he'll pretend to be embarrassed but won't be.

As I'm waiting for the inevitable phone handoff, Mason comes out of the locker room. Sasha's a few feet away and I watch them pass by each other like complete strangers. Something's off.

"Uh-huh," Reeve says, walking up to me. "He's right here." He gives me a huge shit-eating grin and hands me his phone.

"Hey, Ma," I say while giving Reeve the finger.

"Cameron, hon. I must have called you four times in the last day. I was growing worried."

I move down the hallway away from Reeve. "I texted you that we'd catch up Sunday. You know how busy I am right before a game."

"I know, I just wanted to wish you best luck tomorrow. I'll be watching, on TV of course."

I ignore the passive-aggressive jab. I told Mom a while ago Serena and Liam are coming to tomorrow's game, and I'm just grateful she hasn't thrown a fit over it. "Coach says to expect a few scouts at the game, so no bad vibes, Mom. I want you sipping mint juleps and grinning at the TV like some crazy lady."

"Oh, Cameron," she says affectionately. "Mint juleps are for horse races."

"Okay, then get drunk and call me Secretariat if that's what it takes."

She chuckles. "You're in a good mood. Are you still seeing that girl? The one you won't let me meet?"

"The one I was seeing four days ago when you asked me the same question?"

"She must be a special one if you're keeping her away."

I never used to mind talking about my girlfriends with Mom, but something about discussing Lenni with her brings on a weird sense of anxiety. "I better get going, Reeve's waiting on me."

"Hold on, doll, one more thing." Mom takes a dramatic pause. "Is *she* still attending the game tomorrow?"

Just when I thought I'd made it through this conversation without stepping on a landmine. "Uh-huh. She and Liam."

"I see." She sniffs. "You know, Cameron, I've thought endlessly on this, and I kept hoping that eventually it would all make sense, but it simply doesn't."

"What's that? Me inviting my little brother to watch me play football for an afternoon?"

"You being on her side instead of mine!" she says sharply. "We were always a team, you and me. I just can't stand that after all that happened between her and your father, now she's taking my own son away from me."

I take a few seconds to breathe before I open my mouth. My mom's dramatics are fucking ridiculous sometimes. "I get that you're hurt, but Serena's not taking me away from you, Mom. I'll always be on your side. It's one lousy football game, and it's not for her, it's for Liam."

"You know, it's all over town now what happened to our family."

"It's been years, so I'd say it's about time."

"How can you be so cavalier, Cameron? You don't care about our reputation?"

"No."

She huffs. "From the day I became a mother, I devoted myself to raising you properly and creating a well-respected family. My life's work, and he destroyed it! You know, I had to tell Mrs. Petersen the real reason I won't be at your game tomorrow, and she was shocked. A foolish mistake that was. She's probably already told her book club and half the people she passes at the grocery store."

I don't know who Mrs. Petersen is, but I can see Mom's only getting herself more worked up the longer I argue. "I'm sorry," I tell her. "It sucks what Dad did to us, but I don't want to dwell on it. Especially not tonight."

She sniffs, sounding teary, though whether it's genuine or not is anyone's guess. "You're right, hon. I shouldn't be upsetting you before a game like this."

"I'm fine. I'll call you Sunday, okay?"

"Sure. Good luck tomorrow, doll."

"Thanks. G'night, Ma."

"Oh, Cameron?" Suddenly, her voice is crystal clear. "She's not to attend another game ever again. Not as long as I'm paying your tuition." The line goes dead.

Hard to believe there was ever a time when talking to my mom left me in a good mood. The shitty legacy Dad left us just won't quit.

When I walk out of the building, Reeve's chatting up a couple of girls leaning against a blue Jeep. Field hockey girls. I don't want to talk to them, so I check my email and find a message from my ethics professor saying midterm essay grades will be posted by six a.m. tomorrow. My mouth feels dry. I'd give the world for a fast-forward button on life right now.

Reeve finally notices me and heads over.

"You didn't have to wait for me," I say.

"Don't flatter yourself, stud. You have my phone, remember?" He holds his hand out expectantly.

"Like I wasn't going to give it to you at home?"

"I'm waiting on a text from this cute sophomore who's been on me. Great blow jobs, I hear."

I hand him his phone, but I notice he doesn't even check it before sliding it into his pocket.

"So why you dodging Minnie's calls?"

"Next time, why don't you just eavesdrop and save me the trouble of having to update your busybody ass."

Reeve shrugs. "It's my family too."

"You know why I'm dodging her. She's pissed about this weekend, and I don't know how to handle her when she's pissed."

Reeve snorts. "Yeah, you do. You *yes, Mother* it up. You've been doing it all your life."

"Maybe I don't feel like doing that anymore."

He gives me a sidelong glance. "Now you know why she's pissed."

He's right. For the first time I can remember, I'm not being the son she wants me to be. "She's not getting her way."

"Uh-huh. Glad I don't live in that house anymore." After a minute, Reeve adds, "I don't get the whole thing about you and the kid, though."

"Liam?"

"Yeah. You're basically telling your mother to fuck off so you can spend time with her husband's mistress."

For a minute, I just seethe. Not because he's wrong, but because I'm afraid he's right. "He's my brother," I finally say through a clenched jaw.

"Because you share some genes? Big deal. Doesn't make you brothers."

"That's literally what it makes us, you asshole."

"You know what I'm saying. Family isn't about blood." He only meets my eye for a second, but it's enough; he's living proof of his words. We pass The Phantom, where the smell of cigarette smoke wafts from the groups of already-drunk students on the back patio.

"I'm just trying to give the kid what my dad didn't," I say.

"You're not his father. And once that lady gets enough money out of you, she'll probably up and disappear anyway. Minnie's not going anywhere."

"Damn, you're as pissed at me as she is, aren't you?"

He scowls. "No."

I was kidding, but looking at him, I think maybe I'm right. "You are. Look at you."

"I'm not pissed, I just think you're being a bit of a shithead."

"Oh, yeah? How?"

"It's your mom, dude!" He turns and looks at me like he's shocked by what a stupid asshole I've turned out to be. "You're trying to make up for what your father did, but you're only fucking her over even more. And with the same woman too! Shit, why don't you just marry this Serena chick and give your mom the ultimate fuck-you grandchild?"

"Jesus, Reeve, chill out, I'm not fucking her over. Minnie's mad at me because I'm making it harder for her to pretend the Forresters are the most perfect family that ever familied."

"Yeah, okay, she is. But that's not what's really tearing her up. You're the one she's always relied on, and now you're pushing her aside for Serena. Just like him." He looks away and we start walking again.

Just like him.

Reeve has this thing about my dad. Mom was always Reeve's favorite, but I think Dad was the kind of man Reeve wanted to be: successful, well-liked, beautiful wife, perfect family. Dad welcomed Reeve into the sort of family Reeve had always wished for. After the truth came out, I don't think Reeve ever forgave him for shattering the illusion. For the second time in his life, Reeve lost his shot at having the family he always wanted. Or maybe I've just thought about this a lot because it's easier than thinking about my own feelings for my dad.

"I'm not the only one Minnie relies on." I sound defensive and lame. "She's always got you to come to her rescue."

Reeve stares straight ahead, his jaw set. "I'm not really her son."

We walk in silence.

I wonder what I was thinking back when I decided that

getting close to Liam was the right thing to do. What made me so sure? It doesn't feel right anymore. It feels just as bad as turning my back on him and Serena in the name of loyalty to my mother.

I think I'm screwed.

"We need to stop for beer?" he asks when we pass a convenience store.

"Nah, we got plenty."

He nods. "What time's the basketball game start?"

"Eight, I think."

"You seeing Lenni tonight?"

I shake my head. "You know my rule: no sex the night before a game."

Reeve makes a noise like he doesn't buy it. "Yeah, but you're breaking a lot of your rules for Lenni." But there's no hostility in his voice. "Let's grab sandwiches or something. Everything in the fridge is moldy. We need to get a few freshmen over to clean it out."

"Yum. I can think of a certain sophomore we can feed the leftovers to."

"Since when do you let Connery get to you?"

"I'm not. Just seems like he's ready to fuck things up at any minute."

"Big mistake to think that way. He's a powerless little fuck and you've got it all: the game, the grades, the girl. It doesn't get any better than this."

But that's what scares me. Having it all means having everything to lose.

cameron

MY ALARM BLARES but I'm already awake.

I'm not dragging ass this morning. It's Saturday. Big day. I sit up to grab my phone, squinting at the harsh blue light, and open the Shafer website to navigate to the grades portal. I have to try three times to enter my password correctly, my eyes bleary and my stomach knotting tighter after each attempt. Finally, I'm in. I click on the link for my honors ethics class. My knee bounces hard enough to shake the whole bed as I wait for the stupid page to load. Then there it is. My grade for my essay. Ninety-seven percent.

"Holy shit." *Ninety-seven percent.*

I flop back onto the bed, pull a pillow over my face and just smile. I feel amazing. Relief has got to be the all-time most underrated emotion. I might actually pull off an A in the toughest class I've ever taken.

I try to savor the feeling, holding at bay thoughts about everything else that awaits me today. I want to call Lenni and tell her. I want to show Reeve the grade. I want to text Cash and Lorenzo and Mom and spread the word around, but it wouldn't mean much to them, and anyway, I don't want them to see how much it means to me. And already the glow is fading, giving way to familiar anxiety because the essay isn't the only reason I couldn't sleep last night. In a few minutes, I need to be up getting ready for a much more public test of my abilities.

The house is silent while I take my shower. Normally, this is when I let my pregame nerves really unravel, wash them down the drain, but the fear that's been on my back since I found out about the scouts attending today's game just isn't there. When I close my eyes, all I really feel is the usual low-level anxiety—that I can deal with. Because here's the thing, I'm as good as I'm gonna get. I might be good enough to impress some scouts, I might not. But I have other options. When I shrink my world down to just me and my brain, here's the truth: this game isn't do or die.

Of course, it's easy to think that way when you're standing naked under the cool spray of your shower and really feeling yourself because you aced a killer midterm paper.

It's another thing when you're doused in sweat that's more from nerves than physical exertion, and Coach's yelling has finally brought his elusive forehead vein throbbing to the surface, and you realize you actually *might* die because he's going to kill the entire team if we don't start showing up to play.

"What the fuck is wrong with you bunch?" Coach Haskins throws his clenched fists out to the side. "We can't afford one more mistake if we want any shot to get back in this game. Not one! Get your heads out of your asses and make a play!"

It's the fourth quarter and we're only down by two points, but the scoreboard doesn't begin to tell the story of our awful showing. At least the scouts watching will be just as disillusioned with the rest of the team as they surely are with me by now.

We came into this game heavy favorites, but our execution

on offense has been horrible, and if not for our defense, we'd probably be down two touchdowns by now. It's now or never to get this going and keep our season on track. A loss to an unranked team at home would destroy our chances of making it to the national championship—not to mention be a complete humiliation on the worst day possible.

We take the field under Coach's menacing glare and huddle up. We run the ball on first down, but in keeping with the day's trend, we only pick up a yard. On second down, the play comes in and my number is called. It's a play action designed to get the ball to me on a deep post route. I line up to the right, the ball is snapped, I see the safety biting on the run fake, and I know I'm gonna have a chance to make a play; one that could turn this game around.

I beat the corner off the line, and I'm pushing upfield to get behind the safety. I'm in full stride and I see the football airborne. Reeve's put crazy air under it, and as I watch it come down, I know I'm going to have to lay out to bring it in. I dive hard and instantly feel the ball on my fingertips. *Thank fucking god.* I start to haul it in, but I crash to the ground harder than expected and I can't hang on—the ball pops out.

Incomplete.

That was our chance for a big play. It was in my hands, and I should have had it. I can't believe it. I look up and see the fans with their hands on their heads as an unmistakable sigh of disappointment sounds throughout the stadium. On the sidelines, Cash throws his helmet down and a couple guys have dropped their heads in frustration.

Much as I'd love to take a dirt nap right now, I peel myself off the ground and get back to the huddle. We have another chance to pick up a first down and keep the drive alive, but it's third and long. Not easy when the best thing we've done all quarter is gain a single yard.

"We need to pick up a first down here!" Coach threatens. Like this is Pee Wee football and we had no idea our entire season hangs in the balance.

Reeve turns to me. "We're coming back to you again. This one's got your name on it." His eyes stay on me, and he nods; we've been here before, pulled through far worse together, though at the moment it's hard to remember anything worse than this game.

We break the huddle. Pretty simple play: I just have to beat my man, get to the chains, and catch the ball. At the snap, the corner gets a strong jam on me, and I have to fight to get off the line. I push upfield, but he squeezes me toward the sideline. The defense blitzes Reeve and he's forced to get rid of it quickly. To complete the pass, Reeve throws it low and away and I have to break hard back to the ball to make the catch. It's on target and I reel it in as I go to the ground. But my heart plummets when I look up. I'm a yard short of the first down marker.

Three and out.

We have to punt it again.

I slink off to the sidelines. What the actual fuck is wrong with me today? With all of us? My teammates greet me with subdued pats on the helmet, but I can't look any of them in the eye. I should have made the catch the first time. I should have gone deeper on the route. No wonder Coach is talking to us like we're a bunch of elementary schoolers in gym class. The mistakes we've made—*I've* made—shouldn't happen; not for anyone who expects to get to the next level.

The other team picks up a few first downs while I loiter uselessly on the sidelines. I'm sweating as they get into field goal range. The defense is able to hold them to a field goal to keep us in the game, but that leaves us in a deeper hole—down by five points. With less than thirty seconds on the clock.

I'm getting loose to go out with the offense when the

special teams coach yells at me, "Hey, dickhead, what are you doing? You're up!"

That's when I see Jace, our usual kickoff returner, on the bench getting treatment for his ankle. He must have rolled it on the last drive. My stomach drops. Great. Now the game's in my hands.

I grab my helmet and run onto the field. Our only chance of salvaging this game is if we get a big play out of this, and I haven't had a chance to return a kick in a game all year. My heart pounds as I stand on the goal line. I'm looking at a clock with nineteen seconds left to play. We're down five with our season—and my future—on the line. I've gotta make a play to give us a shot.

I glance around the stadium. It's a blur of red, fans on their feet, a few tense voices shouting out either encouragement or threats. I try not to hear either. I know Lenni's out there and I know she's standing, her fingers probably white-knuckled and twisted around each other because even though she doesn't really care about the score, she cares.

But I'm not going to think about how she'll want me just the same if I blow this play because for once, that's not serving me. I can't let myself off the hook. I have to make something happen.

The other team kicks the ball. I thought they might squib it, but they went ahead and kicked it deep. The ball soars high and far down the field toward me. I watch it moving in slow motion. My heels were on the goal line, but I have to drift back a little into the end zone and to the right to settle under the ball and catch it. Should I just take a knee and down it? Let our offense take the ball at the twenty-five? But no. In a split second, I decide I'm gonna try to make a play and run it out. So off I go.

I catch the ball and head up the field, picking up speed. I hear the first wave of pads colliding with a crunch as the coverage team streams down the field and my teammates start picking up blocks. I make the first man miss with a move to the left and find a seam heading up the hash. That alley collapses quickly, and I pinball off two would-be tacklers and stumble toward the sideline, but I'm able to keep my feet and regain speed. I see daylight ahead, but I still have a man to beat. And it's the kicker.

I take off up the sideline, but I cut back across his face around the fifty-yard line. Then the whole field opens up ahead of me. It's a foot race from here. I turn on every ounce of speed I have. I'm vaguely aware of the roar of the crowd as I hear my team blocking behind me and defenders grunting as they dive at my feet while I blaze down the field.

Thirty yards. Twenty-five.

My lungs burn but my muscles feel amazing, strong, every step like fuel on the fire.

Twenty yards. Fifteen. Just ten to go.

Then I feel my shoulder pads tug. Someone's caught me and starts dragging me down. I fight him off, reaching back to stiff-arm the defender, and manage to keep my feet. As he climbs on my back, I fall into the end zone. The ball is over the goal line.

Touchdown.

My ears fill with the screams of the crowd and the shouts of my teammates as they mob me in the end zone. Lorenzo grins as he jogs toward me, clamps his arm around my helmet and pulls me in for a hug. Other guys batter my back and my shoulder pads excitedly and shout over the crowd. We just saved our season. It was ugly, but it put a smile on Coach Haskins's face, who gives me an approving nod when the guys around me finally clear. It put a smile on all our faces.

I turn around and look for Lenni in the crowd.

THIRTY-ONE

I MADE the mistake of telling Gus at the football game that tomorrow he'd have a chance to toss a ball around with my personal friend, Number Eleven. Now I'm paying for it.

We're on our way to the park because Gus insisted all through the rest of the game and at lunch and at my apartment that he has to get some practice in before he meets Cam. Which means me and my butterfingers will be spending the afternoon throwing a football.

Gus bolts out of the car the instant I pull into a parking spot. I call after him to wait, but he's already found the nearest patch of open grass and starts hurling the ball across it with all the force his underpowered body can muster.

I don't know how Mom does it. Other than to wolf down a double cheeseburger, Gus literally hasn't stopped talking about Cam and the other football players since the game ended. And even though it's making me a little nutty, every time he boasts about Cam being amazing and cool and the "king of football," I can't help feel a little swell of pride and think, *Yeah, I know.*

I haven't told him Cam and I are dating because I'm not ready to field the questions Mom would immediately have, but

I'm so freaking tempted. And this is where I am in life, dying to brag to my nine-year-old brother about my new boyfriend. Maybe someday I'll be a real adult.

"C'mon, Lenni!" Gus calls as I get out of the car. "Pass with me!"

"Coming, bud."

Even though throwing a ball ranks up there with watching paint dry on my excitement meter, I have a good time. It's hard not to, standing across from my grinning little brother who busts out laughing every time my passes go awry. It's sobering to realize this is probably the most fun he's had in weeks, but I'm grateful for the reminder. This is why I bust my ass every day. Gus deserves more.

"All right, little dude," I tell him when my arm starts wearing out, "I need a break or else I'm going to fall asleep before dinner time."

I find an empty bench and look around. The park is huge and bustling with people kicking around soccer balls, picnicking, and pushing strollers. A line of trees separates us from the neighboring fields and as I look beyond it, my eye catches on someone familiar. Cam?

It can't be him because why would he be here? After three days apart, I'm craving him hard, so no surprise if I'm seeing him in every well-built, wavy-haired man around. But then I see the guy toss a football down the field and I know it's Cam. No one else moves like him.

I look back at Gus, who's still happily pretending to be a football star. "Stay right here," I tell him. "I'll be back in a minute."

I start crossing the field that separates me from Cam, feeling like a weirdo because I know I'm not going over there to say hello. I want to see what he's up to.

He's playing with a little boy, Liam, I guess. But the boy is tiny, far younger than Gus. So young, in fact, that Cam's not even throwing the ball to him, he's demonstrating his throw while the little boy bounces and claps a few feet away. He looks like Cam with his wavy brown hair cut almost the same length as Cam's, and even from here I catch the blazing amber color of his eyes.

I smile as Cam runs toward the boy, dodges an imaginary opponent, throws the ball, and then scoops the kid off the ground, light and easy as a baby, and tosses him over his wide shoulders. My heart squeezes with emotion.

I wish I could go to him, but somehow it feels like I'm intruding. He didn't say anything about spending time with Liam after the game; in fact, he said Liam would be leaving right away. I recognize the feeling that hits me, yet it takes me by surprise. It's that heavy, stomach-churning sensation of suspicion. Mistrust. I thought I knew better than to feel that way about Cam after all the times he's proven me wrong, but here it is.

I decide to ignore it. He's not doing anything wrong. In fact, I'm the creep who's spying on him. I'll give him his space now, and I'll ask him about it later. I'm not going to indulge the conjecture that's landed me in so much misery before.

I'm about to head back to Gus when I notice the woman walking up to Cam. She's blond and tiny and young. She reaches out to take the little boy from Cam's arms, kisses him and sets him on the ground. She and Cam turn their backs to me as they watch the boy trot down the field, giving me an unadulterated view as she places her hand around my boyfriend's arm and smiles up at him.

My stomach plummets.

My brain scrambles for some logical explanation. Cam doesn't have a sister. And I know his mom is pretty, but this woman isn't even thirty. She's not his mother.

And that's it. I'm out of explanations that don't make me want to cry.

Gus and I spend the evening at the upscale arcade across town that caters to parents and kids alike with their greasy pizza, wine by the glass, and gourmet cupcakes. I skip the wine because of Gus and eat three huge cupcakes because of Cam.

Back at my apartment, Jade, Gus, and I play three rounds of Jenga with a bowl of popcorn between us. I tuck Gus into my bed and lay with him while he tells me about his two new friends from fourth grade who love soccer and how he's too embarrassed to tell them the real reason he can't sign up for the township team with them is that Mom can't afford the registration fees on top of the swimming lessons he takes. She shouldn't have told him that, she should have told me. Or Nana and Grandpa. Someone who might be able to help instead of the one person who's helpless.

"Is it too late to register?" I ask Gus.

He nods his head sadly. "There's another season in spring, but Mom already said she needs to save if I want to do summer camp again."

"I'll pay for spring soccer," I say before I have time to think, weakened by my baby brother's sweet brown eyes and my own memories of growing up without any extras.

Gus snaps his head toward me. "You will? Really?"

"Of course. Easy peasy lemon squeezy."

He grins. "Cool! Thanks!"

"You got it. Now lie down and tell me more about fourth grade."

Gus enters into a fresh story about his P.E. teacher while I think about what I've just done. I have no clue how much soccer registration is, but I'll find a way to swing it somehow.

Worst-case scenario, I'll borrow from Cam; *if we're still together by then*, I think darkly. But I won't go there, not until Gus falls asleep at least.

When he finally does, I sneak out of my bedroom and find Jade. We pour a little wine and I lay out the story of what I saw at the park.

"If this were a movie, that would be his secret love child you saw," Jade says once I've filled her in.

I can't admit this is actually my leading theory. "And in real life?"

She looks thoughtful, then her mouth quirks. "Hate to say it, but . . . secret love child."

I groan. "That's too crazy. I mean, what kind of secret would the kid be if he parades it around at the park a block off campus?"

"Maybe it really is his brother."

"The kid looked barely out of diapers. How long has his mom been birthing kids, twenty years?"

"Why not? Periods are the gift that keep on giving."

"It doesn't matter anyway, my problem is with the woman. Who the hell is she?"

"Hey, you know how you could find out? Ask him."

"And admit I was spying on him?"

"It's a public park!" Jade gestures with her wine glass, sloshing what little liquid was left onto the counter. "Fucking sleazo."

"So you think he's cheating."

"Well, I was just starting to really like him, and we know I'm shit at judging a man's character," she says bitterly. And drunkenly. Sam still isn't telling her what she wants to hear. "Are you still gonna see him tomorrow?"

"I can't cancel. Gus would be crushed."

"Good. Get some answers."

She's right. The last time I made assumptions about Cam, I came dangerously close to losing him altogether. Of course, that time didn't feature a pretty blonde on his arm.

I just need to find some courage.

WHEN I LIE DOWN next to Gus that night, I'm no closer to making sense of it. And without facts to go on, my fears run wild.

I found a good man, one who just keeps proving to me my fears have no place in our relationship, yet here I am, still gripped by worry and mistrust. When will I ever stop wondering what secrets he's keeping from me?

THE NEXT MORNING, Gus and I meet Cam at the park; the same one where I saw him with the mystery blonde.

I barely look at Cam when we get there, but he plays along, probably because he knows I'm not telling Gus that we're more than friends. But once they're out on the field together, I can't take my eyes off him.

He's even better with Gus than I imagined he would be. He's sweet and encouraging but doesn't baby him. He shows him how to throw a football and how to run without dropping it, asks him all about school and his life back home, then actually listens to Gus's answers. When Cam kneels down to double knot the shoelace on Gus's sneaker that keeps coming loose, Gus looks over at me with the world's biggest smile, and my heart swells.

I know this is hardly Cam's idea of a great Sunday morning, but you wouldn't know it by the way he acts. And he's doing it for the person I love most. I don't know how to square this Cameron with the one I saw yesterday. I have to ask him, but

I'm not ready. I'm afraid of the lies he might tell as much as I'm afraid of the truth.

When Gus is finally worn out, we walk back to the parking lot, where Cam lets Gus sit in the driver's seat of his truck, pop open the glove box, crawl into the bed and generally treat it like his own personal playground. As I finally drag my brother away, Cam offers to take us out for lunch, but I say no, we're meeting my grandfather to eat before he takes Gus back home. I see the flicker of confusion in Cam's eyes at my chilly goodbye.

"Meet me later?" he asks quietly as Gus hops into my old beater and busies himself with his seat belt.

I barely glance at him. "Probably not tonight. I really need to write."

But as soon as the words are out, I think, *Nope*. This isn't the way. How many times am I going to swallow it down and suffer in silence? That stopped working for me a long time ago.

"Actually, I'll text you when I'm done writing," I say. "Maybe we can meet up."

AFTER LUNCH with Gus and Grandpa, a few tears slip out on the drive back to my place. Saying goodbye to my brother always makes me emotional, especially knowing what he's heading back to. Sure, things are pretty stable at home, and my grandparents give him every ounce of love they have, but I remember what it's like. Just knowing your mom could fall apart any day keeps you in a permanent state of worry and instability.

I park outside my building and head up the sidewalk. That's when I see Cam sitting on the steps. He looks up at me but doesn't smile. I curse under my breath. I'm not ready for this conversation. I haven't even figured out what I want to say, and after that I still need to rehearse the words in my head 6,000 times or until they lose all meaning.

"Hi," I say coolly when I reach him. "What are you doing here? I said I'd text you."

He makes no move to get out of my way. "I know what you said."

"So let me finish what I need to do, and then we can talk."

I try to step around him. He stands up, blocking me easily. "What are you pissed off about?"

I open my mouth, my instinct to deny, deny, deny, but I catch myself. I take a breath and try again. "I'm—" I begin, but a siren howls around the corner, silencing me.

Cam squares his body to mine, ready for whatever fight I'm about to drag us into. But am I? A fire truck turns onto the street and races past us, siren blaring. Questions simmer inside my head, things I have to ask him. I'm afraid of the answers, but I can't sit agonizing over them any longer. Another fire truck speeds past, and an ambulance wails a few blocks away. I nod at Cam and move for the front door.

THIRTY-TWO

Lenni

"WHAT DID you do yesterday after the game?" I ask as soon as we're upstairs in my apartment.

He looks taken aback, like this wasn't the accusation he was expecting. "Um, grabbed food, said goodbye to my family, went to The Phantom with a couple guys from the team and went home."

There's an ugly silence.

"What? What's wrong, Lenni?"

"I saw you at the park with a little boy. And a woman who had her hands all over you." Cam would suck at poker because his face immediately reads guilt. "Who are they, Cameron?"

"That's my brother. You knew he was visiting."

Even though I told myself I'd dismissed the ridiculous love-child theory, relief floods me, nonetheless. But I have to steel myself for the next question. "And the blonde who couldn't keep her hands to herself?"

He scrubs his face with his hands, heaves out a deep breath. My heart is pounding furiously, and I want to scream at him to hurry the fuck up and just break my heart already if that's what's coming, but I can't seem to say anything.

"That's Serena, Liam's mom."

I stare at him, trying to put these pieces together into a coherent story but failing.

"Serena was my dad's mistress. One of them. We didn't know until after he died that they had Liam together."

And my heart does break a little, just not for the reason I expected.

Cam sinks down onto the couch, his shoulders sagging. My heart tells me to reach out and touch him, but the hurt and confusion haven't quite left me.

"Why didn't you tell me?"

"I don't know. I wasn't trying to keep it from you, I just never felt like talking about it. It's so fucked up, Lenni."

The pain twisted into the lines on his face is too much to bear. I sit close to him. "But you didn't do it."

"Doesn't make it any easier. I'm embarrassed by what my dad did to us."

His words send a chill of recognition up my spine. If I haven't shared that sentiment about my own dad a million times in my life . . .

"You don't have to be embarrassed with me. My dad was the clear winner of the shitty dads competition, remember?"

That earns me a small smile. "Actually, it was a draw. And that was before you knew about Liam."

He's right; that's a kind of betrayal I can't imagine. At least my father never pretended to be someone he wasn't—namely, a halfway decent person. "But you love Liam, don't you? You can't really hold him against your dad."

He nods. "I guess I do love him. It'd be easier if I didn't, though. My mom's so pissed I've been in contact with Serena."

"Oh. Your mom. I didn't even think about that."

"It sucks. After Dad died and we found out what he'd been up to, Serena was enemy number one for both of us. It felt good to have someone still alive to be angry at. It's only in the last year I've come around to talking to her and meeting up."

"That's really big of you, Cam."

"You might not think that if you saw what it does to my mom. But what am I supposed to do? Fuck Liam over like my dad did?" He shakes his head.

"I wish I had the answer." I feel my heart opening to him; to this side of him I never knew before. The depth of him overwhelms me.

He takes my hand and rests his forehead against it, closing his eyes. "I'm sorry I didn't tell you about yesterday. About all of it."

"Family stuff is hard to talk about." I slide closer until our bodies are touching. He opens his eyes but doesn't let go of my hand.

"I would have told you eventually if you let me get to it. I'm not great about sharing personal shit."

I nod, thinking of all the things he still doesn't know about me.

"But Lenni, give me time. Please? We can't keep ending up in this place where you assume the worst about me."

I drop my gaze. "I know," I say quickly. "I know I have some work to do."

"So we both do." He squeezes my fingers inside his palm. "Just understand where I was coming from. I wasn't ready to bring the Forrester family ugliness into you and me. I'm happy when I'm with you. It felt like that other side of my life doesn't belong anywhere near you."

"But I don't just want the happy side, I want all of it. All of you." I force myself, for once, to say what I feel instead of hiding. "I want what's real."

"So do I." He leans in and curls his finger under my chin. "No more hiding."

I nod. "For either of us."

He kisses me, his mouth warm and familiar, and I wait for a sense of ease, but it doesn't come. I understand his reluctance to share his family's ugly secrets. The man sitting next to me is even kinder and more loyal than I already knew, someone whose heart is too big to take sides. But fear is a hard lump in my throat that I can't reason away. How many times will we have this conversation before we realize the selves we're hiding behind our shiny exteriors just aren't compatible? And what will I do if the truth is even uglier than it first appears?

I kiss him harder, wanting to fall into the haze of sex where I feel too good to think. But when I try to pull Cam down on top of me, he winces, exhaling painfully through his teeth.

"Are you all right? Did I hurt you?"

"It's fine, honey. No worries. Just some of yesterday's tackles catching up with me."

"You want me to check the medicine cabinet?"

"I'm good."

"What about a hot bath? I'll give you a good soaping if you want," I tease.

His eyebrows go up. "Will you be naked?"

"That's the point, isn't it?"

TEN MINUTES LATER, Cam sits squeezed into my little tub, hot water steaming around him. He looks ridiculous and sexy all at once.

"Do you really want me to soap you up?" I ask as I undress for him.

"No, I want you to get in here with me."

I laugh. "Where? A rubber ducky wouldn't fit in there."

"Get in. We'll find a way."

We do. I lie against him, my back to his chest. The water

doesn't cover my front half, so he yanks a hand towel from beside the sink, soaks it in the hot water and drapes it over me. His arms encircle me, holding me close, and I relax for the first time all day.

"You're a real Romeo," I tell him, closing my eyes. "Five-star dinner dates, Sunday baths."

"Oh, yeah," he says sarcastically. "A date I was too horny to make it to and a bathtub so tiny a single rose petal wouldn't fit."

"It's still more romantic than anything anyone has ever done for me."

"Low expectations, huh? A guy could get used to that." He kisses my shoulder. "But you shouldn't. You deserve so much better."

"Better than what? Cam . . ." I swallow, willing myself to find the courage to bring the words to my lips. "Cam, you're everything I want." Thank god I can stare at the ceiling instead of his face.

His arms wrap tighter around me. "I want to be everything you want," he says quietly. "I really do, Lenni. I've had a lot of girlfriends before, but this feels different. I'm still figuring out how to do this."

"How is it different?"

"Because *we're* different. The rules were clear from the get-go with those girls; that's why I picked them. With you, nothing was clear except how good it felt to be near you."

I'm glowing. "You don't have to try harder for me. You're already there."

I feel him exhale under me, and I hope it means he's as happy as I am right now. Because this moment is perfect; I don't need fancy dinners or grand gestures. I just need everything we have to last forever.

cameron

WE'RE HALFWAY through football practice when I realize something's up with Mason.

He's on the sidelines with a few other backups, watching me out on the field. We're working on a new play, and Reeve throws a great ball that I proceed to drop. Mason's got the perfect opportunity to pull out one of his recycled insults, but nothing comes.

I steal a glance at him. I can tell he's trying not to look at me.

Now that I think about it, he hasn't said a word to me since the game on Saturday, and that doesn't sit well. One show-stopping play doesn't erase the ugly memory of my mistakes. If Mason told me I played like shit for 90 percent of the game, I couldn't argue. I almost wish I hadn't returned that kick for the game-winning touchdown.

Okay, that's a lie. Thank god I did. Thank god I gave those scouts at least one reason not to forget my name. But I don't deserve the praise I've been getting since Saturday, and everyone who knows football knows that. That A-plus ethics essay is my future, not this game.

Coach yells at us to do it over. We run the play again, and this time, I snatch it with one hand. I look at Mason. He gives me a quick nod like we're old buddies or some shit. Who is he kidding?

Fuck you, I mouth because I know he can't resist. But Mason looks away, pretending not to notice.

That's it. Something's up.

All I can think of is the Sasha photo. If that's what Lenni was talking about, it means Mason—or one of his slimy friends —let that photo get beyond the locker room. He knows how easily I could pin it on him. He's trying to fly under the radar and not piss me off.

Meanwhile, I'm still hoping to hell that the rumor Lenni heard has nothing to do with Sasha or Mason or anyone I know.

Our offensive coordinator blows the whistle, and we head to the sidelines to let a few other guys take the field. I take up position next to Mason, who doesn't look at me.

"Question for you," I say, quiet enough that no one else can hear us. "Where's the picture of Sasha?"

"I deleted it."

"After you sent it to how many people?"

He scowls. "I did what you told me. It's gone."

"You realize if it gets out, she'll know exactly who to blame, right?"

"Who said I took it?"

I stare at him. I'd be an idiot to believe anything this kid says, but how dumb was I to assume that picture was proof he slept with Sasha? They acted like strangers the other day after the football meeting. I should have known it then.

I spit on the ground. "You never fucked her, did you?"

He still refuses to look at me, but he keeps blinking, and that drop of sweat slipping down his face definitely wasn't earned on the field.

The whistle blows. "Connery!" Coach yells. "On the ball!"

"Fucking dirtbag," I mutter as Mason takes off toward the field.

So the picture probably didn't start with Mason. Which means Lenni's right about athletes passing around photos. My athletes. What the hell am I supposed to do now?

After practice, Coach Haskins orders me into his office. I sit across from him, and he looks at me, his crooked fingers tented under his chin. His face is serious, contemplating me. I look back, keeping my face carefully impassive like my high school coach taught me to, but now I'm worrying about that stupid picture and whether I'm about to be interrogated.

"Saturday wasn't your best game, was it, Forrester?"

"No, sir."

"But you showed up when we had to have it—made the biggest play in the biggest moment. That's the mark of a special player."

"Thanks, Coach. I guess I caught a lucky break."

"No, that's just it, it wasn't luck. You laid your talents out there and those scouts saw it. No one else grabbed their attention like you did on Saturday." He leans forward and hammers his fist on the desk. "You proved you've got the talent to make winning plays. *That* separates you from the field."

Pride pumps through me hearing the excitement in his voice. Coach has his ups and downs with other players, but he's always been pretty even-keeled with me; a little praise, a little criticism, but never much excitement either way. Seeing him animated about my performance feels like a wake-up call. I can make things happen. If I want to play pro badly enough, I'm the only one stopping me.

"But you've got to be more consistent, Forrester. All the talent in the world isn't worth jack if it can't be counted on when we go to you on that last drive."

I nod. "I don't know what happened to me."

"You were asleep, that's what happened, and I don't really care why. You got something on your mind? Get rid of it. Personal problems? Nobody cares. You're an intelligent kid, son, but you need to learn when to turn off the thinking and just perform."

"Yes, sir."

He stares at me, eyebrows raised like he expects a more impressive answer. "I mean now. Today! Before you blow the opportunity being handed to you."

"I hear you, Coach. I won't be bringing any bullshit onto the field."

He nods. "What I like about you, son, is as long as you put on a great show on the field, I don't have to do a damn thing else to make you look good. When those scouts come through and want to interview the staff about you and what sort of character you have, I know they're gonna walk out thinking they've found someone rare."

After he releases me, I linger in the locker room. So Coach thinks I have character. Funny. What would someone with actual character do in my situation? Tattle on Mason and open the entire team up to scandal? Or do nothing and pray no one ever sees that photo again?

I could go to Coach Haskins, or maybe my offensive coordinator—he's easier to talk to—and tell them what I know. Maybe that's the right thing. But what do I actually know? Nothing. Zero facts to go on. Which leaves me to do what . . . launch an amateur investigation?

I head out to the parking lot, wrestling with the unfamiliar feeling of wishing I wasn't seeing Lenni tonight. When I think of her, all my uncertainty solidifies into a weight that drops straight into my stomach.

I wait all day for the nights and all week for the weekends

when I can touch Lenni and wake up next to her and breathe her in. When I'm with her, all the bullshit that swirls in my head is just problems to be dealt with, nothing more. When I'm near her, everything is okay. When I see myself in her eyes, I like what I see.

But tonight I feel like I'm dragging Mason and his mistakes home to her, and I can't think of anything worse than the two best and worst people in my life converging into a shitstorm.

lenni

"THAT THING you do with your hips is unreal," Cam tells me as we lay in his bed naked except for the thin sheet covering us. He slides his hand over the curve of my waist and down my hips. "I'm not gonna ask where you learned that."

I like his assumption that I had wild sex before him, so I don't tell him I didn't learn it anywhere, it just happens when I'm with him. "Just trying to keep up with you."

I reach for my phone and realize Cam and I have been in bed for almost two hours. "Shoot, I'm going to be late." I hop out of bed and grab my clothes off the floor.

"For what?"

"I'm meeting Jade, remember?"

He wraps his arm around my waist and pulls me back onto the bed. "You live together. She can't spare you for another few hours?"

"She didn't come home after her date last night." I wiggle my eyebrows. "I need to find out what happened."

"Sam's in the rearview mirror, huh?" He almost sounds sad.

"What, you liked him?"

"He's a smart guy. You know I love my meathead friends, but Sam was interesting."

I wiggle out of his grasp and start getting dressed. "If you really want to get on Jade's bad side, you're welcome to strike up a friendship with him."

"Yeah, right, and get my nuts chopped off."

"Oh, don't exaggerate. She'd only cut off one ball, max."

He grabs his crotch and groans.

"I'll be home after dinner. Come over and keep me warm?"

He shakes his head regretfully. "Can't. I've got that exam tomorrow."

"The Intercultural exam? You've already got that in the bag, cutie."

"I need to study." He gets up and steps into a pair of jeans.

"You know there's nothing higher than a 4.0 GPA, right?" I joke.

"I don't have a 4.0."

"What do you have? Three nine five?"

"I don't know, 3.8 maybe."

"Whoa, I didn't realize what a dumbass you are!" I tease. I step closer and run my hands up his bare chest before he can put a shirt on. "So study while I'm out with Jade and then come see me. You could spend ten minutes on the material and still ace that exam."

His mouth is tight. "Coach wants me to rest up anyway. A sleepover probably isn't a good idea." He moves past me and reaches for his T-shirt, which I'm standing on. He gives it a tug but doesn't say anything.

"After your last game? I would have thought Coach would want you to celebrate."

His eyes linger on mine like he's trying to decide whether I'm accusing him of something.

"I mean, you played amazing. You saved the game."

"Right, what about the other fifty-nine minutes?"

"Come on. What are you even worried about? You're one of the best receivers in the country."

He gives a humorless laugh. "What do you know about football, Lenni? Seriously?"

"I know what they write in the school paper."

"You mean Hero Worship Weekly?"

"What are you getting so mad about? I was—"

"I'm not mad." But his clenched jaw says otherwise. He turns his back to me and buttons his jeans.

I replay our conversation in my head, searching for the words that set him off. "All I was saying is relax a little. Your grades are amazing, you're playing great; you don't have to be perfect."

He whips his head around to look at me. "No? Because I thought that's what you liked about me. That I'm fucking perfect."

"What are you talking about?" I take in the flushed skin on his bare chest. I've never seen him upset like this.

"That's what you said, that I'm the perfect guy."

I huff out a laugh, not because it's funny but because it's ridiculous. "And? Am I supposed to apologize for that? It was a compliment."

His eyes latch onto mine, and a flash of pain passes through them. It's gone by the time I blink. "Well, you're wrong." Cam yanks his shirt over his head. "Don't make that mistake."

"Okay. I'll try to be more cognizant of your flaws." I can't help the snarkiness in my tone.

His nostrils flare. He's itching to say something back, but of course he stays silent. Annoyance surges inside me. He's always so in control, so cool under pressure, so . . . perfect.

I taste the words I want to say, trying them out, knowing they'll piss him off even more. I'm afraid of an argument, but wouldn't I rather his anger than his silence? His composure is a wall I don't know how to break through, and I'm sick of being on the wrong side of it.

"You know what?" I put my hands on my hips. "I'm not going to apologize for how I feel. I've never known anyone that even comes close to you, Cameron, so maybe perfect is the only word in my vocabulary that I have!"

"Fine. Just don't expect me to apologize when you end up disappointed."

I move close so he has to look at my face. "What the hell is it? Go ahead, disappoint me right now and let's get it over with."

He looks at me, trapping me in the storminess of his gaze.

"What is it?" I repeat, but my voice has lost its fire. "What, are you morally opposed to being called perfect, or do you need to confess something?"

"Yeah." He nods. "There's something I haven't told you."

I freeze, my heartbeat pulsing in my throat.

"I thought I could wait until I knew for sure but . . ." His voice is tired and defeated. "I'm not sure of anything."

In the three seconds of silence that pass, my mind fires up a dozen different images of the ways he's about to break my heart. "Well?" I whisper.

He swallows. "I don't know if I want to play pro football. I mean, even if I got the chance . . . I still might turn it down."

I wait for more, but Cam's anxious gaze is on me. That was the whole confession. "That's it?"

His brows draw together. "It's a big deal. I've never told anyone."

"So you're . . . quitting football?"

"Quitting?" he repeats, his voice an octave higher. "No, Lenni. God, no. I want a chance at the pros as badly as I ever have."

I'm still confused. "I don't get it."

"I'm saying maybe that's all I want. The chance to turn it down."

I feel light with relief. "Why would you think you have to keep that from me?"

"Turning down an opportunity like that? For something I've been working toward since I was twelve?" He scowls. Apparently he'd hoped for a bigger reaction. "It's settling."

"Not if it's what you really want. And did you think I didn't already know you might have other plans? Your hints aren't subtle."

He shrugs. "I thought you'd be disappointed."

"For wanting something different?" I take his face in my hands and kiss him. "You don't owe me perfection, Cam. You don't owe me anything."

He closes his eyes for a long second, then nods.

"So is that all?"

Silence for a beat. "Yeah," he says as a flicker in his eyes instantly tells me otherwise. Of course that's not all. This tiny confession doesn't balance out against the simmering anger that consumed his whole body just minutes ago. The anger that I still feel just under his skin, cooling and hardening into something too solid to spill out of his control again. I swallow the lump in my throat and try to pretend I don't know this.

We don't say much as he walks me downstairs to the front door.

"Catch up tomorrow?" I ask. "After your exam?"

He nods, then places a brief kiss on my lips. "Have fun with Jade. Be safe."

I turn to go. Before I can pull the door shut behind me, he reaches for my wrist.

"Hey," he says quietly. "Come over late tonight? I need you to do that thing with your hips again."

I smile. "If you're sure Coach would approve."

I'm already running late to meet Jade, but I don't hurry. She's always late, and I don't want to show up with the sick, unsettled feeling inside me written all over my face.

I think about how Mom always used to tell me to date around before getting serious with someone, and I finally understand why. I have no idea how to do relationships. I was meant to be practicing on dime-a-dozen frat boys who ignore me in front of their friends and need a roadmap to find the clit. I was meant to be so sick of bullshit fuckboys that when a man like Cameron Forrester came along, I'd know exactly how to hold on to him.

Instead, I'm waiting around for everything I don't know about him to fall down on me, and I have no clue how to get out of the way.

I'm in the newsroom toiling over edits for an article I wrote about the school's new scuba diving club. And actually, it's pretty good. So good it makes me want to join the scuba diving club even though wearing a swimsuit in front of my peers sounds as traumatic as it was the summer before eighth grade when Mom forced me to join the swim team.

Out of nowhere, Darren plops down on the desk next to me. "Well, your story's got legs."

"The volleyball one?"

He leans closer. "The photo. Looks like there might be facts to back up the rumor."

I swivel toward him.

"Someone else sent in an anonymous tip saying they've

seen a nude photo of a female student who definitely didn't know her picture was being taken. They might even be entertaining the idea of talking to us as long as no identity is revealed. Apparently, they've got texts that could implicate the original source."

"So it's real."

His knee bounces up and down. "It's far from proven, but we obviously can't ignore it any longer. Have you heard anything else?"

"Not a word. I was starting to think it was all blown out of proportion."

"Could be, but I don't think so."

"So . . . I'll see what I can dig up?"

"Nice try, but when I said, 'your story,' I was being facetious. Every source so far is crystal clear about this going back to the football team. That hits a little too close to home." He gives me a questioning look. "You're still dating Forrester, yes?"

"Yes. Would things be different if I weren't?"

Darren laughs. "You mean if he were your ex? That'd take conflict of interest to the next level. Sorry, Lenni."

"And if some information happens to come my way?"

"Facts? You send them to me to verify. We can't publish locker-room gossip." He offers me a conciliatory smile as he gets up. "I know it sucks when you can't have the story you want, but don't think your tenacity goes unnoticed."

An hour later, Cam is waiting for me outside the building. I tell him I have a headache and he should get dinner without me. I have to ask him about the photo again, but not with my emotions running high. If I questioned him now, it would only come off as an accusation.

While he walks me home, I make a furtive study of him. He

looks the same as always, not like a man guarding a secret that could take down his entire team. Even as team captain, it's entirely possible he hasn't heard the rumors. But his words run through my head, warning me he isn't as perfect as he seems.

After he drops me at home, I try to tackle some homework, but my conscience is working overtime. I can't let the story go. A good journalist doesn't shy away from a tricky lead, and she doesn't take direction from an editor who would just as soon assign the story to one of the many dudes on the paper who are little more than Shafer football worshippers with decent writing skills.

I could make it a story not about suspended football players or a perfect season coming under threat, but about the real victims. I'd write about the danger every woman on campus faces because she pays thousands of dollars every semester to attend an institution that values the athlete over the student. So much so that the men in question don't just think they're above the law, they don't even bother to consider the humanity of those who live within its limits.

Dramatic? It might be, but I'm not wrong. This story has been inside me since that awful night in high school. I want to tell it.

SAM LOOKS suspicious when he finds me at his door just after nine that night.

"This isn't about Jade," I assure him before he can say anything.

"Then it's the other thing." He doesn't sound relieved. "I don't know anything more than I already told you."

I believe him. Integrity—not personal loyalty—is what motivates Sam. "Can I come in?"

"Just for a while. I have someone coming over. For tutoring."

"At nine-thirty? Let me guess. She's pretty."

Sam just steps aside for me, stone-faced.

Once inside, I waste no time. "You saw the photo, right? With your own eyes?"

"Well, yeah. It was on my phone."

"And it was a regular girl? Not something from the internet, but an actual Shafer student?"

"How can I know that? It wasn't a professional photo, but I don't know the girl."

"But you saw it. So you know it's real." Sam's looking at me like I'm crazy, so I add, "It's just that I need to verify the photo actually exists if I'm going to do anything about it."

"I said I saw it."

I hesitate. I know what I want to ask next, but it feels wrong. "You erased it from your phone?"

He nods.

"From your recently deleted too?"

He pauses, then realization hits him, and he sighs. "Guess I overlooked that." He pulls out his phone. "Let me get rid of it."

"Wait."

Sam glances up from his phone.

"Do you think I should . . . ?" I trail off. "Because I'm supposed to—you know, to verify."

"Hold on, Lenni. Everything I know about that picture suggests it was taken without consent. I'm not going to be caught passing it around."

"You're not passing it around. And do you really think I would turn you in? You know I love you, Sam."

He eyes me, and I can guess what he's thinking. Breakups happen and alliances change. But Jade or not, he and I have been solid since the day we met. "I just don't want any involvement with it. Period."

"You already involved me by telling me. And now I have to do something about it."

Sam looks irritated by my logic. "So you want to see it?"

I really don't want to see it. I don't want to be one more stranger looking at this girl's picture without her permission. I look at Sam. "Do I?"

"You know I can't answer that."

I think about the story I want to write. Can I justify invading someone's privacy in order to verify a fact?

"Look, just go to your deleted folder and delete it permanently. And before you do, let me glance at it for one second. I just need to know it's real."

He makes a show of being put out, sighing as he looks down at his phone. "By the way, does Jade know you're here?"

"Yeah, I'm going to run right home and tell her all about my secret meetings with her ex," I say impatiently. Then, to remind him where my loyalties lie, I add, "You broke her heart, Sam."

He avoids my eye, tapping and swiping on his phone while I wait. Music bubbles in from another room, something soft and jazzy. I twist my fingers around my necklace to keep from snatching the phone out of Sam's slow hands. My heart pounds like mad, afraid for reasons I can't explain. Maybe it's not about the football team or a story for the paper or what Cam does or doesn't know. Maybe it's about me.

"Here it is," he finally says as he holds up his phone for me.

But in the half second he gives me to look at the picture, it offers no insight. It's a blond girl asleep on a bed, her breasts exposed, her naked butt partially covered by a bright-blue sheet. I'm hit by some faint sense of familiarity. Do I know her?

"Satisfied?" Sam taps his screen and deletes the picture.

"Yeah," I say. I'm not at all. "Thanks."

There's something off.

I know no more than I did before. The picture is real, the girl exists, and she's a stranger to me. Nothing has changed. But with the image burned into my brain, my heart keeps up its quick, uneasy beat all the way home.

It doesn't hit me until I turn out the lights and lay back on my pillow, but when it does, it's like running into a brick wall. I know those bright-blue sheets that the girl was lying on, and the curved, black, '80s-looking headboard behind her. Not long ago, I lay in that same place trying to seduce a guy I didn't know or even like.

That photo was taken in Reeve's bed.

cameron

AS SOON AS I see Lenni waiting for me after practice, I know the news is bad.

"Hey," I say, hurrying over to her. "You okay?"

"I'm fine," she says, but her face is drawn with stress. She doesn't even attempt a smile.

Behind me, a couple guys make some smartass comments that I barely register. Lenni apparently does, though, because she glares at them over my shoulder. Okay, maybe she's not stressed, maybe she's pissed.

"Come on." I steer her away from the players coming out of the building while my mind runs down the list of reasons she might be mad. When we're alone, I turn to her. "What's wrong?"

Her scowl doesn't let up, but she bites her bottom lip like she's trying to hold back.

"Talk to me, Lenni. Did something happen?"

"I saw the picture."

Oh, shit. Please don't let her be talking about what I think she's talking about. "What picture?" I ask cautiously.

"Oh, please. You know what picture, Cam."

I can't believe she's seen it. I can't believe my team is so fucking stupid. Why did I let it get this far?

I've asked a few friends on the team if they know anything about the photo, hoping to hell Mason's the only one involved, and this doesn't become a team issue. I need facts, but I'm trying to keep it quiet because if no one else on the team is involved, I want to keep it that way. And I can't mention it to Reeve because he'll beat Mason's ass, and anything that jeopardizes our season or Reeve's career isn't an option. I look down at Lenni, not knowing what to say.

She squeezes her eyes shut, and I realize she'd been holding onto hope that I knew nothing about it. When she opens them again, she doesn't look at me.

"Lenni, I'm sorry—" I start to say but she snaps her head up.

"Did you take it?"

It takes me a sec to realize what she's asking. "Take the picture?"

She nods impatiently.

"How can you think I'd be involved in that?"

"Because I just found out I don't know you at all. You lied when you told me you knew nothing about that picture."

"I wasn't lying. When you asked, I didn't know what you were talking about. I'd heard someone mention the picture weeks earlier, and I completely forgot about it."

"Until when? This very second?"

I swallow hard. I'd convinced myself I wasn't doing anything wrong, but the truth is right here between us. I fucked up. "It hit me later, but I had no idea if we were really talking about the same thing. I didn't know that picture ever went farther than one phone."

"Whose phone? Yours or Reeve's?"

I shake my head. "Why do you keep putting this on me? I had nothing to do with that picture."

"Then your best friend did!" she shouts.

"What are you talking about? Is that what Mason told you?" My fingers curl into my palms, anger surging inside me.

"That's what I saw, Cameron! I saw the picture. Blue sheets, ugly black bed. And if you'll remember," she says bitterly, "I know exactly what Reeve's bed looks like. Who the hell else would take that picture but him?"

"No way," I say through gritted teeth. "Not a fucking chance."

"I saw it," she says grimly.

Doesn't matter. Maybe she's right about the bed and maybe she's wrong, but I know Reeve. "Listen, I'm sorry I wasn't upfront with you. Maybe I should have told you as soon as I made the connection, but I just didn't. It seemed like something that I heard about and that went nowhere. And Reeve has no involvement."

"Even if he's not involved, I can't believe you didn't think this was a big deal." Her voice wavers, frantic. "You think it doesn't matter that only a handful of guys have violated her privacy like that? Or that thanks to the internet, that photo is forever? That she stands zero chance of erasing it from existence and has to worry for the rest of her life where and when it'll pop up?" Her voice cracks, tears welling in her eyes.

"Lenni," I say softly. "Baby, don't cry." I reach for her, but she stands stiff and tense in my arms. "I'm sorry. I was stupid, but I wasn't trying to lie to you."

She turns her head away. "It's not just that."

"Then what?"

She stands frozen, staring at nothing.

"Lenni, what is it?"

Fear builds in me with every second that she doesn't speak.

Finally, she recites for me in a toneless voice what happened. How those piece-of-shit football players from high school didn't just play a joke on her, how they videoed and humiliated her, how their punishment meant nothing. "I wondered every day of high school who might be watching the video at that exact moment," she finishes. "Sometimes I still do."

I struggle for words. I wait to feel anger or sadness, but the feeling instead is something new. It's a deep, gutting loss at knowing this happened to her. That it's over and I wasn't there to stop it. That I missed my chance to save her.

"There's one more thing." Her eyes are trained on some faraway place beyond me. "The guy who passed around the video? I didn't just know him—he was my friend. We grew up together, played at each other's houses when we were little. By high school, we weren't exactly best buds, but I thought I knew him. But our history didn't mean a thing compared to his team."

I stand there paralyzed by the feeling of uselessness. "I wish I knew what to say," I tell her feebly. "I wish . . . shit, I wish I could have—"

"It's okay," she says, saving me from my sputtering nonsense. "You don't have to say anything. Whatever you're wishing, I wish it too."

She rests her forehead on my shoulder and this time she lets me hold her. I try not to think about the depth of pain she must have felt because I'll probably lose my mind and that's not what she needs. Later, when I'm alone, I can feel those feelings but not right now.

"Thank you for trusting me enough to tell me," I murmur against her skin. "I don't ever want you to feel alone."

She nods. I kiss her head and hold her tighter. For the first time, she feels small against my body. I've always loved how tall and strong Lenni is, how completely she shatters the "fragile woman" stereotype, but I realize now how vulnerable she is. Without warning, I feel choked by emotion, overwhelmed by the strength of everything I feel for her. It's pure and it's unlike anything I've felt before.

Lenni looks up at me. "I probably should have told you sooner."

I swallow hard, fighting to get a grip on myself. "Not if you weren't ready."

She takes my hand. "Let's go home."

I don't speak until we're inside her apartment.

"I see why this picture thing hurts you so much," I say while she sorts slowly through a pile of mail on her kitchen counter. "I'm sorry I didn't get it."

"You didn't know."

"No, I'm a shithead. I should have done something. I wasn't really thinking of Sasha's feelings. I don't know why, I just . . . didn't think of it that way."

"Sasha? That's the girl?"

"Uh-huh."

Lenni looks up. "So you know her?"

"She hooks up with a lot of football players. Including Reeve." As soon as I say it, I realize I'm totally confirming her suspicions.

"Which explains why she'd be in his bed."

"But doesn't mean he took the picture."

"What if he did?"

"He didn't."

She puts down the envelope in her hand. "What if he did?"

"Then he deserves to be punished for it," I say carefully.

She gives me a satisfied look.

"Wait, Lenni. What are you after here?" She turns to leave the kitchen, but I reach for her. "I know you're mad at Reeve, and I don't blame you, but you're on the wrong track this time."

"I'm not mad at him, but if he's guilty, he deserves to be outed. Don't think I would protect him because he's your best friend."

"Protect him?" It dawns on me what she's saying. "You're writing a story about this?"

"Someone will; if the facts are confirmed and it's traced back to the football team."

Suddenly, this whole conversation looks different. It's her story that Lenni is so concerned about. "And who are they asking to confirm the facts, you?"

"I'll provide any information I have, and if I have good reason to think Reeve is involved, I'll say so."

"Lenni, no. You can't do that."

"Why?"

"Because it's not a fact, it's a suspicion. This is professional journalism, right? Not some gossip column? A story like that fucks with the entire team; it destroys careers."

Lenni looks so unaffected that it chills me. I don't even recognize her, this girl who would gladly drop Reeve's name in the center of a scandal. And for what? Revenge doesn't seem like her taste. Some symptom of the trauma she went through in high school?

"Whatever is published will be based on facts, just like any investigative piece would be," she reminds me. "If your best friend isn't involved, you have nothing to worry about."

"Bullshit! You have no facts and you're still about to drag his name through the mud. That's not the kind of damage you can undo."

"Why are you so worried about him? The guy has everything! He's a spoiled celebrity who gets away with whatever he wants, all because he can throw a stupid ball."

"So that makes it okay for you to pin this shit on him?"

"I'm only following the lead that was dropped in front of me."

"You're wrong about him."

"Tell me how I'm wrong."

"He doesn't have everything, he has one thing. Football. He had a shitty life growing up: no siblings, a dad who took off before he could walk, and a mom who could barely hold it together for more than a couple weeks at a time. He grew up in the meth-head section of town that I bet you didn't know existed; I didn't until we'd been friends for two years."

"Well, poor Reeve," she says coldly. "So his life isn't perfect. Just like all of us."

"So you have every intention of implicating him in this bullshit."

"If he's guilty, sure. A rough childhood doesn't cancel out a sexual crime."

"What's with you? Why are you so casual about taking down someone with no evidence? You're not waiting to see if he's guilty; you've already decided you want him to be."

"The truth will come out," she says flatly, like even she doesn't believe the trite garbage she's spewing.

"And by then it'll be too late for Reeve's reputation, you know that? Scouts won't touch him if there's even a hint of a scandal around him. And maybe that makes you glad, but if you're bringing down Reeve, you're bringing down the entire team. Including me."

Her face is unreadable.

"Don't do it, Lenni. Please."

I watch the chill in her eyes thaw as she stares back at me. A sob bubbles up out of her without warning. "You told me you'd be the man I deserve. Remember that?"

"Of course I do."

"What happened?"

"I'm trying. I want to be what you deserve."

"Yeah, just not as much as you want your football dreams."

"This isn't about my fucking football dreams."

"Then what is it about? Your teammates? Reeve?"

"It's about you not trusting me. You never have!"

"No," she says quickly. "It's about the fact that I'll always come second to your team, won't I?"

I'm silenced. She couldn't be more wrong. But let her take down my best friend? I won't let it happen. Her eyes blaze as she waits for an answer. I should say something, but my brain is spinning with her accusations, her revelation about her past and my own confusion at finding myself smack in the middle of the shitstorm. She wants me to take her side, but for once, I can't. So I say nothing.

"Leave," she demands when the silence goes on too long. "I don't want to see you."

"Lenni," I start.

"I mean it, Cameron. Leave my house and leave me alone."

Good, I think. I don't want to be around her any more than she wants to be around me right now.

But as I turn to go, she adds, "For good."

I stop to gape at her. She's lost her mind. "Just like that?" I feel a strange, cold smile come over my face and disappear just as quickly. How did we end up here? "Really? We're over?"

"Really. We're over." She nods. "Go."

I don't know why I'm listening to her—this is bullshit—but I walk to the door. If she needs space to figure out she's gone completely off the rails this time, she can have it. Before I go, I turn to look at her. "You can bring down the entire football team if you want, but it's not going to touch the guys who hurt you, Lenni." My voice is low and angry. "It won't fix you."

lenni

I LISTEN to his footsteps recede down the hallway, steps that never hesitate. And even though I want desperately for him to turn around and come back to me, I'm amazed by how right it feels that it's over between us. I can be alone. Better to be alone than to be second choice. And now I know for certain that's the most I can be. Cam is the wall that protects Reeve, and I'm never getting past it.

I feel raw with jealousy and even more ashamed to feel it. I want to be the one that Cam defends to the death; I can't believe how much I want it. But if I can't have it, fine. So I'll be lonely; there are worse fates than being alone.

This sentiment lasts me the rest of the day. It's when the sun goes down and the world turns dark that I realize alone is so much lonelier than it was before Cam.

EVERY MORNING when I wake up, I'm greeted by the same double gut punch: Cam isn't mine anymore, and I let it happen.

I trudge through the days, asking myself how I could have

been so certain I was right to break up with him, wondering how it's possible to feel so drained by my own rollercoaster of emotions while also feeling utterly empty inside. Everything reminds me of him. Couples holding hands, guys with wavy hair, any mention of football which of course is never-ending considering it's November in America.

My only comfort is the satisfaction of being right. I always knew Cam was unattainable; sooner or later, he'd choose football.

"You want to go to the game tomorrow?" Jade asks Friday evening as we cook spaghetti in our kitchen.

I do a double take. "The football game?"

"Sure. It's Saturday."

For a brief, wonderful time, the word Saturday had magical meaning. I watched every Shafer game, marveling at Cam's body and his skills and my own incredible fortune.

After home games, I'd wait in bed for him to walk in, his hair still wet and his skin smelling like soap, and he'd lie down exhausted and happy and let me take over. I was in control on Saturdays. Sometimes I'd take it slow, torturing us both as I explored every hard curve of his body, trying to figure out all the ways I could make him groan or twist his hands in my hair or sink his teeth into his bottom lip like he always did when he was close to coming. Other times, watching him on the field for three-plus hours would have me so worked up, I couldn't wait to get him inside me. Saturday sex was always the best sex.

I yank myself out of the memories. "No," I tell Jade a little too harshly. "I don't want to go to the game."

"Oh," she says like she's actually surprised. I eyeball her. She's been sweet and supportive since the breakup, but she's barely said a word about Cam. Highly suspicious for someone who lives for trashing men. "So you haven't told me what you think about my look."

I take in her hair, which has just been dyed an odd shade of green. "It doesn't flatter your skin tone."

She laughs. "I like you when you're grumpy."

"But I respect what you're doing." Sam was always vocal about green being the one color he didn't want to see on Jade's head. "Now, can you tell me what's going on?"

"With what?"

"You've been weird about me and Cam breaking up. You think I was wrong?"

"Nope. He was dishonest."

"You were starting to like him, weren't you?"

"Ugh." She makes a face. "In his dreams."

"Then why haven't you had a single mean thing to say about him?"

She busies herself stirring the boiling spaghetti. "You want marinara or just butter?"

"I'm not eating." Save for a few packs of Hostess cupcakes a day, I haven't had an appetite. "Why haven't you said anything about Cam?"

"No real reason. I'm just not going to trash the guy until I'm sure."

"Sure of what?"

"That you're over for good." She looks at me like she's hoping for some kind of big reaction.

"Oh, trust me, we are. His team will always come first, even if it means protecting his friend from owning up to his shitty behavior."

Jade bobs her head from side to side like she's not sure she agrees.

"That's not what happened?" I challenge her.

She turns to me. "This photo thing is really personal to you, as it should be. I just wonder if it's giving you tunnel vision."

I cross my arms. "How so?"

"You're jumping to conclusions. Reeve could be guilty, but if this were any other story involving anyone else, you'd be putting in hours of research before you even considered that you might have an answer.

"This isn't about journalism, it's about my life."

"Right. Your past life walking straight into your present and complicating things."

"And he couldn't handle that complication. Come on, Jade, are you actually—"

"I'm not excusing Cam," she says.

"Then what are you doing?"

With a maddening lack of urgency, she fishes a strand of spaghetti from the pot and takes a bite. She shakes her head, unsatisfied. "You made an assumption and you're hurting because of where it led you," she finally says. "I don't care if you're with Cam or not, but sooner or later, you're going to start questioning your assumptions."

"Well, I can't exactly prove Reeve did it. I just have to trust myself."

"Forget Reeve and forget the photo; that's not what I'm talking about. Lenni, you need to make sure you understand the choice Cam made."

"I understand what he chose. Football."

She doesn't say anything, but her eyes say it all. *Are you sure?*

"He did, Jade. You weren't there. It was crystal clear."

"Okay," she says simply, turning back to the spaghetti. "So fuck him."

Of course there's truth in what Jade says. I assumed Reeve was guilty. I let my own complicated past tear down what I had with Cam, and I didn't leave room to consider Cam's past. But it doesn't change the fact that he stood there and told me—without saying anything at all—that football comes first. In the long, horrible silence, he could have told me I was wrong.

I won't question my assumptions because it would only be an exercise in pain. To consider that Cam might still be the man I fell for is a door I refuse to open. I can't get it wrong again.

THIRTY-SEVEN

Cameron

ANGER COVERS me like an extra layer of skin.

I like it because it's always there. When I start thinking about Lenni, anger is there to take over and remind me that if she didn't care about her stupid article more than she cared about me, we'd still be together.

Problem is, anger is a thin layer. One minute of actual reflection and I've cut right through it. It's not really about the article. It's her pain and her past and all the things I didn't say when she asked me to choose her; that I'd give up football in a second if it meant keeping her, but that I can't take it away from my best friend, not when he needs it in ways even I don't understand. That I can't take it from Cash and Lorenzo and the dozens of guys on the team. For some of them, it's life.

At first, I think she just needs time to cool off, but days pass with no word from her. So maybe it was always bound to turn out this way. There are feelings and then there's real life; no matter how much I adore Lenni, I won't throw my best friend under the bus so she can move past her bad memories. And no matter how much she cares for me, life did her wrong, and she's looking for signs that it hasn't stopped.

But rationalization doesn't blunt the pain.

What we had was so good, so real, and we'd only just gotten started. Now that I've tasted what my life was missing, what am I supposed to do without it?

WEDNESDAY NIGHT, Reeve finds me in my room after practice. I haven't told anyone what went down with Lenni because I didn't expect us to still be broken up.

"Hey." Reeve flips on the lights. "Jerking off in the dark again?"

"Nah."

"Where'd you disappear to after practice? We were looking for you to grab dinner with us. I thought you'd be at Lenni's."

"I wasn't hungry."

He sits at my desk chair and takes in my pathetic appearance as I sit hunched on the edge of the bed. "What's wrong with you? Girl problems?"

"Yeah. It's over."

"Over?" He laughs and scoops a miniature football off my floor, tossing it between his hands. "It just started."

"No kidding."

"Chin the fuck up, man. A couple months together isn't enough to earn you a broken heart." Met with silence, Reeve drops the smile. "All right, clearly she dumped you. What happened?"

"What happened?" I look at him for the first time. "You fucked Sasha James, that's what."

He spins the ball in his hands. "What are you talking about?"

Fucking Reeve, leaving messes everywhere he goes.

Suddenly I'm furious. "Have you heard about some guys on the team having naked pictures of Sasha?"

"I mean . . . not really, but she's probably sent nudes to half the team so it's not shocking."

"She didn't send this one. Someone took it without her knowing."

He pauses. "That's fucked up," he says dumbly.

"Yeah, it is, especially because the picture was taken in your bedroom."

"Hold on. No goddamn way."

"Yes. No question about it."

Reeve shakes his head. "I didn't take any pictures of her."

"Did you hook up with her in your room?"

"Once."

"When?"

He scowls. "I don't know, man. I guess it was at that big party we had the week school started. But I never took a picture of her."

We stare at each other for a moment before I turn away.

"Hey!" Reeve stands up and the football rolls onto the floor. "I didn't fucking take pictures of her, Cam. You know I would never do that!"

I do know. Reeve goes through girls faster than toilet paper, but he isn't dishonest and he doesn't treat women like that. But then I think of Lenni and the guys who hurt her all those years ago, and doubt hits me all over again. Maybe I'm wrong to think I know Reeve so well I can be sure he wouldn't play some stupid drunken prank. It wouldn't be the first time someone I trusted turned out to be a stranger.

"Cam. Say something, man."

I blink, trying to push away the anger and let logic take over, but everything is swirling inside me. "It was your bed," I say. "Who else would have taken a picture like that?"

I meant it as an accusation and Reeve takes it as one, flinching like he's been slapped. "Literally anyone at the party could have done it. I left her sleeping in bed and came back downstairs, remember?"

I remember. Some of the guys had whooped and clapped as Reeve came down the steps and there were a few comments about losing track of how many guys on the team Sasha had slept with. I swallow hard, knowing I laughed along. I remember looking around and seeing the one guy who wasn't laughing: Mason. We all remembered the way Sasha had very publicly shot Mason down last year, and not just once. It was hilarious because no one had ever known Sasha to turn down a football player's advances.

"Not literally anyone," I say. "You'd have to be a pretty big piece of shit to do that."

Reeve flares up. "If you think I did it, then grow some balls and say it, Cam."

"I know you didn't."

Reeve's features shift with relief.

"I think I know who might have, though."

"Oh, yeah, I see those wheels turning. Put that big-ass brain to work for me, brother. What are you thinking?"

"Connery."

Reeve looks disappointed. "No, dude, Sasha would never fuck him."

I roll my eyes. "Catch up, dumbass. He doesn't have to fuck her to take a picture of her. He's a fragile little weasel, and she humiliated him."

"You mean that creep was slithering around my room?"

"It has to be him. There weren't that many football guys at the house that night. And let's be real. Our team is a bunch of animals, but they aren't shitty enough to do this."

Reeve nods and sits back down. "So Mason's confirmed

subhuman. But why does that have you sitting alone in the dark and pining like some douchebag from a soap opera?"

The heaviness returns. "Someone let Sasha's picture get beyond the locker room. The paper's working on a story about it, probably trying to identify players and expose them. As sexual assailants."

"Shit. That's bad."

"No kidding, Reeve. Especially because you're the one who looks guilty."

"They think I did it?"

"Lenni does. She's seen the picture, and she's been in your bed, remember?" We look away from each other. It's an ugly memory.

"Shit. You gotta tell her she's got it wrong."

"I did. Hence"—I gesture to myself— "sad soap opera douchebag."

"So she dumped you for taking my side."

"She's got some . . . shit from her past. The story's personal to her."

He nods slowly, then looks down at his lap. "Sorry, Cam. And . . . thanks."

I don't deserve Reeve's gratitude when five minutes ago I was waiting for him to tell me he was guilty. "It's not doing us any good if Lenni still thinks you did it."

Reeve runs a hand through his hair, his expression spreading into a grimace. "A story like that would destroy me." He says it slowly, like he's only now beginning to imagine the possibilities. "And sink our team."

My head feels heavy, and I let it drop into my hands. I don't tell Reeve that while the idea of a team scandal and Reeve's career being on the line fills me with dread, it's the thought of Lenni that makes my heart twist with pain, what her obsession with this story is doing to her. What it'll always remind her: that I let her down.

"So what are we gonna do about this?" Reeve asks.

"No clue." I shut my eyes. "But we're gonna do something."

AFTER PRACTICE THE NEXT DAY, I skip the shower and head over to where the field hockey girls play. They're still practicing, so I watch for a few minutes. When Sasha and three of her teammates finally head my way, I catch her eye and wave. Her friends exchange knowing smiles, but Sasha looks surprised as she breaks away from them to meet me.

"Hi," she says uncertainly.

"Hey. Sorry to ambush you. You have a few minutes to talk?"

"I guess so. Is this about Reeve?"

I shake my head and start walking in the opposite direction as her teammates. She falls into step next to me. I realize I know almost nothing about Sasha. There's a lot of talk about her on the team, and I've heard more descriptions about what she's like in bed than I want to. I've seen her boobs and her ass, thanks to that fucking picture. But I don't even know what she's studying. I feel unexpectedly ashamed.

"How have you been?" I ask.

"What's wrong, Cam?"

I clear my throat. I should have planned this better. "I guess I was wondering if you've heard anything about a, um, photo. Of you."

She glances over at me, then looks ahead. "Yeah. You've seen it?"

"Just for a sec." I feel like a complete asshole.

"Has Reeve?"

"He didn't know about it until I told him yesterday. Listen, I'm really sorry someone did that to you."

She shrugs, but she won't look at me. "You didn't do it."

"But I'm a team captain, which makes me responsible for the crap that goes on in the locker room. Whether they know it or not, consider this an apology from the whole team."

"Oh, wow. Does this come with an official certificate or something? Maybe a signed football?"

I know she's trying to minimize it, but I can't bring myself to smile. "Do you know who did it?" I ask.

"Mason, I assume. He hit on me again that night at your house and I rejected him. I guess I was a bitch about it, but he doesn't seem to understand the word 'no'. Whatever. He called me a slut, and a week later I hear about the picture."

"That's who I thought too."

"How come?"

"He was the only one at that party who's asshole enough to do it." I look down at the ground. "And he's the one who showed me the picture."

She nods like she's unaffected but keeps her gaze straight ahead.

"It was a split second. I didn't know what he was about to show me, he just held up his phone and—"

"It's fine, Cam. Don't stress." Guilt churns in my stomach. Here she is trying to make me feel better when she's the one who's hurting. Why did I think I could have this conversation and not feel like a jerk?

"I tried to shut it down when I saw it, but I guess I didn't try very hard. To be honest, I didn't give a whole lot of thought to how you'd feel about it. I'm sorry, Sasha."

"It's not that big of a deal," she says, but I don't buy it. "I know people talk about me. I just ignore it."

"Talk is one thing."

"Yeah, it's a little more than talk, isn't it?" She sniffs. "Anyway I should head in. I have a lot of studying tonight."

"Sure. Sorry if this was . . . weird."

"It definitely was," she says with a brief smile. "But thanks."

I nod, not wanting her to go yet. I'm not sure if what I've said has had any meaning at all to her, or if I've just embarrassed her more.

"What, Cam? You want to say more, I can tell."

"I'm just thinking . . . you don't have to ignore it, you know."

Sasha looks up at me, and this time she looks sad. For the first time, I notice how blue her eyes are.

"You could go to the school. The athletic director. You'd have every right."

"You don't actually want me to do that."

I swallow. "I'm only saying that you don't have to take it. If you do, I worry you'll regret it."

She studies me. "This isn't just about me, right?"

"It's about you. And someone else I know."

"Someone with regrets, I'm guessing?"

"I don't really know, actually."

She nods. "Well, I'm sorry this someone might or might not have regrets, but I'm not interested in going to the school or anyone else."

"Then tell me what I can do."

She looks exasperated. "Nothing, Cam. Leave it alone. I just want to forget about it, and I want you to do the same." Sasha shakes her head. "I gotta run. See you around."

I watch her head for the building, then I turn to cut across the grass toward the main part of campus. I really wanted that conversation to be simple, the problem fixable. I wonder if I just made everything worse for Sasha.

Realization comes down hard on me: I'm responsible. Whether it was one player or a dozen, part of my team did this.

And what kind of captain do I want to be? The kind that's flooded with relief at knowing Sasha wants to sweep the matter under the rug, probably just like captains before me? Or the kind that has the strength to change myself and maybe even the whole team? That answer, at least, is obvious. I need to do something, whether it's for Sasha or some future girl I'll never know. I just don't know what.

My stomach churns with a sudden rush of nerves. I've always been proud of the type of team captain I am: quiet, calm, leading by example. Turns out, that's not enough. I've had that role dialed in for so long, I never thought I'd have to change. To be outspoken, to call people out, to force all of us to think beyond what's best for the team might as well be speaking a foreign language. Where do I begin?

"Cam!"

I turn around to see Sasha jogging toward me, field hockey stick in hand.

"Maybe there is something you can do," she says when she reaches me.

"Shoot," I say. Maybe Sasha has the playbook I desperately need.

"Kick his ass for me, Cam."

I study her face. It's dead serious. "Really?"

"Really. When he thinks of that picture, I want him to remember his humiliation, not mine." At her side, her fingers have gone white, wrapped tightly around her stick.

"As you wish."

cameron

"IT'S SO nice to have you home," Mom says, sliding a glass of iced tea across the marble countertop toward me.

It's Sunday and even though home is close to campus, it's the first time I've been back since September, when we celebrated my grandparents' anniversary.

"Good to be here. Nobody does laundry quite like you, Ma," I tease. I've been trying all afternoon to keep things light. When it's just the two of us like this, Mom's got a sixth sense for when something's wrong. "You catch the game yesterday?"

"Of course I did." She leans against the kitchen island. "Harris and I watched it together."

"I thought you were done with that fucko."

"Cameron! Language!"

I shrug.

"I might be done with him. I'm still deciding." She gives me a coy smile. Suddenly, the new sparkly red gemstone necklace she's sporting makes sense. "Quite a season you boys are having." Mom gives me an appraising look. "Think I'll be permitted to attend another game this season or is the stadium only big enough for one woman that your father—"

"Mom!" I cut in. I don't want to know what she was about to say. "We both know the stadium isn't big enough for both of you. But Serena won't be there anymore. I told her she better just catch the games on TV from now on." It wasn't an easy conversation, but when Serena called a few days back asking about the next game, I told her we'd have to find another way for me to see Liam.

She smiles and reaches across the counter to squeeze my hand.

"Just don't blow it out of proportion. I'm still going to see Liam, so I have to see Serena. But she's not family. I'm just here for my brother."

Mom furrows her brow like she's trying to decide whether this is good enough for her. "You feel responsible for him?"

"Yeah. And I like him. I love him, actually."

"You always did want a baby brother." She sighs, her face relaxing.

"Might not be too late for you and Harris, huh, Ma?"

"Good god, Cameron. I'd sooner die." She takes a long drink, then looks out the window. "I always knew you were a better man than your father." She doesn't want to seem too pleased, because she didn't get everything she wanted. But I can tell by the smile she keeps trying to push down that she's happy. "Well, Harris was quite impressed with your game on Saturday. You looked as good out there as you ever have. There's no reason why you shouldn't be at the top of any team's list." She looks at me directly, making it clear this is a question, not a comment.

"Maybe. There are a lot of good receivers my age."

She waits for more, but I've got nothing. "You don't seem terribly invested in impressing a future employer. I admire your confidence, doll, but perhaps it's getting the better of you."

"I'm working my ass off on the field, I just have other things I need to work on too."

"Well, of course. Your studies are always important, but you've never had to work hard for good grades."

"I'm not just talking about grades." I take a swig of iced tea to buy myself a few seconds. I've been waiting days—years?—to tell her this, but my conviction is wavering. I push through. "I've been talking to a PR firm in Atlanta about an internship next summer."

Mom blinks at me. "Oh. I didn't imagine you'd have time for an internship given summer training ahead of your senior season."

"Coach is cool with it."

"Hmm. I'm not sure how much value PR experience has for a football star."

I bite the inside of my cheek. Now I'm not just a presumed professional player, I'm a star. Christ. "A pro career isn't a sure thing, you know that." It's the first time I've said these words to her, but I wonder how many hundreds of ways I've managed to imply them before.

"Barring a major injury—and that's a notion I refuse to entertain!" she says dramatically, looking up as though she's just daring the heavens to mess with her grand plans. "There's no reason you shouldn't end up playing pro. That's always been the plan, and it's all but done now."

It would be so easy to just nod like I always do and let her continue riding around on her fantasy cloud, but I'd only be hurting her more. And hurting myself. My world didn't shatter when I told Lenni my life might not look like everyone expects it to, and it won't shatter when I tell Minnie, either. At least that's what I've been telling myself all weekend.

"Mom, there's something I should have told you a while ago."

She freezes with her glass halfway to her mouth and puts her hand to her heart.

"You can breathe, okay? I'm not coming out of the closet. I just want you to know that pro football might not be the road I want to take, even if I get the chance."

She stares at me, speechless. I think she would have been less surprised if I *had* come out as gay.

"I love football, but not like I used to. Being a pro is a lifestyle, not a job, and I don't know if I want to devote every day of my life to that."

Mom blows out the breath she was holding and presses her glass to her forehead. "Cameron," she mutters, closing her eyes.

"It's not the end of the world," I say, annoyed. "I can be successful in another field."

Her eyes open wide. "We've spent the last decade preparing you for this! Every weekend, every summer. The people we socialized with and the sacrifices we made; it all revolved around you and your team, Cameron. It's who we are as a family!"

I knew she'd fight me on this, maybe even faint just to make me feel extra guilty, but I didn't expect these to be her reasons. She should be telling me I can't turn my back on football because I love the game. Instead, she's saying I owe her one.

Meanwhile, she's still going. "I'm sure you'll accuse me of being dramatic, but football has always been your destiny! You can't just walk away from it." For once, she's not being dramatic. Football has always been my destiny. But now? I don't know.

"But I might, Mom."

She shakes her head rapidly, her lips so thin they've disappeared. "And then what? What do I tell everyone who's just waiting for draft day to see you in the top ten?"

"You tell them you were wrong about me."

Her nostrils flare and she turns on her heel to walk away.

"Mom." Normally a Mack truck couldn't stop Minnie from flouncing out, but this time, she hesitates. "This has been on my mind a long time, and the only reason I didn't tell you was because I didn't want to let you down. You did everything for me, and you deserve a lot more out of life than the shitstorm Dad left you. I just don't know if I can be the one to deliver."

Mom blinks slowly and then strides out of the kitchen, no doubt headed for her bedroom where she'll flop theatrically onto her bed. I think I've witnessed more of Mom's dramatic exits than I have her cheering from the sidelines. When I hear her bedroom door slam, that's my cue to follow her, knock tentatively and then sit on the edge of her bed and console her.

But today I think, *Fuck it.*

I don't owe her an apology, and I definitely don't owe her a pro football career. I remind myself of this preemptively, before the feelings of guilt come rushing over me like always. But surprisingly, they don't come.

Actually, I feel good.

I head for the laundry room and gather my clean clothes into my duffel bag. I put Mom's glass and mine into the dishwasher, then take the container of food she saved for Reeve out of the fridge. I don't like to leave without saying goodbye, but I'm not getting drawn into her web today.

As I head out the side door near the driveway, I'm surprised to find Mom sitting on the steps looking out into the garden.

"I'm heading back," I tell her. "Thanks for the food, Ma. For all of it."

"You're always welcome." She doesn't look at me.

"I'll call you tomorrow." I head down the steps past her.

"I love you."

"Love you too."

As I pull the truck door shut, she comes down the steps. I

roll the window down and take a breath, readying myself for either a chewing out or a tear fest.

Mom rests her hands on the window frame and looks at me. "I mean it. I love you, Cameron, no matter what."

"I know you do."

"And I'm proud of you, no matter what, football or not."

I want to tell her I know that too, but I don't.

Her gaze goes soft, looking past me. "It's not easy for me to see the dreams I had for you change."

"For me, either."

"I suppose not. But it's important you know that if you do choose a different road, I won't be any less proud of you." The smile she offers is weak, a little sad even, but it's real.

I've thought a hundred times about how Mom would react to me changing my plans, but I can't remember if I ever thought about how she'd feel. "You've had your eyes on the title of pro football mom for years now. Maybe I can't blame you if you're a little disappointed."

"That shouldn't be your concern. Even if someday your choices do disappoint me, I'll still love you even more than I did the day before."

I put my hand on hers. "Thanks, Ma."

As I back out of the driveway and head up the same street I've driven a thousand times before, I breathe a little easier. Everything that waits for me at Shafer is still a crushing weight on my chest: Lenni, my mistakes, my team, and the promises I still need to fulfill.

But I told my mom the truth, and the world's still spinning.

***

Practice on Monday is a struggle.

My muscles teem with energy and anticipation, but for once

there's something more important than football I need to save it for.

Afterward, I wait until the locker room's half empty before I stroll past Mason's locker. "Hey, Connery. Hang out with me for a bit, would you? Maybe we take a walk, grab a beer."

Mason stares at the smile on my face, trying to figure out what the hell is going on, then looks around like he's about to be ambushed. It's just me, though. He gives me a hard look and starts to turn back to his locker. "Yeah, right."

"Yeah, okay, I guess if you don't want to talk, I could go chat with Coach instead."

He hesitates as it sinks in. "Fine," he says, glaring at me over his shoulder. "Gimme a minute."

"Nah, now's good." I've put away the smile, and not without effort. I always thought fighting was stupid as hell, but I'm actually fucking excited. I finally have something worth fighting for.

Mason hasn't taken his eyes off me, but they've turned from cold to wary.

I motion toward the door. "After you," I say and follow him out of the locker room.

lenni

WHEN SOMEONE KNOCKS on the door Thursday evening, I almost don't answer. Jade's been busy treating every guy who glances her way like he owes her big, so her dating life is raging. A lot of dudes come knocking lately.

But this guy is persistent; he knocks again, then, after no answer, a third time.

I open the door and there's Reeve. Ugh. That's what I get for not using the peephole. We look at each other for a few cold seconds.

"Hey," he says finally.

"Hey."

His eyes dart from the empty hallway to me and then back again.

"Um, something I can do for you?"

He looks at me like he just remembered he's the one who came bothering me and not vice versa. "Yeah, I need to talk to you. We need to get straight about some things."

"Cam already told me his side of the story. I don't want to hear it from you."

"He doesn't know I'm here. And it's not his side of the story you need to hear, it's mine."

I study him, trying to figure out what his motive could be. "Why? You don't even like us together."

Reeve looks at the floor. "You know why, though."

Do I? Oh, god. Does Reeve have actual feelings for me? All this time, I thought our short-lived flirtation was him playing games for the fun of it, and maybe hoping for an easy hookup. But was he jealous? Did he actually—

"I know you can't stand me," Reeve says, interrupting my runaway thoughts. "I was afraid you'd talk shit about me, and sooner or later, Cam would get on board."

Oh.

"Anyway, I'm sorry about that, okay? Seriously. I was just being . . . insecure, I guess." He mumbles this last part, catching me off guard with his puppy-dog eyes. And okay, maybe it's slightly endearing.

"It's fine. It doesn't matter now anyway." I'm surprised by the sadness the words bring.

"Don't get ahead of yourself," Reeve says. "So can I come in?"

I bite the inside of my cheek. I don't want Reeve inside my house, but I'd be lying if I said I'm not curious. I can't think of anything he could say that would change the ugly facts of what went down between me and Cam, but maybe, just maybe . . .

"Just for a little bit," I tell him.

Inside, he shoves his hands in his pockets and glances awkwardly around the apartment. It's odd to see his larger-than-life personality shrink inside the four walls of this small space. He follows me to the kitchen where I get us each a sparkling water.

"Thanks." He looks around again, probably so he doesn't

have to meet my eye. "This isn't what I expected your house to look like."

"What did you expect?"

"I don't know. Books?"

"Yeah, I have those. Just not in the kitchen."

"Right." He nods. "Listen, uh, I came to talk about Cam, but I guess there's something I better say first."

I take a drink.

Reeve studies his shoes before raising his eyes to mine. "I'm really sorry about what I did to you that night in my room. I was surprised, but it's not an excuse for treating you so badly." He closes his eyes for a second, and when he opens them, I have to concentrate on not looking away. "I made you feel like shit, and that's the last thing I ever wanted to do to you. I'm sorry, Lenni."

The sincerity of his apology makes my already raw emotions swell dangerously. I swallow hard against the threat of tears. "I understand," I say, grateful my voice doesn't sound as shaky as I feel. "I wouldn't want to be judged for my actions on that night either."

"So you'll think about forgiving me?"

"I already do. It's in the past now."

His expression eases and he lets out a deep breath. "Thanks."

I nod toward the sitting area. "Come on. Tell me what you came here for."

We sit opposite each other, Reeve on the edge of the couch and me in an armchair. He gets right down to it.

"I didn't take the picture," he says. "I had nothing to do with it, and neither did Cam."

I sag with disappointment. "I thought you were going to tell me something I haven't heard a dozen times already."

"It's a fact, Lenni, and I don't know why you won't accept it. Cam isn't protecting me. Do you get that?"

"That's just it!" I snap. "He *is* protecting you, whether you took the picture or not."

He tilts his head. "What?"

"It doesn't even matter anymore who took the picture. He's protecting you, he's protecting the team, he's protecting his football career. And I'm a distant second."

Reeve leans forward. "Why shouldn't he protect me?"

"What?"

"He didn't tell you about us growing up together, did he?" he asks, a little too haughtily for my liking.

"Yes, he did. You had it rough growing up, so you spent a lot of time with his family. You guys were like brothers."

He gives a rueful smile. "I know you two were all loved up, and I'm sure you've shared a lot. But that's the version of the story Cam tells when he doesn't want me to look like a total fuckup."

I wait for him to go on, feeling uneasy.

"Yeah, my mom rarely had her shit together, and the Forresters basically took me in as their own. They turned my life around. But I turned Cam's upside down too. He lied for me all the time. When my mom would forget to pack lunch or I'd pull out my brown bag and there'd be one frostbitten, still-frozen waffle in it, he'd pass me his food all sly-like so none of the other kids would know. It got to a point where the running joke among our friends was that the Forresters needed to fire their housekeeper because she only remembered to give Cam lunch half the time. I didn't have jack, and he shared everything —his clothes, his car—and never said a word to remind me I was just borrowing.

"He even took the fall for me twice in high school when I got into fistfights with this punk on our football team." He gives me a hangdog look and shrugs. "I was an angry kid back then. If Coach knew, I'd have been off the team just like that. Cam got away with a short suspension because he was a good kid, and probably because his family funded an entire wing of the school, but whatever. He didn't need football; he could have been a fucking rocket scientist if he wanted. Me? All I had was football. He protected me because he could."

I should be surprised, but I'm not. After all, he's only telling me what I already know about Cam. He's thoughtful, generous, loyal to the bone. It's Reeve, actually, that's making my heart squeeze with the fierce way he tells his story like he's trying not to get emotional. Like he's just daring me to disagree, so he has one more reason to talk up Cam.

But despite that, my bitterness only grows. If Cam can do all that for Reeve, why not me? "You're only proving my point," I say. "He protects you."

Reeve looks at me like he's only just remembered I'm here. "You don't need to be protected."

I laugh shortly. "You don't know that."

"Look, Cam hasn't told me any details, okay? Not a word. I only know the photo thing hurt you on a different level." His face softens, and I look away. "I guess you have your own story, and I don't pretend to know what that feels like. I only know that I hated you two as a couple because I used to be number one, and then I wasn't. He steps up for people he loves when they need it, not when they don't. And this time he stepped up for me."

"You think he took your side because I didn't need him on mine?"

"What would you think of him if he didn't stand up for me?"

I slump into the chair. I don't know what to think anymore. "Maybe I'd be glad," I say truthfully. "Someone needs to pay for what happened to that girl."

"Someone did. You know Mason Connery?"

"No."

"Lucky you. He admitted he took the picture, and he got his ass beat for it." Reeve looks proud.

"You beat him up?"

"Yeah, right. Look at these hands. Pristine." He holds up his large, smooth hands. "Nah, your boy took care of that."

I stare at him. "Cam beat the kid up?"

He grins, thrilled to be the one to break the news to me.

"I just . . . I can't picture him doing that."

"She asked him to."

"Who?"

"Sasha."

This stirs something deep in the center of my chest. "He did that for . . ." I almost say me, but I catch myself. "For her?"

Reeve nods. "He protects people when they need it. And he kicks people's asses when they need it."

I try to imagine the quiet, self-possessed Cam releasing all his strength on someone in the name of loyalty. It makes me ache for him. "Is he okay?"

Reeve snorts. "He's a lion taking on a weasel."

For a second, I let my mind wander to memories of his bruised, sore muscles under my fingertips, but I quickly shake it off. "If Cam didn't ask you to come here, why did you?"

Reeve fiddles with a cluster of candles sitting on the coffee table. "I dunno. Until now, I would've loved to be the reason you two broke up. But the reality isn't so cool, you know?"

"Why not? You've got your best friend to yourself again."

"He didn't go back to the way he was before you. He's

someone else now." He shakes his head. "And it doesn't look good on him."

AFTER REEVE LEAVES, I pace the apartment. The desire to see Cam is urgent. I want to run to him, breathe in his scent and let him wrap his arms around me. But then what? I don't know. I don't know if I forgive him or if there's even anything to forgive. A sinking feeling hits when it occurs to me. Maybe I'm the one who needs forgiveness.

It's so obvious now how completely out of my head I was threatening Cam with a story that would take down his best friend and maybe his whole team. I need help. Therapy. Something. I can't deny it any longer. I wasn't acting like a journalist, I was acting like a wounded little girl who would rather hurt someone else than try to heal. What was I thinking?

My memory goes back to all the times I told myself that Cam wasn't for me, all the doubts I felt when I pictured us together. I put it all on him, believing he couldn't be trusted. Now I realize those doubts were valid—but they weren't about him. I didn't know how to trust him. Reeve or not, photo or not, I was always going to end up blowing apart what we had.

I feel frenzied and I know my mind's not clear enough for the sort of apology Cam deserves, but I can't let another minute pass. I call him, and when he doesn't answer, I text him.

I'm sorry, I type. *I went way too far.*

I hit send and then type another message—*Can we meet up?*—but I erase it. I try again—*Can you forgive me?*—but I erase it too. Nothing feels right.

What do you say when you've gone too far? When the person who has always fought to win you back—despite your glaring flaws—has gone silent? When do you lose the right to ask for anything more?

After all, if Cam wanted me back, he could have come to me and said Mason Connery confessed to taking that photo. It would have absolved Reeve instantly. I would be wrong and Cam would be right. Again.

But this isn't like the last time.

This time, Cam isn't fighting to get me back.

lenni

I'M DREAMING, or at least I think I am.

It's a bright day. I'm on campus, the football stadium in the distance. Up ahead, I see Cam walking, his back to me. I call out to him, but he doesn't turn. I try to push past the people in front of me, but I'm slowly falling behind, though I keep calling his name. Suddenly, there's nothing but empty space between us. He hears me and turns. He looks at me and I smile. He gives me a nod, then turns away and walks on.

I wake up in the dark, thinking it was the nightmare that woke me. It's 4:12 a.m. But then I hear my phone buzzing urgently on the bedside table. My heart leaps. I'm half-asleep but fully aware I've heard nothing back from Cam in the almost-twelve hours since I texted him an apology. It's not Cam, though. It's Grandpa.

By five, I'm on the road back to my hometown in the dark. The blue matchbox car from my windowsill sits rattling in the cupholder next to me, grabbed in my desperation for something solid to take with me. I don't know exactly what I'll find at home because Grandpa was spare with the details. Mom has been drinking on and off for the last two weeks, but it was only yesterday that things exploded. Her boyfriend called the cops on her after a screaming match, she might not be able to live with Gus for a while, things are a mess, of course. Nothing I hadn't seen in my own childhood.

By the time we hung up the phone, Grandpa was apologizing for everything: calling me, waking me, upsetting me. He didn't want me coming home, but the sound of his voice told me he needed me. When I was growing up and Mom went through her shit, Grandpa always held it together, promising me things would be all right, making it easy for me to forget that Mom was his daughter and that her addiction tore him up too. This time, I could hear his heart breaking. He can't be the strong one this time. But maybe if I'm there, Gus won't have to take on that role.

When I walk into the house just before nine, Gus is sweeping loose papers into his backpack while Grandpa works at a stubborn knot in Gus's sneaker shoelaces, and Nana tucks the breakfast dishes into the dishwasher. All normal and familiar, right down to the grim smiles my grandparents offer when they shuffle over to hug me. Gus jumps on me and buzzes about his new sneakers until Nana ushers him out the door to meet the school bus. He seems happy, but he's nine now. I can't pretend he isn't aware that something is terribly wrong at home. I'm not sure what he witnessed yesterday, but he's old enough to hear everything that's not being said amid the tension in this little house.

Once he's gone, Grandpa pours sweetened condensed milk into a big mug of coffee and hands it to me. "You still take it that way, I hope?" he asks.

"The only way I drink coffee," I tell him.

The three of us sit down, but we don't say much aside from some small talk about school and a few more details about Mom. My grandparents' pasted-on smiles are gone, which I appreciate. Our family is screwed up, but at least we don't pretend otherwise. We can sit here together and commiserate over how much this sucks without saying much of anything.

Finally, I ask the obvious question. "Where is she?"

"Upstairs. Packing." Nana nods toward the ceiling. Since Mom and Gus moved in, Mom's been living in her old childhood bedroom. This makes me feel unbearably sad.

"Should I go talk to her?" I ask, even though it's a needless question. I guess I'm trying to delay the inevitable.

"Sure, if you've had enough coffee and small talk. You need a refill?" Grandpa asks, playing along.

I smile. "I think my sugar high is just kicking in. I'll go see Mom."

I take the stairs slowly. No matter how many times I've done this, and I've done it countless times, it always comes with the familiar concoction of dread and sadness churning in my gut, topped off with the urge to turn and run. Seeing Mom drunk and angry is awful, but this moment is the worst—when she's sober and filled with so much shame she can barely meet my eye, when I want her to know how much she's hurting us almost as much as I want to take her in my arms and wipe away her shame and tell her it's okay, we can move on and leave this all behind.

Her door is half open so I knock and walk in. Mom leans over the bed, carefully laying a pair of jeans into an open suitcase like she's tucking in a baby. She turns to me with a hard-earned smile but doesn't hug me.

"Hi, love," she says softly. "Grandpa told me he called you. He shouldn't have done that."

"Sure, he should've. I want to know what's happening at home."

"Well, I don't need you worrying about me. You've got school and your own life to think about."

I hate how she says this like it's Grandpa's fault I had to come rushing through the night to get home. "It's Gus I'm worried about," I say coolly. I think it surprises both of us.

Mom nods, then turns quickly back to her packing, but not before I catch the quiver in her lip. I know I'm awful for making her feel worse, but I'm so exhausted I can't find the energy to fake it. I'm so tired of being let down.

"Can I help you?" I ask.

"I've got it."

I stand there and watch as she slowly refolds a stack of folded clothing on the bed. "I'll help you," I finally say, sitting on the bed and taking a shirt from the pile. I fold slowly, matching her pace.

"Tell me about your life, Lenni." Mom sounds like a little kid asking for a bedtime story.

I want to tell her about Cam. I know I could get a genuine smile out of her if I told her about the tall, handsome football player with the intoxicating kiss. Nana says Mom's been boy crazy all her life. But that's not my life anymore. I want to tell her how it ended almost as quickly as it began so she can make it better like mothers are supposed to, but she'll only tell me to forget him, move on, find someone better. *The guy's a bum*, she'd say, summing Cam up the same way she's summed up every man she's ever known, save for her own father.

I tell her about school and the extra work I've been doing for the paper. I lay out my master plan for making editor by next fall. I invite her and Gus and my grandparents to drive up for homecoming in a few weeks.

She looks up at me. "I'm sure Gus and Grandpa and Nana would love to, but I can't be there. I'll be in rehab."

"Oh, right." Of course. I feel embarrassed, like I've been caught trying to pretend everything is normal. "Maybe I'll come home for the holidays this year," I find myself saying, though I really don't want to.

"I know you don't like coming home. I don't blame you either. It's just . . . we love having you around."

Guilt cuts through me like a knife. "And I love being around you all. I just don't like being here."

She nods, but I know she doesn't get it, and that makes me angry. She should get it. She knows what happened to me and that coming back to this town brings on a flood of bad memories. What's so hard to understand?

"Look, Mom, this is all just temporary: you living in Nana and Grandpa's house, me being far away, all the things that make life tough. In a year and a half, I'll be graduating, and before too long I'll have a good job in the city and a steady income. And then we can all be together."

She cocks her head. "Be together? In what city?"

I laugh, though it's out of irritation. "I've told you this before. I'm going to get you guys out of here and find you a real job and a good apartment. I'll be able to support this family, with a little help from your job, obviously. If you guys can just hang on a little longer, I'll make it better. I know what I need to do."

Mom pulls back, stunned. "Oh, Lenni," she says softly.

"What? That's always been the plan."

She sits on the bed beside me. "Sure, I've heard you mention that, but I didn't know you really took it to heart. Honey, it's not your job to make it all better."

"Why shouldn't it be? I want to."

"I see that. But supporting a family is hard work. Money and time and stress. And even if you could, you have to know that's not your responsibility. You take on that burden and you'll feel sixty before you even turn twenty-five."

"I could do it," I say feebly.

"No, love, you live your own life, and you make it what you want. That's your responsibility to this family."

"I can't live my life when I'm worried about you guys."

"Then quit worrying. Today when I walk into that rehab center, that's me taking responsibility so the rest of you don't have to, and I'm gonna make it work this time. This is the last time anyone in this family cries over my choices."

I stare at her hands folded in her lap. They don't look like my mom's hands anymore. "I want that to be true as much as you do, Mom. But what if it's not?"

"Then I'll try again. What I won't do is let you set aside your life for mine. You can forget that right now."

Forget that right now. It's right up there with all Mom's greatest hits. *The guy's a bum. Move on and let the past go. Don't let it get you down.* She wants everything to be as simple as saying the words, and it never is.

But this time, I wonder if there might be some wisdom in her advice. I can't imagine what life would look like if I forgot I ever promised myself I'd save this family. But I think I want to find out.

That afternoon, Grandpa and Gus and I stand in the driveway and wave as Nana's old blue sedan pulls away with Mom in the passenger seat. Gus is sad but hopeful. Between the four of us, he's probably been told a dozen times today that Mom is going to a special house full of doctors who will help her get better. I obviously don't tell him that she'd already been to this "special house" twice by the time I was his age and that her stays there amounted to little more than a complete waste of my grandparents' meager savings.

LATER, Gus and I drive into town for dinner and ice cream to give my grandfather some time alone. Gus is subdued until I tell him I've scraped together the money for spring soccer as promised. After that, he bounces around the ice cream shop and recites a list of the top ten soccer jersey numbers he's hoping for, complete with detailed explanations of why each number would be just perfect for him.

We're on the sidewalk walking back to my car when I look up at the young woman walking toward us, maybe a block away, and my stomach drops. Shit. Katie Weatherly? Is it really her? Katie was one of my closest high school friends until the incident with the football players. I stare. She's a little fleshier, but it's definitely Katie. I grab Gus's hand and dart into the alley between two brick buildings.

"What happened?" he asks loudly.

"Nothing, nothing."

"Why are we here? It smells." He gives a disapproving look at the trash carts lining the alley.

"It's a shortcut to the parking lot."

"Nuh-uh. You parked that way." He points in the opposite direction.

"Okay, fine. I forgot you knew left and right. I saw someone I used to know, and I didn't feel like talking."

He nods like he understands completely. "Was she mean?"

"No. She was really nice, actually. You probably don't remember Katie, but you liked her. She used to come over after school sometimes and give you the Fruit Roll-Ups that she didn't eat from her lunch."

"Oh, yeah, I remember those! They were the rainbow kind. She was nice. Why don't you want to talk to her?"

"Oh, I don't know. Maybe I'm just feeling shy."

Of course I know exactly why I don't want to talk to her. After what happened, I shut out all my friends from the "before time." It was easy with most of them because they were back-stabbing assholes who laughed at me or gossiped about me or got angry and called me a slut when the two guys, good old hometown football heroes, actually faced punishment for committing a sexual crime against a teenager. Katie was one of the few who stood by me and defended me and told me it wasn't my fault. But during those dark days, it didn't matter whose side anyone was on. I just wanted to forget what happened and who I was before that night.

Gus is giving me a look like he's not buying what I'm selling. "Mom says being shy isn't an excuse to be rude."

This is true. Kind of like having baggage isn't an excuse to treat the people who care about you like shit. Why do I always learn these things the hard way?

"Come on," I tell Gus. I hurry back toward the street before I can question myself, my footsteps almost as quick as my heartbeat. Please don't let her be gone.

Katie's still half a block away, stopped in front of a coffee shop and staring down at her phone.

"Katie!" I call, but I'm too quiet. She doesn't even glance up. I swallow and try again. My voice feels obnoxiously loud, but she hears me.

She looks up and hesitates, the furrow in her brow slowly deepening. Then a bright smile takes over. "Lenni Crawford? My god!" she shrieks.

She's already closing the distance between us, her arms spread wide to hug me.

I'm glowing the whole drive back to my grandparents' house. Katie and I only talked for a few minutes, but I feel transformed. I didn't think I was capable of seeing someone from high school and smiling without faking it and talking without thinking of what those guys did to me. I didn't think the power of my bad memories would ever lessen its hold on me. I was wrong.

Gus and I are both quiet until we turn into my grandparents' long gravel driveway and Gus gasps.

"Look! That truck looks like Cam's!" He points toward a big gray pickup sitting in front of the house, half-hidden by evergreens.

"No." I wave him off. "Must be one of Grandpa's friends." But immediately I'm going down the checklist of Cam's truck: gray paint, black pinstripe, black hubcaps with that little red logo detail that I know Cam loves because he rubs the dirt off with the hem of his T-shirt every time he gets in or out.

As we near the house, we move clear of the trees and there's Cam leaning against the front of the truck, as at ease in my grandparents' driveway as he is on the football field. The feeling that comes over me is one I don't have a name for. It hits like fear but is somehow delicious.

"It is Cam!" Gus practically shrieks. "You didn't tell me he was coming! Why'd he come?"

"I don't know." I force my eyes away from Cam so I can park the car without crashing. "I guess he wanted to surprise us."

Gus darts out of the car as soon as it stops. I watch in the rearview mirror as he races to Cam, gives him a leaping high-five and then breaks into nonstop chatter. Meanwhile, I sit glued to my seat, my mind racing and my heart hammering. How did he know where to find me? Why is he here? He doesn't text or call or knock on my apartment door, but he drives 250 miles to stand in the driveway and wait for me?

Also, has Grandpa come out yet to yell at him to get that goddamn truck off this property?

I sit for a few minutes, take a few dozen deep breaths. Cam

is chatting away with Gus, smiling and nodding at whatever fourth-grade nonsense my little brother is overflowing with, but he keeps glancing over at my car.

I can't stay in here forever.

lenni

I TAKE my time getting out of the car, avoiding Cam's gaze. When I finally look over, he's staring at me, not smiling any longer.

"Okay, Gus," I say when I reach them. "It's almost bedtime for you. Go shower and get in bed. And tell Grandpa my, um, friend came to visit." I glance at Cam, whose face gives away nothing. "I'll be in later."

Gus sighs deeply but doesn't argue, just gives Cam a long look and waves goodbye.

"See you later, buddy," Cam tells him. "Next time I'll bring my football, I promise."

Gus grins, then turns and runs for the door, calling for my grandfather before he's even made it inside.

When I look back at Cam, all the light that danced on his face when he talked to Gus has gone, replaced by a grave expression. He must know about Mom.

We look at each other, an odd sort of face-off. I notice the small cut on his lower lip and the slight swelling that anyone who hadn't memorized his lips probably wouldn't notice. The remnants of his fight. Something about this scrape on his otherwise perfect face makes me feel raw with tenderness for him.

I break first.

"What are you doing here?" I ask.

"Jade told me your mom's not doing well. I figured it had to be pretty bad for you to come back here."

I nod.

"Is she okay?"

"Mostly. She left for rehab a few hours ago." I trace my finger along the black pinstripe on the side of his truck, once again filled with that sick feeling of wishing none of this were happening. "Her boyfriend called the cops on her. She might not be able to live with Gus for a while."

Cam lets out a slow, heavy breath. "I'm sorry, Lenni. That's terrible. She must be hurting."

"You didn't have to come all the way up here," I say, trying to move away from the subject of Mom so I don't cry. "Four hours is a long drive."

"Just under three and a half for me," he says with a tiny smile, patting his truck. When I don't say anything, he takes a step closer. "I didn't want you to be alone."

My body stiffens. "I'm not. My grandparents and Gus are here."

He looks at me. His eyes are sad, but there's no pity there. They shine with a sort of sincere understanding that makes me ache, and I get it; that's not what he meant. I nod as tears prick the back of my eyes. He's right. I've felt so achingly lonely since I left Shafer, since I left him.

His arms are around me before the first tear rolls down my face, and it feels even better than the first time he touched me. I sink into him and let out a deep exhale. With all the horrible stuff happening at home, I feel bad for feeling so good right now, but I don't want it to stop.

Cam doesn't let go, but he pulls back to look at my face. "You want to take a ride?" He studies me. I hate being babied, but this time his tenderness makes my heart want to burst.

"Yeah." I wipe my cheeks. "Let's do that."

When I climb into his truck, I wonder if any other girls have been here since the last time I sat in this seat. Probably. I think that's what normal people do. Fuck someone new to get over a breakup. But that assumes said breakup has been hard to get over, and I don't know if that's the case for Cam. He never called or asked for another chance. For a second, I hate him. But then I look at him and he's watching me with that penetrating gaze that has never not made my heart skip a beat, and I know what I'm feeling isn't hate.

We ride around town without direction. We don't talk about Mom or us or much of anything. Instead, we listen to music, and I point out some of my old haunts and he tells me about the random oddities of his hometown, the parts of Shafer I've never seen. It's when we drive past my high school and there's not the expected rush of shame, that I realize this is the first time since I was sixteen that I've seen my town this way. Not as a place where dread and dark memories lurk, but just as the place where I grew up. Boring, stagnant, familiar.

Cam gets hungry, so we park in town and he buys two slices of pizza. Walking under the streetlights together, I don't feel the anxious push to get back to the safety of the car like I usually do, that fear of seeing someone who knows my past. I feel safe. And even though I long to take his hand and lean against him and feel the strength of his body like it's my own, I don't need to.

When we get back to the truck, I text Grandpa to let him know I'll be home late and not to stay up. Cam and I haven't talked about what's next, but I'm not ready to go home yet.

"He's a nice guy, your grandfather," Cam says as he backs out of the parking space. "Which way?"

"Doesn't matter. Wait, you met him?"

Cam turns left out of the lot, away from my house. "He was outside raking when I pulled up."

"I'm surprised he didn't brandish the rake as a weapon."

"No way. He invited me inside and everything. I could tell he wasn't expecting company, though, so I just told him I'd wait for you outside."

Even Grandpa isn't immune to Cam's quiet charm.

"Will he care if you're out late?"

"No, it's been a long time since he kept tabs on me on a Friday night." The words remind me of something. "Wait a minute, don't you have a game tomorrow?"

"Yeah, at eleven."

"Don't you need to get back? You'll be exhausted."

"I'll be on the bench; doesn't require much energy."

"What's that mean?"

He glances at me before turning his eyes back to the road. "I'm suspended."

"What? Cameron! What did you do?"

One side of his mouth lifts into a smile. "Take it easy, Mom. It's just one game." He swallows hard, the smile gone. There's no such thing as just one game. "I got into it with this kid on my team."

"Mason Connery?"

"You heard?"

"Reeve told me."

He flicks a surprised gaze my way. "When did that happen?"

"A couple days ago. No, wait, that was yesterday. He came to my apartment. Seems like a long time ago."

"He didn't tell me that. What did he want?"

"I guess for me to understand. He told me Mason's the one who took the picture of Sasha." My cheeks go warm. "I'm sorry, Cameron. I lost my head."

He drives on, his expression unreadable.

"I wouldn't have written a story about him without proof. I just got carried away with my own . . . issues."

He gives a single nod, but I don't know if this means he understands or he's just acknowledging the words to save me from my shame. "We don't have to talk about that. That's not why I'm here."

"Then why?"

His jaw is set. "I would never not show up for you, Lenni. No matter what happened between us."

I don't deserve this man.

"So is that why you beat Mason up? Because of the picture?"

He's quiet for a moment, his eyes steady on the road. "Sasha doesn't want the story out there. This was all she wanted. All I could do, anyway."

Why does this hit so deep? Emotion surges inside me, choking my throat. "Cam, pull over," I manage to say.

"Where?"

"Anywhere. That park on the right."

He pulls into the empty dirt parking lot next to a baseball field. There's a single flickering light over the field, but otherwise everything is dark.

I unbuckle and turn sideways to face him. "I was wrong about Reeve. And about you."

His gaze remains on the windshield in front of him.

"Missing a game is a big deal."

"She needed me to."

"Who?" I can only get the word out in a whisper.

He leans his head back against the seat and looks up at the

ceiling. He reaches for my hand, which he brings to his mouth. He kisses the back of my hand and sets it on the seat between us.

My heart swells, this innocent kiss hitting me like the answer to everything.

I study his profile, the familiar lines and curves of his face, and something locks into place, settling firmly in my mind in a space that was waiting for so long. If I had my laptop in front of me, I could find the words for it, but here in the dark, it's only thoughts swimming in my head. That healing doesn't always happen linearly. That life was once different, and it won't ever be that way again. That there's therapy and apologies and punishments, but sometimes they won't mean anything. But that someone making the wrong choice can mean everything when he's doing it for you.

Is he thinking it too, as he sits there silently? Maybe these aren't the conclusions Cam has drawn. He might be aching to play in that game tomorrow and wondering why he made such a big sacrifice when it doesn't change the past. But when he turns to me, there's not a hint of regret in his eyes.

I slide closer to him. There are things I should say like, *Thank you* and *Forgive me,* but they feel so hollow. His hand rests on the seat just below my leg, close enough I can feel the warmth coming off his skin. I lean over and kiss him.

Everything is like it was before except, somehow, more intense. There's no hesitation as our tongues meet, as he takes me in his lap and slides us to the relative roominess of the passenger seat. I press my body tight to his, taking in his heat. There's no space for questions between us.

I can't make sense of time as we kiss and grope in the dark. His touch is so familiar, but it sinks bone deep like I've never felt before. Our bodies move faster, yet time moves slower as we savor every inch of each other.

Pants are pushed down, though somehow, we never break the kiss. I straddle his lap. His fingers pull my panties aside. I shudder when his knuckles brush the slick heat between my legs.

He enters me with one smooth thrust, drawing a sharp breath from my throat. Cam lets out a low groan. I let my head fall back, luxuriating in this brief instant where pleasure bleeds into pain and back again.

His body settles into a steady rhythm. His fingers dig painfully into my hips as he fucks me, possessing me. I cover his hands with mine, pressing them deeper.

I watch our bodies move together, catching only glimpses here and there like watching lightning illuminate the night sky. The veins that run down his strong forearms, the drop of sweat that traces his sharp cheekbone, his lidded gaze watching me watch him.

I taste his mouth again. His scent is inside my head, dark and male, trapping me in memories of all our nights together. A spark of longing lights inside me, acute as homesickness. I kiss him harder. I don't ever want this to end.

I wrap my arms around his neck, urging him deeper. My hips grind against him. The tension inside me is unbearable. His hands cradle my head, but I have to pull away from the kiss. I cry out as my body breaks like a wave.

Heat and pleasure ripple through me. Cam's thrusts grow desperate until, at last, his body releases with a shudder.

"Lenni." My name drips from his lips. His voice seems to speak every feeling that rages and swirls inside me: need, want, possession, longing. Love. I swear I feel it. Can it be real?

<hr>

When I open my eyes some time later, it's almost one a.m. I don't know how long I've been dozing. As soon as I move, Cam stirs and opens his eyes.

"Do you have to get going?" I whisper.

He rubs his eyes and blinks at the clock. "Guess I better."

I don't bother moving out of the middle seat as we drive back to my grandparents' house. Back in the driveway, I unbuckle my seat belt but don't get out. I don't want to leave him yet.

"I don't know what to say. Thank you," I tell him. "For showing up."

"I always will."

A moment passes.

"Are you okay driving? Do you want some coffee before you go?"

He shakes his head. "I'm awake. No worries."

"Okay. Well . . . good night."

"G'night, Lenni."

I get out of the truck, and he rolls down the window.

"When will you be back?" he asks.

"Sunday night."

He nods, but doesn't ask for more.

Inside the house, I leave the lights off and stand at the window, watching his taillights move up the driveway, then flicker between the line of trees and disappear down the road. I feel weak and confused. I don't know how a night so fraught with emotion and unanswered questions can feel good, but it was such a good night. To know the truth about the photo feels like freedom. And those minutes—hours?—in Cam's truck felt beyond compare. But now the fear is slowly creeping in . . . what if that was the last time?

I'm scared of what lies ahead. What would be worse? To give up on me and Cam for good or to say what needs to be said and face the obstacles together, knowing that even if we give it our all, we might crash and burn?

So many questions and only one thing I know for certain. My heart has never felt fuller than it did the moment I saw him standing there waiting for me.

cameron

SATURDAY SUCKS.

I watch my team win without me, which is only marginally better than watching them lose; at least I didn't fuck up our season for the satisfaction of cracking my knuckles against Connery's jaw.

I have zero regrets. If I could do it all over again, I'd hit him harder. But a couple of the guys on the team are pissed I basically chose to sit out a game for no good reason they can see, and I hate the feeling of being the kind of captain they defer to because they have to, not because they want to. I keep reminding myself of my reasons. Of her.

REEVE AND CASH try to drag me to a couple bars after the game, but it wasn't my win and anyway, I'm running on three hours of sleep, so I say no. The house is silent for once. I lie on my bed and think about how Saturday afternoons used to be: laid out in Lenni's bedroom, watching her naked body move over me, using all the energy I had left just to slide my fingers through her hair and tell her how amazing it felt when she put her mouth on me. I remember thinking how lucky I was, but really, I had no idea how lucky I actually was or how quickly it would all go away.

I should have told her last night how I felt. The words were right there: I miss you, I need you. Please come back to me. But I don't know if those feelings can stand up to the reality of where we are. Lenni's still so deep in her past I don't even know if she wants to hear those things from me anymore. And I'm such a long way from who I want to be.

My mind goes back to the first night she was in my bedroom, tears spilling down her cheeks. I was useless, clueless about what to do and fumbling my way through my desperation to make her feel better.

I close my eyes as the weight of realization hits me. Lenni's seen my flaws since the beginning, and she wanted me anyway. Every time I've tried to pretend I was someone I wasn't, I only hurt her, and every time I was honest, she held onto me tighter.

There's only one way to go if I don't want to spend the rest of my life wrestling with regret.

I try to sleep but my mind just won't quit, the energy inside me building the longer I think about her. I can't call her now with everything she's dealing with, but waiting until she's back seems impossible. My eyes open. I'm wide awake, the sun still bright outside. I can't sit with this feeling anymore, and I can't take the chance I pussy out and stay silent.

I get out of bed and head for campus.

lenni

IT FEELS good to walk into the newsroom Monday after classes. True, I have a shit-ton of work to make up, and with a new issue going out tomorrow morning, I'm up against the clock, but this room is the one place where I always feel like life is moving forward. In here, I can ignore the fact that in three days I'll be in the Student Health Center laying out my life story for a new therapist; I hate telling my story. In here I can put off thoughts of Cam and what I need to say to him and the biggest question of all: whether I've lost him for good.

I haven't heard from him. I don't know where we stand. But with my mom in the relative safety of rehab, I think my head is clear enough to figure out my next move. Maybe I can't get him back, but I'll find a way to tell him how much I wish I'd done better.

Darren approaches my desk after I set to work. "Everything okay at home?" he asks carefully. He knows I had a family emergency but not the details.

"Yeah, things are okay. Thanks."

"Your story on the student-athlete balancing act turned out really well. You didn't have to come through on that one; I was ready to put someone else on it when I heard you had to rush home."

"It was no problem. Against all odds, I think I'm actually starting to enjoy sports writing. Now that I've got the rules of volleyball down, all that's left is for me to learn the other thirty sports at Shafer."

He chuckles and sits down on the edge of my desk. "Funny you should mention that. I've been thinking about asking if you might like to join our side permanently; in addition to Arts and Lifestyle, not instead of."

I look at him. "Seriously?"

"Why not? Jude graduates in a few weeks, so we need another sportswriter. You've got the writing chops, you're just not a sports nerd yet. Think about it?"

I grin. "No need. I'm in."

"Awesome." He claps his hands together. "Just don't take this as a sign you get to grab the football story and run with it."

"I know, I know. Conflict of interest, Mr. Editor."

"That and our tips have dried up. We're putting it on hold for now."

I nod slowly.

"Wait, you're not going to smash your computer or anything? I've been bracing myself all day for this conversation."

I shrug. "I have it on good authority the woman in question doesn't want to talk. She doesn't want the story out there at all."

"Okay, but don't you think that was always the case? Considering she never came forward?"

"That we know of," I can't help saying.

"That we know of. And it seems you've made your peace with that."

Peace? Maybe. I've made peace with the fact that I don't

know the right thing to do. Expose the person who committed a crime? Or let the whole thing stay buried the way Sasha wants it? For now, I'm at peace with having no answers. "I guess I've remembered what I already knew," I tell Darren. "That naming names doesn't magically fix everything."

He pauses. "As a journalist, I'd really like to argue on that lest I find myself obsolete."

"Definitely a bitter pill to swallow. Tell me how this one sits with you: What we call justice rarely changes anything for the survivors."

He pretends to plug his ears. "La la la, I can't hear you."

I smile. "Okay, I'll stop. But I have a different idea I want to run by you."

"I don't know, Lenni, I don't really care for this defeatist attitude of yours. Aren't we supposed to be at least twenty-five before we give up our ideals like this?"

"There'll be a seed of hope in this story, I promise."

"Let me hear it."

"Sexual assault on campus," I say bluntly, watching Darren's face move from neutral to trying-to-appear-neutral. "And don't say anything yet. This isn't about naming names or bringing down a team. It's about the girls walking around college campuses with stories to tell, and the girls who are hoping they never have one. Guys too; they're out there. It would be about trying to break down the stigma of being a survivor. Humanizing them."

Darren's expression is unreadable.

"I know it's not the most original idea in the world. But I'm hoping that would be the beauty of it—giving voice to thoughts and experiences at least half the student population lives with all the time."

"Quite a pivot from the first idea you proposed. What

happened to the fire you had burning in you to see someone punished?"

I know the real answer. It fizzled out when I realized I couldn't think of anything but revenge, that what I wanted for Sasha—to see someone punished—hadn't saved me and wouldn't save her either. That I'm angry and have been for years, and I need to look that anger in the eye instead of trying to find it on another woman's face. And that Cam was right when he said hurting his team wouldn't fix what's wrong with me. But that's all a little TMI for Darren. "I guess it went up in smoke when I realized I was focused on the wrong people."

Darren cocks his head. "Normally, this is the part where I'd ask two dozen questions and then sleep on it. But I think we're better off if I let you run with it and see what you come up with."

A ripple moves through me, excitement and doubt. It's only a tiny seed of an idea, completely directionless. But at the root of it, I feel pure and simple hope.

THE SUN IS SETTING by the time I finish my edits, the room still buzzing with activity. I say a few goodbyes, then head down the hall. I'm almost at the elevator when I hear Darren yelling my name.

"Come here," he calls, gesturing excitedly for me to come back. "You've got to see this!"

I turn back, following his quick footsteps to the computer at the back of the newsroom displaying the layout for the next edition of the paper.

"Look at this." Darren grins, indicating the template showing a page of ads. I have the uncomfortable feeling I'm about to be pranked.

"What am I even looking at here?"

"Are you blind? The biggest ad on the page!" He points to an ad in the center of the paper in big block letters:

HI, LENNI. I LOVE YOU. MEET ME TONIGHT WHERE WE MET.

-FORREST.

My jaw drops. I read it again, then again and once more, my heart throbbing. After the fourth time, I realize Darren is talking to me.

"Someone's in love with you," he says teasingly. "I wonder who."

I open my mouth to argue and tell him the ad wasn't meant for me, but there's no room for doubt. I can't tell if the blazing heat at the back of my neck is embarrassment, confusion, or joy.

"Where did—I mean, when did he place this? Who took the ad?"

"Beats me. Prisha usually handles that."

"I can't believe this," I mutter.

"You two broke up, didn't you?"

I glance at him. "Yeah."

"You want me to pull the ad? I can pull it."

Oh. Right. The paper hasn't been printed yet. No one has seen this but me, Darren, and maybe Prisha. I look at the ad splayed across the computer screen. I could erase it with a click.

"No." A sense of urgency washes over me. I head for the door. "No, don't pull it," I call back over my shoulder before charging out.

I have a hundred questions, but not the mental bandwidth to consider any of them for more than a fleeting second. I skip the elevator and run down the stairs and out into the night air. What did he mean by *tonight*? Was I meant to see it tomorrow when the paper goes to print or today in the newsroom? Or— shit—yesterday? I feel panicked by the idea that he might not be there, that I might have missed him, that I'll never get another chance.

Except, of course, phones exist. I slow down just long enough to pull mine from my bag and dial Cam, but he doesn't answer. I probably look like a madwoman jogging across campus with my clunky bag bouncing against my hip. The November night is cool but I'm sweating under my jacket.

I stop when the garden comes into view. Landscape lights illuminate the stone steps leading into the sunken grounds, but a wall of trees and tall grasses hides everything beyond.

I remind myself that if he's not there, it's okay. It might mean I have the night wrong or that I'm early. He'll call back eventually. I know where he lives. But no amount of reasoning can quiet my heart or the voice that keeps saying, *Now or never.*

I take the steps and freeze on the last one.

He's sitting in the same spot he sat that first night, but I can't see his face. His elbows rest on his knees, head in his hands.

"Cam?"

His head snaps up, and he blinks a few times like he's trying to figure out if it's really me. Then he stands. "You came."

"You put that ad in the paper?" I ask dumbly.

He gives this sexy little half smile. "No, Forrest did."

I let out a choked laugh. "Why?"

"Because I love you."

I draw a deep breath, savoring the air in my lungs, trying to capture these words and this feeling so they never leave me. "You could have called. Or come to see me. Why did you do it like that?" My voice is raspy with emotion.

He walks over to me. "Because I wanted everyone to know I'm in love with you. The written word is forever, remember?"

I do. I remember those words from our interview all those months ago. A lifetime ago. "I'm in love with you too." Tears prick my eyes. "And I'm sorry, Cam. You gave me your best and all I did was think the worst." I feel myself start to crumble. "I'm sorry it took me so long to realize that."

Cam breathes deep and leans closer. "I need you, Lenni, just the way you are. I'm sorry I ever let you think you weren't the most important thing in my world. There's nothing I won't do for another chance to be with you."

I let his words wash over me, feeling like I'm breathing for the first time in so long. "You were only protecting the people you love. I'm the one who let my past get in the way of us."

He pulls me close when I start to cry. "You don't have to apologize for that. Your past is part of you, and I'm in love with all of you." I'm so glad my face is buried in his chest because I'm ugly crying now. I let him stroke my hair and press his lips to my forehead. "You don't have to apologize for anything."

I breathe into him until I can speak clearly. "Yes, I do. I asked you to make an impossible choice."

"We do hard things for each other." He looks at me and reaches out to brush the tears off my cheeks, but I take his hand and squeeze. All I can do is hold on to him, too overcome to find the words he deserves to hear. "And I want you to do something hard for me." He swallows. "Take a leap of faith, Lenni. Trust me. I'll always choose you."

So here we are, in the same place, yet a million miles from where we started. The pieces of me that were buried and forgotten are alive again. A hundred mistakes and hurts lay in our wake, but here we are all the same, ready to face the next million miles. Together.

lenni

IT'S the first week of May, and the orchard is bursting with pale-pink petals and the delicate sweetness of apple blossoms.

Cam and I lie in the grass behind the old house that once belonged to his grandparents while Liam plays nearby. The sunshine and fresh breeze are doing wonders for my hangover, the cumulative effect of the past week's end-of-year parties and last night's celebration of my new role as Arts and Lifestyle editor for the Daily Phantom. I watch wispy clouds morph slowly in the sky and will my mind to match their casual pace.

Cam folds his arms behind his head, drawing my eyes to the curves of his muscles. "What were you scowling up at the sky about?"

"I wasn't scowling." He taps his fingertips on my tensed forehead, and I realize he's right. "Nothing. Thinking about the group mostly."

Back in February, not long after the publication of my article about sexual assault on campus, I worked with Shafer faculty to open our own chapter of a national sexual assault survivor's support group. It was an idea formed suddenly but with such urgency that it was my entire lifeblood spring semester.

The response to my article had been quiet but immense, most of it coming in the form of emails written directly to me by students—female and male—who wanted me to know they felt seen by what I'd written, and who insisted an article wasn't enough. It all seemed so obvious then. One article couldn't contain the millions of words students needed to say and hear. We needed to see each other and tell our stories face to face.

"What about it?" Cam asks.

"I feel like I'm jumping ship for the summer. I don't know how to keep the group going if I'm not here or whether it's fair to ask someone else to keep it going for me."

"It's not your group."

This is true, reassuring, and aggravating all at once. I don't have the qualifications to lead the group—we have a faculty sponsor and two trained grad students in those roles—and I'm only in the beginning stages of working through what happened to me. But I feel responsible for making sure this support space doesn't fail any student who needs it. And I haven't told Cam about the email I received this morning from Sasha James.

I've still never met Sasha in person, but we corresponded a few times through email last winter when she sent me a brief quote she wanted included in the article. I never heard from her after that. But this morning she emailed me asking about the support group and whether it would continue through the summer. I don't have an answer for her. We started small, just a few students, and only managed two meetings before the school year ended. I'm proud of that and worried about what's to come. And I think I just realized how much I've already come to rely on the group for my own needs.

"It feels like mine. Two months is a long time to go without it."

Cam smiles, and I know what he's thinking because I'm

thinking it too. We couldn't have imagined just a few months ago me being so eager to talk about my past, especially to strangers. "You'll have your therapist at home. And I know it's not the same, but you'll have me." That last one is the most reassuring idea of all. Cam extends his arm on the grass, and I lay back against it. "You still feeling okay about spending the summer at home?"

"Okay is a good way to describe it." I ended up taking the job offered to me by Mr. Clemmons, the one Mom was trying to sell me on back in the fall. It pays pretty well, and because the company is brand new, I'll be taking on far more responsibilities than I'd be given at any established media outlet, which is even better.

"Which part aren't you feeling?"

"I guess I'm scared to walk into that town again. I'm ready to stop running away from it, but I don't know what I'm in for. I never pictured myself there again."

Before I took the job back home, I found the courage to be honest with my mom about how broken I still felt by what those high school boys had done to me and why I stayed away from home. It wasn't what she wanted to hear, but she did hear it, and she didn't reason away my pain. So, with some hesitation, I took her up on her offer to live with her and Gus in their new apartment. She's been sober since rehab last November and seems to be in a better place than her last attempt at sobriety. Still, I know there's no such thing as "From now on" in recovery. Life is day by day. I guess that's true for all of us. And I've reassured myself that even if the summer job and living at home is a flop, I'll have an extended visit from Jade to look forward to. She and Sam have waded back into togetherness, and even though they're keeping it more casual this time around, Jade's fiery spirit has returned.

"You're going to blow the whole town away," Cam assures

me. "A place like that can't even hold you." When I don't answer, he leans close so I can feel the warmth of his lips on my ear. "It's okay, Lenni."

I remember these words and the same tender way he said them to me that awful night in Reeve's bedroom. I think that was the precise moment my heart fell for him, even if my head didn't know yet. And just like then, something deep inside me believes him.

"And if things get too hard, come stay with me in Atlanta. Or hell, I'll come to you. Just say the word." He turns and looks up at the sky.

I kiss his cheek, but it doesn't diminish the faraway look in his eyes. "What is it?"

He blinks. "This isn't what I wanted for this summer."

"Stop. This is exactly what you wanted."

"Being a plane ride away from you?"

"Working in Atlanta. Being something other than a football player for a few weeks and seeing how it feels."

His brow creases. "That part's good, I guess." He turns to me and the tension in his face lightens. "You think I'll like it?"

"Being a working stiff?"

"Yeah, that."

"Probably."

Early in spring semester, Cam committed to the internship in Atlanta, and I'd hardly seen him happier. Maybe not dancing-in-the-streets happy—Cam only dances when he's wildly drunk and even then, only when a song comes on that reminds him of high school. But he was walking around like a weight had dropped from his shoulders.

I see it creeping back in though, his mind venturing past this summer and into next year when he'll have to decide whether football is his future or his past.

"What if I hate the internship?" he asks.

I shrug. "Then you'll have narrowed your life down to ninety-nine career options."

"What if I don't make the draft? Then what'll I be?"

"Mine. You'll be mine."

Cam's eyes are awash with color in the sunlight. He wraps his fingers around my wrist and strokes his thumb in small circles over my pulse. "I was always going to be yours."

Liam stands up amid a pile of plastic trucks and runs over to us, an inflatable beach ball clutched between his hands. "Let's play, Cam!"

"You got it, dude."

Liam has zero interest in football, a fact that Cam relishes for some reason I don't quite grasp. Liam likes to tell everyone his favorite sport is "beach ball," which consists, predictably, of tossing a beach ball back and forth. Though with Cam, the game takes a more interesting turn. I watch while Liam throws the ball this way and that, laughing and cheering as Cam breaks and dives for the ball so his end of the game looks more like beach volleyball.

I check the time and feel a wave of melancholy. In less than twenty hours, Cam will be on a plane to Atlanta, and we'll begin our longest separation. For the dozenth time, I wish we weren't obligated to dinner at Minnie's house tonight. Reeve will be there too, probably with some girl he met in the last twenty-four hours. It'll be a good night—being in the company of people that Cam loves is never a bad time—but if I'd had my way, we would have spent this whole weekend alone, stretching out the hours so they felt like days. Maybe Cam would have preferred that too, but he's not saying.

Sometimes I wonder if he can feel the difference between what he wants and what the people who are precious to him want. Loyalty runs bone-deep in this man, and every time I think, *For better or for worse*, I have to stop and correct myself.

For better. Cameron loves few and he loves deeply. Of all the things I am, being one of those few is my favorite.

THAT NIGHT, after dinner and a long goodbye to Minnie and Reeve, Cam and I get into his truck. I slide right up against him, and he puts his arm around me, driving with one hand like having me practically in his lap is only natural.

Cam is glowing. Minnie had only positive things to say about his internship, and when the topic of football came up, his eyes were bright with excitement about football camp and his senior season. I love that he's still holding tight to the things that have brought him so much happiness. It also didn't hurt that Reeve was crowing about a juicy bit of gossip: Mason Connery is talking about quitting the team before the start of football camp. Apparently, most of the players turned on him after finding out how close he came to foisting a scandal on them.

"So are you and Reeve definitely making the trip to see his mom?" I ask as we get on the road.

During dinner, Reeve announced his plans to visit his mother a few hours outside of Shafer. They haven't seen each other in months, and Reeve's anxiety was palpable. He and Cam's seven-word exchange on the matter—*You want to come, Cam?* Reeve asked, to which Cam said, *Yeah, man*—made me wonder how many times they've discussed this before.

"As long as he doesn't back out."

"Do you know his mom well?"

"Pretty well. She's sweet."

"You're the sweet one. Going with him to see her after all this time? You and Reeve are so stinkin' cute."

Cam smiles. "Thanks, honey. 'So stinkin' cute' is just the kind of compliment dudes love."

I laugh. "I'll just add it to the list. Alongside 'romantic' and 'supremely bad planner of first dates.' So when's the trip?"

"August. We'll take a weekend during football camp."

"I thought he said July."

"He did. We have other plans that weekend." He looks over at me and there it is, that gaze that catches you and won't let go.

"What plans?"

"We've got an anniversary to celebrate."

"Whose?"

He chuckles. "Ours. July seventeenth is the night we met."

I stare at him. "It is?"

"So glad it was as memorable for you as it was for me."

"Oh, I remember that night. I remember every detail."

"Like what?"

"I remember your perfect hair." I reach up and drag my fingers through a thick wave of his hair. He's let it grow out since football season ended, and he's never been more popular with girls on campus. "And the way your eyes never dropped below my neck."

"Never worked so hard in my life," he says.

"I remember thinking you were the most perfect guy I'd ever met. And then when I didn't see you again, I almost didn't believe you could be real."

"Dream boyfriend up in smoke. I always knew you were high that night."

"No, I was right the first time." I put my hand on his, wrapping it tighter around me. "The smartest thing I ever did was believe you were for real."

LENNI

Nine Years Later

"MORE CHEESE? REALLY?"

I pause, a thick slab of Parmesan inches from my lips, and look over at Cam, who's watching me from the doorway. "We're hungry," I say with a guilty smile.

"I've never seen anyone eat Parm by the pound." Cam picks up the wedge of cheese from the counter, probably noting how much it's shrunk since his last pass through the kitchen. "And this is the imported stuff too." He bends down to talk directly to my belly. "Slow down, Tiny. Dad's not making pro money anymore."

I sweep a hand through his soft waves, my heart tugging just a little like it does every time he talks to the baby. After over a year of hoping for a positive pregnancy test, the day we finally got one was the happiest we'd felt in years, but since then I've been bumbling my way through my role as mom-to-be. Cam, meanwhile, was a natural from day one, talking to the baby like he expected an answer, searching for a house with the kind of backyard any kid would dream of, and working his ass off as a sports agent so he can spend the baby's first year as a stay-at-home dad.

Cam surveys the kitchen counter, which is covered in half-wrapped cheeses, boxes of crackers, and various containers of nuts and olives. "Maybe you let me take over the cheese plate from here," he says, a smile quirking his lips. "We need to save some for the guests."

"Then what should I do?"

"Put your feet up? People will be here in twenty minutes. Take it easy." He sees my face and shrugs. "Okay, go work if that's what you want. Just don't get sucked in. I need backup when the moms arrive."

Today is our housewarming party, and it's the first time Cam's mom and mine will be in the same room in months. They've never been crazy about each other, and ever since our pregnancy announcement, I feel the competition ramping up for who's going to win the "Best Grandma Ever" award. Spoiler alert: my mom will win on a technicality because Minnie has already forbidden anyone in the family from calling her a grandma. Still, I have to give Cam's mom credit. She never boozes in front of my mom, not since learning about Mom's struggles, and that's saying something for a woman who drinks more calories than she eats.

"Hey, at least you can sneak a couple shots down in the basement," I remind Cam.

"Nope. Sober sympathy, baby."

Upstairs, I grab my laptop from my office and settle in a comfy chair in our bedroom that overlooks the front yard. Liam's old blue matchbox car sits on the windowsill as it has in every place I've lived for almost a decade. It's only family and close friends coming today, but I still feel a flutter of nerves. It's the beginning of something new and exciting, something I've waited my entire adult life and half my childhood for.

In a few months, I'll be a mother and the breadwinner for our family, if only temporarily, and I'll be surrounded by the people I love. Mom and Nana and Grandpa spent yesterday and this morning touring condos and houses as they prepare for their move out here. I don't think I've ever seen my mom more excited about anything.

Gus started college a few weeks ago just a two-hour drive from our new place, and Mom can't wait to devote herself to her new role as grandma. Aside from one brief single incident, she's been sober since her rehab stay all those years ago and has kept the same job. She's worked her way up to a managerial role, and because her company is nationwide, the move will allow her to keep the same position in a new town. Her salary isn't amazing, but it'll be plenty to cover her mortgage once Cam and I make the down payment. So what if that feels like a massive victory? I learned a long time ago it's not my job to save my family, but I can't help it if the fantasy revives itself every once in a while. Life's been better since I learned to dream big again.

I open my laptop and scan the edits I started yesterday. After years as a journalist, I'm back in an editing role for the first time since college and the truth—which only Cam and I know—is that I'm not sure how long I'm going to last here. I work for an online magazine aimed at teaching young women how to apply feminist principles to everyday life, and while I love what we put into the world, I miss being a lowly writer.

Cam spent the first few years after college playing pro in Miami while I wrote for a small indie pop-culture magazine in Tampa where, despite shitty hours, shittier pay, and zero respect, my job was my lifeline. Cam and I had so little time together our jobs became our lives. I needed that; needed the work friends and the structure, and the creative outlet and the knowledge that even if things with Cam fell apart, I could still have a life that meant something to me. They were hard years, knowing that Cam lived surrounded by every kind of temptation, that on any given day there existed the possibility, however small, that I might get my heart broken. But I carried the truth in my heart, and it imprinted itself deeper every time I was in his arms: I'll risk heartbreak for this love. I'll risk anything. So they were beautiful years too.

THREE HOURS LATER, the cheese plate is empty—just a coincidence that I'm seated directly in front of it—and the twenty of us are spread out in the living room, the only fully furnished room in the house.

"Is gift opening over?" I ask hopefully, surveying the floor now littered with tissue paper and boxes.

Nana smiles, pausing in her task of topping up glasses of wine and sparkling cider for everyone in the room. "Get used to it, sugar. All eyes will be on you next month at the baby shower."

"Just one more if you can stand it!" Minnie says, rattling a small box wrapped in beautiful silver paper.

Just behind her, Jade catches my eye with a covert smile. Her hair is the color of strawberry milk, and she smooths a hand innocently over her braid while her foot works to slowly slide a small, overlooked gift bag under the couch where she's seated. She winks at me, then turns to look at Reeve, who's just stood up.

"Hold on, let's give the parents-to-be a little break from the spotlight." Reeve holds his freshly topped wine glass out in front of him. "I'd like to say a little something."

"Always there to take one for the team," Cam jokes.

Everyone turns to Reeve and his imposing form. "I've got a

little reading here in dedication to the beautiful couple and the fucking phenomenal home they've welcomed us into."

"Reeve!" Minnie whispers harshly, cutting her eyes toward my grandmother.

Reeve offers Nana a charming nod. "Apologies."

"She's heard worse," my grandfather says. "Let the man carry on."

Reeve waits until he's recaptured our full attention. "Anyone who knows me—or has just heard of me—knows I'm a man of many talents. I win at basically everything; ask Cam, he'll tell you." Chuckles and eye rolls go around the room. "But there was this one time, years ago in my foolish youth, when I was wrong and Cam was right, and history has it forever preserved. In text message form." He looks right at me, then pulls a piece of paper from his back pocket and unfolds it. Suddenly I'm nervous. "For a long time, I thought Cam was drunk when he sent me this text way back in the summer before we started college. Now I know he was just a little wiser than me."

Oh, god. I can only hope Cam already knows what's coming. But one glance at him and his raised eyebrows tell me otherwise.

"I hope you'll remember there are children present," Cam says, laying a hand on top of my belly.

"Perfectly G-rated, brother," Reeve says.

My mom claps excitedly. "Let's hear it."

Reeve looks down at the paper. "Ahem," he says unnecessarily and smiles, drawing out the moment in classic Reeve style. "A text from Cam, dated July eighteenth, just past midnight:

Cam: *I thought between the two of us we knew every kind of girl that exists . . .*

Reeve: *I do. You're not quite there yet.*

Cam: *Got you beat. Just met a new kind.*

Reeve: *Try me.*

Cam: *The kind that makes you want to stop pretending."*

Reeve folds the paper and holds my eye while the rest of the room breaks out in brief applause and exclamations about how sweet it all is. I should be blushing, but I'm not. I'm too overcome by gratitude for Reeve and everyone else in this room who have gotten me where I am now. I'm too much in awe of how much has changed and how much hasn't. How Cam knew that very first night who I was and how long it took me to figure it out myself. The path out of my past wasn't one I'd wish on anyone, but I don't regret a single step. It's brought me here.

And as Cam's fingers close around mine, here is the only place I want to be.

THE END

Want more Lenni and Cam? Download the free bonus scene by clicking here or scanning the QR code below!

Kristen Vail is a spicy romance author living in the Midwest. When she's not dreaming up her next fictional hero, you can find her cooking, listening to music and rewatching shows from the '90s.

She lives with her husband, two kids and sweet rescue dog.

instagram.com/kristenvailbooks

newsletter

Want early access to book announcements and free bonus content? Subscribe to my newsletter by visiting kristenvail.com